I0820850

I LIKE PEOPLE THAT CAN'T SING

PAUL NELSON INTERVIEWS LEONARD COHEN & LUCINDA WILLIAMS

LEONARD COHEN BUYS PAUL NELSON A CHEESEBURGER, BUT LUCINDA WILLIAMS WON'T

★ ALSO BY KEVIN AVERY ★

Everything Is an Afterthought:
The Life and Writings of Paul Nelson

Conversations with Clint:
Paul Nelson's Lost Interviews with Clint Eastwood, 1979–1983

It's All One Case:
The Illustrated Ross Macdonald Archives
(cowritten by Paul Nelson, with Jeff Wong)

I LIKE PEOPLE THAT CAN'T SING

PAUL NELSON INTERVIEWS LEONARD COHEN & LUCINDA WILLIAMS

LEONARD COHEN BUYS PAUL NELSON A CHEESEBURGER, BUT LUCINDA WILLIAMS WON'T

EDITED BY
KEVIN AVERY

Editor: Gary Groth
Associate Publisher: Eric Reynolds
Publisher: Gary Groth

I Like People That Can't Sing
Paul Nelson Interviews
Leonard Cohen & Lucinda Williams

Cover illustration/design & interior design by Jeff Wong

Fantagraphics Books
7563 Lake City Way NE
Seattle, Washington 98115

www.fantagraphics.com
facebook.com/fantagraphics
@fantagraphics.com

ISBN-13: 979-8-8750-0056-0
Library of Congress Control Number: 2024941953

First Fantagraphics Books printing: January, 2025
Printed in China

For Jack Dylan Gaon

★TABLE OF CONTENTS★

FOREWORD BY SUZANNE VEGA

SCULPTING A CATHEDRAL

Apparently, I met Paul Nelson for the first time backstage at Carnegie Hall, at a Leonard Cohen concert in 1988. I had been a Leonard Cohen fan since my teenage years, and was allowed to come back to meet him. I didn't remember Paul Nelson, but apparently he witnessed this meeting.

My publicist Susan Blond informed me shortly afterwards that a writer named Paul Nelson wanted to interview me. That he had been in retirement for many years. That he would come out of retirement to do this interview. That it would probably take a few days and be a very in-depth interview.

It was.

Doing an interview with Paul Nelson was like sitting to have one's portrait painted. It was a painstaking process, over the course of days, while he watched you with unsparing pale blue eyes, patiently probing with questions in his thorough, slightly dry way, as well as taking in atmospheric details of where we were, and what one wore, while smoking and laughing nervously.

The interview was for *Musician* magazine, and yes, it was sometimes exhausting! But the end result was unlike any other piece from that time. For length, depth, and breadth, as well as his honest take on a person, he was unequaled. Even to have him show interest in interviewing me was a kind of honor, as he had another job and didn't depend on writing for his living.

His piece carried the caption, "The most important interview of her life," as we had plumbed my complicated childhood and family situation. I was very moved by the end result, and impressed with the depth and caring of his questions.

When I ran into him a few years later he recalled my situation immediately and asked whether certain issues had been resolved, which of course they hadn't. It was as though the story never left him and he was still living it, just as I was.

This book shows the process of his interview style. The interview with Lucinda Williams reveals her toughness and need for privacy but also her unstudied blunt-natured character, which I enjoyed very much.

The second interview brought an ache to my heart as I had become friends with Leonard Cohen over the years. There is an anecdote about the purchase of his first sofa which has cleared up a mystery I had often wondered about. The story is this:

After a photo shoot for *Rolling Stone*, or maybe after I sang his song "Who by Fire" at the Canadian Grammys, Leonard Cohen gave me his phone number and asked me to call him next time I was in Montreal. I kept it in my wallet. The day before my thirty-second birthday I was in Montreal, and called his number.

Hi Leonard, I said. It's my birthday tomorrow. Can you have breakfast with me?

No, I can't, he said. I'm so sorry.

But why not? I said. It's my birthday! And you said to call.

The world is too much with me, he sighed into the telephone.

But what does that even mean in this context? I wondered out loud.

I have to wait for some furniture to be delivered, he said. Oh! I wondered whether all his poetry had such prosaic translations and what was so special about the arriving furniture? You will find the answer within.

We were friends for about seven years. During that time we met, had meals, did interviews. He sent me dates at Christmas. When my daughter was born, he sent pink satin pajamas for her in the tiniest size. I still have them. Then came his ten-year retreat to Mount Baldy, during which time he had to declare bankruptcy. I stopped hearing from him completely.

When he came out of his retreat, the world loved Leonard Cohen as never before. In my own hometown of New York City, I went to see him at Radio City Music Hall which holds 6,000, but didn't see him at Madison Square Garden which holds 20,000. One of his promoters told me they began with a date in a small theater in the northwest and it sold out within minutes. And the tour never stopped until his fatal illness.

The last time I saw Leonard was on my fiftieth birthday when he allowed me to open for his show in the UK. I treasure the photos of us backstage speaking and how our body language mimics one another. He passed six years later in 2016.

The interview within brings both men to life again, in real time, in conversations which probe with humor and seriousness the complexities of life and art, politics, love and family. This is the slow pace of the artist's life: thoughtfully, carefully, filled with atmosphere and cigarettes and Coca-Cola.

Paul Nelson was of course, as one of his friends put it, sculpting a cathedral to artists he loved. I am privileged to have been one of those, and it has been an honor to write this foreword.

This book will appeal to those people who more than love music—who have depended on it in times of need in their own lives; for whom music is a sanctuary, for whom it really matters. If you are one of these, you'll love it.

—Brussels, Belgium
November 28, 2022

"No, I like people that can't sing. Dylan, when he said that he's better than Caruso, I completely affirmed it. I think he's a very great singer."

—LEONARD COHEN to Paul Nelson

"I admit that I was a slow writer and I missed some deadlines, but I must have made a lot of deadlines, too, or you would not be writing this story about me."

—PAUL NELSON to Steven Ward

PROLOGUE

If you are reading this book, you probably are an admirer of the often astonishing music of Leonard Cohen and/or Lucinda Williams, and/or you are already familiar with Paul Nelson's brilliant writing. And while it may be argued that the primary reasons for your readership are the two terrific (and primarily unpublished until now) interviews with these ultra-talented singer-songwriters, they could not have been possible were it not for the third member of this artistic triumvirate. For those of you unfamiliar with his work, let me introduce him:

In the 1960s Paul Nelson pioneered rock & roll criticism with a first-person style of writing that would later be popularized by others as "New Journalism." As cofounder of *The Little Sandy Review* and managing editor of *Sing Out!*, he'd already established himself, to use his friend Bob Dylan's words, as "a folk-music scholar." And when Dylan went electric in 1965, Paul went with him.

In the mid-Seventies, after a five-year slog in A&R and publicity at Mercury Records, he distinguished himself at *Rolling Stone* as the last in a great tradition of record-review editors that included Jon Landau, Dave Marsh, and Greil Marcus. Famously championing the early careers of artists like Bruce Springsteen, Jackson Browne, Rod Stewart, Neil Young, and Warren Zevon, Paul not only wrote about them, but often forged friendships with them. Never one to be pigeonholed, he was also one of punk rock's first stateside mainstream proponents, embracing the Sex Pistols and the Ramones as he had the traditional singer-songwriters before them.

But in 1982 he walked away from it all—*Rolling Stone*, his friends, and rock & roll. Nine years later he resurfaced and conducted these interviews. How they came to pass and what happened during those missing years—and afterwards—surfaces in the following interviews. As was Paul Clifford Nelson's strategy, in attempting to tell Leonard Norman Cohen's stories and those of Lucinda Gayl Williams, he was telling his own.

Back in 2011 when I was writing my first book, *Everything Is an Afterthought: The Life and Writings of Paul Nelson*, I found myself with an abundance—anything but an embarrassment—of riches. Thanks to the generosity of Paul's son Mark C. Nelson, as well as his father's many friends who wanted to preserve Paul's legacy, I wound up with more material than I could use. My first-draft manuscript weighed in at a frightful 1,100+ pages. I like to think that what made it into the final book was the result of some sort of literary natural selection, that what didn't make the cut, well, didn't. For example, interviews with Clint Eastwood and crime writer Ross Macdonald deserved books of their own and got them. And now we have this book, recounting Paul's critical misadventures in Los Angeles (to which I only allotted a scant 2,100 words in the original bio-anthology).

Paul was a wonderful writer, but he was a perfectionist, too, and sometimes his perfectionism, among other things, manifested itself in full-blown writer's block. For most of the Eighties he published no writing at all.

Fast forward ahead to February and March of 1991. Paul, who had lived in New York City all of his adult life, and thanks to the kindnesses of friends who wanted him to start writing again, found himself on the other side of the country with an assignment: one week interview Leonard Cohen, another week Lucinda Williams, and write separate profiles to be published in *LA Weekly*.

Responsible for this plan was Paul's good friend and *LA Weekly* editor-in-chief Kit Rachlis. "We didn't pay to fly people out from New York, but I figured I could figure out how to cheat this." Paul would stay the first week with Rachlis and his then-wife, writer Ariel Swartley, then move into a motel. Fred Schruers, another huge fan of Paul's, said, "Look, I know you guys can't afford this, but I really want Paul to write. Let me pay for the motel." Rachlis, who paid for the plane ticket out of his own pocket, repaid Schruers by employing a "dirty little secret of editors": "I assigned Fred a piece, then killed it three weeks later and gave him a kill fee that covered Fred's motel expenses for Paul." Schruers found Paul a motel near the Hollywood Bowl, "an easy stroll away from Hollywood Boulevard, where I felt he could find record stores, Italian joints, and possibly a sense of recapturing old Hollywood."

It is long forgotten who at the *LA Weekly* selected these two particular recording artists for Paul to interview, but the choice was genius. Leonard Cohen with his ever-deepening exquisite growl, and Lucinda Williams with her often mournful twang—two of the world's most distinctive vocalists. As well, Paul found them both not only in the midst of recording new albums but at creative and commercial crossroads in their careers. Leonard, practically a lifelong CBS recording artist, nevertheless seemed a mystery to his label, which seemed at odds with how to promote him and his music in the U.S. Lucinda, no stranger to perfectionism herself, had similar problems being understood and finding a home; from 1979 to 1991, she worked with more record labels (Folkways and Smithsonian Folkways, CBS, Rough Trade, RCA, and Chameleon) than she had albums to show for it.

Paul's three visits with Lucinda Williams yielded five and a half hours of tape, not counting a club date and radio show appearance he attended. A week later he met with Leonard Cohen on three days and burned ten and a half hours of tape, not including time spent sitting in on a recording session for the new album. Then he returned home.

—Kevin Avery
Salt Lake City, Utah
December 4, 2023

EDITOR'S NOTE

"We took about three weeks mixing it [*Stand in the Fire*] down and just fixing little things. When the gal came, she said, 'Wait a minute. What are you going in the studio for?' I said, 'We're just going to fix a few things.' She said, 'Fix?! This is a live album! You can't fix anything!' I said, 'Well, dear, you see, we're making a piece of entertainment here and we measure it by how entertaining it is when we get done. You know, it's not a documentary exactly.' That upset her. It's true to the performance, but there won't be a huge clam that doesn't seem to need to go down in history."

—WARREN ZEVON,
to Clint Eastwood and Paul Nelson

Great care has been taken to preserve the flow of these interviews and Paul Nelson's predilection for circling back and revisiting topics already asked and answered, thereby allowing him to ruminate and dig deeper. In some instances, however, without sacrificing the truth of what was said—if anything, to preserve it—the material has been edited or reorganized to ensure clarity and impact.

PART I

PAUL NELSON INTERVIEWS LUCINDA WILLIAMS

BETWEEN FEBRUARY 22–26, 1991

DISCUSSED DISCOGRAPHY

This list only includes those Lucinda Williams albums discussed in Paul Nelson's following conversations with her. It does not include the albums she would release after 1992's *Sweet Old World*.

1979	*Ramblin' on My Mind*	Folkways Records
1980	*Happy Woman Blues*	Smithsonian Folkways
1988	*Lucinda Williams*	Rough Trade Records
1992	*Sweet Old World*	Chameleon Records

Paul Nelson is with Lucinda Williams in her small Burbank, California, home. She is in the midst of moving out but, because she is under the impression that this will constitute their sole session together, for now devotes all her attention to Paul and his questions. She wears "blue jeans with sort of ripped knees, sandal-like shoes. Black t-shirt with something about an Austin festival on it, and then a pink sweater over it later. She had sort of a blue sport coat over the t-shirt first. She moves around a lot when she talks. Animated. Has sort of a shy smile and a downward look when she smiles." In good spirits other than being tired from the long day, Lucinda laughs easily. Her dog occasionally enters the scene and surveys the goings-on. Paul is Paul, soft-spoken and polite, undoubtedly wearing his trademark newsboy cap and dark glasses. Lucinda has apparently asked him not to smoke. He often refers to notes he has made based on a variety of articles about and interviews with her. As is his habit throughout these interviews when he begins recording, Paul snaps his fingers in front of the microphone to ensure the sound is registering.

PAUL: The guy from CBS in '83, Peter Philbin, is that his name?

LUCINDA: Yeah, he was the first person to take an interest in me from out here [Los Angeles], when I was still in Austin [Texas]. So he was kind of interested for a while, but he didn't do anything.[1]

PAUL: Oh, you didn't make the demo for him?

LUCINDA: No, that was done with Ron Oberman at CBS. That was done after I got out here in about '85. It was his own thing; it was something that he was really interested in. He couldn't find enough other people that were into it, so nothing ever came of it.

PAUL: I know Ron. Ron hired me at Mercury Records actually.[2] So Philbin heard you in Texas live and started talking to you about the songs?

LUCINDA: Yeah, he saw me in Austin first, and then I moved out here. He started talking to me about the songs and maybe some of them needed bridges here and there or something.

PAUL: I don't even know what a bridge is.

LUCINDA: I think he signed Karla Bonoff, and he was into that mentality of writing and recording. I kind of think that's what he had in his mind when he heard me. He had this idea of what I *could* sound like or something. I don't know what was going on in his mind, but anyway.

PAUL: So he was the introduction to the powers of A&R men.

LUCINDA: Yeah, the introduction was, "Well, these are great songs, but we'll see what we can do to fix them." "You're good but you're not ready yet" syndrome. I lived with that for a few years after I came out here. That'll drive me nuts.

1 Peter Philbin was an A&R representative at Columbia Records. A&R, or *Artist and Repertoire*, personnel at a record company are responsible for finding and developing talent.

2 Paul Nelson wrote about working in A&R and publicity in his Mercury memoirs "Out of the Past": "Five good years, five bad years. The same five years: 1970–1975." During those years he most notably signed the New York Dolls to their first record contract.

PAUL: These were basically a lot of the same songs that wound up on the Rough Trade record, right?[3] Done the way you wanted to do them.

LUCINDA: And the ones that didn't end up on the Rough Trade album are going to end up on this next album [*Sweet Old World*]. [*sighs*] All the same stuff that was turned down before basically.

PAUL: Philbin was the first guy to ever deconstruct your songs in every sense of the word, I guess. Was that like a jolt to your thinking in a way? Like, *Oh, my god, I haven't looked at my songs this way before*, and *Should I look at my songs this way?*

LUCINDA: Yeah. I went completely paranoid and started trying to figure out—*Oh, my god, my songs aren't really good enough*—started taking them apart. Big mistake, big mistake.

PAUL: But no one had ever talked to you about your songs.

LUCINDA: No, not really. Not from a business perspective.

PAUL: Was he in some ways a sharp guy who was just acclimated toward the business perspective? I mean, was he intelligent?

LUCINDA: Yeah, he was intelligent, but he's got a business perspective, which is the main problem.

PAUL: When you haven't met that before there's a certain part of you that says, *My god, what if he's right?*

LUCINDA: Exactly. Well, that's why I started getting all anxious about it and questioning myself and questioning my songs. Because the thing is, it had taken me so long and still nothing was happening. So you start thinking, *Well, maybe he's right.* That's the thing: when you come out here, you just started getting all *pulled* both different ways. Because before you come out here, you haven't really asked yourself those kind of questions. You're just going along and playing your songs and singing.

3 When "Rough Trade album" or "Rough Trade record" is mentioned, they are referring to Lucinda's third album, *Lucinda Williams*, released by Rough Trade Records in 1988.

You just have this support group of other people doing the same thing you're doing. So nobody's really questioning whether it's the right thing or not, which I think is real healthy. That's what shatters creativity and what stops the growth of it, and what is so *bad* about getting into the business part of it too much. Because you start getting farther and farther away from the thing you started doing in the first place and the reason you were doing it in the first place. You know?

PAUL: But see, all artists aren't like you. There are a lot of artists who are willing to sell out completely and just take the buck. A lot of people don't care.

LUCINDA: Well, that's true. You get to that point, that crossroads, and you can go one way or the other. For myself, I never considered it a choice. At all. It just wasn't even a question.

PAUL: It's been a fear of selling out constantly that's a big question. I mean, you won't do it, but it's there.

LUCINDA: I have this terrible fear of it. Paranoia.

PAUL: Some of the people that you knew in Houston and Austin *did*, I would imagine. I mean, without naming names.

LUCINDA: Not anybody I know really personally. I wouldn't say that. It depends what you mean by selling out. I don't think I'd know those kind of people anyway.

PAUL: I think there are a whole number of sort of corporate musicians now that don't even go in with personal expression in the first place. They go in like bankers to make the bucks. They imitate whatever is hot at the time.

LUCINDA: Well, that's true. That's a whole nother thing.

PAUL: I think there's a whole lot of music today that is just that, which is why I'm not interested in a whole lot of it; because there's no difference between the corporates and the so-called artists on some of these labels. I mean, which one of them is more corporate sometimes? But you're not that kind of artist.

LUCINDA: Well, there are others like me, too.

PAUL: Oh, sure there are. But I think they're getting to be fewer.

LUCINDA: No, they're there. It's just that nobody knows about them or hears about them because they don't need any kind of recognition.

PAUL: It's hard to because you're formularized immediately and run through the grinder.

LUCINDA: Right. Well, and out here people, when that happens, they just leave usually, I guess. Which is why you don't see that many people like that out here. I know they're here, but I don't see much point in being here unless you're really actively involved in the business. There just doesn't seem to be much support for that kind of music.

PAUL: Well, a lot of people just wear out after a while. They don't have the strength of character to do this for five, six, seven years.

LUCINDA: It just depends on if you see a light at the end of the tunnel, I guess. If you see any kind of progress at all, then you can just keep going. Because when you're in it doing it, you don't realize how long it's taking, until you look back on it.

PAUL: It's kind of a moment of truth when you have to deal with this talk about bridges and songs, talk about structure, and how can we change these. You've lost your innocence at that period. Even though you don't change your music, you're suddenly aware of how everyone's looking at people's songs, and you know that in a way they're looking at you as a commodity as well as an artist. And it's a scary time, I would imagine, when that realization sets in that this is serious stuff, folks.

Which [demo tape] did Henry Lewy produce, then?[4]

4 A veteran sound engineer with many classics to his credit, Lewy worked on Leonard Cohen's *Field Commander Cohen: Tour of 1979* and *Recent Songs*, and *Famous Blue Raincoat: The Songs of Leonard Cohen* by Jennifer Warnes.

LUCINDA: Oh, that was the CBS demo. I don't know what the problem was. I mean, the songs were there. It wasn't a great tape, but it wasn't horrible. It wasn't at the right place at the right time. We sent it to Nashville and they said it wasn't country enough—and they said it was too country here. See, this was before Suzanne Vega came out and Tracy Chapman and all that whole big thing; this was like right before that. So nobody knew what to do with it, nobody knew what to do with me. But that had been going on for years.

PAUL: But the demo tape stuff hadn't been, had it?

LUCINDA: Well, I had made another demo before that in New York in '83. Right before I moved out here, with Brian Cullman.

PAUL: I know Brian. He's a writer and a songwriter. I haven't seen him for years.

LUCINDA: So a lot of these songs have been around the whole time. I can't figure it out. None of it makes any sense. It took somebody from a small label to take a chance, you know, when Rough Trade came along. But on the other hand, Rounder Records came out and heard me and turned me down at one point. Rhino Records.

PAUL: They turned you down?

LUCINDA: Yeah, this is right before the Rough Trade thing. Your guess is as good as mine.

PAUL: And really, on Rough Trade, there was not much precedence to sign an artist like yourself. They had all these strange bands.

LUCINDA: But I think they just wanted to branch out a little bit. They were trying to get away from that.

PAUL: Who was it that signed you?

LUCINDA: Robin Hurley. And then we do the album, and then all of a sudden everybody was able to see what it was. But it was always there before. Maybe it took making a definitive album or something, I don't know.

PAUL: Did he come to hear you live somewhere?

LUCINDA: I think what it was, was a friend of ours, Nicholas Hill, who lives in, uh—what's that town in New Jersey, right outside of the city, where a lot of people live?

PAUL: There's Hoboken.

LUCINDA: Yeah, Hoboken. He was out here for a while, and he had that tape—I think it was that CBS tape—and somehow he ran into Robin Hurley, met him somewhere. At some point there was some connection made and the tapes exchanged hands. I *think* that's the story; I'm not really sure, but I'm pretty sure that Robin heard a tape first. They actually signed me before they even saw me play, just on the strength of my material.

PAUL: And you had some sort of a deal with Pete Anderson, right?

LUCINDA: Well, he was going to produce the Rough Trade album because we had just been talking about doing a record. See, when Henry Lewy produced the CBS demo, Pete was going to maybe produce that. Looking back on it, I should've gotten Pete to do it, but it's just one of those things. Pete and I, we hadn't really known each other that long, and the whole Dwight Yoakam thing was just kind of starting to go; this is like right at the beginning of all that.[5] You just didn't know at the time what anything was going to be. I made a demo with him of about three songs that didn't come out right. Then Rough Trade came along, but there wasn't really enough money involved to be able to pay Pete. So we just decided to do it ourselves. It was one of those fluke things.

PAUL: And they went for it.

LUCINDA: They didn't care what we did. We had total creative control. They left us alone.

5 Pete Anderson used to be Dwight Yoakam's guitarist, music director, and producer.

PAUL: It was the last time you were going to hear those words from a company.

LUCINDA: [*laughs*] Nobody was worried about anything, nobody was trying to second guess anything. See, that's the big word here: nobody was trying to *second guess* is this going to be a hit, is this going to be the single, is this going to do this, blah blah blah. Nobody was trying to construct anything. We just went in and did it. We didn't know if anything was going to happen with it or anything. See, that's what's ruined stuff, is you start thinking about it too much. Everybody gets involved and starts screwing around with it. It's just really overkill.

PAUL: And it's done pretty well. I mean, around the world, too.

LUCINDA: Oh, yeah, I get letters from everywhere. We went across the U.S. and we went to Europe.

PAUL: You got a letter today from Australia. That's kind of neat.

LUCINDA: Yeah.

PAUL: Why did you decide to leave Rough Trade, then?

LUCINDA: The whole thing with that was, the album got a lot of attention, so then here come the major labels: duh da-duh da-duh! [*laughs*] "Now we're interested!"

So I was talking to Capitol, and they were interested. What we were talking about doing in the beginning was like a merger thing with Capitol/Rough Trade, which I thought would have been the ideal situation. The problem I was having on Rough Trade is the usual thing of the record went out to a certain point, and then you can only go so far or do so much because they don't have as much distribution power. The same old song and dance. People were having trouble finding the records in the stores and stuff. So I was talking to Capitol, Capitol here, about doing something with Rough Trade just to get a distribution boost—get things going a little bit more. So I thought that would be the best of both worlds because then I could have the creative control with Rough Trade but have the distribution. See, that's all I think major labels should be; that's what I think their function is, really. That's where I think it should end. It's just, *Here's the money. Go. Here's distribution.* Unfortunately it's hard to get one thing without the other. You get on a major label and then you have to fight for creative control. To me the ideal situation would be like the creative control that you have with a small label, but the distribution that you get with a major label. Which I guess is the idea behind a lot of the labels like Slash/Warners, that type of thing.

So anyway, basically Rough Trade, they didn't want to go for that. And then RCA expressed an interest. So then I was kind of caught in the middle, I didn't know what to do. Then I took all the papers over to my lawyer's, and she was looking at them and she noticed that they [Rough Trade] had failed to exercise their option on time.

PAUL: What's the lawyer's name?

LUCINDA: Rosemary Carroll. She was married to Jim Carroll. Now she's married to Danny Goldberg.[6] Rosemary and I have a good relationship. That's the thing, I have a good team of people with me, around me. So anyway, she discovered that and said, "Well, guess what? You can leave."

You know, before you're on a major label there's a lot about it that's real attractive when you haven't had it before, because you've been busting your butt for so many years. And I have a new manager at this point, and he was really encouraging me to go in that direction and so was everybody else. They said, "You're crazy if you don't take this opportunity. Go ahead and go for it." And RCA looked real good. I went over there and met with Bob Buziak, and I really liked him personally and met all the people. He was head of the company in New York. So it felt really comfortable, it didn't feel like this real corporate thing. I went into his office and sat down in there with him, and he said, "Who do you want to produce your record?" and I said, "We're just going to do it ourselves, like we did before." He said, "Fine," and I said, "Wow, this is great." It's like the best of both worlds *and* a major label—not even an independent label. This is too good to be true.

6 Danny Goldberg, in addition to being a music journalist, record company executive, manager, and publicist, also played key roles in the careers of Warren Zevon and Nirvana. He was good friends with Paul.

And of course it turned out it *was* too good to be true because he got fired because he's real independent-minded. He had signed a lot of on-the-edge type bands: Cowboy Junkies, the Sidewinders. I don't know who actually technically he signed, but these are all bands that were on that label, most of who have been dropped by now: Jo-El Sonnier, Treat Her Right; those are all RCA bands. Cowboy Junkies are the only ones left on that label, of the ones that I mentioned. I couldn't believe it when they dropped Treat Her Right. I thought they were one of the coolest bands to come out of the Eighties that I heard. They're a real groovy little ensemble.

PAUL: What's the time period in this now, when you met Buziak and signed with RCA?

LUCINDA: Well, let's see. I'm not real good at time stuff. It was like late '89, early '90 when this was going on. Then it took a few months to get everything processed and stuff. So when I actually went in to start recording was in May of '90. May of last year.

PAUL: And then he got fired when?

LUCINDA: I think it was in September sometime. I can't remember exactly.

PAUL: And by that point you had done a fair amount of tracks. Some of the ones we're listening to.

LUCINDA: Yeah. But I was feeling real insecure about it because I didn't have that much new stuff on it. There was sort of a different attitude that prevailed when we went in this time compared to when we went in to do the Rough Trade album. Because now I'm on a major label, so there's that stigma of that, and more people are involved. You know, you have an A&R person. I didn't even have an A&R person when I was at Rough Trade; I just dealt directly with Robin Hurley. So it wasn't really the same thing, you know? So everybody was a little nervous and uptight and worried about, *Well, you can't have too many acoustic songs on here*, and blah blah blah.

PAUL: Did you have an A&R man at RCA?

LUCINDA: Since I was out in L.A. they assigned me an L.A. A&R person. Well, he wasn't the right A&R person for me. I mean, I'm sure he would agree with that. You know, everybody just has their own thing.

PAUL: I can't put in that he didn't know what *Blonde on Blonde* was, huh?

LUCINDA: It's not like putting him down or anything even, it's just the simple fact that that's the only way I can communicate with other people. That's the easiest way, let's put it that way, for me to communicate: is to use stuff from some kind of a history of music to use as a reference. You've got to have some kind of reference point. And it's the same with other musicians I play with. I wouldn't be able to play with anyone very easily if they hadn't listened to Sir Doug Quintet or Bob Dylan or the Band or the Byrds, because that's what I came out of. So if I say, "I want this to sound like 'Pale Blue Eyes' on *The Velvet Underground* [*& Nico*] with the banana on the cover," and they go, "What?," then where do you go from there? I mean, I've got to have that as a reference because I can't write music, I can't read music. So it helps if you have people in the same age group, I guess, who came out of the same musical background. It's hard to even verbalize; you either just connect or you don't.

PAUL: You don't write down your songs musically?

LUCINDA: No. We just go in and play, and it either clicks or it doesn't. That's the thing, too: it helps when you go in to record if you've already been playing these songs live, like on the road and all, which we'd been doing when we went in to do the Rough Trade album. See, that was another big difference: when we went in to do this, we hadn't been playing together really that much. So a lot of this stuff was just cold. Here is this song—okay, what do we do with it? It's not even arranged yet really. We just have to play it and rehearse it and see what happens. Because when we go out and play live, we get to work out the song and see how it goes over. So then by the time we go in to record it, you feel real comfortable with it. It makes a lot of difference.

PAUL: Did you feel like the stakes were higher, too, and psych yourself out a little bit?

LUCINDA: Yeah, I was real nervous. *Oh, my god, this has to live up to the other album* and all the rest of it. Intense paranoia set in. I was convinced that *I've got to go back and write some more songs. The material's not good enough.*

PAUL: At that point you *didn't* have enough material in fact really.

LUCINDA: Well, I'm sure it would've been fine, but by my standards it wasn't good enough. I wasn't that crazy about a couple of the songs. We had three songs that I didn't write on there, which was too much for me. I didn't want to have that many non-original songs on there because I don't really feel comfortable with that. Because I don't think of myself really as a *singer*. I'm not really that type of singer. I'm really more comfortable with my own material, because then I won't be compared to anyone.

PAUL: I love the way you sing. How would you describe your voice and your accent?

LUCINDA: God, I don't know. My accent's sort of a mixture of stuff because I moved around so much. See, the twangy thing I think comes more from Texas maybe. I lost a lot of my drawl after I left Mississippi and Louisiana and Arkansas. When I was younger, when I was a kid, I think I probably had more of a *drawl* than I do now. Now it's more of a nasally thing, I think.

PAUL: It reminds me of the big country singers of the Thirties. It just cuts through. It's haunting. It's very hard to put into words, and I was wondering if you had any words.

LUCINDA: God, I don't know, Paul. I can't verbalize.

PAUL: You sing that non-vibrato, too.

LUCINDA: Well, it fits with my own stuff and it fits with some other stuff, but I'm real careful about any other songs that I would cover. I would never attempt to record a version of "I Fall to Pieces." I mean, what's the point? It's already been done by Patsy Cline. It can't be topped. Unless it's somebody like Chet Baker, who would do it so completely differently. That's an exception.

PAUL: You consider yourself more of a songwriter than a great singer.

LUCINDA: Yeah, a singer-songwriter.

PAUL: Suzanne Vega, I interviewed her for a story in *Musician* ["Suzanne Vega: On the Couch"]; she said that she considered herself basically a songwriter when you have to do your own songs. "I can't stand my own voice. It's like a pencil," she said. I always thought that was such a great line.[7] But she never really thought of herself as a singer.

LUCINDA: Yeah, I like her stuff. It's real intimate.

PAUL: Yeah, I do, too. I liked *her* a lot, too. You wouldn't really guess from the records, but she's very funny in person.[8]

LUCINDA: I think I read this article. Did you write that? That was a *great* article. That was the first in-depth article I'd ever read on her.

PAUL: See, you should talk to me. I can be trusted. I can write an in-depth article.

LUCINDA: I know.

Talk turns to growing up.

7 What Vega told Paul was: "I never thought I was a really great singer. I thought, well, I'm a songwriter, so I have to sing my songs. I always considered my voice plain and fine—no big deal. The kind of voice that you use to sing to your children or your brothers and sisters. I like to think of it as a pencil. It's very useful. It's ordinary. Everyone's got one. Mine can carry a tune, but there's no vibrato, no great skill behind it."

8 While being very fond of Suzanne Vega the artist and the person, Paul found her music somewhat impenetrable. To his own frustration and her amusement, his interpretations of her songs were almost invariably off the mark.

PAUL: Your mother's name is Lucille and your father is Miller, right?

LUCINDA: Her name is Lucille but she calls herself Lucy. They met at LSU [Louisiana State University].

PAUL: One story said that your mother played [Judy] Garland and Nat [King] Cole songs.

LUCINDA: Yeah, when I was growing up, those were the kind of the records that they were listening to. We had Nat King Cole records and *South Pacific*. Nat King Cole *Ramblin' Rose*, I remember that. But also Hank Williams.

PAUL: The way that it's phrased in there, I didn't know if it meant she played the piano and sang these songs herself or she had the records.

LUCINDA: Well, she had the music books lying around. But she didn't play professionally, just around the house and stuff.

PAUL: Piano?

LUCINDA: Yeah, piano. She was a music major at LSU.

PAUL: Your father was a big Hank Williams fan.

LUCINDA: Yeah, we had country records and we had his stuff.

PAUL: Has your father regaled you many times about meeting Hank Williams?

LUCINDA: I've heard the story a few times. Yeah, apparently he met Hank Williams at a bar. He had just started teaching, I think. He was a teacher and trying to be like a professor and smoke a pipe and wear a tweed jacket. Apparently the story is he was drinking a scotch, my dad was, and Hank Williams said, "Williams"—I guess they were on last-name speaking terms, like they knew each other's name—"Williams, you ought to be drinking a beer because you've got a beer-drinking soul." My dad was probably in his twenties when that happened, so he was trying to play the role of the professor, and Hank Williams saw right through him. [*laughs*]

PAUL: I'll bet your dad loved it.

LUCINDA: Oh, yeah. He always had immense respect for him.

PAUL: Did you like Williams? Was he a big favorite of yours?

LUCINDA: Well, yeah. I mean, you know.

PAUL: I hear almost more *country* in your voice, like Hank Williams country, than I do blues now.

LUCINDA: Yeah. It comes out. Well, the blues that I do is more country blues anyway. Delta blues.

PAUL: "Memphis Pearl" is like Hank Williams.

LUCINDA: Yeah, I draw on that a lot because that was an early influence. Then I got into Loretta Lynn quite a bit, I'm a big fan of hers. I have a lot of her albums. So those, Loretta Lynn and Hank Williams, are probably my two favorites, yeah.

PAUL: I hear that a lot now in your voice.

LUCINDA: Well, that nasally thing, too.

PAUL: Why did your father move so much?

LUCINDA: I guess because teaching jobs never really paid that much. So always trying to get a better job, I think that's probably a lot of it.

PAUL: Where is his birthplace?

LUCINDA: Lake Charles [Louisiana]. It's between Houston and New Orleans. There's a university there, McNeese [State College, at the time, now McNeese State University]. That's where he was teaching when I was born.

PAUL: When were you born, by the way?

LUCINDA: January 26th, 1953.

PAUL: I love people who can remember the Fifties, I really do. I like that period, with Chet Baker.

LUCINDA: Yeah, but I was too young to be involved in it.

PAUL: Oh, I know, but at least you were in the Fifties. It's just odd, and I don't know why, but all the major myths of the Fifties, like Dean and Brando and Monty Clift and Marilyn Monroe and Baker, all these people are still as big as they were in the Fifties. They've lasted better than any generation I can imagine. You go into Poster Stops now and you still see Brando and Dean and Marilyn, and they all date from the Fifties. It's very strange. I wish I knew why that that particular decade seemed to make such a strong impression on people's imaginations.

So how long did you stay in your birth town?

LUCINDA: About a year. Less than a year.

PAUL: Do you remember the succession of towns?

LUCINDA: We lived in Lake Charles and, let's see, Jackson and Vicksburg [Mississippi], and Macon and Atlanta, Georgia, and Baton Rouge [Louisiana]. Santiago, Chile, for a year, in '63. Back to Baton Rouge, New Orleans, and Mexico City for a year in 1970, and Fayetteville, Arkansas.

PAUL: Which was the longest stretch?

LUCINDA: Well, they're still in Fayetteville. Not my mother; they're divorced. She's in New Orleans still, but my dad and my stepmother [Jordan Williams] are in Fayetteville.

PAUL: When did they get divorced?

LUCINDA: Sixty-five or something. That's when I started playing guitar, that year.

PAUL: Were you a close family when you were growing up?

LUCINDA: Yeah.

PAUL: And with your stepmother after the marriage broke up, you got along with her as well?

LUCINDA: Yeah.

PAUL: "Crescent City" mentions your mother, doesn't it ["Mama lives in Mandeville"]? Your mother lived in Crescent City.

LUCINDA: Yeah. Crescent City is New Orleans; they call it the Crescent City. See, because the kind of family I grew up in, I got introduced to a lot of artists from older people. Like, college-aged people were always hanging around at the house, staying over for dinner or spending the night. We had parties a lot. I had hip parents. My mother, I remember, brought over a copy of *Joan Baez, Vol. 2*, so that's how I first heard about her. And one of my dad's students one day brought over Bob Dylan's *Highway 61 Revisited*. That was the first one I heard, and then I went back and got the other ones.

PAUL: Was Baez the first one you heard that made a big impression?

LUCINDA: Well, that one and Bob Dylan probably. I was already into Peter, Paul and Mary big-time at that point.

PAUL: This was before you got the guitar or right about the time you got the guitar?

LUCINDA: The same year I got the guitar. Well, even before that, though, I think. Actually the story that I hear is Bill Harrison the writer—Bill Harrison who wrote *Rollerball*—he's in Fayetteville; he's an old friend of ours—he left a guitar over at the house, and I just picked it up and started playing it.

PAUL: He was a guitar player himself?

LUCINDA: Oh, well, you know. I mean, everybody had a guitar.

PAUL: He didn't just leave it because you were interested.

LUCINDA: I don't know. I think it had a crack in it or something. He'd been over visiting and he just left it there, so I picked it up and started messing around with it. Then I got a guitar. I think my first guitar was a Silvertone from Sears. Basically I had all the songbooks. I had the big, thick *Peter, Paul and Mary Song Book*. I had the John and Alan Lomax *Folk Song U.S.A.* book. I had the *Bob Dylan Song Book* that everybody had. And I had the albums that went with them. I couldn't read music. I would listen to the records and I would remember the melody in my mind and just use the songbooks for the lyrics and the chords. And I'd just figure them out. I used to spend hours and hours in my room by myself doing that. That was all I did.

PAUL: This was when your mother was still there, then.

LUCINDA: No, this is after the separation, but we would still see her. I'd go over to her house. So we still spent a lot of time together. And then in the meantime Jordan, my stepmother, was listening to Johnny Mathis records, who I also loved. I'm just trying to think of other records that were around that would have influenced me, besides the usual ones like the Beatles and stuff. I remember Ricky Nelson on the radio. That was when I was about ten, so I remember that.

PAUL: They didn't capture you like Baez and Dylan, though.

LUCINDA: Well, I wasn't really old enough at that time, either. I remember singing the songs and everything. I was always singing. It's just that the folk thing sort of coincided with the age I was. When I got to be about twelve and thirteen was really at the height of the whole folk thing, which was 1965. So I just happened to get real absorbed in all of that.

PAUL: One of the stories mentioned that one of the first musics you remember is the hymns. From the church.

LUCINDA: I always forget to talk about that stuff. Well, both of my grandparents are Methodist ministers. We didn't really go to church—I mean, we did a little bit, but not really full-time. I just went to church, I think, when my grandparents were alive. If we were visiting them, we might've gone to church with them. I heard my grandfathers preach in church.

PAUL: I remember when I interviewed Bruce Hornsby ["The Virginian: Bruce Hornsby Finds His Way Home," in *Musician*]. He came from a really fundamental religious area, like I did in Northern Minnesota. It was really fire and brimstone, and it seemed very Southern to him that I would grow up next to the Canadian border and hear people yell fire and damnation all the time. Is that your kind of religion?

LUCINDA: No. See, my grandfather on my father's side was a CO in World War I—a conscientious objector—and he was a Christian in the true sense of the word. Liberal-thinking.

PAUL: That was not like I experienced in Minnesota, where it was sort of an offshoot of Lutheranism, but it was very fundamentalist and evangelical stuff.

Side A of the first cassette runs out and, in the amount of time it takes Paul to flip it over and press record, talk of religion runs out, too. Instead, Lucinda is pressing him how much longer the interview will last.

PAUL: I really want to do a good, long, detailed Suzanne Vega-type story. We just have to talk to do that. You'll be less tired next time. Think of it that way maybe. I could play you some Chet Baker stuff.[9]

9 Back in his Manhattan apartment, Paul had boxfuls of Chet Baker recordings; but he also had seven and a half hours of nothing but Baker vocals that he carried around with him in his leather bag. Once he told her about it, Lucinda had to have a copy, and more than once Paul used the promise of this musical holy grail to get what he wanted from her.

LUCINDA: I've got to get a copy of that tape.

PAUL: Yeah, well, you have to talk. I'm thrilled that you like Chet Baker. I don't know that many people that like him.

LUCINDA: Really? God, I can't imagine anybody not liking Chet Baker.

PAUL: I find a lot of rock fans to be absolutely—you know, they can see about this wide. They've got no breadth of taste at all.

LUCINDA: Wow. My dad is a big Chet Baker fan, so that's how, you know. Doug Ramsey's a big friend of ours. He wrote for *Down Beat*. Did a *lot* of liner notes.

PAUL: No, I don't find rock fans particularly receptive to him [Baker] at all. I don't find rock fans like Leonard Cohen very well. When I was at *Rolling Stone* and made Leonard Cohen lede reviews, the people at *Rolling Stone* thought that was stupid. "You don't make Leonard Cohen a lede review." They didn't like him at all. That was a prevalent attitude—it's *still* sort of the prevalent attitude—among rock people, I think. I don't think they're the most open-minded souls in the world, necessarily. I just like all sorts of stuff. I mean, I love the Sex Pistols, I like Jackson Browne, I like old folk music, I like Chet Baker.

LUCINDA: You know what I really like are Bobbie Gentry albums, early Bobbie Gentry. I *love* her stuff. I started collecting all her albums.

PAUL: I just remember—god, what's the name of it?

LUCINDA: "Ode to Billie Joe." Yeah, but there's some other stuff that's really great. I like a lot of stuff that some people might consider kind of corny. Like, I love some of the stuff that Glen Campbell did. "Wichita Lineman," you know: [*sings*] "I am a lineman for the county." I love that stuff that just has a nice melody. I love vocal stuff, like really good voices. Like, I love some of the pop songs in the Sixties. Like, remember the Sandpipers? And I love that song that Fifth Dimension did ["Up, Up and Away"]: [*sings*] "Wouldn't you like to ride in a beautiful balloon?" I love that stuff. [*sings*] "Up, up and away / In a beautiful balloon." I love that song. And that song the Cyrkle did.[10]

PAUL: Have you ever heard June Christy sing? The jazz singer.

LUCINDA: Julie Christie?

PAUL: No, *June* Christy. I'd seen her for a while with Kenton's band [the Stan Kenton Orchestra], but then she went solo on Capitol. Beautiful stuff. Baker is I guess my favorite jazz singer—man jazz singer—and June Christy my favorite woman jazz singer. I think I brought them with. You might like her. I think she's really great.

LUCINDA: I get kind of funny with records because I get something and I just play it over and over and over and over again and over again. To me an album is such an emotional thing; I just fall in love with an album. That's why it's hard for me to listen to a lot of new stuff. I'm always playing old stuff because it feels real comfortable and familiar to me. Like, one of my favorite albums is the *Best of Gordon Lightfoot*, which I just found on CD and brought it home. And my other really favorite album is Judy Collins's *Wildflowers* album with that Jacques Brel song on it ["*La chanson des vieux amants* (The Song of Old Lovers)"].

You know what other thing that I used to listen to a lot? A friend of mine had these albums and he made a tape for me. Um, what was her name? Oh, *Claudine* Longet! She made these records that she had this soft, breathy kind of a voice with a French ac— [*sultrily sings 1967's "Hello, Hello"*] "Hello, hello / I like your smile / Hello, hello—" I love it! And people go, "*God*, you like *that*?" I don't care. When I first started playing guitar, I used to just take whatever songs I liked and sing them. I'd figure out the chorus and I'd sing them. That's how it all started, the whole different variety of stuff that I do. I never really thought, *I can't do this song because* … Like, I used to sing this Jimi Hendrix song ["Angel"]: "Angel came down from heaven yesterday." It's beautiful! It's like a ballad.

10 She is most likely referring to one of the band's two hit songs: either "Red Rubber Ball" or "Turn-Down Day."

PAUL: Rod Stewart sang it, too.

LUCINDA: I love that Jefferson Airplane album that has "Today" on it. *Surrealistic Pillow*. It has these really pretty soft songs on it. I like all that real sweet, sad, kind of romantic songs. Like, Jefferson Airplane had a couple songs like that on their first album. [*sings* "Comin' Back to Me"] I love that kind of stuff. "Triad" [from the Jefferson Airplane's 1968 album *Crown of Creation*]. I used to do those and I used to do that J. J. Cale song "Magnolia": [*sings*] "Magnolia, you sweet thing." And Jesse Winchester, I used to do a couple of his songs. This was before I really had a lot of my own material. But I guess I never really felt like I did them justice, so I kind of just started writing out of, you know. Because I figured that way I wouldn't have to be compared to the original performer of those songs.

PAUL: More so than feeling, *Yeah, thinking about this, maybe I'll try to write a song*? Or more so than being influenced by it?

LUCINDA: Well, no. There was that, too, definitely. And also, I think a lot of it was I got frustrated because I never could figure out how a song was supposed to be, or I couldn't figure out the key in it. It never would sound right, it never would *feel* exactly right to me. Maybe every now and then one would. Unless it was something real obscure like—well, a lot of the blues stuff I felt pretty comfortable doing that, some of the Delta blues stuff, because I could stretch those out and really do whatever I wanted to with them, because they're more open types of songs.

PAUL: The Byrds influenced you quite a bit, too, I bet.

LUCINDA: Oh, yeah, definitely.

PAUL: In one of those articles you say, "It seems to me I do the same thing that the Byrds do. Everybody thinks that's country now."

LUCINDA: A lot of the bands I grew up listening to did an assortment of styles and music; that's what I was saying. And now people make such a big deal about that. Buffalo Springfield did different kinds of stuff. I love that song they did, "Kind Woman": [*sings*] "Kind woman."

PAUL: Do you remember your first song that you tried to write?

LUCINDA: Oh, god. Yeah, I remember. It's called "The Wind Blows." I wrote it when I was about fourteen, thirteen or something. I actually was coerced into singing it at a gig in Austin about a year or so ago. [*sings*] "The wind blows, and it blows through the town / And the people in the town hear it blow." Pretty simple. You can see the folk thing and the folk phrasing there.

PAUL: Who knew it in Austin to ask for it?

LUCINDA: Well, my fans there. We were talking about that and somebody said, "What was the first song you ever wrote?" I don't know how it came about. Maybe some kind of stage patter or something. I felt comfortable enough where I was playing to do that; because, you know, I wouldn't feel comfortable doing that here with all these record company people in the audience. See, that's why it's so different: there's too much emphasis on trying to make a good impression here.

PAUL: When did you first start doing it professionally, then?

LUCINDA: Sixty-nine, '70. This is when we moved to Mexico City. I got kicked out of high school. It was a combination of things: I got kicked out for not saying the "Pledge of Allegiance," and handing out these leaflets on campus.

PAUL: What did the leaflets say?

LUCINDA: It was something that SDS was doing.[11] Because I went to an overcrowded, understaffed public school in New Orleans and there was a lot of racism there, and we had this principal who didn't give a shit about anything. There were demands that were being made on this leaflet of demands. So I was handing those out, and then we got sent to

11 Cofounded in 1960 by Tom Hayden, Students for a Democratic Society (SDS) was a national student activist organization.

the office. And while I was in the office, the "Pledge of Allegiance" came out over the intercom system, which it always did every morning, and you had to stand up, put your hand over your heart, and say the "Pledge of Allegiance." And we decided not to say it. The assistant principal was in the office with us. He said, "Did you say it?" "No." "Did you say it?" "Nope!" "Did you?" "No." "Okay, that's going to be added to your suspension." We were indefinitely suspended. Then I got back in. Then right after that there was another big demonstration; the NAACP was involved and all. It had to do with racism in the school, on campus and stuff. So a bunch of us joined in with that. So the whole group of people got suspended indefinitely, whoever was involved with that. Probably about a hundred students or so. So then we all came back to class. One by one we were called into the office and they asked us if we'd been in the demonstration, and I said, "Yeah." I was sixteen. Well, then I got kicked out and I didn't go back in because my dad just said, "It's not worth it. You're not learning anything anyway here. The principal is a real goofball." So I had to go get my books and bring them home and study for a time every day—you know, try to be disciplined about it—which was probably the first time I even read the books since I had them. I wasn't a very good student because I was just real restless. I actually learned more once I got out of school than I ever did in school.

PAUL: Me, too.

LUCINDA: So then we moved to Mexico City in 1970, and I was going to try to get into school down there, but they were so strict and conservative I couldn't get in without any kind of papers or anything. I turned seventeen that year, so I didn't even go to school for a whole year. I just spent a lot of time in my room with my guitar and songbooks.

During that same year, a friend of ours named Clark Jones, who we'd gotten to be really good friends with when we lived in New Orleans—he played folk music. He played guitar and banjo and dulcimer and autoharp and everything. I guess he was about in his thirties then. He lived by himself. He came to visit us in Mexico. Because the whole year we were there, we had visitors all year. We lived there, we had a place, so people would fly in and stay with us for a week. So it was this constant succession of people. So he came and stayed with us for a while. And we knew some people in the state department there. My dad put this thing together with this friend of his, where Clark and I would go around and give concerts at different schools around Mexico. So they put it together, sort of an American "Mexico Meets America." We just went in Clark's car, because he had driven there I think in his car. That was my first real exposure I guess to that kind of thing. I was singing traditional American folk songs and harmonizing with Clark playing guitar. Pretty much just folk stuff and some Bob Dylan stuff like "Blowin' in the Wind" and all that, but mostly a lot of stuff I learned from Peter, Paul and Mary. You know: [*sings*] "Come and go with me to that land / Come and go—"[12] I had all the *Sing Out!* books. I used to *pore* through those, but I could only do songs that I heard on a record because I couldn't read music.

PAUL: You'd get the chords but you couldn't get the melody.

LUCINDA: Right. I used to collect songbooks like a fiend. I'd go into a music store and if I saw a songbook that had songs in it that I knew the melody to or had on a record, I'd get all excited. I couldn't wait to go home. I'd sit there and I'd go through the songbook: *Oh, good, I know the tune to this one!* Then I could figure it out. And that's how I built up my repertoire of stuff.

So we did that that year, and so then the next year we moved to Fayetteville, Arkansas, where they [her father and stepmother] still are. I got into school there as a freshman at the University of Arkansas. I went for a semester and then I quit, and then I went back again for a semester and then I quit. I liked stuff that I was interested in, but I wasn't real disciplined. I took music theory and I failed. I wanted to get out and play.

PAUL: Were you reading a lot of books at the time?

LUCINDA: I used to read like a fiend. The whole time I lived in Mexico City I read everything I could get my hands on. I actually read more when I was younger than I do now.

12 "Come and Go with Me (to That Land)," also known as "Go with Me to That Land," is a traditional gospel blues number originally recorded by Blind Willie Johnson.

PAUL: What were you reading?

LUCINDA: I read *The Stranger* when I was seventeen. I don't know if I even understood it all, but I was just reading everything. I read Flannery O'Connor. My dad knew her. We went and visited her at her house when I was real young. Yeah, I was real influenced. I liked her stuff and Eudora Welty, so that became my favorite kind of stuff. I liked Flannery O'Connor the best, though. I *loved* her stuff. [*sighs impatiently*] So I met a lot of the foremost writers of—

PAUL: The South.

LUCINDA: Not just the South; I mean in general. John Ciardi, who he [her father] was real good friends with; John Clellon Holmes, who was at Fayetteville for a while, teaching there.

PAUL: Does your father write stories?

LUCINDA: He's a poet.

PAUL: Oh, he's a poet. I see. Published books?

LUCINDA: He has several books of poetry out.

PAUL: I didn't realize that he was a published poet.[13]

LUCINDA: He was awarded the Prix de Rome for poetry [in 1976]. It's awarded by the [American] Academy of Arts and Letters in Rome. So they lived in Rome for a year in the Seventies.

PAUL: Is he still teaching?

LUCINDA: Well, he doesn't really teach anymore. Now he heads the University of Arkansas Press, in Fayetteville, and he goes out and

13 Paul, for all his love of literature and lyrics, by all indications was not a great appreciator of poetry. The only volumes of poetry that this editor recalls seeing in Paul's apartment were Leonard Cohen collections.

gives readings. He's done some translations in Italian and Spanish, and some editing.

PAUL: Did you ever want to write more than songs? Or do you write more than songs?

LUCINDA: I did want to, but I'm not a poet.

PAUL: You're a very precise writer.

LUCINDA: Yeah, but it's different from, I don't know. The music fills up a lot of space.

PAUL: You can evoke an awful lot with just like two or three verbs. In "Crescent City" they're *dancing*, where it's brother and sister, and *walking* by the river. It just brings a *whole* night's scene together, just in like six words. I don't know how it does it, but it does it.

LUCINDA: I don't know how it does it either.

PAUL: Just reading it on the paper doesn't really do it on the paper, but when you *hear* it, the whole thing just goes zing into your heart somehow. Those six words just add up to a total picture of it.

LUCINDA: [*yawning*] Well, part of it might be, though, when you're hearing it, because you just said when you see it on paper. See, that's the difference between a song and a poem. When you're hearing it, you have the music there. And it depends on who's singing it. So it all kind of goes together, I think.

PAUL: It does, but they still have to be the right six words.

LUCINDA: Stand on their own pretty much.

PAUL: Well, they don't necessarily have to stand on their own, but they have to be the right six words to go with the voice and the melody to do that somehow. They're not accidental six words.

Your father didn't consider Dylan and these guys poets, though, I gather.

LUCINDA: I remember arguments—late night, parties about that—from the younger students and then my dad's generation. It was more the Fifties generation arguing with the Sixties generation about that. But see, that was what was so great, I guess, because I kind of had both of those worlds. Because I had people like my dad and John Clellon Holmes and people like that. Doug Ramsey. So I had that influence, the Chet Baker kind of crowd for the Fifties, and then the Sixties, the college students, who were students of these people. But they were all like hanging out together at our house.

PAUL: Influencing each other sort of.

LUCINDA: Influencing each other. So I was influenced by them because they were all listening to Joni Mitchell and Leonard Cohen and Bob Dylan. And I had those people as an audience. So I'd go in and sing like at parties. It would be like a real loose, informal kind of environment, and we'd all sit around and we'd bring out the guitar and a couple of people would go back and forth. So I had that as a support group. Kind of spurring me on, to go, to do something, really.

PAUL: Did your father take a rather, you know, *T. S. Eliot is a poet, Bob Dylan isn't a poet*? You know, a poet does meters and does this and that?

LUCINDA: No, it wasn't the meter thing. He really got me into John Donne for a while, I remember. That's a whole different thing. You'd have to interview him. He's a real interesting person.

PAUL: It wasn't a formalist argument, then. "He wasn't a formal poet, therefore he wasn't a poet."

LUCINDA: No. Dylan doesn't call himself a poet. From what I understand.

PAUL: No, true. I don't know if it makes any difference whether he is or he isn't one, as far as that goes. It's hard to say. Leonard Cohen actually *is* a poet. Your father, did he like him at all, or did he know him at all?

LUCINDA: No.

PAUL: He didn't know him or he didn't like him?

LUCINDA: [*bursts out laughing*] He didn't know him, and I don't know if he liked him. I don't think he was a big Leonard Cohen fan.

PAUL: You were, though, I gather.

LUCINDA: Yeah.

PAUL: In a way he was a better lyricist than Dylan, in his own way. He wrote stuff that was *so* different, *so* precise. It was different than Dylan wrote. That song "Joan of Arc" was just an amazing song. I just thought that was like the most perfect song I'd ever heard almost. I couldn't imagine anybody conjuring up this whole scene out of a hundred words or something.

LUCINDA: See, that's how I always wanted to be able to write.

PAUL: I can't even imagine Dylan doing that, covering this whole subject that precisely and that wonderfully. It's like an Ingmar Bergman movie. It was like *The Seventh Seal* in four verses. I was just *stunned* at that when I heard him.

LUCINDA: "Famous Blue Raincoat" is the one I like a lot. And what's that other one? Everybody said it was about him and Janis Joplin.

PAUL: Oh, "Chelsea Hotel No. 2"? Yeah, he says it is.

LUCINDA: I like that one, too.

PAUL: Did you see *McCabe & Mrs. Miller*? [Robert] Altman, the director, I read interviews where he said he let the music influence the movie as much as vice versa. He went to the mood of the songs for much of the movie. That was just a magic movie for me.

LUCINDA: "Hey, That's No Way to Say Goodbye," I always liked that one.

PAUL: That's a great one, yeah. "The Stranger Song" is very scary and weird. Yeah, I'm supposed to talk to him, too, while I'm out here.

LUCINDA: Does he live here?

PAUL: He's got a place here, he's got a place in New York, and I think he might have a place still in Greece. I don't really know him well. I wrote a lot about him early on. I was the first guy to write lede reviews in *Rolling Stone*. I actually assigned them and wrote them myself. He remembers that. I was a real early champion of his, in both *The Village Voice* and *Rolling Stone*. I don't really know him well. I met him for ten minutes once. He's working on a record, but I don't know how it's going. Mikal [Gilmore, writer and good friend of Paul's] says he's really good to talk to, but I do not know. I'll find out, I guess.

[*uncomfortable silence*] I just wanted to get us going because you've got a time problem. I want to talk to you two or three times at least. You know, then talk to him, I guess. So are you getting tired?

LUCINDA: Uh-huh.

PAUL: Want to stop for today? It hasn't been too bad, has it?

LUCINDA: No. It's just kind of been a long day. I got to feed my dog.

Paul stops the tape. Later that night, he sits alone in his room at the Best Western Motel in Hollywood.[14] *He presses record and speaks his audio notes. In the course of doing so he opens a can of, undoubtedly, Coca-Cola and periodically sips it.*

PAUL: Oh, Lucinda. Lucinda came over here and we decided not to do it here. Although she wanted to, I got the feeling it wouldn't work out very well here and I didn't really want it to happen here. So we went in her car and drove for a *long* time and talked a bit. Drove all around Burbank, and she went right by this first hamburger

14 Paul grew fond of the motel. He scribbled in a note that "they show an early Anthony Mann movie I've never seen before on American Movie Classics, but I'm too tired after the late-night Lucinda interviews to watch more than 15 minutes of it. I'd like to just stay in this motel for a long time. You can get CNN, the TV's good, and a six-pack of Coke is only $1.59 at a store just a block away. Perfect."

place—after asking what I like to eat, and I said, "A burger." She seemed to want Mexican or Thai, and we drove past a burger joint and she said, "I know you want to eat there, but we won't. I have to draw the line somewhere." We looked for this place where we could get both a burger *and* what she wanted, but we couldn't find it, so we went to this Mexican thing. She got a kick out of my usual appetite, my Minnesota meat-and-potatoes style. I wound up ordering fried chicken with french fries and stuff and skipping all the Mexican parts.

We talked for a long time there, but I didn't feel really if I should tape everything. A lot about the various people at RCA and the various mixes and stuff and the guy not knowing *Blonde on Blonde* and all of this. We stopped at her money management people, I guess, and she went through her fan mail with sort of ambivalence and pleasure and yet sort of strangeness. This one guy that sent a complaining letter from Australia, saying, "Do they listen to this *Hee Haw* stuff?" and wanting his money back for one of the Folkways records, the first or the second. She was amazed that he wrote all the way, and she was going to send him his money back and a picture with her and Dwight Yoakam and some couple of other record guys. Her funny comment at the end to this woman about *you all*. She has this way of correcting people in a very sweet way, saying, "You can't say *you all* to just one person." The heavy lady and the Black lady got a big kick out of Lucinda making this correction. She said, "Well, I'm a Texan, don't mess with me." She just has this bullshit detector, a sort of correctional way about her. Maybe it could be annoying at times, but it's rather sort of sweet. It just came out and nobody took it wrong in this case. I just get the feeling that she has this take on life, a sort of a critical take, but it's not a bitter take particularly. It came out rather nicely in this case.

Later she was talking about getting royalties for a song, which I have to ask her which song it is. Sort of hoping to make a living as a songwriter, more than as a touring person. I feel like she's very ambivalent about fans in general and music-star life in general. She's more concerned with doing the songs and what the songs mean, and not what fans see as the trappings of fame. I don't really think that interests her much or she's concerned much. The songs really do seem to be her life in a way, like Mikal says. Once I get more into the father and the brother, the mother and that whole business—didn't really get very deep into that. Or also some of the getting arrested in Nashville, she told me about that. I should go into that some more. What her father's attitude was towards her education and things. Some more about the blues, how she got into that. How she proceeded to ramble by herself after the first college couple semesters, then she dropped out apparently. And the whole record business was gone into very superficially. Bring out the fighting for control of her records for the last seven years or something. That didn't really come out very clear in this.

In blue jeans with sort of ripped knees, sandal-like shoes. Black t-shirt with something about an Austin festival on it, and then a pink sweater over it later. She had sort of a blue sport coat over the t-shirt first. She moves around a lot when she talks. Animated. Has sort of a shy smile and a downward look when she smiles.

Bit about smoking. She wants to assert herself and yet make sure you didn't actually do it and you're comfortable at the same time. It's sort of push/pull, which seems to be some pattern almost in her life, I think; a sort of asserting and surrendering at the same time almost. Mixed feelings about this.

A big puppy that she bought on a whim, and was hopping and leaping around, the way puppies do. It's this huge dog named Sam. I think she has somewhat mixed feelings about to have it.

That she's a Chet Baker fan is nice.

I didn't see too much of the house. A small house in Burbank, in the valley. You know, pretty nice. Trying to sell the Volkswagen, I forgot what year. Her boyfriend [Tom Overby], more on him. Why particularly they're going to Texas again. More on the record plans generally. Be more observant of her actions and things and the house and all this. Trying to think what else we talked about the record company. Can't really think of anything else. Well, I'll just have to get into it more and try and make some observations tomorrow and on the radio night. Listen to this whole tape back and make more detailed questions. I guess that's it for now.

Two days later, following Lucinda and her band's evening appearance on KPFK's FolkScene *radio show, she drives Paul to wherever he is going to spend the night (probably with one of his writer friends, Mikal Gilmore, Kit Rachlis, or Fred Schruers). The mechanical din of her VW van often gobbles up their words and spits them back out, and at times it sounds as if the vehicle is going to rattle to pieces before they reach their destination. Over that and the* flap-flap flap-flap *of the windshield wipers, they discuss her and the band's apparently less than impressive appearance the previous evening at Club Lingerie on Sunset Boulevard.*

LUCINDA: They have such a relaxed attitude towards playing. They're all real special.

PAUL: They all seem like such terrific people also. No, they were really all nice and the engineer was very good. It just felt very right, and last night felt really weird.

LUCINDA: Well, the thing is, it's professional without being superficial and without being uptight. You can be professional and be good, but you don't have to be uptight about it.

PAUL: No. It's like tonight everybody just naturally seemed to be in a real opposite mood.

LUCINDA: Well, we all love playing together. We haven't played hardly at all in the whole last year, so this is a real treat. We always have fun playing together.

PAUL: Yeah, I hope that's the kickoff to getting the record done however you want it. That'd be nice.

LUCINDA: Well, for one thing, see, I'm starting to feel more comfortable with the songs. A lot of the songs we went in to record, we hadn't been playing live a lot when we went in. When we went in to do the Rough Trade album, we'd been playing as a band live a whole bunch just around town in bars. So the songs were all together and we just went in and did the songs. There wasn't that much arranging. A lot of it is how comfortable I am with the songs. Because when I'm more comfortable with them, then everybody else is more comfortable. When I write a song, it takes me a while to really feel comfortable with it. I have to live with it for a while.

PAUL: Well, you're still using the lyric sheets on some of them.

LUCINDA: Yeah, a lot of that's just for like security.

As they begin to discuss when to meet next, they pass the Best Western Motel. Paul points it out to Lucinda.

PAUL: That's where I was my first two nights. That's probably where I'll be tomorrow night. Where I'll be Thursday, I don't know yet. I feel they're going to put me up there or somewhere in a similar motel for the next three days.

LUCINDA: Are they paying for it?

PAUL: Yeah. After that I don't know. I might wind up in Santa Monica with Freddie Schruers. I hate to put him out. I don't know, it'll work out. It's odd.

[*uncomfortable silence*] So I don't know, we going to get together tomorrow afternoon, right, to—? And Tuesday afternoon, hopefully.

LUCINDA: If we can, yeah. I'm just going to be so busy. It's just going to have to work around my packing and stuff. We're leaving on Friday. I'm starting to panic.

PAUL: It would be kind of good if we could get a long session in tomorrow, because it'll probably be even harder later in the week. I think Kit's going to take me to wherever I'm going, probably the Best Western again, like at ten-thirty or eleven. Should I just call you when I get checked in wherever I'm going? It should be before noon—eleven-thirty, noon, something like that.

LUCINDA: Yeah, just call me. If we could do the rest of the interview and stuff tomorrow and get—

PAUL: I think we'll need one more after that.

LUCINDA: *We will?* Wha—wha—How much more could you possibly—

PAUL: I need a lot. A lot.

LUCINDA: *God!*

PAUL: Um, I would feel safer if we could do, you know, two.

LUCINDA: [*speechless at first*] Well, okay. You should save this and give it to *Rolling Stone* or something. [*laughs*]

PAUL: Yeah, well, I'd like to. This doesn't have to be the only story I do. You're a lot less liable to screw the story up with the more information you have.

LUCINDA: Yeah, but I don't think for the [*LA*] *Weekly*, though. They wouldn't be able to print that much anyway.

PAUL: [*frustrated sigh*] I don't like to do it half-assed. I have pretty high standards in my writing. I just feel like there are huge areas I know nothing about. It isn't even so much quotes; it's just, if you link something or if you say something, the better you know the person, the more on the mark you're going to be. You know? I get to be really thorough. I really like to know as much as I can know. I obviously can't know it all. I take it real seriously. It's not just something to hack out. My name's on it, I want it to be good. If you've just done an hour or two, there are huge areas you won't know much about that person. Let's try for a long one tomorrow and try to fit another one in, if we can.

LUCINDA: Okay. I want to do it, I'm just nervous because I've got to get—

PAUL: I know, I know.

LUCINDA: I mean, if you can like talk to me while I'm doing things, like as I'm packing dishes in the kitchen or certain things.

PAUL: If you can, you know, stay concentrated doing that.

LUCINDA: Well, some of it's easier, I think. I'm not just sitting there looking at you with the tape recorder. I'm thinking if I'm a little distracted sometimes it's better because then— Damn it to hell, I went too damn far! I did, I went too far.

PAUL: [*as Lucinda re-navigates*] You feel more comfortable with me now, right, and everything?

LUCINDA: Yeah. Sometimes it's better if I don't *think* about what I'm going to say first. Like, when it's more conversational, then it's better.

PAUL: I try to talk about myself, too, and give my opinions so it's like a two-way thing, and you have something to judge by.

LUCINDA: I know. I just do that on my own. It's just like when you're recording music: as soon as they turn on the tape recorder, all of a sudden you freeze up. Like tonight, as soon as I knew they were recording, then I start making mistakes and getting all self-conscious. It's just that *thing*.

PAUL: So I don't even know how much I got tonight. I just wanted to get everyone talking naturally. I wasn't even listening to half of it. I'll have to listen to it. It was just everybody was not even thinking about it. Some nice things pop out.

LUCINDA: I know, that's why I think it's the best. Which is what candid photography is, opposed to posing for pictures. I hate posing for pictures, that's another thing.

PAUL: I can't do this for the whole story, but a lot of the times you get some nice stuff just by just setting the tape recorder and just leave it and walk away. Just let people talk. I'm not even sure what's on here. I mean, I wasn't listening to it all; I was talking to a few people.[15]

15 Alas, Paul's attempt at *l'audio vérité*, consisting of pre-and post-show banter in the KPFK studio, resulted in an hour and twenty-seven minutes of mostly muffled voices, crosstalk, snippets of mysterious conversations about Tim Buckley, Bobby Darin, and Doris Day, a comment from Paul that the show the previous night wasn't very good, and Lucinda rehearsing songs before going on-air. While the musicians tuned their instruments, Paul made small talk with host Howard Larman about Paul's old friend, record industry mogul Jac Holzman.

Towards the end as everyone prepared to leave and Lucinda rehashed information about the goings-on at RCA, Paul retrieved his cassette recorder. Seeing this, she said, "And of course Paul's got his

LUCINDA: [*brings VW to a chugging halt*] Here we are.

PAUL: "Oxford Town."[16] [*sighs*]

LUCINDA: So give me a call tomorrow when you get over to the thing.

PAUL: Yeah, as soon as I get there I will. And it was really wonderful tonight. Believe me, I really needed an *up*.

LUCINDA: [*laughs*] I'm glad you were able to do that, yeah.

PAUL: Well, I'm really glad it went well and hope you can get some sleep.

They meet again the next day, this time in her home office. But it's late—after ten o'clock at night. As Paul refers to his notes and interviews her, she packs for her upcoming move back to Austin. There's the occasional staccato screeching of packing tape as she seals cardboard boxes with her belongings within. Her dog checks on them periodically.

LUCINDA: This guy called me from the *Weekly* to tell me that you were going to be calling me for the interview, and I said, "What interview?"

PAUL: He said *what*?

LUCINDA: He was calling me to tell me that you were going to be calling me. The guy from the *Weekly*.

PAUL: *Today?*

tape recorder going all the time. Oh, shit!" Nonplussed, he said, "I only got half of it. I'm trustworthy, though: I hate record companies."

Based on a note tucked into this cassette's case, Paul concurred as to the recording's value: "radio tape of talk (poor quality)."

16 Why Paul, seemingly unprompted, mumbles the name of this 1963 Bob Dylan protest tune remains a mystery.

LUCINDA: No! Last week, or whenever it was. Because that was the first I heard of it.

PAUL: I talked to Rob before I left New York, along with somebody else at that office, and he sent me your Folkways CD and sent me the Rough Trade EP.

LUCINDA: He didn't tell me. I don't know, there was a miscommunication thing. Ah, well, never mind.

PAUL: It's a massive miscommunications business anyway. Let's not let it wreck our friendship.

LUCINDA: I'm not. *I'm not.*

PAUL: So I'm probably going to skip around a bit on these copious notes. So I hope you'll forgive me if we zap around in time. Uh, when you lived in all these towns when you were a kid and growing up, were there good and bad aspects to this moving around all the time? Or did you feel uprooted sometime or what?

LUCINDA: I don't really remember feeling that way. People always think that, they assume that you would feel that way, but I don't think I ever really did. I think I sort of looked forward to it. It's kind of like an adventure. Like, even now I don't like to be one place too long. It kind of stays with you, I guess, once you get used to it.

PAUL: Do you remember any of those towns as being favorite places that you remember fondly?

LUCINDA: New Orleans was where I went to junior high and high school. Just because of the age I was, it's still a special place because, like Neil Young says in the song "Helpless," "All my changes were there."

PAUL: I've been there twice. It's an exciting place. It's the hottest place I've ever been to.

LUCINDA: That's where I started playing. I got my first gig there. Andy's on Bourbon Street. I first started playing, well, not in New Orleans, but I first started playing guitar in Baton Rouge. Probably Baton Rouge and New Orleans were the most memorable places because I was a little bit older then and those were my teenage years.

PAUL: You took lessons for a while on the guitar when you first started?

LUCINDA: Yeah, I took lessons when I was twelve and a half for about a year, I guess. From a college student, I just took lessons. I guess he kind of just knew a little bit of everything. Well, because folk music was so popular—I think he had a rock & roll band—but he also knew about folk finger-picking and stuff.

PAUL: This was on the Silvertone?

LUCINDA: I don't know, I might've had another guitar by then.

PAUL: Now, you took music theory. Were you planning to major in music when you got into college? I know you said you failed it.

LUCINDA: No, that was just when I was in my short term that I had in college. I thought I might as well take it, but actually I never thought about majoring. You know, when you're a freshman and they always ask you what do you want to major in, and you just pick something? So I picked cultural anthropology as a major when I first—

PAUL: Why?

LUCINDA: Maybe from having lived in Mexico City the year before, I got real interested in the history of all that. The Indians. Because we used to go to the pyramids, Teotihuacan in Mexico, outside of Mexico City or wherever it was, I can't remember. They had some other ones right in the city, too, because they were always digging them up and discovering stuff. So it was pretty interesting.

PAUL: Is that a happy time for you, in Mexico City? You were out of high school and were picking the guitar and reading the songbooks like crazy and didn't have much else to do.

LUCINDA: Sort of off and on, I guess. It was fun when there were other people there who we knew—like, our friends from home would come out and visit us—but we felt a little isolated when we lived there. It was kind of a weird time to be there because it was 1970, and so it was right after they had that big massacre thing and a lot of people had been shot and some people killed or put in prison.

PAUL: This was a coup attempt or something?

LUCINDA: Well, it was really just supposed to be a peaceful demonstration, which they got permission to have. I don't know who the people were who were doing it but they were sort of surrounded and they apparently just opened fire on them.[17] So this was right after that had happened; like, the next year or so. The people we wanted to really hang out and be friends with, the more sort of radical, liberal types, were real suspicious because we were Americans and they were more radical. And plus we were in Vietnam at that time. So we were kind of caught in the middle.

PAUL: Ugly Americans in a way, to some people, I guess.

LUCINDA: Yeah. Because my dad was teaching there, the students—who were the more hipper kind of crowd, they were more radical—they snubbed us a little bit. And then the other half of that was the middle class people in Mexico City, who were *real* conservative and real uptight, they come over to your house and sit there with their arms folded in their laps. So we were caught in between. We had trouble finding people to identify with there, just because of the political climate at the time.

17 *El Halconazo* [the Hawk Strike], also known as the Corpus Christi Massacre, occurred on June 10, 1971, when a government-trained paramilitary group massacred almost 120 student demonstrators.

PAUL: You stayed there one year. Your father taught English language classes?

LUCINDA: I think that's what he was doing. Yeah, he had a grant to teach there. He was just interested in seeing what was happening with the literary scene there because he'd really gotten into it when we were in Santiago, Chile, in '63.

PAUL: Did he teach creative writing or just literature and poetry?

LUCINDA: Well, when he actually started out he had a degree in biochemistry. So he never really had a degree in English, but he just ended up teaching it because that was his field. You know, because it's writing. He started out teaching freshman English and that was what he did for a while. He kind of worked his way up to teaching creative writing.

PAUL: Do you remember Chile very well?

LUCINDA: Well, I was ten then, so I have memories of it. But I remember being real homesick and wanting all those things that you want when you're a kid and you're an American kid. You get used to it.

PAUL: There weren't many American kids, I would imagine.

LUCINDA: The school I went to was English-speaking, so whatever American and English kids were there, they were at that school. We had a few friends, American friends, but—

The circuit breaker trips and the power goes out. Once it gets restored:

PAUL: There we go. It's wired like my place.

LUCINDA: Sorry, I'll just turn the heater off. You can't use the heater with the hairdryer.

PAUL: New Year's Eve, I threw a bagel in—we blew out the whole house—the toaster. Just *boom!*

LUCINDA: People have been coming over to look at the house, and we've been giving them all the lowdown on why they don't want to live here. [*laughs*]

PAUL: [*snaps his fingers in front of the mic*] We're still rolling. Yeah, that's quite something, living in Chile.

LUCINDA: The land and everything, it's just beautiful. But you know, when you're a kid living in another country, it's different than when you're there as an adult. But I know from just having talked to my dad that he was real fond of it and he really loved it and he loved the Chilean people. Well, he got to be real good friends with Nicanor Parra, who's a Chilean poet, and I used to listen to Violeta Parra. I think she was his niece, if I remember correctly. But she was a Chilean folksinger.[18] I used to listen to her stuff a lot. Now that I think about it, that was a real early musical influence, which I always forget to mention because it was so long ago. There are so many of those things that were in my life that I forget when I'm just talking about the normal course of events. Because my parents had a couple of her records; so whatever they were listening to, I listened to.

But she killed herself. See, I don't know if I have this story straight, but her lover was killed during a revolution, some kind of political revolution thing in Chile, I guess in the late Fifties or early Sixties or something. That's the thing when you live in another country like that, the people you meet are all tied in to the whole political thing. It's not really a separate thing like it is here. You can really isolate yourself from it here, from what's really going on. People are just getting more involved there, I think, just out of necessity, I guess. They kind of have to; more like a survival thing, I think. You pick up a lot of that when you're living in another country. You sort of learn more about your own country when you're living in another country. You can kind of see the comparisons and see the stuff that we just take for granted, that kind of thing. Or being able to have demonstrations here. They can't even do that there without getting harassed and hassled. It's a big ordeal.

PAUL: You have one brother. Do you have sisters, as well?

18 Violeta Parra was Nicanor Parra's sister.

LUCINDA: I have one brother and one sister. I'm the oldest. We're two years apart. My brother is two years younger than I am, then my sister's two years younger. So he's in the middle.

PAUL: So this song "Little Angel, Little Brother" is about your brother, obviously. You want to say something about how that came about, or the core for that song?

LUCINDA: I hope when people hear it they get the gist of it, of what it's about.

PAUL: It's a very loving song. It suggests he's had or is having some trouble.

LUCINDA: I wanted to write about just the way I saw it without being judgmental. It took me about a year to finish that song. I started out on one track, then it kind of went over to something else. It kind of kept changing attitudes. And then at the end I was just being, I guess, more in a loving, empathetic way without being judgmental.

PAUL: Is the song about him in the distant past?

LUCINDA: Well, just in the last ten years, I guess. We were sort of estranged for a while, I guess you could say. Now everything's fine.[19] But he was just trying to find himself. He's trying to pursue a career in music. He plays piano; modern jazz, R&B kind of stuff. He just had a lot of trouble like a lot of people do, trying to focus in on something. He's extremely intelligent. When I mention the Shakespeare thing ["Your passion for Shakespeare and your paperbacks"]? That's true. He was reading Shakespeare when he was a teenager. We went to see *Romeo and Juliet*, the movie, and he got interested in Shakespeare and immediately just devoured everything he could get his hands on. I guess I was about sixteen, so he was about fourteen. You know, he just reads like [*makes sound*

19 Paul knew all about estrangement. In his lifetime he only saw his own son Mark half a dozen times after the boy turned eight, something for which he never forgave himself.

As for Lucinda, a 2020 article in the *Sydney Morning Herald* would quote her saying that she hadn't spoken to her brother in more than fifteen years. "It's sad," she said. "I have reached out, and while there's no animosity, he excommunicated himself from everyone."

like pages fluttering], pores through books. Really almost too bright, that kind of thing.

PAUL: It can be curse to be bright sometimes. It can, particularly if the expectations are very high.

LUCINDA: It was just a wild time for everybody, the last twenty years, I guess, through the whole Seventies. I was traveling around, going all over the place at the drop of a hat. It didn't matter how much money I had on me. I didn't have a lot of possessions. I traveled light, like Chet Baker says.[20]

PAUL: He used to travel without a horn and borrow one [for gigs].

LUCINDA: Since I've been out here, this is the longest I've lived in one place at one stretch of time, I think, in my whole life probably. I moved here in the fall of '84. So it's time to move on.

PAUL: Is there a place you consider home these days?

LUCINDA: I sort of have three homes: Austin; Fayetteville, Arkansas; and New Orleans.

PAUL: You left [University of Arkansas] after one semester, a break, and then another semester. And then what happened after that? That's where we left off.

LUCINDA: Well, I think what had happened was, in between, at one point when I'd been in school, I guess, and then when the summer rolled around, I went to visit my mom in New Orleans. She'd lived down there all this time; she's always still lived there. So I went to visit her, and I think that's when I got that gig at Andy's. Maybe this is after I'd already been. I can't remember exactly what followed what, but at one point I got offered that gig and I told my dad about it, and he said, "Well, go for it. [*yawning*] Don't worry about coming back to school, just stay down there and do it." That was probably one of the turning points.

20 Lucinda is referencing Baker's version of Trummy Young and Jimmy Mundy's 1942 song "Trav'lin' Light," with lyrics by Johnny Mercer.

PAUL: And can you describe what it was again? The club.

LUCINDA: It was called Andy's and it was on Bourbon Street in the midst of all the strip joints and stuff that they had there. It was like a folk club, and tourists would come in. It was kind of one of those open-in-the-afternoon-late-until-the-sun-came-up.

PAUL: You said it was like revolving singers or lots of singers in one night.

LUCINDA: Yeah, somebody would come in in the afternoon, like from three to six or whatever, and somebody else would play from six to nine. Kind of take shifts.

PAUL: What kind of money did they pay?

LUCINDA: I think it was just tips. I think you just passed the hat.

PAUL: Could you do fairly decently? Enough to stay ahead?

LUCINDA: I guess I did because I was paying my own rent and everything. My rent was only like seventy-five bucks a month.

PAUL: God, let's bring back those days.

LUCINDA: Eighty-five dollars in rent. I think I had a roommate even with that, so my rent was like forty-something dollars a month.

PAUL: Oh, man. Yeah, those were the days. Were you doing any of your own stuff at that point?

LUCINDA: [*yawns*] I think maybe I was doing a couple of things, but it wasn't until about '74, when I moved to Austin, that I really started singing songs that I wrote. I think during like '72 and '73 was this whirlwind of here and there. I guess I'd already been in school for a couple of semesters when I started playing in New Orleans. I can't remember if it was between semesters and then I went back—that could have been what it was—or if I'd already been and then that was the end of it and I started playing. Because at some point I was back in Fayetteville, and I had a chance to go audition at Opryland in Nashville in 1972. So I went to Nashville and stayed with some friends of ours, friends of the family's. One of the musicians, he used to play with Tom T. Hall.[21] He was on the road, so his wife and kids were there; so I stayed at their house. I think his name was Glenn Ray. This was in 1972, so while I was in Nashville that year—I wasn't even there a whole year—I auditioned for Opryland. Of course, I didn't get accepted, and I ended up just staying there. I ran into some musicians. That's where I met [guitarist] Mickey White, who later ended up playing on the *Happy Woman Blues* album. He was living in this house with these other people and he told me that, so I moved in. My rent was about twenty-five dollars a month. There were about six of us living in this big house in Nashville. Rodney Crowell had a band; he was playing in this bar there. That was before he started playing with Emmylou Harris. I think that's the year I met Townes Van Zandt; he was there. And I met Guy Clark that year. And [bassist] Rex Bell, who also played on the *Happy Woman Blues* album. Mickey and Rex ended up in Houston playing with me later. I was exposed to a lot of good music there.

Really I guess the main thing that I remember about Nashville those few months was at one point we were in the house and we were all playing music upstairs. You know, just a kind of a late-night jam thing. Apparently somebody called the cops. It was like a three-story house. I came down to the top of the stairs and looked down, and there are some policemen down there. So they came in and that whole bit. They went all around the house and searched the house and found marijuana paraphernalia and maybe a roach or something somewhere. But we all had to go down to the jail; even the people who were sleeping and didn't have anything to do with this, they woke them up. To this day we don't know who called the cops. Maybe the neighbors did, I don't know. So we all went down there and I ended up having to spend the night in the jail, where they first take you. Because I was from out of town, I couldn't just write a check because I had an out-of-state checking account. So a few of the other people—Rodney Crowell being one of them; I don't know if he remembers this—but apparently they all went around and got some money together and bailed me out. So the next morning I got out, and then

21 Paul, during his stint at Mercury Records, publicized Tom T. Hall.

we had to go through all the red tape with, you know, blah blah. *So* that was the big marijuana bust of my life, in Nashville.

PAUL: Did they put you in a cell by yourself?

LUCINDA: No, I was with some other girls.

PAUL: It wasn't like a prison movie, though.

LUCINDA: No. But it was all like dope busts and hookers and stuff. Black girls with rollers in their hair dancing to the transistor radios. I still had the same clothes on I'd had all day. One night was enough for me. So that's what happened then.

And then I just got this wild hair and decided to go to San Francisco, so I got a ride off of a ride board like people used to do. I had about fifteen dollars in my pocket and I got a ride to San Francisco. So I went out there for a while. Just stayed with this girl whose number I'd gotten from someone, and played in—what was it?—Ghirardelli Square for tips and stuff. I was always playing on the street and playing wherever I could. And *that's* the year that I met—

PAUL: This is what, '73 probably?

LUCINDA: Well, '72, late '72, or early '73. Whatever. *That's* a real big jumble in my mind.

PAUL: Who did you say you met? I'm sorry.

LUCINDA: I met Don Leady and Steve Doerr, who later became the LeRoi Brothers. At the time they were playing as an acoustic duo and then, coincidentally enough, they were playing the street in Ghirardelli Square and stuff, too.

[*yawns*] Let's see, then I think I went back home to Fayetteville for a while to kind of cool out. Yeah, so this was '73. So I went back home and just hung out there for a while. Then I went to Austin in '74 because I met someone who ended up going down there, and he said, "You should come out here, it's great. There's a lot of stuff going on," and all that. So I went to Austin.

PAUL: Which was a big scene then.

LUCINDA: It was like a real magical kind of place. I was playing on the street there, playing for tips, and just staying with some friends. So I went there for about a year and a half, and then I moved to Houston and played around a lot there.

PAUL: Why did you leave Austin for Houston?

LUCINDA: It was just really inundated with that kind of, you know, Jerry Jeff Walker, that whole scene. For a while it was more like acoustic, more folk-oriented, and then it got away from that, away from the singer-songwriter thing and more into the bar-band syndrome kind of thing. So a lot of the clubs were changing their format and they were not really interested in hiring solo acoustic performers anymore. At that time I wasn't playing with a band at all—I never had—I was still just playing by myself. Well, I'd started going back and forth a lot to play in Houston. The Montrose section in Houston had a real thriving little folk scene going on, singer-songwriter kind of scene.

PAUL: Van Zandt and his guys are there.

LUCINDA: Yeah, he was playing around there. So I ended up moving there because I was playing over there more than I was in Austin at that point. So that's where I met Nanci Griffith and Lyle Lovett and Blaze Foley and Gurf. My guitar player was Gurf Morlix. He was playing there with Blaze Foley. A lot of other people, a lot of other singer-songwriters.

PAUL: This was '75, something like that?

LUCINDA: Yeah, '75, '76, '77. Then I had some problems with my throat. I got nodes on my vocal chords, which has been an ongoing problem. If you're susceptible to it, it's just a hard thing to deal with. I never had voice lessons and felt that I could just do whatever I wanted to, and drink and smoke and go out in a smoky bar and yell and scream, and still get up and sing. You know, no rules. You didn't think about disciplining yourself or, when you're in your twenties, going wild and crazy. So eventually it caught up with me. So I went back home for a while to just recuperate and I took a few voice lessons. I took some speech therapy and lived at home for a while. I couldn't even talk literally for a while. The doctor told me to just—complete silence. I literally couldn't sing for about eight months.

PAUL: Is it a severe pain in your throat?

LUCINDA: No, it didn't hurt. Well, you just start getting real hoarse and it doesn't go away, you just get this hoarseness that's constant. They're like calluses on your vocal chords. So I went back home and dealt with that for a while. Lived back home. [*yawns*] During that period when I was there was when I got the offer to do the first Folkways thing [*Ramblin' on My Mind*].[22] During my travels, during all that other previous time, at one point when I was in New Orleans, I ran into a friend of mine who I'd gone to high school with. He ended up calling me when I was at home in Fayetteville, and he had since put this record out on Folkways. He was a singer-songwriter. His name is Jeff Ampolsk and he wrote political songs. He put this record out called *God, Guts & Guns*. So we were talking on the phone. But at any rate he told me that he made this record for Folkways and that I should make a record for Folkways. He said, "It's not that hard. Just send them a tape." So I did, I sent a tape. Just a cassette of some stuff, and they sent me back a one-page contract. I sent it to Moe Asch.[23] I think I probably talked to him a couple of times. The whole thing was a real low-key, real simple, casual deal. So a friend of ours—a friend of the family's who we'd known for a long time—I went to Jackson, Mississippi, because he knew someone who worked at [Malaco Studios]. We went in one day and cut these tracks with this guitar player John Grimaudo, who I'd been playing with a lot around Houston before that.

PAUL: And it was all other people's songs. By choice?

LUCINDA: [*yawning*] Excuse me. Oh, no, I know what it was, I know why I didn't put any of my songs on it. I *did* have some songs but I was under the impression that Folkways, being the kind of label they were, that they wouldn't appreciate original material; so I had

22 The title was shortened to *Ramblin'* when the album was reissued in 1991.

23 Moses Asch founded and ran Folkways Records from 1948 until his passing in 1986.

to be real authentic. That's what it was. I *knew* there was a reason for that. And then by the second one [*Happy Woman Blues*], I guess I had talked to Moe and maybe asked him about it and I guess he said, "Yeah, you can put your own." I was a little bit more relaxed about it by the second.

PAUL: What was the repertoire when you were in Texas? Some of your own and blues and country and Dylan?

LUCINDA: Mixed up in with a lot of, yeah, contemporary folk: you know, Jesse Winchester, J. J. Cale, Dylan, whatever. Delta blues, country blues, Hank Williams. Just kind of a mishmash of stuff. Even back then I was doing just anything.

PAUL: And Asch gave you 300 for the first and then 500 for the second one. Did you actually make the first one with 300? I know the second, you had to kick in some extra money.

LUCINDA: Well, we didn't make it. My friend Tom Royals, I don't know what kind of deal he made with the engineer over at the studios, but he just kind of took care of that for me, which I'm real grateful for. I've always had a lot of support and help. That was the first record.[24] And so then I went to New York right after that.

PAUL: So that was really the first serious try at getting involved in the business end of the record thing?

LUCINDA: Yeah, I guess it was kind of the first of that sort of thing.

PAUL: So you took your Folkways record around to other companies?

LUCINDA: Well, it came out while I was up there. I didn't take it around to other companies. I didn't really do anything like that. Just playing in the Village, in the folk clubs. And writing more. Some of them songs that were on the *Happy Woman Blues* album, I wrote there. I just lived there for about eight months.

24 Tom Royals, a Jackson, Mississippi, attorney and mentee of Lucinda's father, produced *Ramblin'*.

PAUL: But was this the time when you met some of the people that you'd been listening to records by? You said—I think it was in the car or in the restaurant—that in a way you were born too late, when you met these people.

LUCINDA: Well, I felt like that when I went to New York because I felt like I'd definitely gotten there too late. Let's see, I guess then I went back home for a while to Fayetteville, and then I went back to Houston and did the *Happy Woman Blues* album.

[*still packing*] Look, here's a quarterly *Sing Out!* book.

PAUL: Nice. I used to paste those up with rubber cement on the pages. I'd take them to the printer and stuff.

LUCINDA: Really?

PAUL: Maybe I pasted those pages up. It used to be laid out on boards, and I used to paste the introductions out and the headlines. I used to paste the whole issue up. I pasted up some of *The New Lost City Ramblers Song Book*. I was managing editor of *Sing Out!* for a couple, three years, I think [from 1963 to 1965].

So who did you meet [in New York]? Van Ronk. Dylan, I know.

LUCINDA: I saw Paul Siebel play.

PAUL: I like him. Two really nice records on Elektra. I reviewed one of them. I did the notes for one of them, I believe. I think I did. I don't remember.[25]

LUCINDA: At [Gerde's] Folk City. And Tom Pacheco was playing.[26] I got up and did a few songs. I just met Dylan briefly. Mike Porco introduced us—you know, the original owner [of the club].

25 Paul reviewed Siebel's *Woodsmoke and Oranges* for *Circus* in 1969 and *Jack-Knife Gypsy* for *Rolling Stone* in 1971.

26 In 1976 Paul not only wrote the liner notes for Pacheco's *Swallowed Up in the Great American Heartland*, he reviewed the album for *Circus*. "I never saw that," Pacheco says, "Paul always did stuff but never would tell me about it." The following year he reviewed Pacheco's *The Outsider* for *Rolling Stone*.

PAUL: Dylan, did he say much?

LUCINDA: No. I didn't even recognize him at first really. I had my back turned to him; I was talking to this friend of mine. Mike Porco comes up and says, [*sing-songy, faux Italian accent*] "I want you to meet a friend of mine. This is-a Bob-bee." And I just kind of put my hand out to shake his hand. I thought, *Okay, another whatever*. I still didn't realize who it was. Because, you know, Mike Porco's this little old Italian guy. "This is-a Bob-bee, Bob-bee Dylan." And I just went—it's like when you meet someone like that who's been your idol since you were fourteen—I was just in another time and time stood still for a few minutes.

PAUL: Did you manage to say something to him?

LUCINDA: He managed to get a few words out, and I don't know what I said. I just said, "Here's my record," and unfortunately it didn't have any original material on it, so he probably didn't even—

PAUL: Oh, he probably did.

LUCINDA: I put my home number and address on there. He said something like, "Keep in touch. We're going to be going on the road soon."

PAUL: That was Rolling Thunder.[27]

LUCINDA: Yeah, I think so.

PAUL: You had a record with you at the time and everything, so he actually took it away with him.

LUCINDA: Yeah, he took it away, but you know. Shortly after that he left because people were starting to clamor around.[28] They really left him alone for the most part pretty much in there.

27 Dylan's Rolling Thunder Revue, a legendary band of musicians that included Joan Baez, Ronee Blakely, Ramblin' Jack Elliott, Roger McGuinn, Joni Mitchell, Bob Neuwirth, Mick Ronson, and Scarlet Rivera, ran from 1975 to 1976. The musical movable feast was "documented" (with tongue jammed firmly in cheek) in 2019 in the semi-mockumentary *Rolling Thunder Revue: A Bob Dylan Story by Martin Scorsese*.
Lucinda would eventually tour with Dylan in 1998.

28 Lucinda has stated elsewhere in the press that Dylan kissed her on the cheek goodbye.

PAUL: They usually sneak him in, in the back, when the group goes on.

LUCINDA: He was just sitting at the bar, though. That's the thing, just real casual. But you always expect someone to be larger than life.

PAUL: He's not very big, no. I went to Minnesota with him, the university.

LUCINDA: Yeah, that's what you were saying.

Talk turns to some of the songs on Happy Woman Blues.

PAUL: So there are a couple of songs on the second album that—"Happy Woman Blues" for one—are not really happy songs about New York.

LUCINDA: I wrote that in New York.

PAUL: There's another one about—god, what's the name of it?—where it sounds like you sort of split yourself in two. "Howlin' at Midnight," where it sounds like you're driving back South, and you're talking about another woman who's in New York trying to make it big.

LUCINDA: I wrote that about my friend Lynn Langham, who's a singer-songwriter in Houston—she *was* in Houston and *she* went to New York first, before I did. That was one reason I went up there, too, I think in fact because she'd been up there. Then by the time I got there, she was out here. So at the time I was thinking about her when I wrote it. I always take something, a literal thing, and expand on it. It's just about feeling like you're in a rut and you want to get out. Somebody else is at another place and you're trying to reevaluate, I guess, where you are.

PAUL: Who is "Maria" [in the song by the same name]?

LUCINDA: She's my friend [guitarist and actress] Marie Gabrielle actually.

PAUL: And "Lafayette" is a place?

LUCINDA: That's Lafayette the town in Louisiana, yeah. I just grew real fond of it because I used to stop there and play a little bit there in between Houston and New Orleans. When I lived in Houston, I would drive to New Orleans and visit my mom, and I'd stop in Lafayette.

PAUL: "I Lost It" is a big favorite of mine.

LUCINDA: Remember those bumper stickers that came out in the Seventies: "I Found It"? I think they were these Jesus bumper stickers or something. You saw them all over the place, so I think I got that idea from that.

PAUL: It's a nice song; *It* being sort of nebulous, I guess. One's heart, one's early love, first love, one's virginity, whatever. I don't know what it means. Do you ever do that one yet?

LUCINDA: No.

PAUL: No? Not a big favorite of yours.

LUCINDA: Well, no, I do like it. It's just, I don't know, you kind of outgrow things. Musically it's kind of folky now for me.[29]

PAUL: Who is the poet in "Sharp Cutting Wings (Song to a Poet)"?

LUCINDA: That's my friend Bill Priest. He's an excellent songwriter, who lives in Dallas now. He's really good, and nobody knows who he is. Unrecognized songwriter.[30] I think he has a song on one of the Kerrville albums. But he was in Houston for a while, too, in that period in the Seventies when that whole little folk thing was going on. And then he moved to New York, too, right after I moved up there.

29 Probably for the reasons cited, she would record a more muscular version of the song seven years later for her 1998 album *Car Wheels on a Gravel Road.*

30 Lucinda either misheard the question or confused the songs, as her answer of Bill Priest is more in line with the song "Hard Road" (for whom she wrote it).

PAUL: Still writing stuff?

LUCINDA: I still get stuff. Every now and then he sends me a song.

PAUL: Does he write poetry as well as songs?

LUCINDA: Well, his songs *are* almost like that. I don't know if he writes poetry. Not that I know of.

PAUL: What does it mean to go "to some foreign country / Where nobody knows who we are"?

LUCINDA: Oh, that's just sort of a fantasy thing, just kind of that feeling of you want to get away, I guess. That's from "Sharp Cutting Wings (Song to a Poet)." [*yawns*] It's just kind of a love song. The guy I wrote it about is a poet and he had written a poem with that line in it. It's taken out of context. [*reviews the lyrics*] Actually this is just a fantasy thing because I was pretending like he was feeling the same way I did, but in actuality that wasn't really the case.

PAUL: How do you feel about the records now? Which are your favorites from *Happy Woman Blues*?

LUCINDA: I like this one, I like "Sharp Cutting Wings." And I like "King of Hearts." Jimmie [Dale] Gilmore sings "Howlin' at Midnight," And I still do "Happy Woman Blues" sometimes. I don't know, that's hard to say. I don't just put them on and listen to them. I think that they were good for what I was doing at that time. It's just like a page in my life. They're not really meant to be technically great records or anything. They're just taken for what they are.

PAUL: You did the best you could at the time. They're pretty good. I mean, I'm glad they're out. I think you're much better now.

LUCINDA: Yeah, I do, too. That's why it's hard for me to say. I would never try to compare that with something now. It was too long ago. It's ridiculous to make a comparison. I just accept it for what I was doing at that time.

PAUL: They both came out just under your first name at that time. How long were you just *Lucinda*?

LUCINDA: Yeah, I was doing that thing like Donovan, Melanie. [*giggles*] Oh, before that I was *Cindy Williams*; I wasn't even using *Lucinda*. I just started using *Lucinda* I think in about '74. Somebody else suggested using *Lucinda* instead of *Cindy*, and then I decided to just go with *Lucinda*.

PAUL: A good idea or a bad idea?

LUCINDA: I don't know. It's kind of embarrassing to talk about all this stuff from twenty years ago.

PAUL: [*reviews his notes*] Were you a pretty happy kid during this whole growing up thing? You always describe, whenever I've heard you talk about going to school, being not a very good student.

LUCINDA: God, Paul, that's a whole nother chapter. I don't know if I want to get into all that for the *LA Weekly*. That's a book. I'm serious. There's a lot I could say, but I'm not saying it all because I just don't know if I want to—I don't know. I know what you want me to say.

PAUL: What do you think I want you to say? It was an innocent question really.

LUCINDA: Talk about the whole—my childhood and—

PAUL: The whole what? I don't know that.

LUCINDA: Well, I told you a little bit about my brother already. That kind of thing. Not just that. Just my whole childhood and stuff. I just don't feel comfortable talking about—

PAUL: Then don't, then.

LUCINDA: Okay.

PAUL: It wasn't a loaded question. I just meant, in general, when you talk about going to school, you always use the word *restless* and *not a good student*. I just wondered if you were a generally happy kid.

LUCINDA: Not all the time, no, I wasn't. But who was, I mean, you know?

PAUL: I'm really not trying to pry into any secrets here, honest.

LUCINDA: It's not any secrets. I don't want to have any secrets from *you*. I just don't know if I want it printed at this point.

PAUL: No, but I didn't realize that was a question that would bother you. I didn't really mean it as a *deep* question or anything.

LUCINDA: It didn't really bother me. Well, it's just that I could elaborate on my whole childhood and that would be a whole nother thing.

PAUL: I really meant the school thing, since you didn't seem to really like school that much.

LUCINDA: Well, I didn't really like school and I wasn't a good student.

PAUL: What did your parents think about that, since your father was a teacher and everything? Did they understand?

LUCINDA: They were always real supportive. I didn't get a lot of pressure to get A's and there wasn't any of that kind of thing. I did pretty good in English and Spanish. I didn't get good grades in math, and he would just say, "Don't worry about it. I didn't do good in math either." I really didn't get a lot of that kind of pressure to excel academically. They were just a little concerned at first when I was going to quit college, because they were concerned about me having something to fall back on.

PAUL: He was supportive, though, of you being a singer the whole time.

LUCINDA: Yeah, yeah. But he was just a little concerned about [*yawning*] how I would support myself. Which was true: I had a hell of a time supporting myself for the last twenty years. I'm only just now to the point where I'm self-sufficient in the music business.

PAUL: You waitressed a lot and had a lot of jobs.

LUCINDA: Yeah, when I first got here I worked in record stores and worked at B. Dalton books for a while and did some temp work in offices and stuff. I did everything, yeah. I waitressed, worked in bookstores, worked in record stores, sold sample things in the grocery stores—sausages, you know those little trays? I did that. Worked cleaning houses for those companies where you go and clean people's houses.

PAUL: So there were tough times in there.

LUCINDA: Oh, yeah. My family's not wealthy. I ended up putting my guitars in pawnshops, unfortunately. The person I was living with at the time [bassist Clyde Woodward] got us started on that in about 1980. Well, I never had done it before. It was like just another thing to do to get by.

PAUL: Have you had to do that at all out here, or have you made it pretty good?

LUCINDA: No, no, no. Huh-uh, I would never do that again. Not since I lost a twelve-string Martin in a pawnshop fire.

PAUL: I don't know what these clubs pay, but has it been enough to get by out here?

LUCINDA: I could never make enough money just playing here. No. When I got signed with Rough Trade, they told me, "Don't quit your day job." But then we went out and we toured a whole bunch, so I made money from that.

PAUL: And the record sold enough to make a little, I guess.

LUCINDA: I didn't really get to see that much money from the sale of that. And now that's being tied up anyway because of that lawsuit thingy.

PAUL: They're suing you for getting off the label or something.[31]

LUCINDA: Yeah. Their lawyers and my lawyers are haggling it out. Then I was able to live off the advance money that I got from RCA.

PAUL: So here it's been mainly folk clubs and places that you've played.

LUCINDA: Well, as for the playing with the band, after I did the *Happy Woman Blues* album, that was kind of my first band thing. Before I moved out here, I moved back to Austin in the early Eighties, and I played with some bands around there. I had different people backing me up a lot. And then in '83 I went to New York and did that demo with Brian Cullman.

PAUL: Was that another try to make the record company scene?

LUCINDA: Yeah. Well, friends of mine were just kind of helping. This friend of mine, Hobart Taylor, we knew each other in Houston in the Seventies in that same time period. He had since moved to San Francisco. He knew Brian Cullman because they went to school together, to Brown University. He encouraged me to go to New York and get Brian to help me do this demo. I don't know who all heard it at the time—maybe Rounder heard it, I think somebody at Warner Bros. did—and nobody was really interested. I really didn't get that involved in the music business actually until I moved to L.A. I really wasn't pursuing anything. I wasn't doing all that, because I didn't really know anything about it. I was still pretty naïve about the music business until I moved out here.

PAUL: The Cullman tape didn't circulate to very many companies?

31 Rough Trade went out of business in 1991.

LUCINDA: It did a little bit but, you know. It's not a bad tape. The thing is, it's got good songs. It's got some of the same songs that are on the Rough Trade album.

Talk turns to some of the songs on Lucinda Williams.

PAUL: "Side of the Road" is like one big breakthrough. *Why* do you think?

LUCINDA: I don't know, it just felt real satisfying to me. It's hard for me to verbalize things very well sometimes.

PAUL: You mentioned that this song was influenced by the painting of the woman in the field [Andrew Wyeth's *Christina's World*].

LUCINDA: Yeah, there's one like a farm girl or farm woman and there's a big field. Her hair's kind of blowing, kind of wispy hair. I don't know if I'm imagining it or if it's something I actually saw or what.

PAUL: That song you said is about your [1986] marriage to Greg Sowders, right.[32] Are there other songs?

LUCINDA: Some other songs are, yeah. "Big Red Sun Blues." "Am I Too Blue" is about that.

PAUL: How long were you married?

LUCINDA: About a year and a half.

PAUL: That was the only time you've been married?

LUCINDA: Uh-huh.[33]

32 Sowders, who drummed for the Paisley Underground band the Long Ryders, would go on to become senior vice president and head of A&R at Warner Chappell Music, and sign acts such as David Byrne, Green Day, Katy Perry, and Rob Zombie.

33 In 2009, onstage in Minneapolis between the main set and the encore of her 30th Anniversary Tour, Lucinda would marry her longtime manager Tom Overby. The ceremony would be presided over by her father.

PAUL: So just those songs are about him?

LUCINDA: Um, let's see. I'm trying to think.

PAUL: "I Just Wanted to See You So Bad" isn't about him.

LUCINDA: No, that was written in Houston. That's about the same person I wrote "Sharp Cutting Wings" about. "Passionate Kisses" was written about Greg, I think, with him in mind.

PAUL: Is "Like a Rose" about you and Greg?

LUCINDA: Yeah, I wrote that when I was involved with him.

PAUL: "Changed the Locks"? No? Yes?

LUCINDA: That was before him; that was someone else.

PAUL: That's a pretty terrific song.

LUCINDA: That one just kind of popped out.

PAUL: Do the melodies come at the same time? You have a really good sense of melody in that.

LUCINDA: Yeah, pretty much. I get an idea and I just sit down and fool around with it, toy with it, and do it at the same time pretty much. Because then, once I get a melody structure in my mind, then I can fill in the words. I don't just sit down and write all the words out usually. I write some of the words, then I get a melody, then I fill in the melody with the rest of the words.

PAUL: Can they vary from, like, one will suddenly come and you get lucky and it happens in ten minutes—to three, four months, or three, four years sometimes?

LUCINDA: Yeah. Some songs I have just drag on and on. Like, I might get a refrain or a chorus—idea for a chorus, it'll kind of just pop in my head—but then I can't seem to get any verses to it. Like, I have an idea but I just can't seem to put it together. I don't know, you just have to let it go and just work on something else till—

PAUL: Why did the marriage break up? Without trying to be too personal, I mean.

LUCINDA: Well, some of it was just personal stuff, just not getting along or whatever. That was probably it more than anything. But then, see, his band broke up and right about the same time was when I got the Rough Trade thing. So there's a little bit of a conflict there. It's kind of like when his band broke up he was ready to just sort of settle down and say, "Well, okay, now let's get down to business and start having kids and stuff." I said, "Wait a minute, things are just starting off for me." So I guess that was kind of the straw that broke the camel's back. But it wasn't really just that.

PAUL: Did you write any songs with him or play with him or anything?

LUCINDA: No.

PAUL: "The Night's Too Long" sounds like a sister song to [*Sweet Old World*'s] "Memphis Pearl" in a way.

LUCINDA: Sort of, yeah. The small-town-girl-visits-the-big-city syndrome.

PAUL: Is this made up, this song?

LUCINDA: I was thinking of someone specifically, kind of gave me the idea of it, but then it went from there. So it's a fictional character, but the idea came to me just from hanging out in bars a lot and being in bars and clubs a lot. The same old same old.

> *Talk turns to some of the songs that would be included on* Sweet Old World, *which would ultimately be released by Chameleon Records, a subsidiary of Elektra that had at its helm Bob Buziak, formerly of RCA.*

PAUL: Is "Memphis Pearl" based on a person?

LUCINDA: Um, that one really isn't actually. That's one of the first ones that I've written where—I don't know, I guess the whole homeless thing—that I was trying kind of somehow write about that. The idea came to me. It was just a few lines that I'd written down and I just picked that up and it kind of grew from that. Because sometimes I'll have an idea and I won't really do anything with it and it'll just kind of lie around.

PAUL: "Sidewalks of the City" seems to have homeless people, too.

LUCINDA: That's kind of an urban-type song. That was written after I moved out here. Wrote that shortly after I moved out here in about '85, I guess.

PAUL: The Rough Trade album seemed a more lost-love/sadness-love, and then the new one seems to be somewhat more about other people and less about lost love—and less about *you* actually probably. It seems to be about other people—although I'm sure you're present in these songs in one way or the other—but they don't seem as autobiographical, I guess I'm trying to say. Is that true?

LUCINDA: I guess so, probably. They're just more human condition-type songs. Which I'm trying to expand on more because you can't keep writing about yourself forever, your own experiences—love lost/love found, love lost/love found—it gets kind of old after a while. See, I'm trying to dispel the myth—for my own self, I guess, too—that you have to be miserable and suffering and so on and so forth to be able to write. There are all these other things that you can draw on and write about; because poets and fiction writers have proven that for centuries. I mean, my dad is happily married and has been for however many years, and he's still writing. He didn't quit writing when he got into a satisfying relationship. Eventually you have to start thinking about other things to write about. When you get into a better relationship or whatever you're doing, you can't like always be screwing up your own personal life just to be able to write, to have stuff to write about. It's always easier to write about this stuff, that's the thing. *I feel really horrible. So-and-so really fucked me over. Nobody loves me.* Blah blah blah. That's the easiest stuff to write about. That's why most of the songs you hear, that's what they're about. But it's not as easy to write about other stuff, outside of yourself. On the other hand, I've heard other writers say the opposite, that it's easier for them to write about other stuff and *not* about themselves. But most of the songs I hear are about unrequited love.

PAUL: Of the new songs are there any directly about you?

LUCINDA: Oh, "Something About What Happens When We Talk," that's autobiographical.

PAUL: "Pineola" is sort of autobiographical. It's about the dead poet.

LUCINDA: Yeah, it's a true story. So you could consider that autobiographical. I wrote the song about Frank Stanford, the poet. He put a couple of books out. He was a friend of ours. He was a friend of my dad's, just from the whole writing scene.[34]

PAUL: Are you prolific?

LUCINDA: No, I don't consider myself prolific. I've written some other songs, but I don't even count those unless I would feel comfortable singing them. *Now*, you know? I have a lot of stuff I've written over the years, but I've kind of just thrown those aside. I still have them but I'd be embarrassed to sing them now.

PAUL: When you were talking on the radio last night, you seemed to consider revising some of them at least.

LUCINDA: Well, "Hot Blood" is one that I revised. I wrote that probably ten years ago, and I didn't sing it at all because it just bugged me. I had the refrain, I always had that part, but I didn't like the

34 Frank Stanton committed suicide a couple of months before his thirtieth birthday at home in Fayetteville.

verses and I just revised it just last year when we were getting ready to go in the studio.[35] [*yawns*]

PAUL: You write—I don't know what number it would be—maybe an album's worth a year or something like that?

LUCINDA: I guess. Although, like this time when we went into the studio, in May last year, I had writer's block, I guess, just for a while before that. Like, ever since the Rough Trade album came out and I started touring and getting more involved in the business part of it and blah blah, I just got really sidetracked and, I don't know, it was just real hard for me to write for whatever reason.

PAUL: It seems to happen a lot with second albums when people have had some success with the first album. I think there's always extra pressure on the second one for some reason.[36]

LUCINDA: Well, then I finished five or six new songs that I'd been working on and some that I wrote just brand new, and some I finished before we went in the second time. So maybe it was out of pressure, I don't know. That's usually the way I do, is I'll write three or four songs at a time and I'll finish—because I get on a roll and I get in the mood—and I'll do that for a month or so, and then I won't finish anything for, you know. It just really depends. I used to write more often. It just seems like the last couple of years I haven't been doing it again. I don't know what it is.

PAUL: Maybe this comes with getting better and having higher standards. That you realize that something you'd written five years ago that sounded like this would have pleased you, but now it doesn't. It's like, *I've got to be as good as my last good one*, which is a hard game to play.

LUCINDA: Yeah, that probably has a lot to do with it.

35 The song would be included on *Sweet Old World*.

36 This isn't the only time that Lucinda and Paul seem to regard *Lucinda Williams*, her third album, as her "first album," and the upcoming *Sweet Old World* as her "second" one, not her fourth, as if the first two don't count because they weren't on a bigger label.

PAUL: What were your feelings about the radio show last night? You all seemed to have the feeling that you could build off that for the record. Because everybody seemed really rejuvenated and feeling great last night.

LUCINDA: Yeah, it just felt real good.

PAUL: Everybody sort of seemed to say, "Gee, I wish it had been like this in the studio."

LUCINDA: Well, I think that we just had to get away from it enough for a while to be able to get *back* to that place. Because everybody just got a little inundated with the whole stigma of the major label syndrome and feeling a little bit of pressure because of that. Well, I've got a little bit better perspective now, and I think everybody does, for having been able to step back and see.

PAUL: You said last night on the radio that writing is pretty much a therapeutic process, which was an interesting statement, I thought. How so?

LUCINDA: Well, all I mean, they're songs about me and my life, and just getting them out of my system kind of thing. Because it just feels good when you get a song finished, it just feels good to write about something and just get it out of your system.

PAUL: Does it make you understand the situation better? That's a sort of a cliché, you write about it and then understand it, but it may be true to a certain extent, too.

LUCINDA: I don't know. I never really asked myself that, but I guess maybe it could. I wouldn't get that analytical about it. I was just saying that it's therapeutic in the sense that it's a release thing, not really like going to a therapist. I just mean for your own personal satisfaction. [*sets down a box hard, drags it across the floor, and sighs*]. I'm getting tired.

PAUL: Um. I don't know, do you think we can do one more session sometime?

LUCINDA: [*sighs again, heavily*] Yeah, but can we quit this one now?

PAUL: Yeah, if we can do another one.

LUCINDA: Well, that's fine. Is that why we're going so late? Because you thought this was the only—

PAUL: No, I just I wanted to go as long as we were getting something.

LUCINDA: But I don't know about tomorrow, because the problem is with this photo session now for me. I have to be over there at four. I was thinking, if you want to come down to the Palomino maybe, we could kind of just sit back.[37] I'm going to be there for *so long*.

PAUL: Yeah, I was just thinking, you've got all your L.A. friends there, and you probably want to say goodbye to them, and don't really want to have somebody with a microphone. I mean, it involves a couple of hours of uninterrupted talk.

LUCINDA: I know, but I'm going to be there early, is what I'm saying, before all the other people get down there. I'm going to be there from eight o'clock till *whenever*. It's not going to be that frantic and hectic really till later on, till about eleven or eleven-thirty probably. I was trying to get it so we could finish everything by tomorrow, so I could have Wednesday and Thursday to pack everything, and I've got to clean the whole house up. I'm only going to have two days.

PAUL: Where is the Palomino? Is it further out than this or less far out?

LUCINDA: On Lankersham. It's close to here. And it's not far from where you are. Can you get a ride over there tomorrow?

37 The Palomino Club was a North Hollywood institution from 1949 to 1995. At the time of these interviews, the venue hosted an every-Tuesday-night showcase for local musicians, the Barndance, playing traditional and alternative forms of American roots music. Though he apparently (and understandably) doesn't remember, the Palomino was brought to Paul's attention before. Prominent exterior and interior scenes of Clint Eastwood's *Every Which Way but Loose* were filmed there. Not only did Paul interview the actor-director about the film in 1980 (for a never-realized *Rolling Stone* cover story), Eastwood and costar Sondra Locke specifically discussed shooting at the Palomino.

PAUL: I can try. You think we could sit and talk for a couple of hours without problems, huh? Will we be able to hear each other?

LUCINDA: Yeah, we can go backstage. There's a little room, and we can go back there.

PAUL: And you're going to get there about eight?

LUCINDA: Yeah. I'm going to the photo session, and from there going to have dinner at this Mexican restaurant near there at six-thirty. Meeting a few friends there, and then from there going to the Palomino. So I'm not even coming back here. So that means I have to start getting ready to go to the photo session like around two, one-thirty or something, so I have enough time.

PAUL: I'll be there at eight. I thought it went well tonight.

LUCINDA: Yeah.

The next day, back in the sanctuary of his Best Western room, Paul dictates his interview notes. He sounds as if he has just walked barefoot along several miles of gravel road. He opens a bag of chips and munches on them throughout.

PAUL: [*heavy sigh*] Oh, man, this day was truly miserable. *Truly miserable*. The day was supposed to start with the call to Lucinda at eleven-thirty or so, and then getting together very early in the afternoon: twelve, one o'clock. Leave a message. Calls me back at two-thirty. "Well, now I've got to work out. Maybe about eight? Come out at eight." I said I could do three hours. "Three hours?!" She just doesn't seem to understand how long it takes.

Just when I was going to go out and get something to eat at like five o'clock, I get this call from her manager, who's in New Jersey—she's twenty minutes away—telling me that she doesn't understand why she has to come get me—which *is* a drag and everything, but why can't *she* just say that instead of having her manager call me from New Jersey?

Call Mikal, call Bud [Scoppa, friend and music critic]—can't get a ride. Call her and ask when. Now the interview starts at ten o'clock at night. Wonderful. And she's ticked off that they're going to take her photo and it's going to take two hours to take a photo. She's just ticked off generally. "I hate the paper. Nobody's told me nothing." And I'm pissed. I try to settle down and I don't really manage it.

Anyway, I take the cab out to Lucinda's. Take the goddamn cab out there. Get there ten-to-ten. She's in a *really ticked off* mood and just starts wailing about, "I don't even know if I even want to do this interview! I hate the *Weekly*! You make them reimburse you for this. I don't know why I should care about this article!" Just whiny and awful like a two-year-old. Just really *nasty*. Not so much *at* me—at the *Weekly*—but it's not what you want to walk into, which was even much worse than she was over the telephone. I really felt like just walking out the door and saying, "Screw it." "Nobody told me that this was going to be a possible cover and a photo, and nobody told me that it was going to take this much time! I didn't know anything about it until a few days ago!" I said, "Your manager knew about it, he knew it was a possible cover. He knows it's realistic to want to talk to somebody for six or seven hours on a piece like this. You agreed to do it. We have to do it or both our names are mud. Can't really do you any great harm. They're not going to like it if you don't do it, and they're not going to like *me* if you don't do it." Yeah, she just went on and on. Life isn't fair. What can I say? I think half of her felt guilty that she didn't come and get me. So she felt [*sic*] this incredible sort of harangue at the *Weekly*, trying to stick it off on them instead of the circumstances. I really, the first five minutes out there, just figured, *This ain't going anywhere*.

A big Labrador puppy kept crawling over me and biting my hand and jumping up in my face, and I just thought, *Oh, god, this is just hopeless*. It's like ten-fifteen now and she's in this *pissy* mood and we're just getting *nothing* done. We go back to her little office space, which is pretty small, and she brings a box back there to pack books. Without any real hope at all, I read off the first question and she sort of gets this sweet smile and amazingly enough, once we started to talk, it was a good interview. It was better than the first day's. She was pretty good on some of her answers and she most of the time was pretty forthcoming. One time I think she thought I was trying to trick her with a question about whether she was a happy kid, but I wasn't. For the most part I got *much, much* more than I ever thought I would tonight. I thought

I'd get zip. I don't know if I covered even half the stuff I wanted her to answer, but at least there's a fighting chance for this thing with the information I got tonight, which was—oh, god, what was it?—probably close to two hours maybe. Something like that.

Unfortunately, she wore out after that amount of time. Amazingly I wasn't mad anymore and I was putting the pieces together mentally, and I could see her just yawning and yawning through the last forty-five minutes, the last thirty minutes. I just ignored hints that she was getting tired and kept rolling until it became apparent that she wasn't going to go any further.

I called a cab again. She offered to take me back, but it wasn't a serious offer, I don't think. If I would've said yes, god knows what she would have done tomorrow. Sixteen dollars to get there. Same to get back, except the Chinese guy—very nice, sweet guy—didn't know where he was going and took three times as long. I get home at one forty-five after spending an hour and a half trying to get back.

Anyway, she purported this scheme about the Palomino at eight tomorrow, which doesn't thrill me, but I don't have any real choice. She says it'll go well. Hopefully. We have a lot to cover tomorrow. Hopefully I can get a ride out there, too. I don't know, this is almost over. It's been a truly horrific day. I'm amazed and thank god that the interview went well. And may I get another two hours like it tomorrow. Ooh, boy, what a story this is turning out to be.

The tape runs out. Since yesterday, Paul has purchased new batteries for his tape recorder. When he commences recording again, Lucinda and he are in the darkness backstage at the Palomino Club. The loud music from the club— and the multiple conversations and the ringing of the telephone, combined with the roar of aircraft of all sizes arriving and departing from nearby Burbank-Glendale-Pasadena Airport—often drown them out. Sometimes they have to shout to be heard.

PAUL: This is one of your favorite places.

LUCINDA: Yeah. A lot of people I know come down here. On Tuesday nights, it's kind of fun like this. The band that was up just now is the house band for tonight. They go on and they do a set and then they get off, and then like four other bands get on and do like twenty-five minutes or twenty minutes or something. And then the house band gets back up again.

PAUL: [*adjusts the recording level*] If you don't mind, I'm going to crank this up as high as it will go here. Can you talk just a little about some of these songs that we didn't talk about yesterday? "Six Blocks Away" is a New York song.

LUCINDA: I can't remember if I wrote it while I was there or right after I left there, but it was right around that time, yeah. Written for my friend Bill Priest, the same person I wrote "Hard Road" for on the *Happy Woman Blues* album.

PAUL: We played through all those songs that you'd recorded for the RCA record, and there was one that you didn't have a tape on, you mentioned.

LUCINDA: You're right. It was on the rough mix tape that never did get mixed because RCA didn't like it. They didn't want it to be on the record, so it didn't get mixed. It's called "Well Well Well." It's not one of my best songs. I wrote it real fast. I may end up revising it. It's kind of like a little jug band thing. It's real kind of lighthearted, kind of country, folky type of thing. It's kind of too, um, I don't know. They didn't get it.[38]

PAUL: One of my favorites is "Sweet Old World."

LUCINDA: That was actually inspi—no, I don't know if I should say *inspired*. Whenever I talk about some of these songs, it's the same problem I was having when I was on the radio show Sunday night, is how to describe—well, I did describe it that night a little bit.

PAUL: Yes, as an anti-suicide song.

38 A recorded version of "Well Well Well" wouldn't surface until 2008 and Lucinda's ninth studio album, *Little Honey*.

LUCINDA: Right. Or I should say a celebration of life song. It sounds better. A friend's father had killed himself just this past year. I didn't know her real well, but just the whole idea of it just really struck me. It was just so sudden and everything. I heard about that, and then just the other one that I knew about from before that I wrote "Pineola" about. They didn't come close together, but just the whole idea of it in general. I think that was what prompted me to write this, was when I heard about this friend of mine in Austin's dad just like shooting himself out of the clear blue.

PAUL: It's not about one specific person, it seems like.

LUCINDA: Right. And I may have already even started writing something on it before and that may have just been the thing that allowed me to finish the song.

Seminal rock critic John Morthland's name comes up.

LUCINDA: I talked to him, by the way, yesterday. Did I tell you? I told him that I was getting together with you, and he said, "*Really? Paul Nelson? Wow.*" He said, "Out of that whole New York writing crowd, he's about the only one there I really felt was so nice and that I really liked."

PAUL: That's really nice to hear. I always liked John, too.

LUCINDA: I told him that I gave you his number, and he said, "Oh, good."

PAUL: I had it and I lost it, and then he sent me a Christmas card, and he didn't put an address on it. So I didn't know where to get him, because he's unlisted. I know he's unlisted because when he sent me the number, he said, "This is for *no one*." I always have numbers on little sheets of paper, and I always wonder whose number they are.[39] [*strikes a match to read his notes*]

39 By the time of Paul Nelson's demise, over fifteen years after these interviews took place, a good amount of every flat surface in his apartment, horizontal or vertical, would have Post-it Notes affixed to them, and scraps of paper of varying shapes and sizes, bearing reminders and phone numbers (some of them with corresponding names, many not). A half dozen of them would contain this editor's name

LUCINDA: Need a flashlight.

PAUL: Tell me that White man's blues story—

LUCINDA: Oh, god. Well, I was just doing this interview for, I don't know, it might have been the *Boston Globe* actually, and they asked me what kind of music I did. He said something like, "How can you sing blues and country both?" and I said, "Well, country is White man's blues," you know, to use an old quote. The two go hand in hand.

PAUL: It's a Hank Williams quote, isn't it?

LUCINDA: I don't remember. Don't say that because I'm not sure.

PAUL: I think it is, but I'm not sure either.[40]

LUCINDA: I've seen it before, I've heard it before. It's saying a lot in a few words, and you either understand what that means or you don't. So first of all, how anybody could ask me how I can sing both country and blues, is obviously not very hip and not going to get it. How are you supposed to answer that? "How can you sing country *and* blues?" Where do you go from there with a question like that? So I said, "Country is the White man's blues." They quoted me, "Country is White people's blues," and I saw that and I was furious, absolutely furious. It just defeats the whole point of what I was saying. How anybody can be so unhip sometimes. God! It never ceases to amaze me.

PAUL: Do you ever feel like a role model for women? Do you *want* to feel like a role model for women?

LUCINDA: You don't really *feel* that way. It's not something you feel like.

---

and phone number and reference my desire to work with him on a book collecting his writings. Of these, one in particular will always intrigue me; not what it said ("The book guy" along with my name), but its placement approximately one foot off the floor inside the door frame leading from one room to another. On nights I cannot sleep, I often wonder why Paul chose that particular place for the note and under what situation he would have ever known to find it there.

40 Over the years the quote has also been attributed to Ray Charles, Little Richard, and Jimmie Rodgers.

PAUL: No, but do people view you that way? Let's put it that way.

LUCINDA: Well, I don't know. See, it's hard to know that yourself, because unless people come up and tell you that—they don't always tell you. But I've gotten the impression that that's probably true to some extent, because I have a big following of women who like my music. I know *that*.

PAUL: Well, I think they like somebody who has fought to get the music really the way she wants it.

LUCINDA: Well, also what I'm singing about, what my songs say, they just relate to. Like, "Side of the Road" is real popular with women because it's a song about searching for your independence while you're in a relationship and you love the person you're with. You don't want to leave the person you're with, but at the same time you miss being by yourself; you kind of long for that feeling of how you used to feel when you were alone. Actually what the song is about is losing part of yourself in a relationship, which women do a lot. As soon as you get in a relationship you lose something that you had before. It's a constant battle with a constant struggle, and *that's* what that song is about. It's not the other person's fault, it doesn't have anything to do with that. It's just this thing that women do when they get in relationships. So you start realizing that and start thinking about it. That's what makes you want to leave sometimes. It's not even the person, it's that you lose part of yourself when you're in this relationship. So the only way you can get it back is to leave and be by yourself. But then it just becomes a vicious cycle. Then you just get into another relationship and you just do the same thing all over again. It's not the other person, it's you. You have to do that. I mean, unless you're in a real abusive relationship. I'm talking about if you're just in what could be a normally happy, healthy relationship. It might even be that way, but you might still feel that way. It wouldn't even be the other person necessarily.

PAUL: Some of the articles refer to an ambiguity, a push/pull quality, and it's in "Side of the Road." I think she wants to stay and she wants to leave. I think that's present in a lot of your songs.

LUCINDA: It is. Most women relate to that because that's what everybody does. It's like a real honest kind of thing.

PAUL: Is that one of your characteristics, do you think?

LUCINDA: Of my personality? Probably, yeah.

PAUL: Can you describe what kind of a person you are? What are some characteristic traits?

LUCINDA: I've got to think about that for a minute. Whatever I say, it's going to be pretty indicative I think of most people. Some people have a hard time just *being* happy, knowing how to be happy. You have to learn it. I'm not real easily satisfied. I get bored real easily with things. If things are going along fine, I tend to think something's wrong. *What's wrong? There's nothing wrong*—so I've got to make something wrong. That's a real typical thing. Everything's fine, and then you look for something to get nervous about or anxious about or whatever. It's like you're not comfortable unless you're uncomfortable. [*sounds as if a 747 is about to land atop the club*]

PAUL: Say that last part again. I missed it.

LUCINDA: I'm real aware of it, so I'm working on that. But that's not uncommon, I don't think. It's the stuff that most people toss off as "Well, she's an artist" type of thing. Or "He's an artist" or something, so you get away with it. People who are in music or whatever, in arts, have those similar things. But a lot of people do.

PAUL: Let me phrase it a different way as I segue into another question which I usually ask people: what do you think your best qualities are, the quality that you're most proud of, and what do you think your worst qualities are, both as a person first and then as an artist or a writer? That one always stumps people for a little while.

LUCINDA: Yeah, because I don't really feel comfortable talking about myself that much. Um, I'm real generous. If I had a lot of money, I'd just loan it to friends. That type of thing. Um, I think I'm pretty much a giving kind of person. I'm real sensitive, a romantic.

PAUL: Always gets one into trouble, doesn't it?

LUCINDA: Aquarius.

PAUL: Yeah, me, too.

LUCINDA: Um. I tend to give people the benefit of the doubt all the time, which sometimes gets me into trouble. I like people in general, I'm pretty much a people person. I think I'm pretty open with people. [*drowned out*] A lot of planes coming in at the same time!

But the thing is, because I tend to be open and I'll let people come in pretty easily and all, and I'm pretty sensitive to stuff, sometimes I have trouble with that because I'm overly sensitive. I tend to get defensive sometimes, or I'll take things the wrong way. I tend to forget to have a sense of humor about things a lot of times. I take things way too seriously. I need to lighten up. That's the only reason I'm moving back to Austin: I'm trying to find something that I feel like I lost a little bit over the past ten years. Well, part of it might just be with age. Maybe that's what I'm feeling. I don't know what I'm feeling, but I'm trying to. I've just been feeling somewhat alienated or something lately.

PAUL: It might be Los Angeles also, I suppose.

LUCINDA: See, I don't know if that's what it is, but I'm going to try to find out. I'm going to leave here and see if it makes any difference. I haven't felt real inspired a lot. The creative flow just hasn't been happening.

PAUL: It doesn't sound like L.A. is a town that you particularly like. Seems to be a town where people know each other but never see each other somewhat.

LUCINDA: I like to have people around me. I like to come into contact with people, with friends of mine. I like to have that kind of feedback. That's what I really thrive on, and I'm not getting that enough here. I could spend weeks, months, in my house and never leave and never see anyone, and nobody would think twice about it! I can't live like that![41] I get depressed when that starts happening. Like, I have to have more stimulus, and I don't mean walking down a crowded street with a bunch of people. Not that kind of stimulus. I'm talking about going out and seeing people you know and people dropping over; and you live close enough so that somebody can just drop by your house. You know, everybody lives fairly close to each other and there's some kind of center going on. Even in a big city you can have that. If that's true and if that exists, then it's great. Like the way the Village used to be in New York at one point. But if you're in a big city and you don't have any kind of center like that, then you can feel really isolated.

PAUL: Yeah, I don't feel like I have one in New York. I have about six people I know in the city now that aren't even close.

LUCINDA: See, it's different for everybody. Some people like that feeling of aloneness. I tell people I'm moving to Austin and they say, "Well, that's all fine and good, but everybody knows your business because it's a smaller city and smaller town," and blah blah blah. *So* you're not going to find a perfect place to live. And anyway the music community here is the same way: everybody knows your business. It becomes that same kind of circle. Anytime you're in any kind of situation like that there's still going to be a certain element of that. But that's why I come down to these things on Tuesday nights, because I know I'm going to see a lot of the same people and there's camaraderie. I come in and everybody goes, "Hi, how are you?" and I see all my friends and it feels real warm and comfortable. I found myself only coming here to the Barndance things and I started thinking, *What am I living in this humongous city for? I'm going to one club one night a week. I don't belong to anything else here.* It's like, what's the point?

PAUL: Going back to the other part before, the best points about your character and the worst points about your character, how

41 Paul *did* live like that. When he died in his apartment, a week would pass before his body was found.

about as a singer? Performer? Writer? What do you think you do the best?

LUCINDA: Well, writing. I think melodies, with lyrics also. I really consider myself more of a singer-songwriter, but I don't consider myself a vocalist. Although sometimes I get asked to sing backup on somebody's record, but I don't really feel that comfortable doing that. I'm not like a professional backup singer or something like that.

This friend of mine's playing. Do you mind if we take a break and go hear her a little bit?

When Paul turns the tape recorder back on, he's still backstage at the Palomino Club but now he's by himself, in what appears to be a storage room, surrounded by cases of beer and portable space heaters. Sounding as if he is freezing, he speaks somewhat clandestinely, whispering into the microphone. Sometimes he is still barely audible over the bands, their audience, and the jets above.

PAUL: Lucinda and I are sitting way back in an offshoot of the Palomino, in a back room, on a cold night in utter darkness with two candles, and I can't read my questions hardly. We're sitting with this ten-foot board fence around us and way back. There's a big back room with chairs and tables, a couple of them, and we're in yet a third one, which has a bunch of old junk in it, sitting here in the dark doing the interview. But she's very receptive and she looks really well. She looks good and friendly today after the photo session.

Did about forty minutes of it—no, about thirty minutes of it—when she runs into the club to hear her friend. Also, the harmonica player is here from the record and a bunch of people she knows. She's talked about the club. The back is like the front: it's this *huge* board fence; sort of looks like a fort with doors in it. As she goes in to hear her friend, there's one light pointing out, and I move our little tiny, square two-foot table over under the light so I can see my questions. Seems like a great idea.

It's a very great atmosphere. You can see the front sign of the Palomino from here: a horseshoe with a yellow horse rearing in the middle in neon and a blinking sign of a cowboy. It's going really well. Anyway, I think I'm going to change the tape and put a fresh tape in. All right.

When he begins recording again, Lucinda has joined him in the new locale. The audio challenges within and without the Palomino have subsided somewhat.

LUCINDA: So, um, are we almost done? What else do we need to do?

PAUL: Yeah, almost done. Almost done.

LUCINDA: [*feigning a breakdown*] Come on, Paul. You want me to tell you something that nobody else knows. I already have.

PAUL: You've told me a *lot* of stuff.

LUCINDA: I've been pretty, you know.

PAUL: Yes, you have.

Talk turns to songwriting.

PAUL: I was always a liberal, but I had a tough time listening to all those bad topical songs. They didn't give me much pleasure. I love Phil Ochs as a person, but I hated most of the topical songs. He knew it and we got along great. We talked about movies and stuff.

LUCINDA: [*yawns*] Well, it's hard to write a good topical song.

PAUL: It's *very* hard.

LUCINDA: Bob Dylan's one of the few artists I've ever heard be successful at that. And until I can write a song that comes close to "Masters of War," I'm not even going to try to do that.

PAUL: No, because you don't want to wind up preaching to the converted.

LUCINDA: "The Times They Are a-Changin'"—I mean, he wrote all the best. He was able to do that—he *is* able to do that. One of the things that I wish I were able to do better.

PAUL: "[The Lonesome Death of] Hattie Carroll," do you like that one? That's my favorite because he really makes you feel for that person. Rather than preaching at you, you feel for the person.

LUCINDA: Right. Well, the stuff that I do, that I'm experimenting with writing about, aren't really political songs. But to me, even if I did write a quote-unquote *political song*, it would be more from a humanist perspective, the human condition, which is what it's all about anyway. It's not really about politics, it's about day-to-day life, the human condition. Like, "Memphis Pearl" could be considered a political song. It's about a homeless woman with a baby, who's destitute and down and out and maybe she's a prostitute or whatever. Whatever you want to read into it, that doesn't really matter. The song is about her, but it still says something. It has a message.

PAUL: Those are the best kind, where you feel the person and then you feel the larger picture as well. You seem to be political and very much anti the war and things. You're obviously liberal, I think.

LUCINDA: Yeah, although that word now has such different connotations.

PAUL: Well, you know what I mean. I don't think there are very many left. But I always found I was for all these things, but they produced so much bad art that I just didn't want to sit through. You need a Picasso or a Dylan to pull this stuff off.

One of my big favorites is the first song on the Rough Trade album. Is it a deliberate thing to write like that, where it ends where most songs like that would begin and the structure is sort of oblique?

LUCINDA: Not really a conscious thing. What are you referring to?

PAUL: "I Just Wanted to See You So Bad," where she goes up to see him, and then when she sees him the song ends. A lot of people would've started at that point. What happens to them when they do get together? But you end it at that point, and I think that's so neat. I really like that. It's what you do in a few of the songs—which maybe drove Peter Philbin crazy—but the song sort of ends where you think it would begin. Some of them, they tell you so much, but no more, about a character, and it's very interesting. I think you make that work for you. They're very quirky songs with quirky structures in places and it really works nicely.

LUCINDA: [*giggles*] That's the kind of stuff I don't think about, I'm not conscious of when I'm doing it, I don't think.

PAUL: Just instinct and intuition. Willie Nile, I talked to him a few weeks ago [for the *Musician* article "Willie Nile's Good Luck/Bad Luck"], and he said he wants to write songs with a lot of elbows in them. I thought that was a nice term for odd little quirks and angles and stuff. Your songs have a lot of elbows.

LUCINDA: Well, I like to throw in little angles.

PAUL: And they make your songs unique, which is probably why people can't figure them out sometimes. You can't guess what happens.

LUCINDA: I try to sit back and think about how *I* would feel if I were hearing it and what I would think if I were hearing it. Does it sound too corny? Or does it sound too pedantic? Or does it sound too clichéd? There's just a fine line between familiarity and—

PAUL: Triteness.

LUCINDA: Triteness, exactly. That's where the craft comes in, I guess, is knowing just how many familiar words to use, so it's not too *heady*. But at the same time you want to write intelligently. So I try to find that balance somewhere, because I never want to be elitist about it. I hate that kind of self-indulgent—

PAUL: Genius, self-indulgence.

LUCINDA: Yeah, and that's boring. You've got to bring people in.

PAUL: The folk-country base brings them in, too, I think.

LUCINDA: Yeah, the music, but I mean lyrically. You can't be a snob about it. You can't just write these songs that only you understand. Nobody is interested in sitting and hearing twelve verses of what somebody did when they were in kindergarten or from the time they were in kindergarten through high school. You've got to make it interesting, but so that it's not too much of that intellectual folky thing.

PAUL: A lot of this came from your father, this no clichés, no stereotypes, other kind of stuff, I guess, too.

LUCINDA: Yeah, he used to say that all the time.

PAUL: Was he an active critic of your songs? Did you take your songs to him and say, "What do you think?"

LUCINDA: I show him my stuff.

PAUL: You still do that? And he's helpful?

LUCINDA: Um-hum. Sometimes just a word or two. He'll suggest, "Why don't you use this here instead of this? It makes more sense." It's the same thing I was just saying about intelligent writing. It's okay to use fantasy in there and create poetic license or whatever; but still, there's a fine line. It still has to make sense. You can still be poetic or whatever, but it still has to make sense. I don't know how to explain it exactly. It's got to be grounded. Country music for me has helped me stay grounded. That's what I draw from, and you have that first. Then you embellish it. But first you have to be grounded, and that's what people identify with. That's the gut thing. And then this, the mental head part, that's the interesting part of it. But you have to have that grounding, solid thing. Country and blues, that's what that's all about: it's all gut. See, that's what I see people getting away from too much. Like, a lot of the folk stuff got too far into the head thing.

See, I never got too far into that. I was into the folk thing, but I never allowed myself to get too far away. I've stayed with this country-blues. I drew more back on that, because I was in folk bars and coffeehouses, and sitting there, like [*snores*], yawning, listening to *no roots*—like, *all head* and no roots—which is *really* boring. It's not going to capture an audience.

See, I could play anywhere. I've played everywhere: coffeehouses, bars, clubs, hotel lounges, Holiday Inn lounges, on the street, I mean, everywhere. I've always challenged that. I can tell what people are reacting to, and so over the years I've been able to just build up a real good ear. I can tell what draws people in. It's just that balance, that fine line.

Some people are traditionalists and they deliberately do it in the traditional vein, and it's sometimes done really well. Like Jo Ann Kelly, I *love* her stuff.

PAUL: I've heard of her. I don't know her stuff very well.

LUCINDA: She's White and British and she sounds Black and Southern. It's amazing. She emulates Memphis Minnie to a tee. It's absolutely incredible. If you closed your eyes, you'd think you were listening to Memphis Minnie. And if you'd see her, you'd never put her face with her voice. Some people might not appreciate it because she does that on purpose, I think.

PAUL: As long as it has heart and soul and it works. It's not one of my favorite genres—Koerner, Ray & Glover and the blues are—but I mean White guys singing blues aren't.[42] But you and Ray and these people don't have any of this preciousness about it, with museum quality about it. It's just—there it is.

LUCINDA: I don't try to be something I'm not, for one thing, and I only do ones that I feel comfortable with. There has to be some kind of thing there. I don't just sing anything.

42 Paul produced *Blues, Rags and Hollers*, the first album by the Minneapolis trio: "Spider" John Koerner, Dave "Snaker" Ray, and Tony "Little Sun" Glover.

PAUL: No, you seem to make them completely a part of you. A lot of times too many folk artists, when they try it, it just becomes precious. You hear any of this stuff and you just can't believe a word of it.

LUCINDA: Not that many people can do it and get away with it. I just happen to like her stuff because I like that kind of music so much.

PAUL: Yeah, I like it, too. Like, Dave Ray and Koerner and those guys, they seem to be able to do it, and you do it really great.

LUCINDA: Well, see, I got into this album in 1965 that was one of my favorite albums of all time, on Elektra, *The Blues Project*.

PAUL: Do you know who wrote the notes for *The Blues Project*?[43]

LUCINDA: The compilation album? You wrote the notes for that? God, I can't believe it, and here we are talking.

PAUL: Look at your copy.

LUCINDA: I ate that album up. I mean, I lived with it. I played it over and over and over. That was like one of the most influential records for me of my life, that album. That White, urban folk-blues kind of stuff. Because I was still listening to like Mississippi John Hurt and stuff like that and Lightnin' Hopkins and all; but this was a new entryway for me and I was able to see how to apply it. Also, because it wasn't real identifiable; it was blues, but it was in-between. I just loved the fluidness of it. Geoff Muldaur's voice, I just loved his voice and that kind of vibrato. There was something just real spooky and kind of, I don't know how to describe—like the way he sings "Ginger Man" on that. And I love the picking, all the, you know. So, yeah, that album was real important for me. That's so ironic that I just brought that up.

43 Not to be confused with the band by the same name, this 1964 album compiled sixteen White folk-blues numbers performed by Dave Van Ronk, John Koerner, Geoff Muldaur, Dave Ray, Danny Kalb, Ian Buchanan, Mark Spoelstra, Eric Von Schmidt, and Bob Landy (a.k.a. Bob Dylan).

PAUL: We do know a lot of the same people.

LUCINDA: Your name keeps popping up every time I turn around.

PAUL: When you went to New York, you met some of these people from *The Blues Project*.

LUCINDA: Well, I met Geoff Muldaur here at McCabe's [Guitar Shop, in Santa Monica], and I met Dave Van Ronk in New York. He was going to give me guitar lessons, but that never transpired.

PAUL: How big a part do you think coming from the South comes into your songwriting?

LUCINDA: Whole hell of a lot. Well, it's such a rich culture and it's such a soulful place. I love the South. I'm a Southerner all the way and that's how I was raised. I was raised in the South and I was raised to be real proud of being a Southerner. I absorbed a lot of Southern literature. That became my favorite kind of stuff. I really identified with it. Because I like the underbelly, the dark weirdness kind of stuff, which was also reality, it was just real life.

PAUL: Do you remember the first real concert you saw with a big name that you really liked?

LUCINDA: One of the ones I can remember was when I was about fourteen, when I lived in New Orleans, I was able to see some concerts there. I used to always see Peter, Paul and Mary when they came through town. They probably played like every year at Loyola, on campus at Loyola, so I went to see them a few times. They were my big heroes. I was a kid, thirteen or fourteen.

PAUL: Some of their stuff's pretty good. It holds up pretty well.

LUCINDA: I loved them. Um, and I saw Donovan at that time period. And I saw the Lovin' Spoonful and Buffalo Springfield, and I saw Hendrix, which I barely remember because it was out in this football field or something.

PAUL: I never saw him. I never saw the Beatles either. I saw the Stones, but not the Beatles.

LUCINDA: I never saw the Beatles or the Stones, and I never saw Dylan back then.

PAUL: I'm trying to speed through this. You mentioned "Side of the Road" as a breakthrough song. Can you think of any others that you thought of as breakthrough songs?

LUCINDA: Well, in a way I guess "Passionate Kisses" was, because now it's sort of like a pop song, which I never really meant it to be, and I didn't know it was going to end up like that. But I never really considered that, you know, *that way*. In a way, maybe "Like a Rose," too, because I was able to get real slow and intimate. It was a more naked kind of song. It's hard to do those kinds of songs, lyrically and musically. It's real soft and everything that way, and real close-up, like "Which Will," that Nick Drake song.[44]

PAUL: I love the way you do that.

LUCINDA: When I wrote "Like a Rose," I think the influence for that came from Velvet Underground, from a couple of their songs, like "I'll Be Your Mirror." Actually that's the way I meant to record it, but it didn't really come out that way. It came out more folky and real pretty. I wanted it to be real pretty, but I wanted to put an electric guitar in it or something to sort of—that contrast, you know?

PAUL: You like the Velvets. You mentioned them a few times.

LUCINDA: I went back and discovered them when I was older. I didn't really get into them that much in their heyday.

PAUL: I never saw them either.

LUCINDA: There was that Velvet Underground song "Pale Blue Eyes." And "Sunday Morning."

44 *"Which Will"* would be included as *Sweet Old World*'s closing cut.

PAUL: Do you have that Velvets live '69 album on Mercury?

LUCINDA: No. I don't have any of their albums.

PAUL: I put together that one. It was after they had broken up. It's a double live album. Some of it's from Texas actually. You can tell it's from Texas because I put in all of Lou Reed talking. He says he'd seen a football game with the Cowboys, so it's obviously Dallas.[45]

Maybe it's just one song of many that influenced you, but we were talking about Leonard Cohen and "Famous Blue Raincoat," that you really wanted to write like that. You know, precise. Was that a big song for you?

LUCINDA: Those were my standards. That's why I was so hard on myself, because I always felt it's got to be this good or else it's not good enough. I always wanted to write a song like "Sad Eyed Lady of the Lowlands." And Van Morrison, he can do no wrong. To me that's what I set myself up against, those kinds of songs.

PAUL: I talked to Cohen briefly today and I said I was interviewing you. He said to say hello.

LUCINDA: Really? He knew who I was? *Really?*

PAUL: Yeah.

LUCINDA: Well, actually I know someone, one of the girls who's been singing harmony with him, Julie Christensen. She's actually from Austin, but she lives out here now. I know her, so she may have mentioned me to him or something.

PAUL: In one of the interviews you were talking about men and women together. Fighting various father figures in one's life. Do you remember that? You were struggling against various father figures, not necessarily meaning your father literally, but you said throughout

45 After convincing his higher-ups at Mercury Records to spend twenty thousand dollars to acquire the live recordings that became the essential *1969: Velvet Underground Live*, Paul was responsible for curating the tracks and producing the album. For some unknown reason, Irwin Steinberg, Mercury's president, always confused the band with Deep Purple; otherwise he probably wouldn't have sanctioned the project.

your whole life I guess it included people who wanted to change your mind as well.

LUCINDA: Well, it's real easy to fall into that role of letting someone do something for you. Because a lot of times you might be the only woman among a group of all men recording in a studio. You have a male engineer, you have a male producer, you have male this and male that, and so it's real easy to get into that role: [*sounding mousy*] "Okay, whatever you say" type of thing. So it's a constant battle to *not* allow yourself to fall into that kind of thing; because it's real easy to just sit back and take direction, as opposed to taking charge. I'm still learning how to do that. I know a lot of women have that problem in the studio, because I've talked to them about it. I know friends of mine who've had the same problem in the studio and they end up making demo tapes and records that they don't like. You say, "How did you allow that to happen? You were right there." Well, I know how it happens. Because it's really easy to get intimidated and you *assume* someone else knows more than you do because they've had more experience or whatever. And it's a double-edged sword because it also makes it harder if you're the only woman, and you have a male engineer and a male producer, and you subconsciously just sink back into that subservient role. So it's like a constant battle to just be aware of that and say, "No, I don't like the way this sounds, goddammit, and I want to do it over again. So fuck you." And even if they yell at you, you can't, like, go cowering off into a corner. Somebody might yell at you, but it's not the end of the world. It doesn't mean they don't like you and it doesn't mean they don't love you. But rather than risk that kind of confrontation, it's a lot easier to just go [*more mousy*], "Well, okay. Whatever you say." And then you go home later and you listen to it and you hate it and you go, "Why didn't I say something?" I've seen that happen over and over and over again, and I let it happen one too many times with these demo tapes I've done. I didn't take charge and I didn't have any kind of focus or direction. Like, when I did that Henry Lewy thing, I mean, he's real experienced and all this stuff, but I just *assumed* too much. I *assumed* that he knew what I wanted, and you can never assume that. You have to stay on top of it all the time, constantly. So by the time I went in to do the Rough Trade album, I had been through a few of these scenarios like that, where I was feeling really frustrated because I wasn't getting across what I wanted to get across on tape. People just weren't getting it because I had yet to make a decent demo tape or a really good record with all these songs I had. I had all these songs—I didn't have a record out since the *Happy Woman Blues* thing—I just kept getting passed back and forth from one A&R person to another, and nobody knew what to do with me. I fell in the cracks between country and rock & roll. And part of it was that I just hadn't had that kind of focusing and direction. I allowed myself to be led around too much. Even though I'm a real independent kind of person, it's still real easy to do that if you're a female. As strong and hardheaded and independent as you might be, it's real easy for you to just fall into that role.

PAUL: One of these guys wouldn't even let you play guitar. Pete Anderson, is it?

LUCINDA: Well, yeah. When we were doing that demo, it was just easier if he did it. He's a great guitar player, but that's not the point, that's not the issue. I wasn't going to play all the lead parts, I was just going to play the basic kind of whatever it is that I do with the songs. But no, he did all of the guitar parts. It's a control thing.

PAUL: You could find better guitarists than Neil Young that play the guitar, too, but you'd never get the same impact as Neil Young. I mean, technically you could find better ones.

LUCINDA: I don't want to put him down in the story, but that's probably the most accurate kind of example of that. But that hasn't been the only incident like that.

A couple on their way out find Lucinda and Paul in their spot of light in the dark. She introduces them to him and mentions that he used to write for Sing Out!

MAN: I was in a band in New York when *Crawdaddy* was first starting out.

PAUL: Yeah, I was writing for them then.

LUCINDA: I was just talking about this great album on Elektra called *The Blues Project*, that compilation album with Geoff Muldaur on it and Eric Von Schmidt that came out in about 1965. One of the most influential albums of my life. He wrote the liner notes for the album.

MAN: Oh, too much!

LUCINDA: It's so funny.

WOMAN: It sure is.

PAUL: I don't think it was the liner notes that affected you. I think it was the music.

LUCINDA: [*everyone laughs*] I know. But I mean, you know.

WOMAN: Mutual connections.

LUCINDA: Yeah.

PAUL: A lot of them.

After more small talk and exchanging contact information with Lucinda, everybody says their goodbyes. Her friends leave them again alone.

PAUL: Just a couple more here. Why do you think it is you never learned to write music?

LUCINDA: Technically? Music theory and stuff? It's too mathematical, I guess, for me. My brain doesn't work that way. What do you call it when you think with your—you know, they talk about the right side of your brain and the left side of your brain?

PAUL: I don't think I think with either one. [*laughs*]

LUCINDA: I don't know, I have this mental block when it comes to numbers and stuff. It just never really appealed to me and I always got frustrated trying to learn it.

PAUL: Can you tell me just a little bit, and we can get it on tape, about how it was easier in the Seventies to get by and all?

LUCINDA: Well, just because of the economy of it all, because rent was so cheap, that you could work a little part-time job a couple of days a week and sustain yourself. The change in the economy I think has made a huge difference. Because having that kind of freedom, that much free time, has *got* to make a difference. It just gives you so much creative freedom, so much time to just hang out and play and jam and write and whatever.

PAUL: Yeah, there really were no yuppies then. People were different. The people today that are just into business, they don't read books, they don't listen to music, they don't buy anything cultural. It just seemed very nice in the Seventies, and everybody had enough money and could get by without killing themselves or selling their souls.

LUCINDA: Yeah, I wouldn't want to have to start now.

PAUL: You can't live anyplace!

LUCINDA: Well, there are places to live that are more like that, but I don't think L.A. is one of them.

PAUL: New York's not one of them. And now you're dealing with different types of people, too, at the *top* than probably were on top in the Seventies. They're all bank presidents or something like that. I think they were different creative people.

LUCINDA: Well, those people are out there.

PAUL: No, I mean in the record companies and in the high places. They're different people than there were in the Seventies that were in the high places. It seems like money is at the root of this.

LUCINDA: It's the root of all evil. Always has been. That's why we're in war right now.[46] That's what it all boils down to.

PAUL: [*checking his notes*] That's probably about it unless you can think of anything else.

LUCINDA: Well, you can call me and ask me stuff, too.

PAUL: I just have one more. When you were going through the fan letters at the office, I just had this feeling, and maybe it wasn't even the right feeling, that you liked getting letters from the fans and you wrote them back in many cases.

LUCINDA: Well, I try to. I'm really behind with all that.

PAUL: But that it wasn't about—and maybe this is wrong or maybe I'm not going to put it right—but it wasn't about what people thought of you on the stage and fan adulation. That performing and writing it was your life, and it hardly, really, didn't make that big of difference what people did think. Is that wrong? Right?

LUCINDA: Well, yes and no. I was doing this before anyway. Of course it matters what people think. Everybody cares what people think. I think what you mean is, if I weren't getting fan mail and stuff, would I still be doing this anyway?

PAUL: Yeah. The satisfaction comes from doing it really well, not that the people are saying, "She's number one. She's the greatest." And that if you did get to be number one on the charts that it wouldn't be *that* important, as the songs being good. That the songs be your life, not being number one be your life.

LUCINDA: Yeah.

PAUL: I guess that's what I mean, if you get what I'm talking about. Maybe it's just bullshit, I don't know. But I'm trying to make sense out of this point.

46 At the time these interviews took place, the U.S. was in the midst of the first Gulf War against Iraq.

LUCINDA: I have to admit that I like knowing that people like what I do. It's just kind of icing on the cake. It's the ultimate compliment to have someone write you a letter like that, who you don't even know, and tell you that you touched their lives in some way. But it still surprises me. It affects me on one level, but on a day-to-day level it doesn't really affect how I feel about myself or what I do from day to day. I still have the same old problems that I always had: trying to learn how to be happy in a crazy, mixed up, depressed society, a depressing world for the most part. It doesn't necessarily make you happy. It's nice and it's great, but it's not going to change how you feel about yourself or anything else. It's just sort of reinforcement, I guess.

PAUL: Everybody likes to be liked. I like it when people read an article and they like it. It's just that writing that article means more to me than people saying they liked it.

LUCINDA: Of course, otherwise you wouldn't be a good writer. That goes without saying. If you were just writing for the *glory* of it or whatever, I don't think the two go hand in hand. You wouldn't be able to do that. Although, actually, I guess it is done because look at all the stuff that's real popular that people supposedly like, and it's crap.

PAUL: Yeah, Harold Robbins and all this stuff is just churned out.

LUCINDA: He probably gets fan letters. Maybe he likes what he does, maybe that's what he thinks is good. You can't really put yourself in that place and say, "He's unhappy and miserable because his stuff sucks."

PAUL: I mean, if you got as famous as the Beatles, it would still be about writing the songs well and that would matter more than fame.

LUCINDA: That really makes me nervous to think about it. It makes me extremely uncomfortable. I have no desire to be that famous. I want to be able to make a nice living—

PAUL: Have a pen that writes.

LUCINDA: —but I still want to be able to come to the Palomino to the Barndance and be with my friends. I'm real uncomfortable with any kind of star stuff and all. I don't like that. I'm real uncomfortable with it and I feel real silly. I had to do a video for this song. The whole idea, I have no interest in doing videos or any part of that. All the stuff that you're supposed to do as you go along through the music industry holds no fascination for me at all and I don't really want to have to do it. I'd like to be able to do what I do without doing *that*. And the hard part is once you start doing it, it's like a snowball-rollercoaster. Suddenly you're surrounded by people pulling you along through all the little political scenarios or whatever that you're supposed to do. I *hate* that part of it.

PAUL: That's what I sensed when you were reading the letters.

LUCINDA: That's one reason I'm leaving L.A. That element, there's too much of that. Like, I talk to my friends back in Austin and as far as they're concerned I'm still the same person I was when I left. They think it's funny. I talked to this friend of mine in Albuquerque, and she lives in a trailer with her husband and they have a bluegrass band, and she said, "I guess you're kind of famous now. I was talking to a friend of mine and he said, 'You know Lucinda Williams? Wow, you're a friend of Lucinda's?'" She said, "That's hilarious." Like, she wasn't intimidated by it. And those are the kind of people I want to be around. I mean, I'm glad that I'm able to exist on playing music and all that. Support myself. I like that part of it just because I've had to eat shit for so many years. So it's good not to have to worry about the rent. But having a record deal on a major record label is not the be-all and end-all of my existence. I mean, it *does* make a difference. It feels good for the critics to like your stuff and all that. It's great because those are people whose opinions I really respect, like Ed Ward and John Morthland and Mikal Gilmore and Steve Pond. They all like my stuff, and it feels great. I'm glad.

Then I found myself getting all paranoid and uptight. I got caught up in that thing of, *Oh, my god, I'm going to make a second album* and *What if they don't like it?* and *What if they're going to compare it to the first one? Oh, my god, I can't stand for the reviews to come out. What am I going to do?* I just wanted to go run and hide in a cave somewhere, I just wanted to disappear and not be visible. I just didn't want to do it anymore because I couldn't stand the thought of being exposed anymore. It was different before because I wasn't expecting it, and now all of a sudden I'm doing it, I'm in the music business. It's like I woke up one day and went, *Oh, my god! I'm becoming sort of successful! Oh, my god, people are looking at me completely differently. Oh, my god!* And I just started reevaluating everything. What was I doing and *Do I really want to be doing this?* Sometimes it felt okay, but a lot of times it didn't feel okay. All of a sudden I had a manager and a lawyer and a business manager and a record company and a booking agent, and I didn't have to worry about the rent anymore. But I still felt the same way I did before and it didn't make me any happier. And then I just had all the hassles of business and stuff. I was getting totally paranoid worrying about stuff that I never worried about before. Before I worried about the rent; now I was worried about what some record company person is going to think about my songs. I don't know which is worse. So I kind of had to just grab hold of myself and say, "Wait a minute, wait a minute." Like, with this whole scenario of making this album [*Sweet Old World*], I just went through a lot of changes with this thing, just a lot of confusion and disillusionment and disappointment. *So this is what it's like to be on a major record label? This is it? This is what I've been striving for all these years? For twenty years? This is it?* You know, that kind of crisis/change thing that everybody goes through. So that's what I've been kind of going through for the last year, that whole thing of like, *This is it? Big fucking deal, I don't even know if I* want *it anymore. Just get back, leave me alone, because I don't want what you think I want.* It's hard to control it, though. It's hard to say, "Okay, I'm going to take this, some of this, but I don't want that. I just want this." It's like it's all or nothing.

Some more of Lucinda's friends stop by to bid their farewells, and she introduces Paul as "a friend of mine." He turns off the tape recorder and, when he turns it back on, it's just the two of them again.

PAUL: Finish it off, whatever you want to say. You're free. You have the last word. You can make up your own question or not make up one, whatever. We're done.

LUCINDA: [*laughs*] I don't know.

PAUL: You don't have to say anything. You can just say, "Thank god!"

LUCINDA: Oh, I didn't tell you about my song ending up in a porno movie. We might as well just talk about it now. What the hell.

PAUL: What song?

LUCINDA: Well, it just goes to show that you need to be real careful when you sign a publishing deal, and read the fine print. But anyway, what I was going to say, Folkways had this brother-sister relationship with Alpha Music. I signed this little dinky contract, and they always say in the contract they can use your songs and whatever. So I get this call from our friend John T. Davis in Austin, who's a journalist in Austin. We were talking on the phone, this was when I first moved out here, and he said, "This fan of yours called me up and said that he heard this song of yours in this porno film and he recognized the song." And I said, "Oh, yeah, right, ha ha ha," and had a big laugh about it. I said, "What was the name of it?" and he said, "*All American Girls in Heat Part 2*." I said, "Come on. No way. You're kidding." This is like a big joke. Of course the caller didn't identify himself. Gives you an idea the kind of fans I have. I don't where he was watching this, at a theater or at home, but he knew the song because it was off the *Happy Woman Blues* album. It's called "One Night Stand," ironically enough, and it's this tongue-in-cheek kind of country song. So anyway, my manager at the time of course had to research it, so he went out and rented the thing and sure enough it was in there. Needless to say, I was appalled. I didn't know whether to laugh or cry. I felt completely exploited and angry. So we called the guy up. "What's the meaning of this?" "Well, nothing you can really do about it. It says we can use the songs, and I let them have it for a hundred dollars and you're going to get fifty percent of that. You'll be getting fifty dollars pretty soon." Of course I never got any money, not a cent, which isn't the issue. And you can't track those people down because it's all, like—

PAUL: They're all PO boxes.

LUCINDA: Yeah, right! There's nothing on there that says anything that has anybody's name on it; it's all fake names and stuff. But it's this hardcore porno film—we're talking hardcore—and there's my innocent little song off this innocent little album. They obviously built the scene around the song. [*sings*] "Just another one night stand." Here comes this girl in a cowboy hat and a miniskirt: [*western twang*] "Hi, honey. Wanna fill up my cup? I need something *hot*." So they get into this whole thing and there's a pickup truck and the whole bit. First they drive up in this bus, just the two girls with the guy on the bus, and then she gets off the bus and they're at a gas station with a truck stop. All the clichés. And meanwhile the song is going on loud and clear: [*sings*] "Just another one night stand / Just another man to forget." I couldn't believe it. And of course I was petrified—*petrified*—that people are going to think that that was on— So let me set the record straight now, folks, I had *nothing* to do with it. *Nothing at all* to do with it! And by the way, if anybody knows where I can find a copy of it. [*laughing*] I want to have it in my archives.

Are we done?

PAUL: We're done!

LUCINDA: On that note—

Paul presses the stop button. When he begins recording again, alone in his motel room, he snaps his fingers in front of the microphone and lights a Nat Sherman Cigaretello, his smoke of choice. It's around midnight.

PAUL: On that note we were done. That was a really fabulous night. Just great. This is the Lucinda I wanted to see and hadn't seen until this point. Really wonderful. Instead of short answers there'd be long answers. I was actually trying to move along because I thought I wouldn't get all the questions in, and she just kept talking and talking.

It was all terrific, introspective stuff, which I didn't expect. Back with the beer cases and what I thought were bug traps, but they were heating things. And I got this brilliant idea to move the table and everything to this wonderful place to conclude the interview, and she was really on. I expected her not to be in that good a mood, with the photographer's thing, which kept her very late. I was quite stunned, particularly when she didn't show up until, oh, an hour and a half late. I thought, *Oh, I won't get anything*. Then we couldn't find a place in the back for a long time before we could talk. I just thought she would more or less talk a little and friends would interrupt, and that we wouldn't get anything much at all—if half an hour, I thought, especially when she was so late—that I'd get nothing out of this. But it certainly didn't turn out that way. It was by far the best interview, and she really seemed relaxed for the first time. Maybe because the end was near and she's staying the extra day, but it was really terrific. I wish the rest of it hadn't been so rocky at times, though. I had to run right afterwards because the car was waiting and I was a little late with it. She seemed to understand. They gave her a cake onstage. I didn't get to see her perform, which I'd have liked to have done; but if I'd stayed, it would've probably killed me. Probably will anyway. I was exhausted and it would have been a very late night. It's just a great relief for it to be over.

She had on a little gray jacket tonight and brown boots, cowboy boots with metal tips, and blue jeans. Wonderful lot of friends, they all seemed just terrific. I met a lot of them, but I don't remember who they were. One of them [Mandy Mercier] is the woman who was there when she met Dylan. They all seemed to be warm and wonderful. She really opened up and talked tonight for the first time. You got the feeling this is what she's like when she's relaxed and happy. The introspection tonight really seemed to *not* be a pain in the ass for her to deal with, since she wasn't suspicious like she was the other times. A complete surprise. The club itself is pretty wonderful. It just made the story basically. Now I've probably got *too much* instead of too little, but thank god literally for that. But I really needed an *up* at the end of this story and it really happened that way. It's going to be a pretty terrific story, I think. And I really don't even think there are too many holes to fill basically. I doubt that there are. Probably won't need all this other stuff from people to fill in the blanks. So I think it will be a very good story. This is the best setting, I think, also that I've got to write with. The outside stuff and the club and the whole scene, and what she said about the club, that sort of makes the whole business. The Barndance night, how she comes down all the time, it's wonderful stuff. So I'll check to make sure it's here [*on tape*] now. Thank heavens I got the batteries, too, or I would've been totally out of luck.

Paul turns off the tape recorder.

ENTR'ACTE

Paul's final meeting with Lucinda Williams is on February 26, 1991. From what evidence we have, namely his papers and tapes, he doesn't record anything else until eight days later, on March 6, when he begins interviewing Leonard Cohen. What does he do with his time in between, from February 27 through March 5? For certain he doesn't return to New York, as his funds wouldn't allow it.

Kit Rachlis doesn't know. "At that point, Paul was no longer staying with Ariel and me and had moved into the motel on Highland Avenue that Fred Schruers paid for. But what he did during that stretch is a mystery. We talked once the next week when he interviewed Leonard Cohen, but our conversation focused on how it was going, not on what he had been doing. I think he got together with Mikal Gilmore at least once during the period, but I don't know for certain."

Fred Schruers recalls: "I'm sure we got some hang time during those several days of downtime between interviews in February and March, but nothing stands out. I do recall being along for a portion of a Lucinda meetup and trying to communicate, however subtly, that for this fairly seasoned *RS* contributor and Paul confrere, this was all well worth her time. It takes nothing away from her musical brilliance to say she wasn't exactly a piece of cake. Despite a somewhat eccentric upbringing, she was perhaps a little shy of the patience that might have eased the process and led to a better result."

"I'm guessing," says Rachlis, "but I suspect he mostly stayed alone in his motel room listening to Julie London and Chet Baker, as he did in our guest room."

PART II

PAUL NELSON INTERVIEWS LEONARD COHEN

BETWEEN MARCH 6–10, 1991

DISCUSSED DISCOGRAPHY & BIBLIOGRAPHY

DISCOGRAPHY

This list only includes those Leonard Cohen albums discussed in Paul Nelson's following conversations with him. It does not include the albums that would be released after 1992's *The Future*.

1967	*Songs of Leonard Cohen*	Columbia Records
1969	*Songs from a Room*	Columbia Records
1971	*Songs of Love and Hate*	Columbia Records
1973	*Live Songs*	Columbia Records
1974	*New Skin for the Old Ceremony*	Columbia Records
1975	*The Best of Leonard Cohen*	Columbia Records
1977	*Death of a Ladies' Man*	Warner Bros.
1979	*Recent Songs*	Columbia Records
1984	*Various Positions*	Passport Records
1988	*I'm Your Man*	Columbia Records
1992	*The Future*	Columbia Records

BIBLIOGRAPHY

This list only includes those Leonard Cohen books discussed in Paul Nelson's following conversations with him. It does not include volumes that would be released after 1984's *Book of Mercy*.

Novels

1963	*The Favourite Game*	Secker & Warburg
1966	*Beautiful Losers*	Viking Press

Poetry Collections

1956	*Let Us Compare Mythologies*	Contact Press
1961	*The Spice-Box of Earth*	McClelland & Stewart Limited
1964	*Flowers for Hitler*	McClelland & Stewart Limited
1966	*Parasites of Heaven*	McClelland & Stewart Limited
1968	*Selected Poems 1956–1968*	McClelland & Stewart Limited
1972	*The Energy of Slaves*	McClelland & Stewart Limited
1978	*Death of a Lady's Man*	McClelland & Stewart Limited
1984	*Book of Mercy*	McClelland & Stewart Limited

Paul Nelson meets Leonard Cohen at the Chariot, a bustling coffee shop on La Brea and Wilshire in Los Angeles. Leonard sips a cup of coffee while Paul most likely drinks his customary two Cokes. Leonard is "wearing a gray striped suit," and "Looks like Dustin Hoffman sort of when he smiles. A really wonderful, open smile. Battered good looks." Conversation comes easily between the two, and they often open up to one another or share a laugh.

LEONARD: Are you here alone?

PAUL: Yeah. The [*LA*] *Weekly* has been rather strange. I've been trying to get out here since December. "Well, we can't do it for just one artist. You'll have to do another interview with another artist." So they gave me Lucinda to do, which was all right, and then they had to wait like a month to buy a cheaper air ticket for me. I don't know how much expense they're going to pick up and how much I'm on my own.

WAITRESS: Would you like some cream for that coffee?

LEONARD: Yes, ma'am. Some milk please. [*takes out his cigarettes*]

PAUL: God, you smoke, Leonard. Great, I can have a cigarette. Not too many of us left.

LEONARD: Help yourself.

PAUL: [*lights up*] I've always sort of felt a kinship to your music. We're about the same age. I was born in '36. I was born sixty miles from Canada. Warren, Minnesota, a little bitty town.

LEONARD: You're from Minnesota, eh?

PAUL: Fifteen-hundred, yeah. Dylan and I actually went to the U of M together for the small time he was there. I knew him before he was Dylan, actually.

Cold country. It was forty-five below the day I was born. January 21st. I mean, I didn't know any better. I thought the whole world might be forty-five below. Who knew? You were from an even colder place, I guess.[47] Or as cold.

LEONARD: As cold.

PAUL: You also remember the Forties and the Fifties, which is also rather wonderful. Not many people do. What was your birthdate? I know it was '34.

LEONARD: Twenty-one September, '34. I'm two years older.[48]

PAUL: I guess I was an early champion. I wrote a lot of early reviews.

LEONARD: I know you did.

PAUL: Took a lot of abuse for it, I must say. [*laughs*]

LEONARD: I imagine, over the years.

47 Leonard Cohen was born in Westmount, Quebec.

48 To be precise, Leonard was one year and eight months older than Paul. At the time of the interviews they were fifty-six and fifty-five, respectively.

PAUL: Including from Columbia Records—even your record company. They were trying to make Billy Joel a lede review once and I said no. And they didn't like it.[49]

LEONARD: Yes, I've had a long and curious relationship with CBS.

PAUL: *Various Positions*, they just pulled out, more or less.

LEONARD: They just neglected to put it out; I don't even think they pulled out. Because it was treated with sublime indifference, they didn't even tell me that they were not putting it out.

PAUL: I remember I got it on a cassette. I couldn't find it, then Mikal Gilmore, who's a friend of mine—I think you know him—

LEONARD: I do know him.

PAUL: —he sent me a cassette of it finally from here. I was proofreading at *Time* and someone borrowed it on my shift and stole the tape.[50]

WAITRESS: [*brings Leonard's order*] Grilled cheese. [*to Paul*] How about you?

PAUL: Nothing right now, thank you.

LEONARD: [*to waitress*] Thank you, dear. Thank you so much. [*to Paul*] Do you want half of this grilled cheese?

PAUL: Oh, no thanks. I had something a little earlier.

49 At least once during his five years as record-review editor at *Rolling Stone*, Paul was overruled and forced to make the occasion of a new Billy Joel album a lede review. Having the last word, he reviewed 1980's *Glass Houses* himself, a 1,000-word negative notice that's best summed up by its final two sentences: "Billy Joel writes smooth and cunning melodies, and what many of his defenders say is true: his material's catchy. But then, so's the flu."

50 Because of their disinterest in 1984's *Various Positions*, Leonard's seventh studio album, Columbia Records (part of the CBS Records Group, which is owned by Sony Music Entertainment) declined to release it in the U.S. until 1990. The album was initially released on the independent Passport Records label.

LEONARD: [*between bites*] *Various Positions*, huh?

PAUL: Yeah, that's a big favorite of mine.

LEONARD: Since that *Various Positions* I've been working nonstop. I need some rest.

Talk turns to his work in progress, the album that would ultimately be released the following year, 1992, as The Future.

LEONARD: I have two tracks. I'll play them for you in the car. One I produced myself and one I produced with a man by the name of Steve Lindsey, who's a very talented young player and producer.

PAUL: You haven't worked with him before?

LEONARD: No, I bumped into him. He was doing a record with the Temptations. My favorite engineer, Leanne Ungar, who's done most of my last records, she was doing the engineering for him, and she introduced me to him. There was a song I liked very much that was written by Frederick Knight, called "Be for Real," that nobody seemed to have heard of. I don't know what the destiny of that record was, but I heard the song and I liked it very much, so we've done a cover of it. It's not quite finished, but I've got enough of it to play it for you in the car, and you can get an idea of it. And then I've got my song "Democracy," which is a long song I worked on a long time. Um, I may do a track with Don Was or with the band Was (Not Was). I'm friendly with those people.

PAUL: You're on one of their records.

LEONARD: Yeah, I did that Elvis song [Was (Not Was)'s "Elvis' Rolls Royce" in 1990]. I like the guys very much and I like Don Was very much. It's just that I find it very hard to translate my intentions, which are often very cloudy, even to myself. It's difficult to collaborate because people generally then move immediately to a kind of music that they know. Which is often good, but often not good for me.

PAUL: Is Don the producing Was and the other one doesn't?

LEONARD: Don is a producer, yes. I think David Weiss also produces or helps in the production. I'm very fond of both of them. I'd like to do a track with them somewhere down the line. If it isn't for this record, then somewhere down the line.

PAUL: And the last one [1988's *I'm Your Man*] you [produced] yourself. Talk to me about that one.

LEONARD: I thought it was my best record. It was a desperate move because I couldn't really find a producer and ended up doing about half of the record myself—playing the keyboard myself on it.

PAUL: Various small keyboards. You've collected them over the years.

LEONARD: I have favorites at different moments. They're really sophisticated toys, they're not like real synthesizers. They have preset factory rhythms and drums; sometimes I replace them, sometimes I don't. Sometimes I just put it right on, like in "Tower of Song."

PAUL: These are all like Casios and things like this?

LEONARD: Technics is my preferred company. It's not terribly expensive. The ones I have now are quite good. I'll show them to you at my house. It's just around the corner, my house.

PAUL: I think it was a very early book by Michael Ondaatje [*Leonard Cohen*, in 1970], back in the footnotes was a quote: "My first mythology was radio," which was certainly also mine. What particular things did you listen to?

LEONARD: Happily, some of the radio stations here, National Public Radio and KPFK, have been rebroadcasting some of those old shows: *Amos 'n' Andy* and *The Shadow*. *Lux* [*Radio*] *Theatre*. *Green Hornet*. Of course, [*The Adventures of*] *Superman*.

PAUL: You were from a metropolitan area. We were so far away from a big city, we didn't even get TV, so I grew up totally without television. I saw my first television when I was seventeen years old in Minneapolis in a department store window. I think we were there for a high school basketball tournament or something. But we were still so far away that we couldn't get it; but people would have it in their living rooms like religious totems, waiting for the tower to be built at Fargo or Grand Forks [North Dakota], so we could get it. People would turn it on, and there'd just be static, and look and flip around. Very strange.

LEONARD: I saw my first one when I was fifteen, maybe sixteen. I went to a family wedding in Cleveland, Ohio, and the people we stayed with had a television set. I didn't leave the living room. I knew I'd never be lonely again.

PAUL: Both of us missed the golden age of television completely. I went to college, and I just wasn't interested in it. I never missed it because I'd never seen it, so I don't think I got my first set until my mid-twenties. But radio was a big deal. Every night there was this lineup of stuff, so you sat and listened to the radio. In *Beautiful Losers* [Leonard's second novel, published in 1966] you mention the radio a lot.

LEONARD: I used to listen to the Armed Forces Radio station coming out of Athens [Greece]. A really good station, it had wonderful stuff on there. They had very good country music on that Armed Forces Radio station. They had a country hour every day. They had *Top of the Pops* or whatever they called it, and then they had some good R&B programs, I guess aiming at the Black personnel. It was kind of set up that way, the daily programs. I got covered every which way on that radio station. That was around the years '60 to '67.

PAUL: Seems like you were really into music early on. There are passages in *The Favourite Game* [his first novel, 1963] with Breavman and Krantz riding in the car, listening to the radio.

LEONARD: That's what we used to do. Krantz played banjo and the trombone. I played clarinet in my high school band, and he took up banjo about the same time I took up guitar. He played trombone in the McGill College band. So we used to play a lot together. I was playing a rhythm guitar and we had a mouth organ and a bucket bass, and we played barn dances mostly.[51] It was early years of college. They used to have a lot of square dances and barn dances as recreation in the high schools. We used to play for those setups where one of the guys knew how to call dances and we'd just play. It was very nice, it was fun.

PAUL: When we were talking about *The Favourite Game*, I mentioned Krantz, and you were talking about a real person who Krantz was based on, I gather.

LEONARD: *Based* is not quite accurate, but *suggested* anyhow. He's still very much in my life. We've always lived pretty much on the same street. We grew up on the same street and we roomed together at college and we got little houses together in the East End of Montreal, where we lived. *Krantz* came from *Rosencrantz*. His real name is Rosengarten. They used to call us Rosencrantz and Guiltencohen.

PAUL: What was the first name?

LEONARD: Morton. Morton is an extremely good sculptor in Canada. Wonderful sculptor.

PAUL: *Based* isn't the right word, but they're not literal either.

LEONARD: Not literal, no. Like Breavman, whoever he is exactly, I'm not exactly myself either. But that friendship and those kind of buddies. I mean, those drives are right out of that period. We'd get his parents' car and drive down to Lakeshore [Ontario] and all around.

PAUL: Was the novel rewritten five times?

LEONARD: Well, it started off as a book called *Beauty at Closed Quarters*, which is probably a much better book. I wrote that in England in the winter of '59 and then I took it to a publisher

51 While at McGill University, Leonard formed a country & western outfit called the Buckskin Boys.

in England, and they said, "Very good, but it has to be refined." And I'm sorry I refined it now because it was a better book.

PAUL: More like *Beautiful Losers*?

LEONARD: It was much wilder. Much wilder and truer.

PAUL: It was *too* wild for them?

LEONARD: It seemed to be. But I had no confidence in myself as a novelist at that time, and also there was much in me that admired and appreciated that very precise kind of writing. So, as you know, I had to choose whether I was going to be Thomas Wolfe or Flaubert. So I decided to become Flaubert. I started working on the thing and throwing everything out and producing this little autobiographical novel rather than this kind of wilder expression of … [*doesn't finish his sentence*]

PAUL: Does the original version still exist?

LEONARD: At a certain point I sold all my papers to the very kind University of Toronto Library, which was buying Canadian manuscripts at a certain point, so I gave them most of the stuff I had around the house.

PAUL: So it was rewritten a number of times. Were you happy being Flaubert at that time, and it was just later that you thought, *No, I shouldn't have done that.*

LEONARD: Well, I've thought that about many things that I've overworked. I think that's my little aesthetic battle.

PAUL: You think you have a choice in that, though? I've always wished that I could knock them out like [Jack] Kerouac, but I never would do it. I don't really think I have a choice.

LEONARD: Within the range of your own nature, I wouldn't necessarily believe what the Beats go by and believe, which was "First thought, best thought."[52]

52 Usually attributed to Allen Ginsberg.

PAUL: No, I don't agree with that either, that the first draft is the only draft. But, god, it would be nice if it worked out that way, wouldn't it, and you didn't have to sit with it for months and months and months and torture yourself about it?

LEONARD: But somewhere between that and refining it into some kind of spun glass that breaks at first handling. It's a very rigorous enterprise and it really can drive you crazy.

PAUL: I guess to some degree there was a choice because, after the last album, it was like a breakthrough record into a simpler style in a sense and a more personal style, if that's possible.

LEONARD: More direct, I think, yeah. On this one also. Getting that way.

PAUL: But that doesn't make it easier to write. Or it *does* make it easier to write?

LEONARD: When they gave me this award on Sunday night, some well-meaning but mistaken people came to me and said, "It's about time." And I said that the Academy [the Canadian Academy of Recording Arts and Sciences], "both in its graciousness and hospitality *and* timing, was impeccable. Because if this had happened to me at twenty-six it would've turned my head; at thirty-six it would have confirmed my flight to a kind of morbid spirituality; at forty-six it would have rubbed my nose in my sense of failing powers; but at fifty-six," I said, "Hell, I'm just hitting my stride. It don't hurt at all." [*they both laugh*] And I feel that. You pick up a few things along the way. Also, I think you go through various periods where you're singing better than others, where the material *and* your voice have some kind of harmony. Real harmony. And I think that I've produced a number of records where my voice and the material were not well-married. [*lighting a cigarette*] You know? What I like about *I'm Your Man* is that I feel that it's there, as it was in the first record [1967's *Songs of Leonard Cohen*], that the voice and the material are perfectly matched. And I think I was just getting there with *Various Positions*, I was just starting to get that again, and that previous to that a number of records didn't have that. The material was good and there was a certain poignant vulnerability that was attractive in a certain way, but I hadn't really mastered the song.

PAUL: There were changes musically, too.

LEONARD: Yeah, well, I started playing keyboard then, in the few years before *Various Positions*, so the songs started to have a different structure. I could lean on the time, on the rhythm, and I could do things because of factory presets that I could hear but could never reproduce on my guitar. My musician friends, they're fond of saying—you know the expression *chops*? Well, for me they say *chop*. "Leonard's got a great chop." [*laughs*] And when it moves out of that, you can't reproduce the rhythms that I hear. With these little toys I'm able to establish them and *then* say to musicians, "This is the groove." So I can get them now.

PAUL: It changed your writing.

LEONARD: It changed the writing, yeah.

PAUL: Different writing with a guitar with different chords than it is writing with a keyboard. No more songs composed on the guitar at all?

LEONARD: I composed a country song called "Closing Time" on guitar. It goes [*recites different lyrics than appear in the final version, some of which would show up in "Never Got to Love You"*]:

> *The parking lot is empty*
> *They switched off the Budweiser sign*
> *Back from here to St. Jovite*
> *It's dark all down the line*
> *They ought to give the night a ticket*
> *for speeding*
> *It's a crime*
> *I had so much to tell you*
> *Yeah, but now it's closing time*

Fifty dollars in your pocket
but you cannot spend a dime
When the boss has got his coat on
and it's closing time

They're stacking up the chairs
wiping down the bar
Hardly started telling you
how beautiful you are
So I'll say goodnight, my precious friend
and to my bed I'll climb
You fall in love forever
Yeah, but then it's closing time

PAUL: That's nice. It's sort of a country song and a comment on a country song at the same time. At least it sounds that way to me.

Talk turns to family.

PAUL: Your father was a relatively young man when he died.

LEONARD: Fifty-two. My father died when I was nine. My father's name was Nathan Bernard Cohen.

PAUL: Your mother was how old?

LEONARD: Seventy-two. My mother came from Russia eight or nine years after the revolution, and her name was—they used the name Kline—it was Klonitsky.

PAUL: E-I-N or I-N-E? I wasn't sure.

LEONARD: I've seen it spelled both ways. I don't think they ever got it straight themselves. My mother's name was Masha. My mother and her father and a brother originally went to Atlanta [Georgia]. I'm not sure what it was, I don't think my mother was allowed to stay in Atlanta.

PAUL: By the government, you mean?

LEONARD: Yeah, I don't think her papers were in order in some way. They were refugee immigrants. My mother's sister married into a very old Jewish family in the South, in Atlanta, the Alexanders. Her sister's name was Manya [Klonitsky-Klein], I believe, and she married this Alexander [Henry Aaron Sr.] who was actually a Republican candidate for governor at one point. My mother couldn't stay there for some odd reason, and my grandfather didn't want to stay there—he wanted to go to New York where there was a Yiddish culture—so he went to New York and found some cronies and never really learned to speak English. My grandfather, her father, was a distinguished writer, a Hebrew grammarian. In fact he was known as the Prince of the Grammarians, that was his nickname. His name was Rabbi Solomon Klonitsky-Kline. He wrote, among other things, a lexicon of Hebrew homonyms and a thesaurus of Talmud interpretations. He was a very wonderful man and a great scholar. And he was the disciple of a very famous scholar in Lithuania by the name of Yitzchak Elchanan [Spektor] … He had a yeshiva that was famous enough to have boys from England attending it. It was one of the foremost yeshivas of the day. And my grandfather closed his eyes when he died. He was a beloved disciple of the man.

PAUL: I worked for a paper in New York for three years called *The Jewish Week*.[53] So I got some sort of grounding in Judaism for three years. It was quite fascinating.

LEONARD: My father's father founded the first Anglo-Jewish newspaper in North America. *The Jewish Times*, I believe it was called. It later became *The* [*Canadian*] *Jewish Chronicle* in Montreal. His name was Lyon Cohen.

PAUL: Do you think it helped your love of language, the Talmud and all this scholarly writing that you read? Very precise and very getting down to the bone.

53 Paul sometimes had trouble with remembering time. He began work at *The Jewish Week* on September 7, 1987, and was laid off a few days short of one year later, on September 2.

LEONARD: I think it's in the tradition. Because, you know, there's a tradition that the Almighty created the world with letters. It was with vowels and consonants that the world was made manifest. So there is a sense that the language is the creative vehicle in the cosmos. It's well established within Judaism. Some branches emphasize it. The Hasidim emphasize the importance of the language and they examine each word, sometimes giving each letter a numerical value. A *gematria*, a kind of numerology, developed. And then the other treatment of the language is taking the words and changing the letters within them to create other words that somehow resonate within that word, so that meanings can amplify and echo.

PAUL: Was your path very religious?

LEONARD: I suppose it's what you would call traditionalist. Conservative. In some places in the United States it leans toward liberalism, but in Montreal the conservative movement leans toward orthodoxy. The religion, the rituals, and the laws were observed quite rigorously.

PAUL: They weren't orthodox or they weren't Hassidic?

LEONARD: They weren't orthodox in the sense that they didn't educate their children in separate schools, they didn't wear the fringes, the *tallis*, all the time, they didn't cover their heads all the time, but Friday night the Sabbath was rigorously observed, but not as rigorously as an Orthodox. For instance, we were allowed to turn on the lights or turn on the radio or turn on the stove. Where in an Orthodox home you have to observe—

PAUL: You can't use electricity.

LEONARD: Yeah. You can't kindle a light. So there are those kinds of degrees of difference; but the complete involvement in the community, in the calendar, *that* they shared with the Orthodox. Tradition. And the training of the children was not as rigorous. We went to Hebrew school three times a week, but we didn't go to an exclusive Hebrew school every day.

PAUL: This has certainly been contained in all your songs, this background in Judaism.

LEONARD: It's been there, yeah. And biblical reference. In any case, the familiarity *with* a tradition, just the respect for a tradition, whether I used it or not. It's the background of a certain point of view, that there is something that is inherited, there is something which binds the generations, one to another. We are not just floating—

WAITRESS: More coffee?

LEONARD: Uh, yes, dear. Thank you so much.

PAUL: Your father was an engineer.

LEONARD: He was trained as an engineer. Our family was in the dredging business, dredging the canals around Montreal, until the government changed and the business evaporated. A new regime.

PAUL: The new regime did not want any dredging.

LEONARD: Well, they didn't want dredging from this particular outfit. So the old order changed and a new pharaoh arose who did not know us.

PAUL: Then he was in the clothing business?

LEONARD: Yes, he was in the clothing business—but he was a sick man most of his life. It seems like after the war, the First World War, his health deteriorated considerably, so I'll always remember him as a man in bed or a man in the hospital.

PAUL: Was he a soldier?

LEONARD: He was a soldier. He was part of the Canadian Expeditionary Forces that took over Germany in the First World War. He was a town commandant of a little town on the Rhine. He loved the army and he loved the empire. He was an Edwardian gentleman. He'd go out in the evenings with a monocle, spats, cane.

PAUL: Well-educated man, I guess?

LEONARD: He was reasonably well-educated. He went to McGill, as I did. He was born in Canada. His mother was born in Canada. My great grandfather Lazarus [Cohen] came from Poland to a small town in what is now Ontario, called Cornwall. It was before Confederation, which was 1867. So around 1860 they came to this small town and my great grandfather learned English with a Scottish burr. He would appear at rabbinic counsels in New York and astound people by this fluid Scottish delivery.

PAUL: How did your father meet your mother?

LEONARD: My grandfather Lyon, who devoted himself to establishing institutions in the Montreal Jewish community that are still going, he was a man to whom a lot of Jewish immigrants applied either for work or for help. Somehow my mother's father, when he came to Atlanta, was put into contact with Lyon Cohen in Montreal when my mother had to go to Montreal. She was received by Lyon Cohen in some way and she was introduced to his oldest son, which was my father, and they fell in love. There was nineteen years difference between them. My father fell in love with her and, according to my mother, he loved her very much. And they married. My mother was a nurse at the time in the Hospital of Hope in Montreal.

PAUL: Was your father wounded in the war in some way?

LEONARD: I think he did receive a minor wound, but I never got that story straight.

PAUL: But it was not a particular wound that set off his bad health.

LEONARD: No, no, no, no.

PAUL: What was the trouble? Was it his heart?

LEONARD: There was a heart condition, yeah. I think he had a broken heart for some reason or another.

PAUL: [*laughs wryly*] That could do it. So when he was hospitalized, it would be for months at a time.

LEONARD: Yeah. He was a very kindly figure. Somewhat militaristic. There was a great emphasis on neatness. Your shoes had to be together under your bed, that kind of thing.

PAUL: Does this carry over to you?

LEONARD: When you're dealing with disorder in your own mind, it's agreeable to have at least your surroundings well-ordered. I find it's important.

PAUL: Were you the oldest?

LEONARD: No, my sister's five years my senior. Esther [Cohen]. She lives in New York, but she and her husband [Victor Cohen] are frequent fliers and they rarely touch the ground. I'm very close to my sister and brother-in-law.

Back to Leonard's "long and curious relationship" with his record company.

PAUL: I went to Columbia and tried to get some clips, but they didn't have any.

LEONARD: We can give you stuff. A young woman by the name of Kelley Lynch takes care of my affairs.[54] We just moved the office here.

54 Kelley Lynch, Leonard's business manager for many years, more than took care of his affairs. In 2004 he would fire her for embezzling five million dollars and leaving him broke. He filed suit and won a default judgment ordering that she pay back $9.5 million. In 2012 she would be convicted on five counts of harassment and be sentenced to eighteen months in prison with five years' probation. Broke and in need of an income, in 2008 Leonard would have no choice but to commence touring again, which he did up until his last concert on December 21, 2013.

PAUL: I called Columbia, I guess it was late summer, saying, "The *Weekly* wants to do a cover story. Who do I talk to at Columbia?" They kept giving me the name of different PR people, saying, "Try this one."

LEONARD: None of whom had heard of me.

PAUL: Well, they'd heard of you.

LEONARD: Leanne, my engineer, she phoned up CBS/Sony here, trying to get hold of some *I'm Your Man* albums. Not only did that not have any *I'm Your Man* albums, but they didn't know who I was.

PAUL: Even though CBS awarded you its Crystal Globe Award for selling over five million copies of *I'm Your Man* outside of the U.S.

LEONARD: I've got the thing; it's a very nice award. It's the nicest one I've ever seen. When they handed it to me, I said, "Over the years I've been deeply touched by the modesty of your interest in my work." I made a little speech that made me chuckle a lot and, as soon as they understood it, they began to chuckle, too. I said, "You know, often when I'm walking along Sixth Avenue, the Avenue of the Americas, I look at the CBS Building on Fifty-second Street and I think to myself, *The Tomb of the Unknown Record.*"

PAUL: [*laughs*] It was the only time I've ever said it's for a cover story on an artist and they didn't seem to care. They'd just say, "Well, try this one," and then "Try that one." I tried three in New York and then they gave me somebody out here to call. She gave me yet another one. I think I went through six PR people. *Nobody* called me back, nobody knew anything: "No, we don't know that record." Finally, I got Kelley Lynch's name from one of them. But this went on for like six weeks!

LEONARD: I have no trouble believing this story. [*chuckles*]

PAUL: No, this just doesn't happen. Am I that much of a has-been that they don't even call me back?

LEONARD: I don't think it was your *has-been-ness*.

PAUL: Well, I'm a has-been, believe me. [*laughs*] I'm making a comeback in my whatever—my career, if I can call it career.

LEONARD: Well, I wish you well. What have you been doing?

PAUL: [*sighs*] I've done about six pieces in the last year. The first one was Suzanne Vega.[55]

LEONARD: In Canada we have the JUNO Awards, which are our version of the Grammys, and they just had them this last weekend in Vancouver. They inducted me into the Canadian [Music] Hall of Fame this weekend, and Suzanne Vega was kind enough to cross the continent and come up and sing ["Who by Fire"], she and Aaron Neville ["Bird on the Wire"] and Jennifer Warnes ["Joan of Arc"].[56]

PAUL: Who else is in the Canadian [Music] Hall of Fame beside yourself?

LEONARD: It's Guy Lombardo, Oscar Peterson, Hank Snow, Wilf Carter, the Crew-Cuts, the Four Lads, the Diamonds, Glenn Gould, Neil Young, Gordon Lightfoot, the Band, and Joni Mitchell. And Maureen Forrester.[57]

PAUL: You and Suzanne had your picture taken for *Rolling Stone*.

LEONARD: She was kind enough to identify me as one of her mentors.[58]

55 In addition to Suzanne Vega, he profiled Chet Baker, Bruce Hornsby, and Willie Nile for *Musician*, where he also reviewed Bob Dylan's *Under the Red Sky*. For *Rolling Stone* he reviewed *Room to Roam* by the Waterboys.

56 While the song is titled "Bird on *the* Wire," it often is sung as "Bird on *a* Wire." The incorrect title even found its way to one of Leonard's own releases, 2002's compilation album *The Essential Leonard Cohen*.

57 Leonard forgot one other inductee: Paul Anka. When he ascended the stage at the ceremony to accept the honor, he said, "I want to salute those who have stood here before me, the residents of the Hall of Fame," and recited the complete list. "Two women of genius among all that exuberant masculine prominence, it causes me to reflect that it's going to be hard to get a date in the Hall of Fame."

58 "Sweet Inspirations," *Rolling Stone*, September 21, 1989.

PAUL: Have you spent much time with her?

LEONARD: I don't know her at all. Well, let's see, maybe we've met on three occasions. I met her when we did that picture together, and then I went to her concert here at the Wiltern, and then this time.[59] I think she's a wonderful woman.

PAUL: We sort of stayed in touch. She was like my first comeback story. Actually I saw her backstage at Carnegie Hall at your concert [July 5, 1988], and somebody said to you, "Would you mind taking a picture with Suzanne?" and you said, "I hope this doesn't compromise your career, dear." [*they laugh*] She just looked interesting to me and I thought, *Gee, if I ever do write again, she'd be a nice one to do.*

LEONARD: I'm very fond of her.

PAUL: Yeah, me, too. She sent me a really nice letter from Sweden or Norway. They cut the story a little bit, and I sent her my complete version of it. She wrote me this really nice card saying, "You did a really good job" and "I really cried when I read the article. I've been thinking about these things for years." It's very nice to hear that, particularly since I hadn't done a piece for seven years or something like that. This turned out to be a very long piece. I was nervous about it. It was a praiseworthy piece, but you just never know what people are going to think. I've had articles where I've been nothing but praiseworthy towards the artist and they've never spoken to me again. You just don't know.[60]

LEONARD: I find her interest in my work very touching.

59 In addition to a photo shoot for the aforementioned *Rolling Stone* feature on "Musicians and Their Mentors," Leonard's subsequent meetings with Suzanne Vega would include a 1993 co-interview wherein he queried her about her recently released album *99.9F°* and she asked him about his new one, *The Future*. Afterwards they went out to dinner together.

Vega told Dublin's *Hot Press* that "Leonard then gifted me the best 50th birthday present possible when he asked me to play with him at the Mercedes-Benz World concert just outside of London. That was seven years ago and the last time we met face-to-face." The date was July 11, 2009.

60 Perhaps the best example of this is Rod Stewart. Once good friends (there was a time when Paul used to recommend songs for Stewart to record, and when Stewart would acknowledge Paul in the liner notes), after Paul wrote the laudatory *Rolling Stone* article "Rod Stewart Under Siege," Stewart brushed him off and stopped taking his calls.

PAUL: Her favorite songs of yours are "Avalanche" and "So Long, Marianne." She said you couldn't imagine what it was like sitting there, living in the worst part of New York—it was a very turbulent family situation—trying to figure out "Avalanche." *What does this song mean?* I'm not sure I ever *have* figured out "Avalanche." I went back to it after she had talked. I think it may have something to do with the Christ figure, but I'm not sure. Maybe you could tell me.

LEONARD: Maybe I could resurrect it.

PAUL: [*chuckles*] When did you come up with the women backup singers?

LEONARD: From the beginning. I've always liked that. I think it came from the R&B records that I loved during the Fifties.

PAUL: Like, when you were how old did you start listening to music? I don't know if *seriously* would be the correct word, but where it became an important part of your life.

LEONARD: My mother used to sing very beautifully around the house. Even my father, who had no voice, would sometimes pull out the Kiwanis Club songbook and we'd sing songs like "K-K-K-Katy, beautiful Katy." Wartime songs. But then the cantor in our synagogue was inspiring to me, and the use of the voice with the choir, that interplay, always touched me. By the time I was fourteen I started collecting a lot of folk music. I went down to the Harvard record library [Widener Library] one summer [1953] and just went through everything I could find.

PAUL: Your mother sang. Did you say she played any instrument?

LEONARD: She didn't play an instrument, but she had a beautiful contralto voice. An untrained voice, but she sang with great enthusiasm and with great melancholy. She sang Russian folk songs, Yiddish folk songs. She liked a couple of popular songs of the time that I remember. One was "Amapola." [*sings*] "Amapola / My pretty little flower." And the other song that she loved very much was "Donkey Serenade."[61] [*sings*] "There's a song in the air / But the fair senorita doesn't seem to care /For the song in the air." And my father loved Gilbert and Sullivan. We had a lot of those thick seventy-eight [RPM] Gilbert and Sullivan records. He also liked [Scottish singer and comedian] Sir Harry Lauder.

PAUL: Do you remember the first concerts you saw or who they were? [Pete] Seeger was mine.

LEONARD: Seeger might have been my first concert. No, I think it was the Weavers.

PAUL: Yeah, the Weavers, Pete Seeger. And [Frank] Sinatra and Chet Baker and Peggy Lee and some of those people also.

LEONARD: Peggy Lee, did she do "Tennessee Waltz"?

PAUL: No, Patti Page.

LEONARD: Patti Page. That was a song I fell in love with. I was doing it in my '85 tour.[62] There's a song I love very much—[*he can't remember the title, but softly sings*]: "My heart cries for you / Sighs for you, dies for you / My heart longs for you / Oh, please come back to me."[63] I think we should revive that. It's a good idea.

PAUL: I find myself listening to this stuff again. I think I'm trying to get back to the Fifties as far as I can go. I'd even take the 1850s if I can't take the 1950s. I miss hearing that stuff over the radio. Pete Seeger, when I saw that, that rang a bell.

LEONARD: He had the integrity, of the voice and the man. He was very inspiring.

61 Made popular by Allan Jones and Jeanette MacDonald in the 1937 film *The Firefly*.

62 Leonard would include a live version of the song from the tour on his 2004 album *Dear Heather*.

63 Borrowing an Eighteenth Century French melody, "My Heart Cries for You" was written by Carl Sigman and Percy Faith, and scored on the pop charts with versions by Guy Mitchell with Mitch Miller & His Orchestra, Vic Damone, and Dinah Shore.

PAUL: It inspired a friend [Jon Pankake] and I to start something called *The Little Sandy Review*, which was a folk magazine. We started it for somewhat altruistic reasons, but also because we were students in college and couldn't afford to buy the records. So we figured, *What if we reviewed them?* There didn't seem to be any great writers out there in folk journalism, so we figured, *We can write about this stuff and they'll send them to us*, and it actually worked. They did.

LEONARD: You said you were making a comeback. Did you leave the scene for a period of time?

PAUL: I did. Yeah, I left for what seemed to be solid reasons at the time, but then my whole life sort of fell apart. My mother got cancer. I left *Rolling Stone*. I was reviews editor at *Rolling Stone* and writer.

LEONARD: I know.

PAUL: I just couldn't take what was going down there, which was like no opinions on anything. I would get memos from Jann Wenner every day practically, saying, "This is wrong, that was wrong. You can't compare one artist with another, because it implies one artist is worse than the other." That's not why people do it. Sometimes, if you only have a paragraph or two, it's a shortcut, it's a description, it's not a comparison. That doesn't imply one is worse than the other. No, I can't do that, I can't write about the artist's history or compare early songs to new ones. And then, finally, the worst thing was—and being a poet you would understand this—each review had to be eighteen lines long in the space.

LEONARD: Oh, a sonnet.

PAUL: I was having trouble keeping writers anyway because of all these ridiculous restrictions, and I thought, *My god, eighteen lines of* Rolling Stone *space is about three sentences.* I wouldn't be editing for content anymore, I'd be editing for line count. "I don't care what you say, it's got to be eighteen lines." And I figured he was trying to make me quit.

LEONARD: In retrospect do you think he was?

PAUL: I was the only one there that was a troublemaker, I guess. Because I really did care about it. I cared more about that than I guess staying there and having a career and a paycheck.

LEONARD: You were taking it very seriously.

PAUL: I did, yeah, which is a curse sometimes. He was quite stunned when I left, and didn't want me to leave. I signed a contract with Doubleday to do a Neil Young book at the time and thought, *I'll do that and support myself writing this book*. A few months after that, or a month or two actually, my mother came out for Christmas and discovered this lump in her throat. Cancer. Lymphoma.

LEONARD: See, I went through a scene like that. With my mother, yeah. Leukemia. I was down here studying with Sasaki Roshi, and I moved back to Montreal to try to be helpful in those last couple years.

PAUL: We went through about the same things probably, then. Oddly enough, my mother was actually cured of it after two and a quarter years.[64] She got so sick during much of the process that it just continued to elongate before they could finish the radiation. They actually cured the cancer, but she said, "If it ever comes back, I'm never going through this again." She went back to Minnesota, a shell of herself, really weighing nothing and trying to gain some weight, and she died in two months. She died sitting up looking at the TV with the remote in her hand and a smile on her face. I've got to say the cancer probably did kill her, or the cure for cancer did—whichever. It just wrecked her health so totally that I think she probably would've really done herself in if the cancer came back, rather than go through that again.

LEONARD: I think that would have been my mother's viewpoint, too. I understand that the chemotherapy has been refined so much in the past ten, twelve years, but in those days it seemed to be more like the way they treated witches: like you dunk them in the water and if they,

64 Paul always told the story this way, when by all accounts only approximately one year transpired from his mother's diagnosis to cure.

you know. It was like they poisoned you. They brought you to the point of death, they killed everything, and then if you could make it back …

PAUL: Just spending two and a half, two and a quarter years seeing people dying—little kids dying, teenage girls dying—I'd just go home and stare at the wall and sank into clinical depression. I was unable to write a word, was basically unable to go to Los Angeles because I couldn't leave New York. So I blew the Neil Young book, I just eventually canceled it. I just cracked up, basically.

LEONARD: Oh, it's very painful—

The tape runs out. Paul turns over the cassette and continues recording at the Chariot with its background of chattering patrons, clacking plates and clanging utensils, the occasional shattering glass, and someone whistling a tune.

LEONARD: You get to that moment where a room starts tilting and you lose your balance and you fall to your knees and you don't know how to get from one moment to the next. I'd lose my balance and I'd fall down and I'd just cry out.

PAUL: Yeah. That's what I was doing. And the psychologist said, "Hey, if you wonder why you're depressed: your mother's in the hospital, you're going to lose your apartment, you have no money, you don't know where *anything's* coming from, you don't have a roof over your head in the next month"—because I was losing that apartment because I couldn't pay high enough rent—he said, "It's no wonder you're depressed." The thing is, you don't know how depressed you are.

LEONARD: Did you read [William] Styron's very beautiful evocation of clinical depression [*Darkness Visible: A Memoir of Madness*]?

PAUL: No. I'm sort of afraid to.

LEONARD: You should read it. It's probably the first time someone with that kind of talent has evoked the mood of clinical depression.

He says *depression* is a very inaccurate word for it; he calls it a *mind-storm*.[65] And there doesn't seem to be any relief. You wake up *into* the nightmare.

PAUL: You went through this yourself on a couple of occasions.

LEONARD: I know it very well. There were two years that were very rough. The pressure of the work, the breakup of my family. [*pauses*] It's involved with loss, loss and pressure. Do you find yourself similarly, you think? It's just your melancholy nature?

PAUL: I've always had that.

LEONARD: So you keep giving that description to it somehow, you think you're going to snap out of it, and then two months go by, five months go by, and you realize that your mood hasn't really changed. It's worsened.

PAUL: This happened in '85, '86?

LEONARD: Yeah, '85, '86, '87.

PAUL: The breakup of your family was with [Suzanne Elrod], the mother of Adam [Cohen] and Lorca [Cohen]?[66]

LEONARD: Yes, that happened in '79, but there were troubles. You know, the troubles arose. They moved to France.

PAUL: After you broke up you still were able to see the children?

LEONARD: Yeah. Things like that. The pressure of the work had a great deal to do with it. Starting with that record [*Various Positions*] in—well, I started writing the record around '83, '84. And I think it's got to do with one's age and the sense of failing powers. I felt profound displacement.

65 The term Styron uses in his book is actually *brainstorm*.

66 Elrod was Leonard's common-law wife. They met in 1969 when she was nineteen. She is not the Suzanne who inspired one of his most famous songs of the same name. That was Suzanne Verdal, a dancer/choreographer whose relationship with him was platonic.

That's a displacement that the music wasn't *it* somehow, that the magic had gone out of the enterprise. The pointlessness of the enterprise.

PAUL: Of the whole music scene? Or are you talking about just your music?

LEONARD: One's own music, the whole enterprise.

PAUL: There was a certain degree of truth in that.

LEONARD: I think so.

PAUL: I worked for Mercury Records in the Seventies as an A&R person. It seemed to me the artists at that time at least had something to say, or *thought* they had something to say, and were idealistic at the start. Maybe later they got corrupted by the business, but nowadays I think a lot of them come in just wanting to get rich and not caring *at all* about whether they have anything to say or not. They're more corporate sometimes than the corporation, it seems like.

LEONARD: I remember, on a more comic side, one began to see that the artists were the straight men, and the managers and the lawyers and the accountants and the record executives were the flamboyant *enfants terribles*. They're the ones with the clothes and the dangerous habits and the glamorous, doomed atmosphere about them.

I had those things happen to me [at CBS] as recently as my last record, in New York. I sat down with people, they told me how they were going to hire independent promoters and do this. And the record had received very extravagantly positive reviews. It was called a "masterpiece" in *The New York Times*. And, uh—

PAUL: Nothing.

LEONARD: Evaporated.

PAUL: Did it wind up selling better than the other records in the States or about the same?

LEONARD: Well, I toured extensively in the States—

PAUL: I saw three of those concerts [in New York in 1988 as part of the *I'm Your Man* tour: the Ritz, Carnegie Hall, and the Beacon Theatre].

LEONARD: —and I pretty well sold the record, and people couldn't find it. I still get mail, not a very great deal of mail, but a bit of mail, saying, "Do you know where we could find a copy of—*anything*."

PAUL: Unless you're in a big city you can't find the record, basically.

LEONARD: Not even in a big city. [*chuckles wryly*]

PAUL: Suzanne [Vega], when I was talking to her for the *Musician* magazine story, said she thought you were working on another live record.

LEONARD: I have been gathering the tapes. I want to have them in the can anyhow, even if it's only for myself, because we had some good performances and we have some good recordings of them. In Europe, Toronto. We have a tape from the *Austin City Limits* we did.[67]

PAUL: Also, you did a jazz program, a TV thing with some jazz guys.

LEONARD: Well, I played on that show that was called *Sunday* [*Night*] with David Sanborn.[68] That's where I met Was (Not Was). I did a song with Sonny Rollins, backed up by some of the Was (Not Was) singers, Sweet Pea and Sir Harry [Bowens], and my own singers [Perla Batalla and Julie Christensen]. We did "Who by Fire." Sonny Rollins, as you know, is a master. He is so kind. We only had one or two rehearsals and he said to my singers, "I hope Mr. Cohen likes what I'm doing because I know he's a sensitive cat." His work on the song was stupendous.

67 Some of these performances may have shown up on 1994's *Cohen Live*, 2001's *Field Commander Cohen: Tour of 1979*, or *Live at the Isle of Wight* in 2009. The *Austin City Limits* broadcast was released in album form in 2018.

68 The NBC late-night show, produced by Lorne Michaels, changed its name from *Sunday Night* to *Night Music* by the time the episode aired in 1989. Jools Holland cohosted.

PAUL: He knew your work.

LEONARD: Well, I don't know whether he knew it, but I played a tape for him of the song. And they were very accomplished musicians in David Sanborn's band. Sonny Rollins, it took him about twenty seconds to get a handle on the thing. The solos he plays in it are really something.

PAUL: Were you a jazz fan also?

LEONARD: I used to go to a lot of jazz clubs in Montreal. I used to like listening to it. I like the atmosphere of the clubs really almost more than the music. I don't know where it stood in the hierarchy of jazz at the time, but I liked those evenings. Charlie Parker passed through Montreal at a certain point and turned on a lot of people in all ways possible. Alfie Wade had clubs in Montreal at the time. He was a friend of mine. So I was *there* in some kind of way. And I worked with Maury Kaye, who was a kind of jazz composer, and we did poetry and jazz together in a little club in Montreal for a while during that period [Dunn's Birdland, upstairs from Dunn's Famous Delicatessen]. I guess there were only us doing it: Ferlinghetti in San Francisco and Kerouac in New York, and I was doing it in Montreal and the reading, too.

PAUL: Did you hear Parker?

LEONARD: I never heard him play.

PAUL: I gather you did poetry readings with Irving Layton and A. M. Klein.

LEONARD: I never read with A. M. Klein but I knew A. M. Klein. Those were the figures in our little world in Montreal. There's A. M. Klein, Frank Scott, Irving Layton, Louie Dudek. Those were the poets of the city.

PAUL: These books sold rather well?

LEONARD: Well, compared to what, you know? I mean, 400 copies was considered a large sale. It was a very wonderful training ground for a writer. There were no prizes around. It was a *very* tiny mode of expression in Canada. You knew everybody who was writing verse, more or less, at the time. We would gather, a group of us, several times a week and read each other poems, and there would be a rather formal and rigorous and vicious examination of everybody's poems. So it was taken very seriously. It was very elitist in the sense that we'd pride ourselves on not being part of the popular culture. Which wasn't bad at the time, incidentally. I mean, at least there *was* something you could at least resist, which is not the case today.

PAUL: I don't know what the case today is. Everyone's a total stranger everywhere it seems like, as far as popular culture. You go to a movie and it's incoherent.

LEONARD: I have this song on my new record called "If You Could See What's Coming Next." It goes like this [*recites*]:

If you could see what's coming next
If you could read the hidden text
You'd say, Give me war,
give me poisoned rivers
You'd say, Give me the ozone layer,
with that little hole we can't repair
You'd say, Give me crack, give me television
'Cause things are gonna slide in all directions
And nothing will be measured anymore
The blizzard of the world has crossed the threshold
And broken down the secret inner door
When they said repent, I wonder what they meant

If you could see what's coming next
If you could read the hidden text
You'd say, Give me love or give me Adolf Hitler
You'd say, Kill that fetus now,
we don't like children anyhow

You'd say, Give me filth, give me bloody murder
Just get me out of this mirror

If you could see what's coming next
If you could read the hidden text
You'd say, Give me crime, give me law and order"
You'd say, Give me back the Berlin Wall,
give me Stalin and Saint Paul
You'd say, Give me Christ or give me Hiroshima
Just get me out of this mirror

'Cause things are gonna slide in all directions
Nothing will be measured anymore
The blizzard of the world has crossed the threshold
And broken down a secret inner door
When they said repent, I wonder what they meant[69]

PAUL: Yeah, that sums it up, doesn't it? I think New York is already about one verse into that song. I don't know if you've been to New York lately, but it's pretty horrible. I don't think there's enough money or will or status to ever put that city together again.

LEONARD: Times that try the soul of man.[70]

PAUL: I'm sure it's here, too. Since I haven't been here for ten years, I thought it would be in a bigger state of disrepair than it seems to be.

LEONARD: Just go downtown.

PAUL: People have already told me, "Stay out of downtown."

LEONARD: I think there are great reservoirs of goodwill in the country that haven't been tapped.

69 The song would appear, renamed with considerably reworked lyrics, as the title cut of *The Future*.

70 He is paraphrasing the opening line of Thomas Paine's 1776 pamphlet *The American Crisis*: "These are the times that try men's souls."

The din at the Chariot has swelled, and a boisterous child at an adjoining table causes him to lose his train of thought.

Let's go over to my place and sit down.

When Paul turns the recorder back on, they are in Cohen's two-story home (in the vicinity of Lew Archer's fictional pre-divorce two-bedroom stucco cottage in West Hollywood). The new locale is not without its own aural challenges, from inside and out: chirping birds, phones ringing, children playing, dogs barking, lawnmowers, fire engines, police sirens, hammering, sundry aircraft, and the occasional chainsaw.

On the drive over from the Chariot, Leonard played the instrumental track of one of the upcoming album's new songs.

PAUL: What was the name of this song?

LEONARD: I don't have a name yet. Probably called "Anthem" or something like that. It goes [*recites*]:

Heard these voices just the other day
Start again, I seem to hear them say
Don't dwell on what has passed away
Or what is yet to be

The wars, they will be fought again
The holy dove be caught again
And bought and sold and bought again
The dove is never free

Ring the bells that still can ring
Forget your perfect offering
There is a crack in everything
That's how the light gets in

What will I call it? "A Crack in Everything" maybe. Or maybe "That's How the Light Gets In."[71]

71 Ultimately the song remained titled "Anthem."

PAUL: So all the songs are written for this record?

LEONARD: Pretty much, yeah.

PAUL: When are you going in again to cut some more of it?

LEONARD: I'm covering another song on Thursday. It's the song "Always" by Irving Berlin. It's written in 3/4; I'm cutting it in 4/4. I've always liked that song and I was experimenting with different time signatures for it. It works very nicely.

PAUL: I'm trying to think what else you've covered. "The Partisan" you didn't write.

LEONARD: "Passing Thru" I didn't write. That's it.[72]

PAUL: You're just covering them because you like these songs?

LEONARD: I don't know if they'll find their way onto the record, but I think "Be for Real" will, because I'm happy with that song.

PAUL: It would be nice if "Always" made it, too.

LEONARD: Yeah, I love that song. The lyric is very beautiful, you know? "I'll be loving you always / With a love that's true always." The construction of that song, oh, yeah, that's really the reason right there that intrigued me. I started studying it, playing it, and it's so *kindly* constructed. Melodically and chordally. It's a very beautiful way it turns on itself.

PAUL: When you started playing, you got a guitar when you were fourteen, but were you musically literate as far as chords and how songs went?

LEONARD: I had the piano lessons when I was a kid. Miss McDougall. Everybody in the neighborhood studied piano with Miss McDougall.

72 He forgot one: the traditional tune "The Lost Canadian [*Un Canadien errant*]" on the *Recent Songs* album.

PAUL: And were you good?

LEONARD: Never distinguished, by any means. I *knew* how to read music. Now I know quite a lot of chords.

PAUL: You began writing songs at the same time you were writing poetry.

LEONARD: Yeah, I was always playing around with song. I never distinguished between the two.

PAUL: Some of the songs are also in the poetry books.

LEONARD: Sometimes I've put them in there when they were too embarrassingly slim—slipped a few songs in there. It's curious, sometimes a song will stand as a poem, often it won't.

PAUL: So there weren't any that were written as poems and then converted to songs?

LEONARD: No. They were all written as songs and sometimes they seemed to be able to stand on a page alone. But usually songs aren't so dense as a poem. A song *has* to move quite swiftly. I've certainly violated that precept more than most songwriters.

PAUL: They're there to be violated, I think, to some extent. Not all the time. It always amazes me because I can see myself *maybe* writing lyrics for a song, but I can never conceive of myself thinking of melodies and doing the music part of it. I'm just wondering if this came easy? If this came hard? Because you've written some beautiful melodies, and I've always claimed and written that you were the best lyricist in rock & roll. I think your music is terrific.

LEONARD: Well, that's kind of you. I remember sitting with Dylan after a concert of his in Paris two years ago, and he praised a song of mine called "Hallelujah," which he was doing in concert. And he said, "How long did it take you to write it?" I said, "I'm embarrassed to say, but it took at least a year, maybe two, before I got the thing together."[73] And then I praised a song of his from—I think it was *Slow Train Coming*. I think it was the song "I and I."[74] I praised that song and said, "How long did it take you to write it?" He said, "Fifteen minutes." I believed it.

PAUL: Well, I'm of the slow school myself.

LEONARD: I think Hank Williams could do it in half an hour. Only one song in my life ever came that way. It wasn't half an hour, it was all night. It was "Sisters of Mercy." I'm not sure, maybe I had some of the guitar patterns before that, but usually it's very, very slow.

PAUL: They come together, music *and* lyrics?

LEONARD: Usually a phrase of music and a line, then a few more phrases, a few more lines; then a verse is established. And then it keeps going back and forth: a revision of the verse, then a revision of the music, a revision of the music, a revision of the verse. For "Democracy" I've got at least—I can show you.

He retrieves a legal pad and a smaller notebook, showing Paul page after page filled with "Democracy" lyrics.

PAUL: Are these verses that are eliminated or endless rewrites of verses?

LEONARD: Both.

PAUL: I know at least one other songwriter who has notebook after notebook: Jackson Browne would have pages and pages and pages of one verse with maybe one word change, if that. It would take him two or three years to write an album.

LEONARD: That poor devil rewrites, too.

73 Retellings of this story to various journalists have Leonard claiming that it took as many as seven years to complete "Hallelujah."

74 "I and I" appeared on Dylan's album *Infidels*.

PAUL: So will I.

LEONARD: The position for "Democracy" was tricky to establish because I didn't want to write an anti-American song, I didn't want to write an antiwar song. I didn't want it to be claimed by the Left, I didn't want it to be claimed by the Right. I said that—"I'm neither Left or Right / I'm just staying home tonight / Getting lost in that hopeless little screen"—to establish that position: "I'm junk but I'm still holding up this little wild bouquet." I had a *lot* of verses. There are lots of verses treating a whole lot of things.[75] And this is during the Gorbachev honeymoon; I was writing: "It ain't coming to us European style / Concentration camp behind the smile / It ain't coming from the East with its temporary feast / As Count Dracula comes strolling down the aisle." It was taking in the whole world. [*laughs*] Genesis.

PAUL: How *would* you characterize this song? What stance do you think it *does* take? A nonpolitical stance? It's a very tricky song.

LEONARD: It's hopeful, I feel. The appropriate hope. I've always said, "What is the appropriate behavior in a catastrophe?" I tried to say that in "The Gypsy's Wife": "Too early for the rainbow, too early for the dove / These are the final days, this is the darkness, this is the flood." Now, what is the appropriate behavior in a flood? You're holding onto an orange crate in the stream, and how do you greet the people that you bump into? What is the cordiality and the etiquette of a catastrophe? Because, as you know, we can't just surrender to the catastrophe. There has to be a mode of hopefulness to establish.

When Lester Bangs comes up, Paul attempts to explain his "method."

PAUL: He was a rock critic who, sometimes when he was feeling particularly cynical, would just look at the cover of a record and *guess*, and wrote a review from that. [*laughs*] And never even open the record.

75 He told at least one journalist that he had more than fifty verses to the song before he commenced discarding them, and that there exists at least three or four versions of "Democracy."

LEONARD: Yeah, I thought of doing that with you. I thought like, *Well, just come on into the house and look around. Open the drawers, look at the notebooks.*

PAUL: That's it? No, I don't know if I'm back in form. Do the tea leaves maybe.

It's a nice house. There's something about Los Angeles, it's always reminded me of the Midwest.

LEONARD: [*deadpan*] It's the palm trees.

PAUL: Yeah, it's the palm trees. I remember knocking the snow off the palm trees in the winter. [*chuckles*] Not this neighborhood, but there are a lot of sort of nondescript, just house after house, that's sort of Midwestern. I don't know why, just the first time I got here I thought, *Jeez, a lot of this is just like the Midwest.* Maybe it's just the difference from New York.

LEONARD: I think somebody said on the radio once, "When you leave New York, you're on a camping trip."[76]

PAUL: In a way. Having never been to Europe and seen London or Paris, I guess we're the only really large city in America that's a comparable city, for all the good and bad. I moved there after seeing it in the movies in Minnesota. That was all there was to do in the town. At that time there was a great romance with New York, but that's evaporated in the last decade.

LEONARD: Now it's a marriage. [*chuckles*]

PAUL: It's a bad marriage. Did you give up your place there? You had a place in the Seventies I heard there.

LEONARD: I've had little flats there from time to time, but I haven't lived there since I lived at the Chelsea. I lived at the Chelsea for a year or so. I had an office there. My lawyer was there; he used to handle all my stuff. After he died, I took it over myself. He was a very wonderful

76 In the late 1800s, vaudevillian Nat Goodwin popularized the saying, "When you leave New York, you're camping out."

man by the name of Marty Machat.[77] We were together for about eighteen years. He represented everybody from Nancy Sinatra to Sugar Ray Robinson, and had a stint with Genesis and Peter Gabriel.[78]

PAUL: You also stayed at the Royalton Hotel.

LEONARD: The Royalton Hotel has now been turned into a very chic hotel on Forty-fourth Street between Fifth and Sixth. It's directly across the street from the Algonquin. It used to be a wonderful hotel where you could get a suite for like a tenth of the price of the Algonquin. But yeah, I had a lovely room there. It's the only time I ever made a deal with a hotel manager. I was staying by the month. He knew my work—that's what gave me the courage to speak to the guy, because I'd come in there and he'd come over to me and he'd say, "I know your songs and I like them very much"—so I thought, after I'd been there a week or so, I would ask him. And he did, he gave me a very, very nice, very, very good deal.

PAUL: When you came to New York, Judy Collins was an early champion of yours.

LEONARD: Judy did that really beautiful version of "Suzanne." And "Sisters of Mercy" and "Hey, That's No Way to Say Goodbye."[79] She was very helpful, very kind. She brought me along to her concerts.

PAUL: I remember seeing one in Central Park where she introduced you. And this was after your first record?

LEONARD: No, it hadn't come out yet. I was in the midst of recording it. I started recording with John Hammond, and then he had a heart attack—or he wasn't well, I don't know if he'd actually had a heart attack, but he was feeling poorly—and the

77 Machat's former legal assistant was Kelley Lynch.

78 According to Peter Gabriel's website, after Machat introduced him to Leonard, the two men "ended up as partners in a New York art gallery founded by Avril Giacobbi called the Art Palace."

79 In addition to these three songs, which appeared on her 1967 album *Wildflowers*, over the years Collins would record a number of Leonard's other compositions: "Dress Rehearsal Rag," "Priests," "Story of Isaac," "Bird on the Wire," "Famous Blue Raincoat," "Take this Longing," "Democracy," "A Thousand Kisses Deep," and "Night Comes On."

producer was changed to John Simon. But I recorded several of the tracks with John Hammond.

PAUL: That aren't on the record? I didn't know that. Which tracks, do you recall?

LEONARD: "Stranger Song," "Hey, That's No Way to Say Goodbye." I think that was it.[80]

PAUL: It's rather nice being signed by John Hammond, who's one of the true legends. His record has proven that he was a wonderful judge of people and talent. Going all the way back to the Twenties or Thirties, I think.[81]

LEONARD: He was a very hospitable man. Both warm and aloof, down to earth, and *immensely* stylish at the same time.

PAUL: I met him but not for very long. He's a guy I really respected. [*sighs*] That type of A&R person doesn't seem to exist anymore, as far as I can tell.

LEONARD: I don't know. Fortunately I don't have to.

PAUL: I don't think you want to know, I gather, from hearing Lucinda Williams's horror stories about it.

LEONARD: Yeah, everybody's got a few of those, eh?

PAUL: The songs you wrote when you were fourteen, fifteen, somewhere in there, uh—

LEONARD: It was mostly in that period I was listening to music, collecting music. There were a few things that I wrote, but I didn't really bring anything to completion.

80 According to the 2021 documentary *Hallelujah: Leonard Cohen, a Journey, a Song*, Hammond also recorded "Suzanne."

81 Hammond began his career as record producer in 1931. After joining Columbia Records, he discovered, in addition to Leonard, the likes of Bob Dylan, Aretha Franklin, and Bruce Springsteen. He also signed Pete Seeger to the label.

PAUL: Were they imitative of what you listened to and liked, or were they very personal songs?

LEONARD: It was a little bit different. They were more like rap.

PAUL: Really?

LEONARD: More like rap, more like chanting. I'd get a rhythm going on the guitar, or with Maury Kaye with his band, with rhythmical speech, metrical speech, on top of it. [*delivers an example from memory, forgetting a couple of the words*] That kind of incantatory—

PAUL: Does that song have a name?

LEONARD: No, no.[82]

PAUL: Did you perform these, as well?

LEONARD: Sometimes.

PAUL: Not with the Buckskin Boys?

LEONARD: No, that was a completely different mode.

PAUL: Just instrumental only or did you sing?

LEONARD: Buckskin? Mostly instrumental. Occasionally "Red River Valley" and that kind of thing. But mostly there was somebody calling. For the dance.

PAUL: I was out at the Palomino for the first time. I did one interview with Lucinda out there. Square Dance Night they call it or Dance Night or something.[83] She never missed it. It reminded

82 The song per se may not have a name, but the first verse was part of "Twelve O'clock Chant," which appeared in Leonard's 1961 poetry collection *The Spice-Box of Earth*. Along with some frantic guitar-strumming on his part, Leonard performs the song in the documentary *Ladies and Gentlemen, Mr. Leonard Cohen*. The second verse came from "Prayer for the Messiah," which in 1993 would be included in *Stranger Music*, a collection of poems and song lyrics.

83 Paul is referring to Lucinda Williams's beloved Barndance.

her of Texas and the South, and she'd gone to them all. It was the only club she liked.

Talk turns to Suzanne Elrod.

PAUL: Wasn't she the last person you really were involved with in a serious way?

LEONARD: Suzanne? No. Because, well, we stopped in '79, so fortunately there's been some comfort since then.

PAUL: Are a lot of the songs still about Suzanne or no?

LEONARD: No. I never really wrote much to her. The records of that period are, well, maybe I wrote a lot to her. Who knows? Because I guess you incorporate your experience somewhat. I first met Suzanne when I was doing *Songs of Love and Hate* [1970 to '71]. Well, "Joan of Arc" was written around the time I started to go out with her. And then there was *Death of a Ladies' Man*, which was a great disaster.[84]

PAUL: Yes, I remember the one time that we met, you telling me you never heard the final mix before the record came out.

LEONARD: No, I never did. I never did any final vocals. They're all scratch vocals. I never got it. I was in very bad shape while I was making that record. Working with Phil [Spector] was no holiday either.

PAUL: No, I remember the .45 pistol pointed at you in the studio.

LEONARD: Oh, yeah. There were guns and bodyguards and—it was very unpleasant.

PAUL: Has he spoken to you afterwards and apologized for this?

84 Elrod is seated to Leonard's left on the cover of the *Death of a Ladies' Man* album; the woman to his right is their friend and Québécois model Eva La Pierre. The photograph is credited to Martin Machat.

LEONARD: No, I don't think he feels any—I don't think Phil is given to remorse about the— I guess he felt that I'd done as well as I could. And he may have been right. You know, I didn't have the confidence at the time. I don't know if I would have been able to master the lyric and the performance in the way I want it. It was the first time I'd ever sung anyone else's tune. It probably would have taken an unreasonable amount of time for me to get it. To give Phil his due, he was acting as a producer and he probably said to himself, *Well, you're not going to get much better. He doesn't have it. He doesn't understand this kind of music.* It's not going to really swing in the way he was used to great singers. He's a good singer himself.

PAUL: We met briefly in New York once. I think you told me that some songs you really thought were good songs but that the treatment was—

LEONARD: Yeah. I thought "Iodine" was a real good song. I think a song like "Memories" is a wonderful song. I think that "Paper Thin Hotel" is a really good lyric and a good song. In fact, I was just talking to Steve yesterday. I gave him the record, I said, "Listen to these. I'd like to recut some of these songs. And 'Death of a Ladies' Man,'" I said, "If you can bear it, try and listen to the whole thing. I think we could do something with it." "Death of a Ladies' Man" I would really love to recut with Steve with a really nice groove.

PAUL: I've never seen a concert where you've sung any of those songs.

LEONARD: I used to do "Memories" with various bands.

PAUL: You've never done the title song in a concert?

LEONARD: No.

PAUL: In a way that's sort of a lost album, too, in the sense that you never know what it would've come out to be if you'd been allowed to participate in it more.

LEONARD: I feel I know so much more about the studio at this point. You know, it's twelve years. More than twelve. Fourteen years. And it taught me a lot about the studio. A kind of a painful education, but something came through. That's why I say I don't know if I ever *could* have gotten on top of it at that time at that point in my life, even if Phil had been more cooperative. The arrangements were so far from my own style, you know, there was no place for me in the arrangements.

PAUL: It takes two or three cuts to even try to get a handle on what's going on with the arrangements. And if you stay with it, it does somehow jell in a berserk way. Depending on the mood you're in when you're listening to it, sometimes you can penetrate it.

LEONARD: Yeah, I can't. I don't listen to my albums, in any case, but I certainly wouldn't listen to that one. [*chuckles*] Yeah, it's weird. It's a strange moment. But yeah, I'd cut that song again now.

PAUL: It's a *very* odd record.

LEONARD: It's a very odd, very eccentric record.[85]

PAUL: On the *Death of a Ladies' Man*, the album, they're all credited as "Spector & Cohen" songs. How did that break down? Who did what?

LEONARD: By and large it was my supplying the lyric and then Phil would do a tune, and then, on the basis of where the tune went, the necessity for a hook or one thing or another, I'd adjust the lyric to the song. Those were wonderful days, incidentally, and it was a great pleasure working with Phil in those days, in the days preceding the actual recording. Just one-on-one he was charming and very hospitable.

PAUL: This was mostly at his place.

85 "Odd" and "very eccentric" would continue to define Spector's life. The progenitor of the Wall of Sound would be convicted of the 2003 murder of actress Lana Clarkson (he shot her in the mouth) and spend the rest of his life in prison. He was eighty-one when he died in 2021.

LEONARD: All at his place. And we'd work late into the night. I remember it as a very, very good time. In the studio something else happened. It was a great change. When there were other people around, Phil tended to assume other roles that weren't altogether that agreeable from my point of view.

PAUL: I think you're being very kind to him in those statements myself. I think you should have at least had a shot to sing the vocals and certainly hear the mix.

LEONARD: I had the clear sense that I wasn't in control. Phil was very interested in those matters having to do with control, and I'd never come up against anybody like that. I'd always come up against people who *deeply* wanted to cooperate with me. So it was a curious thing and, as I say now, I was in quite a bit of trouble personally at the time and I just simply didn't have the inner strength to resist or to insist. I was going under.

PAUL: One of your bad periods.

LEONARD: One of the bad ones.

PAUL: At one point you went to a monastery?

LEONARD: Well, I started studying with an elderly Japanese monk, Roshi. Roshi is just an honorific title that means *venerable old coot*. His name is Joshu Sasaki. I've been studying with him now for about eighteen years. Studying Zen. He officiated the marriage of a friend of mine, and I met him. Then I began to sit in his *zendo*, his meditation hall, and I've continued to do that over the years. I generally spend between a month or two out of every year at a Zen center. There's one in New Mexico and there's one on Mount Baldy. Mount Baldy is about an hour and a half southeast of here.

PAUL: Are you a religious person? An odd question maybe.

LEONARD: Zen isn't really a religion.

PAUL: No, I know. I'm thinking of the Judaism.

LEONARD: I couldn't call myself a religious person. I like to light the candles on Friday night, and I've studied the tradition in a small way and respect it deeply. It's given continuous nourishment. In that sense I suppose I could be called religious; but as an observant Jew, no, I don't qualify very highly.

PAUL: You don't go to synagogue much?

LEONARD: No, I don't. I go to the meditation hall in the morning and the evenings.

PAUL: When I was at *The Jewish Week*, the question of Jesus always came up. They were all very anti-Jesus at *The Jewish Week*. Yet you're fascinated by Jesus.

LEONARD: The figure of Jesus, yes, is extremely appealing, and a case could be made that he is the highest expression of the Jewish prophet. I don't think there's anybody that has taken the stand like he did really with the outcast, really with the criminal and the prostitute. Think of it today, think of the man who would really stand there and make the case, you know, validate their beings. There's nobody. Maybe Mr. Snyder, who killed himself recently.[86] Mother Theresa. As I say in "Democracy," "From the staggering account / of the Sermon on the Mount / Which I don't pretend to understand at all." Yeah, it's such a radical expression, the Sermon on the Mount, that teaching, "Blessed are the poor in heart."

PAUL: Was your mother very religious?

LEONARD: We didn't think of it as religious; it was a way of life. There was no separation between our daily activity and what would be called religion. We lived Jewish lives, so there was no objectification of the activity.

PAUL: [*takes out his New Canadian Library paperback edition of* The Favourite Game, *and opens it to page eleven*] There's one

86 The year before these interviews, Mitch Snyder, a longtime advocate for the homeless who had several times put his own life in jeopardy by staging fasts, hanged himself.

passage, I don't know whether it's fiction or true, but it's wonderful.

LEONARD: I don't have my specs. [*retrieves them*]

PAUL: This one. Maybe this was fictionalized, but it makes it sound like your family was very much in the hierarchy of the Montreal Jewish community.

Leonard silently reads the passage Paul has indicated, the one that begins "The Breavmans founded and presided over most of the institutions which make the Montreal Jewish community one of the most powerful in the world today" and ends with the line that, chuckling, he reads aloud:

LEONARD: "We were civilized first and drink less, you lousy bunch of bloodthirsty drunks."

The phone rings. When Paul starts recording again, memory loss is being discussed.

LEONARD: Something happens to your memory. It's not just that during the midst of those episodes you can't remember things, but somehow you abandon your past.

PAUL: I'm finding mine comes up and hits me in the head quite often, as well. Yeah, you do lose memory.

LEONARD: I think everyone has to undergo a process of self-reform and I think that within that process one has to determine whether or not it's valuable to continue your antique versions of yourself. If your particular path is to dissolve these antique versions of yourself, then a lot tends to evaporate: memories and mechanisms.

PAUL: What parts of yourself did you want to dissolve?

LEONARD: I had no agenda. I just find that to approach the possibility of living in present time, that once you begin that particular motion, that a lot of things fall away and you're not continually keying in to a whole lot of inappropriate mechanisms. There's something very poignant and rather sad about hearing people over forty or fifty talking about their parents in a kind of blaming way, as an alibi. I think there's a moment when you have to put aside childish things, as the Old Book says.

About education.

PAUL: I didn't even know what classical music was when I went to college. We had sort of a *Reader's Digest*-abridged version of literature. O. Henry was the great American writer in our high school. We never read Faulkner. The town library was thirty books. I read all of Shakespeare because that was part of the books. The rest were baseball books, I think, basically. I read all of the books, but I had more books on one shelf than the entire town had in their library. So I was really ignorant when I got to college. Maybe that's why I jumped in feet first when I finally found it. So in a way our growing up I guess was vastly different, because mine was totally devoid of culture. But your mother and father were educated people, I take it.

LEONARD: They swam in a culture that was quite a living culture. They didn't read Faulkner either. We had a full set of O. Henry in our house also and a full set of the *Reader's Digest* also. But they floated on a culture, they embodied it. That was something that was really quite rich.

PAUL: So you went to high school in Montreal and graduated in '51. And then straight to McGill after that?

LEONARD: Yeah, that was the way it was done in those days.

PAUL: That's the way I did it, much to my regret. I think I would have been much smarter traveling around Toronto.

LEONARD: Yeah, it wasn't done where I grew up. That was the trip: you finished high school and you went to McGill. So you entered university at sixteen.

PAUL: In a way it was just like thirteenth grade for me. I never really took advantage of it, I don't think, because I was too stupid. Basically I didn't know anything at that point. I certainly learned things, but I think I would've been smarter to knock off for two years and learn something about life, and then go.

LEONARD: We learned a lot about wine and cheese and poetry. [*chuckles*] *Tried* to learn a lot about girls but didn't do very well.

PAUL: What did you major in at McGill?

LEONARD: Well, the first year, I think the way it was then, you just took a general course; you know, English 101. Then I went into commerce, where I took statistical analysis and accounting. All this is all theoretical because there weren't any classes. I arranged to have all my classes from nine to twelve, and I was getting up around twelve. So I missed the entire year pretty well. I was taking Latin, too. And then I went back into the arts faculty and majored in political science and some English courses.

PAUL: Did you give any serious thought to accounting ever?

LEONARD: I went through these occasional convulsions where I thought I should learn how to do something practical.

PAUL: I wish I had. My father had a Ford-Mercury dealership that sold farm machinery, and also had a couple of little farms. It was a total rural farm community basically. He always wanted me to do that.

LEONARD: That would be a good trade.

PAUL: Well, I guess, but there have been many years, many *bad* years, when I wished I would have learned to do something practical. Victim of beauty, I guess, where I was always wanting to be around the arts or whatever. It's fine as long as it's the Sixties and the Seventies and you can find a cheap apartment and you can get by on your wits. But you can't do that anymore.

LEONARD: No, the marginal life is not pretty. And certainly New York doesn't seem to be the place to pursue it, because [of] the rents.

PAUL: It's exactly the wrong place. You're sitting in this city where there are twenty great options for that evening if you can afford to go see this play or see this opera or whatever, and you can't afford to do any of this. So why aren't you sitting in a cheap apartment somewhere where you could afford to do *something*?

LEONARD: Or even in a small town with a repertory theater where there are people working outside of the marketplace. I imagine, if I had that kind of appetite, that's where I'd go today. If I were really, deeply interested in the arts, I'd go to some place like Winnipeg, where there's the Manitoba Theatre Centre, or Minneapolis. I think many people were beguiled by the notion that you could live this investigative, creative, experimental life *and* make a good living. And you could, but the money dried up.

PAUL: The money dried up, the interest dried up, I think.

LEONARD: The interest dried up. And the enterprise corrupted itself.

PAUL: Most of the people I meet that are younger than me, which is almost everybody, they don't read, they're not really interested in this. A number of friends had used bookstores in New York, who were trying to cling to the culture by selling books. Basement bookstores. They've all gone out of business.[87] If the term is still yuppie, I don't know, but whatever, that generation does not buy books.

LEONARD: My daughter reads, my son doesn't.

PAUL: Did you go to movies at an early age?

87 A notable exception was Paul's friend Michael Seidenberg. Off and on from 1987 until his death in 2019, he maintained, behind the door of his Manhattan apartment, Brazenhead Books, a hidden, by-appointment-only bookstore.

LEONARD: The curious thing about Montreal is that there'd been a fire, I think it was in the Forties, in a movie theater and a number of people had been trampled to death, and a law was passed forbidding children under sixteen to go to movies. So there were movies at school and at churches for the kids. But what you would *try* to do, as soon as you reached thirteen or fourteen, is that you'd try to sneak into the downtown movie theaters. We'd put Kleenex in our heels and put fedoras on our heads. Maybe one out of ten times you'd get in. But that was one of the things you did on a Saturday afternoon: you'd try to get in to see a movie.

PAUL: Forbidden fruit.

LEONARD: Yeah, and they really meant something to us. A movie was the greatest thing you could go to. So we remembered those movies.

PAUL: Remember the first one you saw?

LEONARD: Oh, one of the first movies I saw was the *Kiss of Death*. Richard Widmark.

PAUL: Oh, yeah. Mine was *Commandos Strike at Dawn*. It's with Paul Muni. My father took me to it. I saw it again recently. It wasn't that bad. I was terrified that it was going to be utter trash. It wasn't. *Kiss of Death* is great, though.

LEONARD: Oh, it's wonderful. Wonderful. James Cagney movies.

PAUL: They never did—or did they?—make a film out of *The Favourite Game*.

LEONARD: It's perennially optioned. It's undergoing a film treatment right now. It's a Canadian group and they just—what do you call that?—renewed the option.[88]

88 The book would finally find its way to the Canadian screen in 2003, directed by Bernar Hébert from a screenplay by Peter Putka.

PAUL: Did anybody option *Beautiful Losers*?

LEONARD: Many times. A friend of mine just did a treatment on it, a man by the name of Eric Lerner, who wrote the original script of *Bird on a Wire*, with Goldie Hawn and Mel Gibson.

PAUL: I didn't see it. It got *terrible* reviews.

LEONARD: The script was very beautiful.

PAUL: But I imagine they didn't film the script.

LEONARD: No, they just basically turned it into a forty-minute car chase. But the original script, which I read, by Eric Lerner was very fine.

PAUL: Is your version of the song in that movie also or just Aaron's?

LEONARD: Just Aaron Neville's.[89]

PAUL: Why was that?

LEONARD: Well, I think he sings it better, honestly. It's a pretty good version. It's a different one, though.

PAUL: See, I don't know, I've always liked your singing, let me put it that way. I know there are a lot of these people—"Oh, I can't stand his singing." I guess, to a certain extent, that *you* don't like your voice.

LEONARD: Certain records I like it on and on certain songs I like it on now. It's not bad. A lot of people like it. It's not bad. I think it's getting there.

PAUL: I know that a couple of times that you've said that you felt that it limited your material for what you could do.

89 The recording is credited to the Neville Brothers.

LEONARD: In a certain way that's true. I love to hear my songs done by someone like Jennifer Warnes because she really understands the melody. Her readings of the songs are impeccable also, but her understanding of the melody has always touched me. She really manifests it.

PAUL: My favorite singers are yourself, Dylan, Chet Baker, and people who have limitations vocally but somehow get through the limitations. I don't know how to explain it. It's more interesting than a perfect glass wall if it has cracks in it. Cracks are where the light comes in.

LEONARD: I like those kind of singers, too.

PAUL: They seem to really curl into your soul and, within the certain range they have, they get places other people don't somehow.

LEONARD: I find that to be true.

PAUL: So I've never quite understood when people say, well, they don't like your singing.

LEONARD: When I criticize my voice I'm not criticizing from that point of view, of something technical. No, I like people that can't sing. Dylan, when he said that he's better than Caruso, I completely affirmed it.[90] I think he's a very great singer.

PAUL: Yeah, I do, too. I've just been enamored with Chet Baker lately.

LEONARD: Oh, that's a beautiful voice.

PAUL: I have a seven-and-a-half-hour vocal tape. I just carry it around with me like it was the Bible.

LEONARD: It's in the pocket all the time.

90 In the 1967 documentary *Don't Look Back*, Bob Dylan told a journalist that "I'm just as good a singer as Caruso," adding, "You have to listen closely, but I hit all those notes."

PAUL: I should make you copies of that if you like his singing. It's just all vocals for seven and a half hours. And his songs, who could not like those songs? And June Christy, who actually *could* sing in a technical way as well but has a wonderful directness about her.

The doorbell chimes and Leonard excuses himself. When he returns he is singing "Be for Real."

LEONARD: "You see I, I don't want / To be hurt by love again."

PAUL: When you were at McGill, these other poets we talked about, were they all classmates of yours?

LEONARD: Irving Layton was a generation older than me, and we became friends there around that time. He was a published poet and he was very helpful in getting me published. He took me around to his poetry readings, introduced me to publishers, and really exercised a generosity that's rare of one writer to another.

I was very happy at the Hall of Fame; the man who introduced me was also a student of Irving Layton. His name was Moses Znaimer and he's the founder of MuchMusic, which is the Canadian version of MTV, and he has several television stations. He was a student of Irving's and he cited the lineage. We'd both been students of his. I just phoned Irving yesterday and thanked him. He's a wonderful poet.

PAUL: He's written fifty-some books now. At the time you were writing poetry, as were other poets, was this a renaissance period for Canadian poets?

LEONARD: It was part of what later was described as the *Montreal School* in Canada. It doesn't mean anything over here, but in Canada it has some meaning. It was a group of poets with—I suppose if you are hard-pressed—you could discover a common sensibility. Usually personal poetry. And some pretty good poets still continue. Klein, Layton, Dudek, myself, David Solway, Henry Moscovitch, Arty Gold. Quite a few. F. R. Scott was another poet in that group. A very wonderful man, too. The leading constitutional lawyer in Canada.

PAUL: There was also a film, a documentary.

LEONARD: Around that time there was a little movie made by the National Film Board [of Canada] called *Ladies and Gentlemen, Mr. Leonard Cohen*. That arose out of a poetry tour that Jack McClelland, who was my publisher, organized for four poets' books he was publishing that season [1964]. They were Irving Layton, Earle Birney, Phyllis Gotlieb, and myself. We were going across the country reading at universities, bookstores—and the National Film Board somehow was conned into covering this as a documentary. I'm not sure exactly how this came down, but at a certain point either the film was lost or damaged. What they had was my readings, so they decided to change the focus of the film and make it a film about me rather than the tour.[91]

PAUL: You were not necessarily the most popular poet on the tour.

LEONARD: I would say that Irving was the most well-known poet. Earle Birney also, a very beloved poet in Canada for at least 400 people that cared at the time. I was kind of doing a standup comic piece before each of my readings just to keep myself amused, try to get a laugh or two.

PAUL: Ad-libbing?

LEONARD: Yeah. I'd tell some stories and some of them came out pretty well, and they're in the film. I think that was influential in the decision. They thought, *How entertaining is this picture going to be with four poets, you know, reading?* I just looked at it the other day.

PAUL: What were your feelings?

LEONARD: It was nice to see my friends young.

PAUL: You're still young of course, but they've changed a lot, haven't they? Every once in a while I pull out *The Little Sandy Review*, which is this magazine we started in college, and read the reviews. I wince

91 The good-natured 1965 documentary, in addition to Layton, includes footage of Paul's friends Robert Hershorn and Morton Rosengarten.

in embarrassment in places, but I get the feeling they were really written by somebody else. Yes, I was that person and I know that person. He's got some talent. Somehow I can look at it impersonally and I can't connect the person to it anymore. I like that guy but he's not *me* anymore. Did you feel that watching that picture?

LEONARD: Yes, well, I feel that about things a lot more recent than that. That's what we were talking about the other day, where you develop this benign amnesia toward your past.

PAUL: Reading your early poems now, can you retrace the emotions you had when you wrote them?

LEONARD: Very difficult to look. I tend to look at it anecdotally. I don't seem to be terribly interested in the poem itself. I think, *Oh, yes, I remember, I was in New York at the time where I was living at the Chelsea,* and *I was on Hydra, I was there with Marianne [Ihlen].* When I do look at those things, it tends to just produce recollections of the past. It's very hard for me to look at the work itself. Although I force myself to do it.

My publishers did ask me to prepare a selected-poems. I mean, it's quite long ago that I had selected-poems [1968]. There's been quite a lot of material since then. So I did. I went through all the books, and I suffered through that enterprise. It was hard to do. And I didn't put it out. Somebody else has got to make these decisions, whether this is worth anything. When I was writing, we did have a sense that somehow there was a pantheon or an academy, some invisible academy; that there was a *board* to which we were submitting all this work somehow and that there was a culture that could integrate it; that there was some significance to the whole activity. But I don't feel that any longer. Perhaps there is, but I don't know. Perhaps there still are guardians of the culture. Perhaps there still is a *culture* in the sense that we used the word in those days, although we incidentally never used the word. But somehow there were judges on the other side, as I say in my song "The Traitor."

PAUL: I love that line: "The judges said you missed it by a fraction."

LEONARD: We had that sense.

PAUL: Oh, judges are always going to say that you missed it by a fraction.

LEONARD: I don't know where poetry fits in anymore.

PAUL: Was the Montreal School connected with Beat poetry at all?

LEONARD: Not really. In fact, I think I was the sole member of that school that had a real connection with the Beat writers. They were not held in great esteem. They were considered a little bit too much "First thought, best thought." There was a sense of discipline and training and precision among those poets that they found lacking in the Beat poets. I found it invigorating. Especially Irving and Louie Dudek, F. R. Scott, I think they appreciated it. I remember sitting down with Irving and playing a song of Dylan's. He liked it as a song, but he didn't really embrace it as a piece of writing.

PAUL: Ewan MacColl, who was a singer I really loved—

LEONARD: Wonderful.

PAUL: —hated Dylan, just hated Dylan.[92] Wrote several pieces putting him down as the great fake, for some English magazine. Regarded Dylan as a total threat somehow.

LEONARD: Dylan did an incredible job of synthesizing all these voices that he heard. Yeah, it does sound like a lot of other people that most people had never heard of.

PAUL: Maybe I'm totally wrong in this but I get the feeling that your poetry books sold rather well.

LEONARD: They started to after my first record came out, which was quite popular in America. The books were reissued—well, in a

92 MacColl was best known for penning the songs "The First Time Ever I Saw Your Face" and "Dirty Old Town."

selected volume [*Selected Poems 1956–1968*], they were put out by Viking and it sold very, very well. Also, my novel [*Beautiful Losers*] was reissued in paperback.

PAUL: I remember buying that at Gotham Book Mart when it came out. We thought it was a scandalous book in a sense, but it got a lot of attention. What do you think about *Beautiful Losers* now? Do you think anything?

LEONARD: I hadn't even thought of the book for years until my publishers in Canada asked me to do a selected-poems. So I resisted, and it still hasn't come out. But I looked at *Beautiful Losers* again because I want to use a couple of passages of it in a selected-poems. There's some good writing there, I think, some very exuberant kind of writing. I don't know what to think about the thing.

PAUL: It's sort of a shoot-the-works novel.

LEONARD: Shoot-the-works, exactly.

PAUL: I gather it was difficult to write.

LEONARD: Yeah, they're all tricky to write. Heaven, it's tricky.

PAUL: Both of them were written in Hydra?

LEONARD: Um, *Favourite Game* was written, first draft, in England, and then a second draft in Hydra, and then a third draft in Montreal, and then a fourth draft in Hydra. *Beautiful Losers* I wrote all in Hydra.

Talk turns to what Leonard did after he graduated from McGill University in 1955.

PAUL: Did you leave Columbia [University] just because you were sick of school? Or for what reason?

LEONARD: I'd gone to McGill law school [McGill University Faculty of Law] after McGill. Well, just for a year. And then I didn't think that was going to happen, and I think then I went to Columbia. Same thing happened.

PAUL: Not in law, though?

LEONARD: No, in literature. But in both cases I got lost in the city. In Montreal, at McGill, I really got lost in the city. At Columbia I got lost in New York.

PAUL: One semester or something.

LEONARD: Yeah, and I stayed in New York for that year. Then I came back to Montreal and got a job.

PAUL: Was that your first long period in New York?

LEONARD: Yeah. I visited now and then. I'd spent a summer there. Rosengarten and I went down, we roomed together at International House, we just hung out in New York City. And the same thing happened when I went down there.

PAUL: It's quite a city to get lost in. Wouldn't be nearly as much fun I don't think today to try that.

LEONARD: It was wonderful. And just the people. International House was wonderful, too. It's a residence for foreign students, but it's an independent organization. I don't know who sponsors it. I have a feeling the Rockefellers funded it, I'm not sure. It's still there. It's a wonderful residence with its own activities and a cafeteria and a music room and a program. Roscoe [Lee] Browne, the actor and former track star, he was around at the time. We were friends. Read some of my poems. There were poetry readings. I edited a little magazine there called *The Phoenix*.

PAUL: One that was already in existence or did you start it?

LEONARD: No, we started it.

PAUL: Rosengarten, did he come to Columbia at the same time you did or was it summer school?

LEONARD: No, we went down for summer school.

PAUL: What, it just didn't work out, so you just wanted to go back to Montreal? Or didn't like Columbia?

LEONARD: Well, I found out that you were going to have to work and turn in essays. Of course with William Tindale, who's a great scholar—I think it was him—they allowed me to do, as a term paper, an analysis of my own first book, *Let Us Compare Mythologies*. [*laughs*] I thought, *What is this? Boondoggling of some kind of sophisticated higher order?* And it began to dawn on me that I wasn't a scholar, and I really couldn't keep up with it.

PAUL: You were a scholar on your own time, though.

LEONARD: Yeah, my own time. I read and I was vitally interested in the work, but not from that specific point of view. I mean, I really wanted to be a writer and I was just—

Ooh, there's a hummingbird! So beautiful. Oh, he went around—Oh, god. Oh, jeez, I've got to fill up my hummingbird [feeder]. I let it go. I've got to fill it up.[93]

PAUL: You said about McGill that, basically, you didn't really study much.

LEONARD: There were good students there, but this was pre-Sputnik university. After Sputnik, somehow North America got very sensitive about their *curriculi* and about the diligence of their students and that sort of thing. It was kind of acceptable to just go to McGill and spend those four years in some kind of gentlemanly investigative mode. A lot of the classes, they didn't take attendance. I thought that I was in *Brideshead Revisited*. This may be a completely particular,

93 A hummingbird would grace the front cover artwork of *The Future*. And in 2019, three years after his passing, the last track of his last studio album, *Thanks for the Dance*, would be the spoken-word "Listen to the Hummingbird."

individual point of view—it probably has no reality, what I said about it probably isn't true at all—but that's the way we took it, a number of us. That this was an occasion to learn a lot about wine and cheese and as much about women as you could. And poems, and really not much else.

PAUL: That's pretty much how I went through school, too, I think. There seemed to be a direct correlation between if the teacher was really, really an exciting personality, I would go; and if the teacher wasn't, I wouldn't go. Then I was basically investigating cities rather than anything else.

LEONARD: Fortunately I came into contact with three *very* wonderful teachers. One was Louis Dudek, who was teaching modern European literature and poetry, and next there was Hugh MacLennan, who was the leading novelist of the country. He just died last year. Hugh MacLennan wrote *Two Solitudes*, which is a definitive Canadian novel, and many others; *Barometer Rising* and *The Watch That Ends the Night*. A wonderful novelist and a very great teacher. I studied the novel with him.

Irving Layton wasn't teaching at McGill but he was a close friend of Louis Dudek's and part of what later became known as the Montreal School. So I bumped into him. Knowing those three men at the time was very rich. Although I wasn't doing particularly well in my courses, I got through everything. Really the study of the thing that I wanted, what I was most interested in, which was writing, was really quite intense, even though it took place outside the actual curriculum.

PAUL: When you returned to Montreal, what did you do?

LEONARD: Well, I did a lot of odd jobs; elevators and that kind of stuff. And then I got a Canada Council [for the Arts] grant, which was very, very nice. It was a grant to write. I'd already put out that little book, *Let Us Compare Mythologies*, my first book, and I got a Canada Council grant of four thousand dollars, which was quite a lot of money to me at that time, and I had a plane ticket to visit the ancient capitals. So I had a plane ticket that went from Montreal, London, Rome, Athens, Tel Aviv. I wanted to visit Athens, Rome, and Jerusalem. So while I'm in England I did the first draft of *Favourite Game* and I did the first draft of *The Spice-Box of Earth*, which is my second book of poems. And then I came back to Montreal, after I'd been to Rome and Athens, and in Hydra I bought this little house for fifteen hundred dollars.

PAUL: Hydra is an island where in Greece?

LEONARD: Well, it used to be four hours from Athens by boat, but now with the hydrofoil it's an hour and a half. It's a little island in the Argo-Saronic Gulf, and that's where I had my first house. I rented my first house there for fourteen dollars a month.

PAUL: Oh, god, take me there! I like that rent.

LEONARD: Fourteen dollars a month for a house all my own. You could get a tumbler full of cognac for a dime. And bread was a dime. I always said that my standard of living has deteriorated ever since. At eleven hundred dollars a year I was living in this beautiful house with Marianne, and a woman coming in to help out, and good food, good liquor and wine, good bread.[94] There was a bakery next to my house. You'd smell it in the morning and knew when it was ready. And you'd get your bread on a string because it was too hot to hold. Bring it back to the house, butter it in honey. It was a good economic solution at the time because I had no money.

PAUL: So *Mythologies*, and *Spice-Box* later, did not sell that well till the first record came out?

LEONARD: Yeah, maybe *Spice-Box* at first sold pretty well, I think, in Canada. But when I say *pretty well*, I mean maybe it sold 5,000 copies.

PAUL: Not enough to make a living on.

94 Marianne Ihlen was Leonard's girlfriend from 1960 to 1967 and the inspiration for "So Long, Marianne." Though in real life he pronounced her name *Mari-AN-ah*, in the song he employed the standard English pronunciation (*Mary-Ann*) so that it would work syllabically.

LEONARD: No, I had no money right up to the time that the first record came out. In fact, well, after *Beautiful Losers* came out, I was living in Montreal on Aylmer Street and I couldn't pay the rent, I couldn't buy the groceries. It was a desperate situation, so I borrowed some money. I had written these songs, some of these songs, and I'd been listening to AFR, Armed Forces Radio station, country music for a long time. I love country music, and I thought I'd go down to Nashville and not just make a scene; I had a folly that I was going to bail myself out of my economic dilemma by becoming a country singer. So I borrowed some money from my dear friend Robert Hershorn, who died when he was forty. But he lent me some money, and I started south and went down to New York, and in New York I came head-on to this so-called folk song renaissance that was going on that I knew nothing about in Greece. I bumped into Judy Collins and Phil Ochs and Joan Baez and Bob Dylan, all those great luminaries of the movement, and I kind of got ambushed there.

PAUL: Right. Did they know your reputation as a poet or did they not?

LEONARD: Lou Reed was the only guy who seemed to know. He was very kind to me. I just remember one or two occasions. I'd bump into him at Max's Kansas City. I don't remember where it was I first met him, but he came over to me and said, "I love 'Flowers for Hitler.'" I said, "How do you know about *that*?" He'd invite me over to the table that he had gathered around him and he'd introduce me to a few people.

PAUL: Was he how you met Dylan? Judy Collins?

LEONARD: Judy Collins I met through a woman by the name of Mary Martin. She used to be with Albert Grossman in his office, and she struck out on her own. I think she was the woman that brought Dylan and the Band together. She knew a number of people and was in management at the time, and she became my manager.

PAUL: And then Judy took you under her wings.

LEONARD: Judy was very kind to me. I sang her "Suzanne" over the phone, and she loved it. The first time I met her, I met Earl Robinson, who had composed "Ballad for Americans."[95]

PAUL: These are people whose work you really didn't know.

LEONARD: Well, I knew "Ballad for Americans" very, very well.

PAUL: Yeah, but you didn't know Judy Collins.

LEONARD: No, I didn't know anybody.

PAUL: Even Dylan.

LEONARD: No. And then Judy's record came out, and I believe I was at the Bitter End; I think it was Joni Mitchell performing there. I had heard Dylan's records, and a representative of Dylan's came to me and said, "Bob Dylan would like to meet you." So I went over to another restaurant, and that was the first time I met Bob Dylan. And then we would bump into each other now and then. We seemed to get along well. You know, he's an acquaintance. I feel very friendly towards him. I don't know him terribly well. We've met on a number of occasions and had some good talks.

PAUL: I knew him briefly at the University of Minnesota because my friend and I had this folk magazine, *The Little Sandy Review*, which as I said, we started to get free records. And it worked. We had three subscribers for the first issue. The first one was Jay Smith from Jacksonville, Florida, who we immediately made a monthly columnist because he was our first subscriber. [*Leonard laughs*] He was thrilled at that. Eventually it got up to like 2,000 people subscribing.

Sort of the *enfants terribles*, we actually criticized people. That was never done. And Dylan was around then. I know we played him his first Ramblin' Jack Elliott records because we got them from England, sent to us, and Elliott didn't have an American contract then. I think we played him his first Woody Guthrie records. But I remember he

95 "Ballad for Americans" is a 1939 patriotic cantata with lyrics by John La Touche and music by Earl Robinson.

came, say, like on a Tuesday and listened to some of this Elliott and Guthrie stuff—until that point he'd been singing Odetta and [Harry] Belafonte and Josh White songs—and he came back on Wednesday and he sounded like he did on the first Columbia record [1962's *Bob Dylan*]. He got it overnight, what took Jack Elliott ten years to get, and I just said, "Jesus!" He used to look through records, and I saw his notebook once, and he invariably picked the best song from every record. He just had an instinct about that.

We went to New York at the same time as part of the folk boom. I went to *Sing Out!* All of a sudden they became the going concern because of the folk boom; so they needed to hire a managing editor. Which happened to be the same week I was graduating from Minnesota—I was going to go to New York anyway—so they offered me the job because I got the degree more or less, which was terrific. I defended Dylan in Newport during that whole electric controversy, where *Sing Out!* and some of the topical song movement really didn't like his stuff. He was booed at Newport and at Forest Hills and Carnegie whenever he'd play the electric half.[96] At Carnegie I remember everybody from *Sing Out!* magazine but me made a big point to be seen walking out when he started playing with the Band. Do you know that whole Newport story?

LEONARD: Yes. Well, I guess I don't know as much as you know, but I know that stuff.

PAUL: I'm sorry to be talking too much.

LEONARD: That's all right.

PAUL: But it turned out, the last night of the festival, Seeger had planned a night of songs to be sung to this—I guess she actually wasn't a mythical young baby, I think she was John Cohen and Penny Seeger's new baby—he wanted a sort of utopian night. Dylan, not knowing this was going to happen, had planned on that night to sing "Like a Rolling Stone" as one of his songs, for the first time, I believe, to sort of introduce the song. Seeger was *very* upset by "Like a Rolling Stone,"

96 As he had with his then-most recent album, 1965's *Bringing It All Back Home*, in concert Dylan was dividing his songs into electric and acoustic sets.

which he read as sheer nihilism, I guess, and by the electric band in general, and got in his car and rolled the windows up and told somebody to cut the electricity. It was like crazy. I mean, it's just a song. So, Irwin Silber [cofounder and editor] and the *Sing Out!* people—I don't know how well you know them or if you know them at all—but they were sort of Thirties leftists and they published open letters to Dylan saying, "You've gone Tin Pan Alley," which was as far out of, you know—they just didn't know what he was doing.

Well, I knew what was going to happen at *Sing Out!*; that they were going to really crucify him for not writing topical songs after going electric and selling out, in their terms. I figured wherever this was going I didn't want to go with it. So I wrote this passionate defense of Dylan at Newport, over the utopian night aspect, as virtually my resignation. I didn't trust Irwin Silber to print it, so I went to Moe Asch, who was connected sort of to *Sing Out!* The whole publication and Folkways was supposedly some triumvirate financially. I asked Moe if he would see to it that it was printed as I wrote it, without interference, because they would frequently do this. I can actually say I quit a job over "Like a Rolling Stone." It really moved me enough so that I just didn't want to be part of this. I liked some of the topical songs, but I didn't like a lot of them as songs. I just thought they weren't very interesting songs. I agreed with most of the sentiments but I just didn't like the songs. So I just left at that point.

But Dylan loved that article. I think I was the only folk writer who defended him. He sent me tickets for years to concerts after that article. It's gotten reprinted a lot in various anthologies. We talked on the phone three or four years ago, and it was a strange conversation, because this is arguably the most important rock & roll singer of all time. He was saying that Columbia didn't want to put out his new album and they were going to take it back and they wanted a couple more songs on it. He said, "I'm so sick of playing North America. I do my own songs as well as I can, but some of them I've just sung so many times that I can't get into them anymore, and some of them just don't sing well for me. I try to do a folk song by somebody else and the audience just sits there and talks. Then when I go into something that I really don't like to sing anymore, I bring the house down." He said, "I'd like to go to South America with like three or four people where I could sing anything," and Bill Graham wouldn't book it. He was quite serious about doing this, but Graham said, "No way." And I was thinking, *Jesus, this guy, the number one guy in music, his record company doesn't want his record, his booking agent won't book his tour, and I'm sitting here about to get evicted. We don't sound that different*. This guy was having major troubles with his musical career and Columbia wasn't the least bit understanding about it, nor was anyone else apparently.

LEONARD: I can believe that.

PAUL: He sounded like, "I don't know who my audience is. I don't know if anybody's listening anymore." That was probably the best conversation I've had with him, the most personal, because I never really knew him all that well in Minnesota, and I don't know him all that well now. I think he's always liked the fact that I've defended the electric stuff. Among the folk journalists I was the only one. So he sort of led me into rock & roll. In a way I hadn't really listened to much. The Beatles sort of existed for me on the radio, but until I saw Richard Lester's first movie [*A Hard Day's Night* in 1964], I didn't get them. A long digression here. Sorry about that.

LEONARD: [*chuckles*] We're just sitting around.

PAUL: Were the same songs that wound up on your first record the songs you were taking to Nashville?

LEONARD: Some of them.

PAUL: What did it feel like to be thirty-three at that point, to be trying to break into this?

LEONARD: Most things I didn't give too much thought. It seemed possible. I realized I couldn't make a living writing novels and verse.

PAUL: Was your reputation in Canada considerable even though money was not considerable?

LEONARD: Well, among those people who cared for the whole enterprise, how many was that? Maybe 5,000 across Canada.

PAUL: You weren't a household name by any means.

LEONARD: No, there was no such thing as a household name, not in that deal. Maybe McGill, maybe a few cafes in Montreal you're well-known in. But that didn't bother us any. We thought every time we had a beer together was a historic occasion.

PAUL: What did the other Canadian writers think of your movement into songwriting then?

LEONARD: There was quite a long period—and Irving Layton defended me quite a number of times publicly—a number of people felt that I had really lost it, done something really *bad*. So for a long time I was, in Canada, caught between these two versions of myself. The music people didn't really consider me one of them because I was really a poet; I was really a writer, and the writing people didn't really consider me thoroughbred because I was in the music business.

PAUL: It was somewhat like Dylan going electric.

LEONARD: Yeah, it was something like that, but on a much, much tinier scale. Because you're talking about a few thousand people gathered who even knew about it. It was a very dedicated group of people and dedicated to the craft of poetry. Once you left it there's really not much to say. I think the juices, they've all evaporated by three or four years anyway; it's just that group of people meeting. And we put out a magazine called *CIV/n*, which was the abbreviation for *civilization*, by Ezra Pound. It's really quite rarified, the whole thing. I mean, you're talking about a dozen people who knew or cared about it.

PAUL: Did you consider it a major shift?

LEONARD: No, I always considered it the same thing. But I'd always played music. Yeah, I was on my way to Nashville and I found that there was all this other stuff going on and bumped into Judy Collins. I thought this was a way I could make a living.

PAUL: I saw the Central Park concert where she introduced you, I believe, and you sang a couple together. You mentioned this little hotel on Thirty-fourth Street and Eighth Avenue that you stayed at.

LEONARD: Oh, yeah, the Penn Terminal. Penn Terminal Hotel. I think I used to mention that hotel as a kind of introduction to "Hey, That's No Way to Say Goodbye," which was where I think I finished that. What a place. I don't think it's there anymore. I'd stay there from time to time. It was very inexpensive. It was near the bus station. I'd come down by bus from Montreal.

I never made it down to Nashville, except for years later when I actually did move outside of Nashville, outside of Franklin. I lived there for a couple years; that was '69 and '70. I moved to a little place outside of Franklin, which is a little town outside of Nashville. Boudleaux Bryant [country and pop songwriter] rented me his fifteen hundred acres and a little shack for seventy-five dollars a month. And I lived there. I bought a horse from Kid Marley, who was the Tennessee rodeo champion, and I began to live the life down there. Bought a rifle. Got a horse.

PAUL: Tennessee squire.

LEONARD: I started going to Nashville in '69; between '70 and '71 I lived there. I was living down there with Suzanne [Elrod] in this little cabin, which was beautiful. This little stream. They had some wild peafowl there, peahen and a peacock, and they'd come every morning in front of the shack and they'd do their dance—it was the male, the peacock, would do his dance—and we'd give him bread. I've had some very lovely places.

PAUL: Did you make one of your records in Nashville?

LEONARD: Two. I did *Songs from a Room* there and *Songs of Love and Hate* [his second and third albums, respectively] with [producer] Bob Johnston.

PAUL: I think *Love and Hate* has the single most perfect song I've ever heard: "Joan of Arc." I don't think I've ever gotten over that song.

LEONARD: Oh, god, Jennifer did that on Sunday night. The people were galvanized. Oh, god, you should've seen this thing. She was so beautiful. I almost started crying. I thought, *Oh, god, the old guy is going to cry. This is going to be a charming moment*. But it was *so* beautiful.

PAUL: I didn't think anybody could write a song like that.

LEONARD: Lot of drafts of that one. I love Jenny's version of it. I think it's a good song. I worked so hard on getting it right.

PAUL: Why did you move from Tennessee?

LEONARD: I don't remember what happened there. I guess I moved back to Montreal. Between Montreal and Greece. I put a little money together in Montreal and then I'd go to Greece.

PAUL: Do you still do that now? Do you still have the house?

LEONARD: Yeah. I went, not last spring but the spring before, working a lot of these songs there. It was the first time I'd been there alone in a long time. It was wonderful, even though the island is somewhat more touristic now. The Greeks have really resisted tourism marvelously. And they still have their own music. It's really wonderful. People have talked about how the place has been ruined by tourism. Yeah, the port is touristic, but once you get a hundred feet above the port it's pretty nice.

PAUL: But when you first went there, you rented a place for a while and then you bought one.

LEONARD: Yeah, I rented that place for fourteen dollars a month, and then my grandmother left me fifteen hundred dollars, which was *exactly* the price this house was on the market. My father's mother, Lyon Cohen's wife, she'd left all her grandchildren, I think it was fifteen hundred dollars. And I bought this house and I stayed in it a number of years and I've still got it. It's a wonderful little house.

Talk returns to the Beats.

LEONARD: Well, you know, you were young at the time, that's what you were reading. I was also reading Camus at the time and I was also reading Dostoevsky at the time and I was also reading the Bible at the time. So there were other influences. But of course those were the guys that were on the scene, and I think it was their rawness, their honesty, their, uh …

PAUL: I like that time. I love Kerouac. *On the Road*'s I think fabulous.

LEONARD: I love a lot of his books.

PAUL: Today a lot of people don't remember how big a deal that was. Every major national magazine had article after article on Kerouac and the Beat generation. It wasn't like a one-article phenomenon.

LEONARD: No. That's what I mean to say: that's what it *was*. You were either reading J. P. Marquand or you were reading Kerouac and Ginsberg. It was exciting if you were young, it was speaking for you or speaking to you.

I always loved Ginsberg, and I was sitting in a café in Athens—I'd just come in for some reason or another—and I saw Ginsberg going by. I recognized him from his photograph. I ran up to him and we started talking. I said, "Come on over." So he came and stayed at my house. And that's really where we first met.

[Gregory] Corso *had* been there the summer before or a few months before. I think that may be where Allen had heard about it. I met Corso, I think it was maybe in Greece or maybe in the Chelsea Hotel. I'd bump into him here and there in the world.

PAUL: There was a Norwegian writer there [in Greece].

LEONARD: There were a number of very fine writers there. There was Axel Jensen.[97] He is a wonderful man that lives in a boat now in the Oslo Harbor. He's Norwegian. There's something he said to me once that was really wonderful. He had a small sailboat, and he'd

97 Jensen was married to Marianne Ihlen from 1958 to 1962.

invite me out. I got onto the deck, I was wearing running shoes, but I put a black mark on the deck with my running shoe. And this is a guy that was very, very loose, and he suddenly got very upset about this black mark. And I said to him, "What's the deal, Axel? It's just a black mark." He said, "Look, Leonard, if this sailboat just sank to the bottom of the harbor, I'd walk away without even thinking about it. But while I've got it, I want to keep the decks clean." [*laughs*]

PAUL: So was Marianne divorced from him then, at that point?

LEONARD: No. He fell in love with a young American painter who was on the island and they ran off together. In that boat they sailed away.

PAUL: With a black mark on it. [*laughs with Leonard*] You and Marianne got together later than that?

LEONARD: Yeah, and we stayed together for about eight years or so.

PAUL: Is she the one on *Songs from a Room*, the [back cover] photograph, at the typewriter?

LEONARD: Yeah.

PAUL: And that was your first great love? Or is that wrong? Or you lived with somebody for eight years, I guess it had to have been, right?

LEONARD: [*seems reticent*] She was—she is a wonderful woman. She was just in L.A. and I missed her.

PAUL: Was she a writer? An artist?

LEONARD: No, she wasn't.

PAUL: [*consults his notes*] I've forgotten now where I'd gotten this, but maybe on the telephone you talked about it. Columbia might be considering a double set or something? A best-of?

LEONARD: They wanted to. I'm sorry I didn't do it now, but that was before my son had an accident.[98] If I'd known it would've taken this long, I would've put out a best-of.

PAUL: Volume two [to 1975's *The Best of Leonard Cohen*]?

LEONARD: Well, no, not a volume two, but a long CD. But I wanted to put out a CD that was heavily based on *I'm Your Man* and *Various Positions* and going back. Because nobody knows my work here. *I'm Your Man* sold maybe fifty or sixty thousand copies in America and *Various Positions* sold maybe twenty. As I said to them [Columbia] at a meeting—they said, "We're waiting for your new record"—I said, "You've *got* two new records! Nobody's heard *I'm Your Man* and nobody's heard *Various Positions*." When they were kind of hot on me a couple years ago, they wanted to put out this, and I worked on the list and I had it, and then I thought, *No, I really want to do a studio album*. But then my son had the accident and I was delayed for at least six or seven months. I was living in a little room next to the hospital for three months and not thinking about much except my son. So I really lost contact with my songs. I'm just starting to get back into it now.

PAUL: Writing this batch wasn't nearly as tough as *I'm Your Man*. Or was it?

LEONARD: I haven't finished this record yet, so I don't know. I've got one song I'm working on now; it's to the muse, so to speak. It goes [*he recites seven lines that, in a different order, would appear in the song "Light as the Breeze"*]:

> *There's blood on every bracelet*
> *You can see it, you can taste it*
> *But she comes to you*
> *Light as the breeze*
> *Now you can drink it or you can nurse it*

98 When Adam Cohen was seventeen, he was involved in a horrific car crash that left him with, among other injuries, a broken neck and nine broken ribs, a punctured lung, and a fractured pelvis, ankles, and knees.

It don't matter how you worship
As long as you're
Down on your knees

PAUL: Do you feel you've got most of the material for this record taped?

LEONARD: You can't tell when you do it. When you hear it, I usually find there's something really off that has to be corrected.

PAUL: This will sound somewhat like the last record, you think?

LEONARD: I think they'll move between those two cuts you heard. I have the feeling that they're going to go that way. I've got a techno-pop dance track for a very different kind of lyric, and then that kind of sweet R&B feel for "Be for Real." And there'll be a country song on it.

PAUL: Did you sing country songs, other people's country songs, ever?

LEONARD: Not professionally. Of course I sang them myself a lot.

PAUL: Who did you like?

The tape runs out. Later that day Paul dictates notes from his first session with Leonard. He's back at the Best Western Motel. He lights his nth Cigaretello of the day and draws deeply on it in between sentences.

PAUL: Oh, what a great guy he is. Wow. We meet at the Chariot on La Brea and Wilshire. He's wearing a gray striped suit. Great. Short sleeve. Looks like Dustin Hoffman sort of when he smiles. A really wonderful, open smile. Battered good looks. Tells me a little about the restaurant; used to be a Jewish restaurant, now it's Spanish. A very good coffee shop. We drive to his place. Kelley is there. Set up at the little wooden table that he finished "Tower of Song" on, which is the "Tower of Song" Table. We're in the Tower of Song.

He has this Technics machine, a computer, a workout room (have to ask him about that). We do three hours forty-five minutes of pretty good stuff, I think. He shies away from the breakdown stuff a little, understandably. A *lot* of stuff I didn't go into or follow up on. He is a smoker.

Afterwards, we drive back and stop at the Burger King on Highland. He buys me a cheeseburger, fries, and a Coke, and sort of starts interviewing *me*. We talked about Styron's book on mental breakdown and he went on with this, or maybe I went on with it. He seemed very sympathetic. A lot of people, they call it [depression] *it* and they keep track of each other, like it's the worst place they've ever been. *Suicidalness* is talked about. He said he just sort of didn't know, so we continue. For a long time I had the feeling that that would be an option. [*now puffing midsentence*] Much to my surprise, talking about writing, I said I'm the only writer I know without a computer or even a typewriter that works, and he offered to help me get one and get a job out here. One thing he said that was terrific, talking about the rents and how much he loves it out here, he said, "All I need is a table and a room, a room and a table. I live the same where I am anywhere."

He's got a Buick. Listened to some of those songs. Two great songs on the one cassette, which I'll have to make double sure are on here.

Two days later, Paul is back at Leonard's. The previous evening he attended a recording session for Leonard's cover of Irving Berlin's "Always."

PAUL: Why don't you tell me all about last night and how terrific it all went? It sounded like a great *up* night where things came together.

LEONARD: Last night, let me see if I can recall. It was at Capitol [Records] up on Vine above Hollywood. According to Steve Lindsey, it was the room that Nat King Cole cut his Christmas album in and where Frank Sinatra did all of his Capitol records. None of this was terribly comforting when I came into the room.

PAUL: You were doing a song that fit in with that.

LEONARD: Yes, that's true.

Well, we picked up a bottle of tequila and some cranberry juice, some lemons, Kelley and I, and we came about seven. We made a few Red Needles and the session started.[99] Leanne was working on the board, getting the sounds right. Musicians were in place. The song was written in 3/4; we were cutting it in 4/4. I'd never really sung it out loud. I'd sung it to myself with my Technics many times, trying different rhythms, different approaches. We didn't have anything clear, either the musicians or I, we just felt it had to be sweet and low, a kind of Delta feel. And these musicians were really sensational. So we started playing. The first time we played for fifteen minutes; we had to change the tapes. We just played right through. Everybody was very happy. It was one of the unusual evenings where the pressures of the enterprise don't seem to operate at all. There were just people playing music and singing, and it was very lighthearted, very happy and intense at the same time. I think many people remembered why they'd come into music in the first place. It was one of those mysterious events that has nothing to subtract from its sweetness and excellence.

PAUL: And you did three live takes, or more than three live takes?

LEONARD: We did three full twenty-four-track reels. The last take we did was about six or seven minutes long, which is probably the one we'll work on. That has that tension. It's hard to recreate it now because we're all a little tired, but you picked up how excited people were, still. Those musicians are exceptional. I tell you, I would sure like to get to know them. Every one of those men were playing impeccably. There wasn't a clam the whole evening, wasn't a false note. There wasn't a moment when someone sailed out of the groove or the mood or *frisson* or anything. The modesty of the playing and the precision and the feeling are really quite unusual.

PAUL: This was all live with no overdubs.

LEONARD: All live. The pianist played me some riffs and—he's a magnificent player—I said, "That's great playing. Too many notes for

99 Cohen lays claim to having invented the Red Needles cocktail in Needles, CA, in the mid-Seventies. The only ingredient he didn't mention to Paul was the ice.

the song." He said, "How about this?" and he ran through three or four things as if anything that he wanted was at his disposal. I said, "I don't know, man. Just one thing that I always end up saying: it don't mean a thing if the man can't sing." I always tell that to musicians because I'm often playing with musicians that are very, very accomplished, and I have to cover myself. Because it doesn't matter how good the track is if I can't sing to it. I was really leaning on Steve for pitch. He was right there. Every time I'd falter he'd be right under me with the pitch.

PAUL: Is that a problem with some songs?

LEONARD: Well, it's always a problem for me, staying in tune, especially if there's no pad.

PAUL: What do you mean by a *pad*? I know it's a technical term.

LEONARD: I mean like that horizontal movement of music which is carrying the chord, like the triad C, E, and G. Like, an organ pad would be just laying in that horizontal phrase that would be holding the triad, the chord, right along without any movement, just so that you can move around and know that you're always going to be out of pitch if you hear that thing. A really great singer can sing with just a very few things going on. I could take it away later, but to sing, especially if I'm getting excited and there are a lot of things going on and a lot of people *aren't* playing exactly within the chord, I need that pad later. It's just something to rest on, so it's there.

PAUL: Can you tell when you're singing when you're going off?

LEONARD: Oh, yeah. Oh, it drives me crazy. Always has. Finally, when I learn a song, I can start approaching what is acceptable, or reasonable. But often when I begin—and with very unfamiliar material and with a kind of a tempo, if it's moving fast—I get excited, I lose it. That one I lost about twenty percent; the song is a little off for my taste. But there's a lot of it that is on; but Steve was right there.

PAUL: Did it come out like you had heard it in your head?

LEONARD: Yeah, it did. It had that feel. *Better* than I'd imagined.

PAUL: I don't know what I'd imagined. I guess not that it was going to sound like that. It was terrific.

LEONARD: It's always a surprise. Good is always a surprise, and always a pleasant surprise. But it's the energy and the control at the same time, or the tension of the movement, that the movement creates in the song, so that you're gathered into it. You're never disappointed, you know, the way it moves. Yeah, it's unusual when it happens that effortlessly, but you have men of very high accomplishment playing. That doesn't always guarantee it.

PAUL: It doesn't. Sometimes it just guarantees boring perfection. They've got to be in it emotionally, too.

You were drawn rhythmically to that song and by the way it was constructed musically, rather than lyrically. Is that correct?

LEONARD: Well, I think the lyric is very expert and very beautiful. Irving Berlin is a *very* great songwriter. He's sort of scorned by people who scorn Middle American culture, but the songs are really very beautiful. And this lyric is so simple and so beautiful, and the construction of the song is so kind. The movements in it, the chord changes, are so simple and so perfect. It's a very happy marriage of lyric and chord changes; lyric and music are married very, very tightly. The music produces the exact appropriate emotion for the lyric at every moment. And you finally get those final declarations at the end: "Not for just an hour / Not for just a day / Not for just [a year, but always]." The way the chords are progressing at that moment, you come to that last word: *always*. It is the end, it *is* the solemn promise.

PAUL: Do you think this is an exception, that you're starting to do other people's songs now? Or do you think it will continue?

LEONARD: I would love to be able to do it. I would love to have a modest success with a cover tune so that I could be justified in doing more and more of them. I hope that people find favor in them, because

I would like to be able to do it. There's a number of songs I would love to cover.

PAUL: I'll have to play one for you. I think it's a Van Heusen song. It's called "Deep in a Dream." It's about a cigarette-smoking woman.[100] Very lovely.

LEONARD: Yes, Paul, please send it to me. You know, then I'd be having these conversations with people that are saying, "There's a lovely song ..." You know? And writers could send me songs. I just feel in the mood of doing it, using my voice, just whatever is left of it. Just move it around in the song, and playing it kind of like a sax.

PAUL: Well, it's like I said, I always thought you had an expressive voice, and I think it's good to do that. I think you could do a lot of these songs really quite great.

LEONARD: I would love to give it a shot. Of course I don't want to disappoint the people that have stayed with me all these years, who are expecting to hear something from me that is specifically mine or a specific take I have on things. But I think these songs stand up musically and emotionally.

PAUL: I don't think you write enough, but there's always going to be to-cover songs. I think your fans may be intrigued. I think they'd buy the record because they like whatever—it's not only particular songs, it's the whole persona, the whole personality. These songs obviously mean something to you and I think it's logical to believe they could also mean something to your fans by that extension.

LEONARD: I hope so.

PAUL: And I also think probably that the best chance to get one on the radio oddly enough seems to be cover versions.

100 The music for the song was indeed written by Jimmy Van Heusen, with lyrics by Eddie DeLange. It's been covered by numerous singers over the years, including Frank Sinatra and—most likely how Paul heard it—Chet Baker.

LEONARD: I don't really know the marketplace of the radio programming at all. I don't know what gets on radio anymore, what you have to do to get something on the radio. I don't have any high expectations of these, especially in this country.

PAUL: Still, it would be nice. I know you're not doing these songs trying to make a hit or anything, but for some reason cover songs by people get a little more attention. I don't quite know why, but some of them *have* become hits. I don't know how many either, but I think luck is just a great part of it. Who would've guessed "Luka" as a hit? With its subject matter, I would've said, "No chance."[101]

LEONARD: That's true. Timing is very important. It just came between like a moment where there wasn't much around that was really interesting and before a lot of other female singers emerged. It was just dropped into the pocket, times and melody. Unless you have some kind of huge star-making machinery behind you, it seems to be so capricious what is going to find favor, what is going to insinuate itself into the consciousness of people.

PAUL: I don't think anybody can predict.

LEONARD: I certainly haven't been able to.

PAUL: Your first album got you a lot of attention. And also *McCabe & Mrs. Miller* had three of those songs, and that was a fairly big movie.[102]

LEONARD: Yes, that gave them a bit of renown. It's a lovely movie. I sometimes see it on television.

PAUL: It's his [director Robert Altman's] best movie, I think. Did you meet him?

101 Suzanne Vega's "Luka," a top-ten hit for the singer-songwriter in 1987, dealt with the subject of child abuse in an artful way that didn't diminish its sales.

102 In addition to "Sisters of Mercy" and "Winter Lady," the 1967 film also included, over the credits, "The Stranger Song."

LEONARD: Yes, we became quite friendly. We always see each other once every year or so when we happen to find each other in the same city. He'll often turn up at a concert of mine in Paris.

PAUL: How did that come about, the songs being in the film?

LEONARD: I think that he wrote the film listening to that record. I think that's what he told me. I think I either read that or he said that to me. I was living in Nashville at the time. The curious thing was that I was living out in the country, and I'd come into town a little bit early for my session, a lot early. It was raining and I ducked into a movie house that was showing *Brewster McCloud*. And it was a great surprise, that movie. I just ducked into this movie house in Nashville, and I sat through it twice. I was living out in Franklin.

Anyhow, he called up and it was Bob Altman on the phone that night and he said, "I'd like to use your songs in this movie I wrote." I said, "Could you tell me some of the movies you've made?" He said, "Well, I made a movie called *M*A*S*H*," and I said, "I know it was a grand success. I didn't happen to see it. Is there anything else?" He said, "Well, I did do another movie, but the chances are very slim that you've seen it. It's called *Brewster McCloud*." I said, "I just sat through it twice. You can have anything you want of mine."

PAUL: You weren't on the set for any of it?

LEONARD: They flew me up to Vancouver for some odd reason, just to talk maybe. Oh, yes, he wanted to talk because he needed some additional material. So I did a guitar and my chop behind one of Warren Beatty's soliloquies, and then we mixed some of the music without voice so he could use it incidentally. Some of "Sisters of Mercy" we used without the vocal. And there were a few other little touches here and there that he asked me for. But I never saw the set. I don't believe it was the winter.

And then he shot a few movies in Montreal. He'd come to Montreal and we'd manage to see each other. Then he was in Paris. He moved to Paris for a couple of years and I was in Paris a lot seeing my kids at that point, so we'd meet from time to time. Always good meetings with him. He invited me to a few of his sets. I was at the set of *A*

Wedding,[103] and there was a movie that he filmed with Lauren Bacall in the lead that was never released, called *HealtH*. And he asked me to do the music for *Popeye*. I said, "Have you got three years? It's a lovely idea." [*chuckles*]

PAUL: It was a charming movie, but you wouldn't think it would be able to come off with an actor playing Popeye. But it was very well done, very low-key. Quite good.

LEONARD: Well, he's a very adventurous spirit. That's what we love about the guy. He never stops making movies. He doesn't care what the particular conditions of his life or his career are at the time, he just continues to make films. People come and take his furniture away in the middle of it, and he gets it back. A check comes in, he pays the creditor of the other movie. It's just juggling.

PAUL: Did he talk to you at length about the first album and why he liked it?

LEONARD: I think his wife had found the album and introduced it to him, his wife Kathryn [Reed Altman]. No, we never discussed it. We did discuss *Beautiful Losers*, which was a novel that he liked very much. I would love him to make that.

I've been invited to do scores by a number of people, but I always tell them, "When do you hope to release the film? It's going to take a while."

PAUL: In some cases it would just be music, I guess, than lyrics.

LEONARD: Just the music, yeah. I'd like to do that somewhere down the line.

PAUL: Do you think that would be as painstaking a process if you didn't have to write the lyrics?

103 Towards the end of his 1978 film *A Wedding*, Altman has one of his characters sing "Bird on the Wire" while playing an autoharp.

LEONARD: I'm not sure.[104] I was playing around with my keyboard the other night, pretending that I was writing a concerto.

PAUL: And it was coming all right?

LEONARD: It was coming all right. A friend of mine by the name of Ted Allan, who's a great writer, he wrote *Love Streams* with John Cassavetes. He's a Canadian writer. He had a huge play in Europe called *Gog et Magog* [cowritten with Roger MacDougal]. He's a very accomplished writer. He has books and plays and movies and he worked a lot with Cassavetes. And he wrote a little play [*Everyone Else a Stranger*], and he came over and I played some music for it. So that might be going on one of these days. I wrote the theme for the play. One of the main characters is a composer, so he's sitting at his keyboard a lot during the play or playing. So I composed this little piece. It's quite nice. I'd play it for you but I don't have a machine.

PAUL: Has that begun to interest you more, the musical end of it, or have you always been that interested in the music?

LEONARD: I've been always very, very interested in the music, but I'm quite passionate about it now. I'm very interested in the whole enterprise. In a certain sense, maybe this is just one of the characteristics of getting old. You get deeply and intensely interested in some matter at the same time as not giving a shit about it. I mean, the whole enterprise to me in some ways seems quite irrelevant and insignificant, and I really pine and look forward to the day I can drop it. On the other hand, at the same time within those feelings, I have the most intense and concentrated attention to the matter, much more so than I've ever had. Much more interested in every detail and every movement in the form. It seems like since I began to write *Various Positions*—I guess I started writing around '83; some of the songs are older than that—that it hasn't let up. The kind of attention I've brought to the whole matter has been intense for a good eight, nine years now. I don't remember it being quite this intense. I don't remember sweating quite this much over the lyrics and the music

104 On *The Future* he would include, for the first time on a studio album, an instrumental cut, "Tacoma Trailer." Previously, on *Live Songs*, there had been the guitar-based "Improvisation."

and the performance. I know I worked hard, I know that I was wrapped up in these things, but it didn't seem to be quite to this degree. I seem to remember that I also had a human life that went along with it in the earlier records.

PAUL: And yet at the same time you said you couldn't wait to drop it, in some peculiar way.

LEONARD: There's the possibility of dropping it. Well, as you get old of course you know that your odds start getting higher about leaving in one way or another anyhow. You really do start to understand that every life is hanging by a thread. One always knew that intellectually, but I think as you get older you really do begin to sense that. In a certain way you're sensing it or you've already been around a lot longer than a lot of people that you knew. And *why*? Those three, four months that I spent in the hospital with my son Adam last summer certainly reinforces that sense of the frailty of the enterprise. Especially during the Labor Day weekend, the choppers were coming in; it was like war. From all the highways and rivers of Ontario these broken bodies were coming in every fifteen minutes, and you thought why them and not you. But yet I think with that sense of the frailty of things, the significance of your own activity becomes quite questionable. And of all activity.

Not that we want to descend into this morbid spirituality or anything like that, but you just do get the sense of the frailty of the thing and how important it is. And it is tough, it's very, very, very, very hard work. I've always admired the people who could write great songs in the back of taxicabs like Hank Williams. I was never one of those guys. There's something Norman Mailer says: "One of the few things you learn as you get old as a writer, you know how much it's going to take out of you, the next novel. You can't fool yourself. You know you're going to be spending days like this and nights like last night and a lot worse, and everything good and everything bad you're going to pay for."

PAUL: Graham Greene I think basically stopped writing long novels ten, fifteen years ago because, he said, "I don't have the strength to finish a regular length novel anymore." He wrote novellas. Some writers physically train for a novel.

LEONARD: I think you have to. In a sense, I do. I wouldn't try to do this without keeping in pretty good shape. Going out on the road I always try to get into good condition for it. On the other hand I don't want to be one of those, you know, how tough life is at the top or by the top. I still feel very privileged. I've been able to make a living, and a decent living, over the years. A modest living, but I've always been able to pay my bills and take care of my children. I've never done *one* thing I didn't want to do. I've always said I want to get paid for my work but I don't want to work for pay, and I've been able to do it.

PAUL: And I gather, if nothing else, CBS has never really interfered and said, "Look, we're going to remix your songs," or things like that. Your records are probably not that expensive to make, you're probably a prestige artist for them basically, and now they just put them out. If anybody wants them they can buy them, if they can find them.

LEONARD: No, that's the good side of it. Their appetite for profits was never excited sufficiently for them to be deeply interested in what I was doing. On the other hand, they knew that they could always sell the record in some modest way and they wouldn't lose their tiny advance.

PAUL: I just find that I only want to listen to certain things, with some sort of essence, that mean something. I'm wondering if that's another way to say what you were saying, that in a sense it doesn't matter to me anymore because you're thinking of it differently. Strangely enough, I don't know how to even say this, but when you're thinking about essences, in a way they matter, but you're aware that you may not even be here. They don't matter in that sense. You want to get it done as best you can. Youthful ambition or career dreams, that's not what's on your mind.

LEONARD: Well, I find the paradox interesting, this fundamental indifference. At the same time within that fundamental indifference, a real capacity for attention and for care and for concern. The background of it seems to be indifference or—*indifference* is too cold—but somehow it loses its grip on you. The things—things of the heart, things of the spirit, things of the pocketbook, things of the genitals—you're not quite in the grip; and at the same time like wilder and crazier and more lusty and more greedy and more concentrated and more concerned.

It's close to sundown on Friday evening. Leonard lights the Sabbath candles and sings a brief blessing in Hebrew to celebrate Shabbat, a day of happiness and rest. He pours Paul and himself each a glass of wine.

LEONARD: Have a little glass of wine. Oh, you don't drink, eh? Here, don't drink it, just lift it up.

PAUL: No, I wish I did. No offense, I can't tell the difference between one wine and another. I'll try it and see. No, I often wish I did like wine. I just—

LEONARD: [*chuckling*] If you don't like it, you don't like it.

PAUL: God help me, I like the taste of Coca-Cola better than anything.

After the ceremony, they discuss Scottish writer Alexander Trocchi.[105]

LEONARD: [*cigarette in his mouth, he strikes a match to light it*] Trocchi hid out with me at a certain point when he was on the lam. He was trying to get out of North America. He stayed at my house for a few days in Montreal. I'd met him I think in London. Or maybe not, maybe just in Canada. I'd read his books, and his books had been published by Grove Press—*Evergreen Review*, that period—but I can't say that I ever liked him a lot. I can't say that I was influenced by him.

PAUL: You seemed to have an affinity towards Ginsberg and the Beats.

105 One of Norman Mailer's wounded literary birds à la Jack Henry Abbott, Trocchi, charged in New York City with supplying heroin to a minor, with the help of Mailer was smuggled into Canada, where Irving Layton gave him refuge.

LEONARD: I liked them. I liked them a lot. I liked the public stance. I liked the fact that they were poets who *had* a public stance. In Canada we hardly had any stance at all.

PAUL: You said the group was rather proud to be elitist in the early days. You never felt that elitism in your songs, I don't think.

LEONARD: Well, I never felt that personally. I think there was a sense that there was everything else and then there was this sacred activity called *poetry*, and that we were practitioners of it and it really didn't *have* to relate to anything beyond its own borders. It was elitist in that sense. But I think that actually the real tone of the so-called Montreal School, the tone of the poetry, is very contrary of elitist. It's very confessional, the language is very simple, the themes are simple. It's high emotional content and not-so-high intellectual content. I don't mean that it's anti-intellectual in any sense. I mean there are fine lines in it, like Frank Scott, like Irving Layton, but the tone of it is expansive.

PAUL: I never got the feeling from your poetry that it was elitist.

LEONARD: No, I just meant that in the sense that nobody was worried about making a career out of poetry and could they sell books and would they get grants. There weren't any. There weren't any prizes for the thing. It was totally engrossing and that's what we were doing. And the social activity was based on that, on those meetings. As I said, it's a very rigorous mutual examination of the work. People were just in tears. There were no holds barred. I mean, somebody had to explain a line. You couldn't get away with anything. And only five people in the entire country were, like, concerned with the whole matter. And then there were many evenings Irving and I would spend together where we would take a poem, a poem perhaps by Wallace Stevens—we used to call it *cracking* it; you know, *crack* the code, really find out what it's about and really place every word in it that illuminates the meaning of this thing—and those were wonderful evenings also. It was taken seriously, but nobody would ever use the word *seriously*. That's what the activity was: it was poetry, it was literature, and in a very unacademic surrounding. I mean, there was liquor and there were women poets—that *was* our social life also, it was our vocation. And then Irving and I would do that to movies, we'd go to movies. He became quite a wonderful movie critic, Irving. When he saw a movie being savaged that he thought had real merit, he would go public with it, because he was a well-known personality in Montreal. In Canada at a certain point he was on a television program frequently. For instance, we saw *Night Porter* many, many times. It was being lambasted as pornography.

The phone rings and he answers it. Paul turns off the tape recorder during the call.

PAUL: I don't remember, I think it was 1959, *Advertisements for Myself* came out. Was that a book that had any influence on you?

LEONARD: I didn't read it at the time. I love Mailer. I think he's a great writer. I'm astounded to see the hostility that he's managed to provoke. I thought his last novel [1983's *Ancient Evenings*] was very brilliant. Great masterpiece. I like everything he's written. I just read a piece that he did in *Vanity Fair* about this book *American Psycho* ["Children of the Pied Piper: Mailer on 'American Psycho'"]. I'll give you the magazine.

PAUL: Favorable or unfavorable?

LEONARD: He said the book should be published. It's the first novelist [Bret Easton Ellis] in many years really to take on the nightmare of the American psyche right now, but he wishes he were a better writer to do it. I think that's basically what he said.[106] But in saying that there's a great illumination of what writing is and what the writer's activity is. As he always has, there are, I think, very wonderful insights into the whole enterprise: writing. I always like to hear what he's got to say. I always find it comforting somewhat.

106 Mailer put it this way: "So, the first novel to come along in years that takes on deep and Dostoyevskian themes is written by only a half-competent and narcissistic young pen."

PAUL: He's going to go down as probably the greatest American writer of the last twenty, thirty years.

LEONARD: He certainly has my vote. It's just so *juicy*, his writing's so *meaty*. I read an interview that he gave; he said something quite interesting. He said love is the reward for work in a man's life.

PAUL: I always thought the journalism was just incredible stuff. Also, he's not afraid to look foolish, which is a wonderful quality, I think. He's really tried to belt them out every time. You don't of course. When you don't, you look foolish, I guess, but you've got to take those risks, it seems to me.

LEONARD: Oh, yeah. He takes risks. Listen, I don't even care about his homeruns, I just like to see him swing.

PAUL: You said you didn't read much.

LEONARD: Yeah, I haven't been reading very much lately. But I've been studying a lot with my old teacher, so that didn't leave too much time.

PAUL: How long has the interest in Zen been?

LEONARD: It's been about twenty years.

PAUL: And you get a mental calmness from this, as well?

LEONARD: I don't know what the benefit, or even if there is one, or even if the notion is applicable, but something's strengthened. It helps you hang in there.

PAUL: It sounded in the *Musician* interview that after the difficulty of rewriting *I'm Your Man*, basically, or during that, during all of the dark periods, you went to the monastery as a sort of cause and effect thing. I don't know if it *was* cause and effect.

LEONARD: I often went to the Zen center, one of the two Zen centers, to cool out and put the pieces together. Often it's had that function in my life, and I'm very grateful to old Roshi and to the community. There is such a place, there is a quiet room where you can sit together. There are daily sittings. From a certain point of view that's the fundamental activity, but it's combined with ordinary activity: maintenance of the place, preparation of the food, cleanliness of the cabins and the grounds, gardens. Just the things that have to be done.

PAUL: Suzanne [Vega] is a Buddhist. Did you know that? Soshu Buddhism, I think. She chants about an hour and a half, I think, each morning. Or two hours.

LEONARD: Nichiren Soshu, yeah. She chants the Lotus Sutra. Chanting is very beneficial. Most training involves and most religious discipline involves chanting. Catholics are wonderful with the whole Gregorian chant. The method of reciting the Jewish prayers and the bobbing of the body has a very salutary effect.

PAUL: I remember hymns very fondly as the first music I ever remember. My aunt played piano.

LEONARD: Yeah, all that magic activity is very valuable. I love gospel, I love hymns.

PAUL: Are you familiar with the movies of Max Ophüls at all? *La Ronde*? *The Earrings of Madame de . . .?*

LEONARD: I don't know if I saw that. *La Ronde* I loved. A wonderful film.

PAUL: He's one of my favorite directors. I guess I equated your sensibility to his in a certain way: a reverence for women, and the wistfulness and the transitoriness of everything.

LEONARD: He certainly has that, eh?

PAUL: Yeah, the bittersweet thing. And just the artistry, the precision. It's all this tracking with camera in the most beautiful way possible, and it's the subject matter for the film. In one of his movies—I think it was *La Ronde*, in fact—where everybody's always asking each other what time is it, Andrew Sarris, who is I think a really great film critic,[107] says, "Through the whole movie everybody is asking, 'What time is it? What time is it?' and it's always too late because the moment the moment is captured is gone forever. These people become aware of this." In my mind what I like about his films, I found in your work. Some similarities.

LEONARD: Yes, there's some sense of fraternity there.

PAUL: Also, women can be said to be the major characters for all of the subjects, and I think that's true of lot of your poems.

LEONARD: I think so, the female presence, very much. Irving has some beautiful poems to women, his *Love Poems*.

PAUL: He's your favorite of the poets, right? I have the feeling that you admire him, his work, better than the others.

LEONARD: That might be true. I think he's one of the greatest poets in the language. It's always been astounding to me that he isn't known here. Irving Layton is a very great poet.

PAUL: What was your last book of poetry?

LEONARD: I had a book prepared to put out but I never put it out. The last published book of mine was *Book of Mercy*. I'll give you a copy. It's a book of prayers.

PAUL: You've written some since?

LEONARD: Oh, many.

107 When Paul reviewed the eponymous first album by the Ramones, he did so as a takeoff on/tribute to Sarris's writing. Loving films even more than music, he respected Sarris's criticism. The same was true in return. Though the project never came to pass, the two men once discussed starting a film magazine together with the financial support of Jac Holzman.

Leonard brings out the selected-poems he put together but didn't publish. Shuffling through the many pages, he reads some of his favorites aloud.

This is one I like, called "Paris Models":

The models were changing
for the next shot.
I saw the sex of one
and the breast of another.
A balloon was taped
to a woman's finger,
and they started up
the wind machine.
The dresses came alive
and glorious accidents
of hair and shadow
framed their solemn faces.
The miracle of the balloon
grazing on a fingertip,
while the storm
carried off their bodies
was deeply convincing.
Finally the Chinese food arrived,
and the models walked around
wearing towels
and carrying paper plates.
Everyone was happy
that the magic of womanhood
had worked again.
They could rest a little while
on the great wave,
at the very crest
of confident and effortless allure.
I was happy too.
I felt privileged
to have attended a ceremony
usually restricted to professionals.

PAUL: That's nice, that's nice.

LEONARD: [*laughs*] And this is to my old friend Robert [Hershorn], who OD'd in Hong Kong many, many years ago. This is called "Robert Appears Again."

Well, Robert, here you are again talking to me at the Café de Flore
in Paris. I haven't seen you for a while. I have several versions of
that sonnet I wrote after your death but I never got it right. I love you,
Robert, I still do. You were an interesting man, and the first friend with whom I
ever quarrelled. I'm slightly stoned on half-a-tab of speed I
found in this old suit, it must be twenty years old, and I took it with a
glass of orange juice. It couldn't possibly work after all this time, but
here we are, talking again. I'm glad you don't tell me what it's like
where you are because I have no interest at all in the afterlife. You're a
little pissed off as usual, as if you've just come from something
immensely boring. Here we are, talking about the lousy deal we
negotiated for ourselves. What are you saying? Why are you
smiling? I'm still working hard, Robert. I can't seem to bring anything
to completion and I'm in real trouble. The speed is wearing off, or the
mood, and I can't tell you an amusing story about my trouble, but
you know what I mean. Of all my friends you know what I mean.
Well, goodbye, Robert, and fuck you too. Your disembodied status
entitles you to a lot of privileges, but you might have excused
yourself before disappearing again for who knows how long.

[*chuckles*] These little poems.

PAUL: And that was five, six years ago?

LEONARD: Yeah, it was in a bad time in Paris. This is a most interesting one; I'll read it to you. It's called "When Even The":

Your breasts are like.
Your thighs and your carriage.
I never thought.
Somewhere there must be.
It's possible.
Summer has nothing.
And Spring doesn't.
Your feet are so.
It's cruel to.
My defense is.
Summer certainly doesn't.
Your.
And your.
If only.
Somewhere there must.

But the.
And the.
It's enough to.
Soldiers don't.
Prisoners don't.
Maybe the turtle.
Maybe hieroglyphics.
Sand.
But in your cold.
If I could.
If once more.
Slip or liquid.
But the.
And the.

Sometimes when.
Even tho'.

Yes even tho'.
They say suffering.
They say.
Okay then let's.
Let's.
The sign is.
The seal is.
The guarantee.
Oh but.
O cruel.
O blouse with.
This is what.
And why it isn't.

But what do they.
What do they.
When even.
When even the.
Years will.
Death will.
But they won't
Even if.
Even if the.
They never will.

O deceiver.
O deceptive.
Turn your eyes.
Incline your.
To the one who.
Rotten as.
Hungry as.
Who does not.
Who never will.

But now your.
And your.
And these arms.

Which is lawless.
Which is blind.
If you come
If you find.
Then I.

Like all.
Like every.
If only.
If when.
Even tho'.
Even if.
Not for.
Not for.
But only.
But every.

If I could.
When the.
Then I.
Even if.
Even when.
I would.

He reads another poem, "A Deep Happiness," from the collection.

A deep happiness
has seized me
My Christian friends say
that I have received
   the Holy Spirit
It is only the truth of solitude
It is only the torn anemone
fastened to the rocks
   its roots exposed
to the offshore wind
O friend of my scribbled life
your heart is like mine—

your loneliness
  will bring you home

He pulls out another one, "My Honour":

My honour is in bad shape.
I'm crawling at a woman's feet.
She doesn't give an inch.
I look good for fifty-two.
But fifty-two is fifty-two.
I'm not even a Zen master.
I'm this man in a blue summer suit.
My lawyer took my .32 away
and locked it in the safe.
I'm defenseless against
her arrogance.
When the world is slow
she turns to me for an easy victory.
I'll rise up one of these days,
find my way to the airport.
I'll rise up and say
I loved you better than you loved me
and then I'll die for a long time
at the center of my own dismal organization
and I'll remember today,
the day when I was that asshole in a blue summer suit
who couldn't take it any longer.

PAUL: Is it easier to do those than the songs?

LEONARD: Yes, except for one long poem, which is written in—um, god, I've just forgotten the name of the form now. It's a very complex form. I wrote a lot of the songs for a movie that a friend of mine [Lewis Furey] directed called *Night Magic*, a Canadian movie; I wrote the lyrics for his music and I wrote them all in this form. This one I wrote as a preface to the book of a friend of mine; I wrote in this form. My friend wrote this book [*New Poems*]—he spent most of his life in mental hospitals—I helped gather some of his poems together. He's a very great poet, I think. His name's Henry Moscovitch, and I wrote the preface to his book in that form, which I can't remember the name of. "The Faerie Queene" is written in it. [*finally remembers*] Spenserian stanzas!

PAUL: Spenserian, yeah.

LEONARD: So it rhymes like: this rhymes with this, this rhymes with this, and then this rhymes again, and then this rhymes with this and these two rhyme, and this rhymes with these two. It's quite complex.

PAUL: Yeah. Boy.

LEONARD: You know that Verdun was a great battle of the First World War, but it's also the name of our mental hospital in Canada, in Montreal. So I wrote this up [*reads "Stanzas for H. M."*]:

O perfect gentleman, and champion
of the Royal Throne; O unbroken stone
of Sinai's heart; O hero of Verdun;
our greatest poet until now unknown,
whose banner over death has always flown
in wilds of poverty and solitude;
I thank you for the years you spent alone
with nothing to hang on to but a mood
of glory, searching words that Love could not elude

(We lost you for a while. The doctors tried
their hopeful science on a chosen soul,
but this chosen soul was sitting by the side
of God, and touched by Him, hale and whole
though broken in men's eyes, in His control.)
O friend who pardoned everyone who came
to light your dark and dim your aureole,
accept this awkward homage to your fame
(nor Modesty supply your instant counterclaim).

We do not know the Will or voice that made
you fly from high Décarie's overpass;

we do not know the Hebrew you obeyed
to raise your feet so far from sand and grass
and try the air, O faithful Anabas—
but blessed be the One who saved you there,
and bless His name, His every Alias,
Who gave you, on that insubstantial stair,
the bravest songs we have of loss and love's repair.

Dear Henry, I know you will forgive these
lines of mine, their clumsy antique tone,
for they are true and not mere obsequies,
and for all their rhetoric overblown
a simple gesture to the man you own,
whose friendship is so rare, whose art so pure,
simplicity is dazed, then overthrown—
alarmed and shy my love must I obscure
behind the fallen grandiose of literature.

I don't know where I'm going anymore.
I find myself a table and a chair.
I wait, I don't know what I'm waiting for.
I change the room, the country. I compare
my clattering armored blitz to your spare
weaponry of light, your refined address—
I know you stand where none of us would dare
I know you kneel where none of us would guess
well-ordered and alone, huge heart, self-pitiless.

PAUL: That's really nice.[108] Do you think that if economically, say, as a writer you had made enough money to pay the rent and live in a comfortable fashion, that you would have stayed a poet and a novelist? Or would you have become a songwriter still?

LEONARD: It's hard to say. There's so much excitement attached to the song that happened to coincide with my economic situation as a solution, I think I might've gotten into it anyways. Because I was

108 In 2006 Leonard would include "Stanzas for H. M." in his collection *Book of Longing*. He would dedicate the volume to Irving Layton.

very much involved in collecting so-called folk music and learning to play it and writing my own little songs.

Let me see if I have a *Death of a Lady's Man*.

He returns with a copy of the book for Paul, who offers to send it back when he's finished reading it.

I've got a box of those, and you can't get them anymore.

PAUL: This doesn't have any relationship to the record, right?

LEONARD: No, and it's a different spelling.[109] The only relationship it has to the record is that I used the song in there.

PAUL: It's got one of the most haunting endings, and I don't know why, I don't even know what it means: "It's like our visit to the moon / or to that other star"—

LEONARD: "You got to go for nothing / if you really want to go that far."

PAUL: Yeah, that says it. I don't know what it says, but that says it. I was at a friend's house when that came out on CD, and I just made him play that song over and over, the last part of it. I thought it was just a stunning four lines.

LEONARD: That book had no attention.

PAUL: Really? You consider it one of your best poetry books.

LEONARD: Well, it's a book of poems and each poem has a commentary on it by another persona, and often very vicious criticism of the thing. It has a certain integrity, the whole book.

PAUL: Everybody assumes that you were always yourself in these songs, but is it? Do you use various personas?

109 The album and its song are titled *Death of a Ladies' Man*, whereas the book is named *Death of a Lady's Man*.

LEONARD: I never thought much about it. I certainly wouldn't describe—they're just fleeting selves.

PAUL: One of them, maybe more than one, I can think about is actually from the point of view of the woman: "The Stranger Song." If one was going to read that as an autobiographical song, you'd have to read it as a warning against your persona. You know, stay away from the stranger, which is one side of your persona in song, at least.

LEONARD: I think that kind of song should move all around the circle, looking at that middle of the circle from different points in the circumference. I like that kind of movement in a song. You get different versions of this moment, you know, moving around.

PAUL: Can we talk about *Various Positions* now? I played a lot of this album after my mother died. There are songs that I played over and over and over, "If It Be Your Will" being one of them.

LEONARD: I think that's one of the best songs I ever wrote. I remember beginning it; I began in Hydra.

PAUL: Is this the period after your mother had died?

LEONARD: Yeah. She died around '79 [1978]. *Recent Songs* came out around the same time. I started the song close to that period. I wasn't feeling very good. It was one of those moments that you could really feel what the healing power of your own work was. I remember feeling—I was sitting at my desk in Hydra and my guitar was on the wall—and I just couldn't do anything. You know the state. And I took the guitar down and I just started playing that pattern that spoke to me. It took a long time to write the lyric because of the rhyme scheme; it's very, very difficult, just using that *I-L-L* rhyme over and over again. But I was happy with the song. It was true.

PAUL: That was the song, and Dylan's "Every Grain of Sand"—

LEONARD: A very beautiful song.

PAUL: —I would just play over and over and over and over. It seems like a song that somebody who was going through a lot and—not in a denominational, religious way—just looks up: *If You are up there and You want me to keep doing this, what do You want me to do?*

LEONARD: Yeah, I think that's certainly part of that feeling.

PAUL: This album seems to contain a lot of them. I would imagine that your mother's death had a lot to do with the feeling of this record. Sort of rethinking of one's life at this stage.

LEONARD: Oh, yeah. That song "Night Comes On," yeah. Also a long time in the writing.

PAUL: I know when my mother died I felt, in a way, the things I thought I would feel, but I also felt something else that I didn't expect to feel: it was that the source was gone; that the two people who had brought me into the world, there was no connection with me anymore. It never dawned on me that I would feel that. Did you have feelings like that? That both people who brought you in were now gone, and you were all alone in a sense?

LEONARD: I had a contrary feeling. My mother died, my marriage broke up around the same time. The feeling I had was that my mother's presence became very, very strong. I often get it still, the very, very strong presence of my mother.

PAUL: You were close with her?

LEONARD: I see people with their mothers, and it wasn't like that at all. It wasn't that kind of closeness. It wasn't confessional in any sense. She didn't really know much about my life, but I knew that she was there and I knew that she *really* cared for me, and there was no question about who she was in my life. There was this being that somehow took full responsibility for my life.

PAUL: It seems to me also that this album was either a breakthrough album in one sense, or a summation in another, and moving into another territory.

LEONARD: I felt it had all of those qualities. That was the record where the kind of concentration on the work had become more intense than I'd ever remembered it, the attention to every line and the effort that it took to bring these songs to completion. I think I've told another interviewer that I remember being in the Royalton Hotel, trying to finish "Hallelujah" in my underwear and crawling along the floor, banging my head against the carpet. I found myself in those kind of situations often in that record. But there didn't seem to be another life. I didn't seem to have a life. It seemed to be this.

PAUL: I also felt it was an intensely religious album, and yet in a non-formal sense.

LEONARD: I'm not sure what that means.

PAUL: I guess I'd have to translate it in my own terms how I felt about it. It seems to be some question, if there is a God, then help. If there isn't, then—

LEONARD: Help, anyway.

PAUL: I mean in that sense of *religious*, not a formal religion. A lot of essences seem to be in this record.

LEONARD: I thought it was the best I could do at the time. I had two or three songs on it that I think are as good as anything I'll ever pull off: "Hallelujah," "If It Be Your Will," "Dance Me to the End of Love."

PAUL: But "Hallelujah" you've rewritten since then. I like them both, but I like the old one better.

LEONARD: Well, I wrote a secular version that I sang on the last tour, but I've gone back to the old one. I like the old one better, yeah. I wrote the two versions at the same time. It's often the way that I do it. The only trouble is, I find that you can't discard something until you've written it, and to write it takes as much trouble as to write the thing that you're going to keep. So every one of those verses is worked on with the same kind of care as the verses you keep. So I found at the end that I really did, in this case, have really two completely different songs. The other one I don't think is as good as the original. I mean the recorded one.[110] I just felt like singing that kind of song: "Baby, I've been here before / I know this room, I walked this floor / I used to live alone before I knew ya." I like that first verse.

PAUL: I think the one on the record fits the context of the record better than the new one would have. Because it isn't the secular one, it fits better on this record. It's also got just a gorgeous melody, which "If It Be Your Will" does also. I don't think I will ever understand how people create melodies like that.

LEONARD: If I knew where they came from, I'd go there more often. I don't know how those things arise.

PAUL: "Dance Me to the End of Love" is a great song, too.

LEONARD: I love to sing that.

PAUL: "We're both of us beneath our love, we're both of us above." I love those lines. And "Coming Back to You" I think is one of the best.

LEONARD: Oh, now I remember that record: making it, writing it.

PAUL: "And springtime starts but then it stops / In the name of something new / And all the senses rise against this / Coming back to you." There seems to be a push/pull in a lot of the songs. The thing you want most is the thing you want to get away from, and then when you're away from it, you want to go back.

LEONARD: That motion, yeah: expansion, contraction.

110 Leonard would include the "secular version" on *Cohen Live*.

PAUL: Particularly of the romantic. You write songs from all points of view, I think.

LEONARD: Yeah, that's why I call that one *Various Positions*.

PAUL: Well, I think through your career you've written songs of intense guilt and intense anger, of almost every position one could take. You know, *I'll do anything to come back to you* and then *I've got to leave you*.

LEONARD: I began to feel the dignity of my own life in that *Various Positions*, that it's okay. I'm a guy, I can speak about myself now in a way that is just a little bit different, just with a little more magnanimity or something. I deserve to be here. A certain generosity in the record that I like. But it's fading now, the landscape from which that record arose. I don't remember it too much now, either.

PAUL: Well, it seems like it must have been one of the dark times because "the night comes on." It starts with you at your mother's grave, saying "I'm frightened," and one gets the feeling you wouldn't mind joining her. "She said, 'I'll be with you / My shawl wrapped around you / My hand on your head when you go.'"

LEONARD: Oh, that's nice. She used to put her hand on my head sometimes.

PAUL: And then it goes to your father, I believe. "We were fighting in Egypt"—

LEONARD: —"when they signed this agreement / Nobody else had to die."

PAUL: I didn't understand this part of it until we had talked: "There was this terrible sound / And my father went down." I thought that his father had died fighting in Israel.

LEONARD: Well, of course you could get that impression from there, but Egypt is used in medieval Jewish poetry as that territory that is hostile to the spirit. Also means like the non-Jewish world, but more deeply it means that world in which the soul cannot flourish.

PAUL: I see. So it wasn't a literal agreement between you two.

LEONARD: No. But I *was* in Egypt with the Israeli army during the '73 [Yom Kippur] [W]ar.

PAUL: You were? You went over there to be there during that war?

LEONARD: Yeah, I volunteered in that war. It only lasted a couple of weeks [October 6–October 25, 1973].

PAUL: Did you actually have to fight?

LEONARD: Well, I was—I don't know if I should speak about this. I'll tell you why, so please be judicious about it.

PAUL: You tell me not to use it, I won't.

LEONARD: Yeah. I'll tell you the story. I never speak of it because I'm worried about getting knocked off by a Palestinian crazy when I'm on tour. You know what I mean? I was a volunteer—[111]

PAUL: Why don't we just shut it off?

Paul stops recording. When he restarts, talk has resumed about "Night Comes On."

111 Leonard, then thirty-nine, volunteered in the Israeli Defense Forces, but ultimately found himself entertaining the troops at the front. According to Matti Friedman, author of *Who by Fire: Leonard Cohen in the Sinai*, "He hears on the radio that a war has broken out, and he gets on a ferry to Athens, then gets on an airplane to Israel, without a clear idea of what he's going to do.

"He doesn't seem to have planned to play for troops. It's not exactly clear what he wants to do, although he tells people he wants to volunteer on a kibbutz. He just feels a strong Jewish pull."

Many years later, on September 24, 2009, Leonard played before a sold-out crowd in Tel Aviv's Ramat Gan Stadium, in what was advertised as "A Concert for Reconciliation, Tolerance, and Peace," with all net proceeds going to Israeli and Palestinian peace organizations.

LEONARD: But I identify with my father, then, who was in the army and who had that sense like there's no armistice in this real war that is going on. I forget what the last lines of the thing are.

PAUL: The last line [of the second verse] is: "I'd like to pretend that my father was wrong"—that there was no armistice—"But you don't want to lie … to the young," and then that leads you into I guess Suzanne [Elrod] and Adam and Lorca.

LEONARD: Yes.

PAUL: "We were locked in this kitchen / I took to religion." What does *religion* mean in that?

LEONARD: Well, the daily life was so impossible that you take refuge in spiritual matters. I meant it humorously, too.

PAUL: I don't know how religious I am. I *think* I might believe in a God, I don't know. I don't believe in any church, I guess. My mother's death made me really think about religion. I would guess probably it's a safe bet to say that, of anybody, our mothers were more religious than we were. It would be true in my case; I don't know if it would be true in yours.

LEONARD: I'm not that, uh—yeah, it's hard to say.

PAUL: Well, then, maybe it's not correct. It made me think of God when my mother died, I guess, a great deal. But I'm just maybe connecting what was going on in my head with these songs, too.

LEONARD: I think that if a song is good that's what happens. Poetry is not theology. Irving always makes this point in the prefaces to his books, like it's a different vocation: it's not philosophy, it's not theology, it doesn't have an argument.

PAUL: I don't think I'm saying that.

LEONARD: No, but I think it's completely legitimate to fill a song with your own experience.

PAUL: I mean as a listener. And then as a writer, yeah.

LEONARD: I do. I always do.

PAUL: Suzanne's last record, which in that case it was a lot of her dreams, were difficult to interpret for someone who hasn't had those dreams in some cases, and I came up with a couple of interpretations that held up lyrically but were not really what she had in mind. I said, "At least you got a good laugh over a couple of these interpretations," and she said, "Oh, no, they were very interesting. I never mind how people take my songs. I see them as a sculptor, and you can look at them from this angle and that angle and, if it's a solid song, it doesn't matter." Which was a nice way to put it, I thought.

LEONARD: Yeah, I think that's true. From what I know of Suzanne, authentic examination of her work is something that would please her very much.

PAUL: She seemed to. In one case, she said, "You know, you're absolutely right, line for line you could read the song that way. It wasn't what I had in mind." And then she said, "I don't think it was. I mean, not consciously in my mind."

LEONARD: I have a great respect for that activity. There's a guy who wrote a book; half the book was devoted to an analysis of *Beautiful Losers*.

PAUL: Yeah, Lee.

LEONARD: It was called *Savage Fields*. It's a Canadian book. Lee is a very great poet also, Dennis Lee.[112] Well, I had never gotten over that book, and we became close friends. But the analysis of *Beautiful Losers* is right.

112 *Savage Fields: An Essay in Literature and Cosmology* was published in 1977. In the other half of the book, Dennis Lee devoted his critical eye to Michael Ondaatje's *The Collected Works of Billy the Kid*, a novel in verse. While Paul clearly hasn't read Lee's volume, it is nevertheless unsurprising that he's familiar with it; not only given his interest in Leonard, but also because of a lifelong fascination with the Billy the Kid/Pat Garrett mythology. For him William Bonney represented youth and freedom while Garrett served as the Establishment. Paul even framed a 1930 article, torn from an unknown newspaper, reporting the death of James H. East, a veteran peace officer who'd had a deputy's star pinned on him by Garrett and was part of the posse that captured Billy the Kid.

PAUL: It was a favorable analysis?

LEONARD: It was beyond favorable or not favorable. The fact that he would devote a whole half a book to the thing. I think he put his finger on the flaw of the book. If the reviewer, if the critic, is doing something superficial, you prefer to be praised. But if somebody is really doing a job on you, I don't think it matters what they say. If they have devoted this kind of attention to the thing, it's not a thug's work and they're not trying to dismember you, then I think that anybody would be pleased.

PAUL: But he primarily liked it obviously or he never would have written that much about it.

LEONARD: "A very good book," he said, "but it could have been a great book. But this is where the failure of courage was: right here." I don't remember exactly what it was, it may not even be true, but it was true enough for me to get a little *frisson*, a little shiver up my back when I read it, because, *Yeah, this guy knows*. [*knocks over his wineglass*] Oh, shit.

PAUL: Whoops! [*as Leonard cleans up*] I keep thinking I'm trying to make you religious by suggesting these questions. I'm really not. I'm not that religious myself, but when my mother died I just found myself praying, and I hadn't prayed for years.

LEONARD: Well, you'll see that in that. I mean, I just wonder, because I don't want to talk too much longer, but maybe we can meet again.

PAUL: I'd like to. Tomorrow or Sunday, anytime you want.

LEONARD: Maybe Sunday or something like that.

PAUL: If we could do one more long one it would be a great help to me, and do some more over the phone probably. I thought I talked way too much during the first one.

LEONARD: Nah! You're not going to do a word-for-word from these things—I'm sure you will have quotations and that sort of thing—but I know that you have ideas. I know your writing.

PAUL: Yeah, I'd like to write a good general piece on your work and on you as well. No, I have a lot to say about the songs. I don't know, critics really don't—I think they can help a record in one way. You know, they can give the record company some doubts, but whether to drop somebody or not— When you're a young artist, they can give you another record maybe, but they'll never give you any sales.

LEONARD: For me it's very valuable. And, at least man to man, I don't care particularly anyways about almost anything. And the day that we actually meet, you know—I'm very happy to do this interview with you, and I look forward to reading it.

The thing that I was going to say is that, the question of religion is vital to the thing because that's what I've been doing most my life, is I've been studying this with this teacher and sitting in meditation halls for long, long periods of time. Usually when I'm not recording I go every morning at five and every evening at seven. I get up at four-thirty and I— [*tape runs out*]

I don't know how even to begin with this subject. Those questions have pretty well been resolved for me about the existence of God or the nonexistence of God, or of a Supreme Being or an Absolute Being, through experience, and it's been a great source of energy and comfort in my life. So I'm not really in the questioning condition. I understand that when you address the idea of God, whether there is or there isn't a God, the self that is engaged in this activity of doubt is a limited self. When the self is not limited but that self experiences itself as all things that arise, when the content of the self is all things that arise, then there is nothing outside the self. There's nothing that the self needs to call God, and the self that is produced in this circumstance has no questions about itself. So that experience dissolves all questions about the beginning or the end. You don't remain in that condition, you come back into a limited self, but that self has a residue of the experience of the unlimited self, so that it can use the word the *Absolute* or *God* very easily because it recognizes that it is the limited self that is addressing the Absolute. And it's appropriate, then, legitimate for us to place ourselves in a worshipful condition, if we wish, before this Absolute and to address prayers to the Absolute. But it's also important to realize that there is a self that has no need to objectify a god. I've tried to put this into this poem. It's called "The Embrace":

When you stumble suddenly
into his full embrace,
he hides away so not to see
his creature face to face.
You yourself are hidden too
and all your sins of state;
there is no king to pardon you;
his mercy is more intimate.

He does not stand before you,
he does not dwell within;
this passion has no point of view,
it is the heart of everything.
There is no hill to see this from.
You share one body now
with the serpent you forbid,
and with the dove that you allow.

The imitations of his love
he suffers patiently,
until you can be born with him
some hopeless night in Galilee;
until you lose your pride in him,
until your faith objective fails,
until you stretch your arms so wide
you do not need these Roman nails.

Idolators on every side,
they make an object of the Lord.
They hang him on a cross so high
that you must ever move toward.
They bid you cast the world aside
and hurl your prayers at him.

Then the idol-makers dance all night
upon your suffering.

But when you rise from this embrace
I trust you will be strong and free
and tell no tales about his face,
and praise Creation joyously.

PAUL: That's beautiful. That's an unpublished poem?

LEONARD: Yeah. So generally we have the notion that we are the subject and everything else is the object, and we establish this subject-object relationship with *all* things, whether it's the table or each other. I am at the center, you're over there. And then, either suddenly or with training, a moment arises when you are able to discard the subject-object relationship and this particular point of view dissolves and you have no point of view, and all things that arise are manifesting as yourself. And space collapses. And a dog barks and you're barking. A bird sings and *you* are singing. A shadow moves across the floor and you are moving across the floor. This true self has no outside and no inside and no past and no present. It is the Absolute self. It is the Absolute Being.

PAUL: This comes about through your studying with Roshi, this understanding?

LEONARD: We are already embraced by this experience at all times. We just haven't refined our understanding of it, we just haven't matured our wisdom. We're already embraced by this experience, this *is* our real life, this is our true life. We *are* this manifestation of the Divine, or the Divine is a manifestation of us. We are producing this, this whole affair. This is a very elementary step in the whole training process. It's nothing to get hung up on. It's often an impediment to your own study and training to get hung up on this idea, but I think it's not inappropriate to discuss it from time to time. But this kind of sitting with the self and observing the various selves that arise, and then breaking the identification between the real self and these other selves, the selves arise but you begin to lose the need to identify. Hatred arises but you don't have to identify with it. Hunger arises, you don't have to identify with it. It's just a self that is arising. And behind that is another self, which is just manifesting as these images. Now, that experience comes with sitting. It can come anyways. With me it came that way, that kind of experience.

If you ever are interested in looking into it, I'll be very happy to turn you on to whatever I know about it. But that has been the vital experience of my life and I don't think I probably would have wanted to go on without it. Because my sense of alienation was so intense, to break it down, you know. You only begin this kind of practice because of suffering. It's too rigorous for people who are just checking it out. [*lights another cigarette*]

PAUL: The breakdown sort of—

LEONARD: The breakdown produces the interest in it. I'll keep bopping along until I start to get very anxious again and very separated, and then I'll go back and sit and understand that it's just a fiction I fall in love with. It's the fictional self. No need to embrace it. No need to reject it either. It just arises. It changes like the weather. It'll arise, abide, and disappear. So that practice has meant everything to me. It's basically a sitting practice and a breathing practice, and it then flows into your life in some way immediately. You get loose, you get a lot looser.

PAUL: Yeah, I think in a way that you're not aware of it—I wasn't aware of it when I started—but I think I use running for that.

LEONARD: Yes, that high is very—from what I understand from people who run.

PAUL: It's not a high. It's not like a drug high, it's a feeling of calm and security and well-being. Very calm and able to deal with things.

LEONARD: You're at home in this world. It sounds a lot like sitting. It changes your life.

PAUL: I think people who do not run think these people run because they want to hit a speed. It's not that at all. It just doesn't come with a jolt and then go away in ten minutes, it lasts the entire evening. If you're running a lot, you miss it if you don't. It's addictive in the sense that you want to do it every day so you can continue to feel this good. But the *runner's high* is rather unfortunately named. I suspect it sensationalized it. I wasn't even aware I was going to feel that way when I started running, but I did. In a way it became certainly as beneficial as physical well-being. More so, I think.

LEONARD: Can I smoke one of your cigarettes?

PAUL: Oh, take as many as you want. I just opened that pack up.

LEONARD: Okay, thank you.

PAUL: Some of the lyrics in your songs have changed. "Bird on the Wire" you sing differently live now.

LEONARD: It's a song I never felt I finished, I never felt I got it quite right, and I've been changing it ever since.

PAUL: I think the verse about the beggar was out in the last tour. And there's an ending about "It's been paid for."

LEONARD: Yeah, that's right. There was something that I felt at the time. I forget the words I used now but it was like, "It's finished, it's completed / It's been paid for." *Consummatum est*. I had that feeling in my life. I was coming out of that episode that we've already discussed. You know, I was back on my feet. "Bird on the Wire" definitely changes every tour. It seemed to be the kind of song that I can personalize every few years.

PAUL: Do you think you have a version of "Bird on the Wire" now that you like?

LEONARD: No, I don't think it's there yet.

PAUL: What was the core idea to begin for the song?

LEONARD: I don't really recall. I know it actually had something to do with a bird on a wire, because they had just recently put up telephone wires on Hydra. You were very conscious of those telephone wires, electrical wires. There had been no electricity. It looked imposingly ugly, to suddenly see all these wires going from house to house and down the streets and across the courtyards. So one was very aware of it. And then a little bird came.

Maybe I never got the real feeling of the song, what it was really about: "Just tried in my way to be free." Just an opportunity for some kind of confession. Also, "Like a drunk in a midnight choir," those were all violent images. You hear the guys coming home at night with their arms around each other, climbing the stairs, singing this impeccable three-part harmony in the middle of the night. Nobody minded in those days. I don't know what it's like now, but you were *allowed* to come home from the taverna late, late at night, even though the whole village was sleeping, and to be singing on the streets. It was common. You'd hear it every weekend and often during the week, too. For certain every weekend you'd hear guys coming home at night, stumbling home, singing beautiful songs. That was the other image in the thing.

The second verse, I never got it straight. I used to sing, "Like a worm on a hook / Like a knight from some old-fashioned book / I have saved all my ribbons for thee." I think it asks the listener to make some leaps that are illegitimate. I thought things waving, ribbons and the worm and the knight, but didn't feel it was right, so I changed it to "Like a worm on a hook / Like a knight bent down in some old-fashioned book / It was the shape of our love twisted me." I changed it to that, I thought that was a little closer. But I don't know if I ever got that second verse, if I ever nailed it.

PAUL: I'm curious whether "Joan of Arc" and "Last Year's Man" are connected to each other. The reference to Joan of Arc in "Last Year's Man," if it's accidental or if those two songs are linked in some way.

LEONARD: Well, I don't think the songs are linked in any way. For some odd reason that year the image of Joan of Arc was strong, and I had another poem or two about her. I remember walking down Twenty-third Street with Nico and we were talking about Joan of Arc.

I said, "Do you think Joan of Arc ever fell in love with anybody?" and Nico said, "She fell in love with everyone."

PAUL: You hadn't written the song at that point at all?

LEONARD: No. Perhaps I was in the middle of writing because I wrote much of it—the song took a long time to write and there are many, many verses—but I was putting it together. I think I was living at the Chelsea on Twenty-third. I knew Nico in that period, and she made me think of Joan of Arc somehow.

PAUL: In what way?

LEONARD: Well, physically for one. I thought, *That's how Joan of Arc looks*: the large, strong, regular beauty.

PAUL: Was that the time of the [Otto] Preminger movie with [Jean] Seberg [1957's *Saint Joan*]?

LEONARD: I think that's subsequent to that. I think that's a bit later.

PAUL: When we were talking the other day, we were talking about [author] Myra Friedman and I mentioned she was writing a book on Seberg.[113] You said you knew her, and I wasn't sure if you were referring to Myra or Seberg.

LEONARD: I also met Myra Friedman around that time in New York, although I just happen to know that I met her; we never became friends. But I was in Paris in, I guess it was the '79 tour, and Jean Seberg phoned the hotel or the road manager to get tickets. Curiously enough I had met her in 1960 or '61. I think maybe she had just married the French novelist Romain Gary. The CBC had hired me to do a program in Paris, my first big job, and it was to moderate a panel discussion between Mary McCarthy, Romain Gary, and Malcolm Muggeridge. They sent me to Paris and they put me in a beautiful big hotel, and they gave us all this very elaborate French lunch before the interview. And then we

113 Friedman was the author of *Buried Alive: The Biography of Janis Joplin*, published in 1973.

went to a suite in the hotel—it was one of the grand hotels—and the technicians were there. We set up the mics, and I was supposed to—I did—moderate a discussion on something to do with Western civilization.

PAUL: Malcolm Muggeridge must have been quite a character it sounds like.

LEONARD: He was a grand guy, a grand old man. I wrote about the occasion for the *CBC Times*, I wrote a description of the afternoon. But besides that, for me, it was a wonderful occasion. In one sense I felt that I was like next on the list, that these were the guys we're going to replace. On the other hand I admired all of them. I loved Romain Gary, I loved his work. I kind of got friendly with Romain Gary during that interview and he invited me over to his flat on Rue du Bac. I came the next day, and he was very kind. He was an older guy and I was this young writer. You know, we talked. And Jean Seberg strolled in. He introduced her. I think she'd already made [*Saint Joan*]—had she made it by then? Must've. So it must've been around that time, '61 or '62, that I met her. And then '79—and that was the end of it. I never saw Romain Gary or Jean Seberg—there was no way our lives would intertwine.

So she phoned up for tickets and they were sent to her, and after the concert she sent me a very nice telegram with her phone number on it. So I called her and we arranged to meet at a café, I think right at the bottom of Rue du Bac and the Seine.

PAUL: Jean Seberg was just this young girl from small-town Iowa. Marshalltown. Discovered on some nationwide talent contest by Preminger, which was a hoopla thing anyway. He threw her into this movie, and she wasn't a classical actress, which would have been what would be required. It was really Preminger's fault that the movie was not well done. It wasn't her fault. She really didn't get any guidance through it, which she should have.

Marshalltown, Iowa, wasn't that far from where I was going to college at the time, which was Southern Minnesota. I think I was in college at that point when that movie came out, and she was just so beautiful.

LEONARD: Wasn't she.

PAUL: And *Breathless* of course, she was even more beautiful. She was one of my early distant loves, I think.

LEONARD: Me, too. I loved her.

PAUL: Well, she just got crucified for *Saint Joan*. It wasn't a good picture, it wasn't well directed, it wasn't good in any way. But then she was marvelous in *Breathless*. She couldn't have been better. I got very taken with her and interested and dismayed by what she was going through. I guess she was found dead in a car.

LEONARD: The back of a car, I think.

PAUL: And what Myra said, she just gave up on her Jean Seberg book because she couldn't find anything interesting about her and she was depressing, I just thought, *Myra, there's a lot interesting about her*.

LEONARD: Romain Gary was one of the most interesting minds of the time, and he loved her.

PAUL: I just thought her life was fascinating and tragic.

LEONARD: That fundamental sweetness and beauty of her nature was not at all compromised.

PAUL: She turned out to be a pretty good actress in upcoming pictures. She was good in most everything I saw her in after *Saint Joan*.

LEONARD: Yeah. It's an odd story, I guess. Well, I think her life is one of those symbolic lives. She's the dark side of the Sixties. Her heart was in the right place. She gave all her money away to the Black Panthers. Apparently, they used her very badly.

PAUL: Trying to remember a line from way back when. In some magazine it said everybody's lives changed in '65, I think. Or maybe it was '63.

LEONARD: Yeah, I had that feeling that a lever had been thrown. I don't really recall the year, but probably why people would just put it down for pot talk. Something strange happened, you had that clear feeling. I put it that way, like some lever has been thrown in the cosmos.

PAUL: Changing it in what way?

LEONARD: It seemed like time was different. The way time was passing by was different, the relationships had altered, the landscape had changed. There weren't the same kind of landmarks. We moved from the Nineteenth Century culture, the literary culture, poetry culture, into something else. [Marshall] McLuhan would be able to put his finger on it. A *popular* culture where somehow the university education, higher education, seemed to be irrelevant. That everybody knew the same things. The guy who was sweeping the street knew the same things and was watching the same things as the guy who stepped out of the limousine, which makes for a very volatile situation, when there are no longer any elitists or secret information. Everybody's seeing the same things, feeling the same thing, listening to the same music, seeing the same movies. There's no longer what we thought of as a *culture*. Something changed around then. I'm just trying to elaborate on it now, I don't know how I put it at the time.

PAUL: That happened to be the year that my life changed completely, when you said it. I got divorced and met the true love of my life, and that lasted for three years.[114]

LEONARD: I guess if you say it in any year, a certain amount of people will be able to affirm it.

PAUL: I think that was probably the year where more people would've said, "Yes, he's right."

114 Paul left Doris Gehrls Nelson, his wife (who had also been his high school girlfriend), for Barbara "Bobbi" London. London had been at his side on the night of July 25, 1965, when Dylan went electric.

LEONARD: There was that kind of a geopolitical or geo-psycho language being used, like in the East Village out there, and those kind of people were talking about trying to put things in a wide perspective, I think. Acid had a lot to do with those perspectives.

PAUL: I think it changed quite radically. I remember the good parts of the Sixties, or the parts that I found moving, were if a Stones record or a Beatles record or a Dylan record came out, you knew what ten million people were going to be listening to that night at the same time you were putting it on, in fact. And there was some sort of communal feeling *that way*.

LEONARD: The vital information was in the music.

PAUL: And it was the *same* music everyone was listening to, which couldn't be said at all today, I don't think. There weren't factions or anything. Suddenly what seemed to be enlightenment was turning into disaster in many cases, in many cases not. And you make a statement in a few interviews that everybody went for the money. You know, wasn't idealistic.

LEONARD: Yeah. Some people can survive that. I think a lot of people went for the money and survived it. But a lot of people can't survive it. Maybe the culture, the whole deal, can't survive it.

PAUL: One had to listen to an awful lot of bullshit in the Sixties.

LEONARD: *A lot.*

PAUL: I remember falling in love with several women who were—one of them just a really gorgeous woman, but all she could talk about was "How much dope is left? What's the state of the stash bag? How many more joints can be rolled?" That was her only topic of conversation. No matter how beautiful she is, you get real tired of that real quick.

I remember meeting Tim Hardin—trying to interview Tim Hardin, who I liked a great deal. Looking into his eyes and realizing with true fright there was only about ten percent of him left. That ninety percent of what was behind those eyes was irretrievable.

LEONARD: I met him shortly before he died—I also loved him very much—I just met him at somebody's house, and he threw his arms around me and said, "Leonard, I love your stuff." I said, "Ditto, man. Would you do me a favor?" He said, "Anything." He was about the same width as he was high, and he was *enormously* bloated, which I had begun to understand that was the preface to a certain kind of alcoholic's death. He was a huge man, but skin that looks like it's about to fall away and blotched. And I said, "Will you play 'Don't Make Promises' for me?" He said, "Sure," and we went into a room—I saw the guitar in the car—and he sang a couple of songs for me. It was wonderful.

PAUL: That was one of the most frightening experiences I've ever had. He was barely coherent and the eyes were just dead. I didn't know what to do, I just didn't.

LEONARD: Did you do an interview?

PAUL: Yeah, I did, but it was pretty rambling and incoherent.[115] I was just frightened out of my mind when I looked into his eyes. I think his wife or a girlfriend was more or less leading him around like one would lead a blind man. He would sit with a cigarette in his mouth and just drop ashes all over himself, and she would brush him off. And I was just terrified to the core, I think. I don't think I'd ever seen anybody in that bad shape. I kept figuring all the medicine in the world couldn't get what this guy's lost back. He's not going to be here very long. Just feeling awful. And that was the dark side of the Sixties.

LEONARD: Oh, yeah. Those are the well-known ones, those are the ones we hear about. There were a hundred thousand roadies and musicians and engineers.

115 Paul's interview resulted in a five-part article that appeared in the January 1969 issue of *Hullabaloo* and, after the magazine changed its name, the February, March, May, and June issues of *Circus*. In 1971 the singer-songwriter released "Bird on the Wire" on an album bearing the same name.

PAUL: Hangers-on who wanted to be hip. Yeah, I think the Rolling Stones used up more people than Vietnam almost, if I make any sense. You felt that Woodstock was a symbol of the end of it?

LEONARD: Well, in some way. I was driving back from New York to Montreal during that period. I remember that the highway was uncharacteristically crowded. I didn't even know about it; that's how far out of the scene I was. I wasn't invited and I didn't even know about it. I was with Suzanne [Elrod] in the car and we were driving to Montreal, and I wondered out loud. And then we turned on the radio and they started mentioning that there was this huge festival going on. I was kind of happy I wasn't going to it. I don't know, I'm just saying that in retrospect now, but I guess what they called *the Sixties* would have started for me in '55, '56, around that period when I left college and started hanging around New York and downtown Montreal. Then of course I went to Greece where I got a curious take on the Sixties because some of the great figures like Ginsberg and Corso would come through. But we were living that life already, of great freedom and exuberance. Well, I just thought that went with being young anyways and I didn't necessarily connect it with a huge world movement. When was Woodstock?

PAUL: I think '68 or '69 because I started working for Mercury in 1970 and it had already happened by then.[116]

LEONARD: Yeah, I felt it had perceptibly changed. I felt the old forces had reasserted themselves and it was getting dull again. But also I was just having started to have children and feeling rather constricted and restrained anyways, so I didn't know if it was that or the thing was actually changing.[117]

PAUL: There was something odd, in a way, of 500,000 kids or however many there were, sitting out in the mud, having had nothing to eat. Danny Fields, you've probably met him.

116 The Woodstock Music and Art Fair happened August 15–18, 1969.

117 As noted earlier, his children were not born until 1972 and 1974.

LEONARD: I knew him. What has happened to Danny Fields?

PAUL: He's doing a weekly radio interview show in New York now. I think it was he who told me that the really sad part was that 500 kids would line up for *any* drug. You could have sold them pills saturated with kerosene and they would have swallowed it without question.

LEONARD: Oh, yeah. It's a terrible innocence.

PAUL: And this innocence in a great part was destroying an awful lot of people, I think.

LEONARD: I did an interview with Danny Fields once. I don't know if it ever came out. I know that I talked a lot about the importance of an army, and it was very unpopular as a position.

PAUL: The importance of an army?

LEONARD: Yeah, of a nation having an army, strong and good and in this world. It was a very anti-military period. It was supposed to be for *Interview*, I think, and he said they refused it. I would love to get hold of that. Not that I found myself as right-wing or left-wing, but what may have appeared as a very right-wing and *now* very popular position on. Very unpopular at that point.[118]

PAUL: That was another interesting thing in the Sixties: what one considered *friendly forces*, I guess, in the Fifties, or something like the police department and the government, was all on the enemies list at that period. I've never been particularly political. Every role sort of switched over: the heroes were now the villains. And then it all switched back again, like fifteen years later, in the late Seventies or something.

LEONARD: It must've been hard for you as it was hard for me, being of our particular generation or age, which was, regardless of what your politics are, the kind of rhetoric that was being used against authority simply was

118 "Yes that is the interview," confirms Danny Fields, "putatively for *Interview Magazine*. They never even read it because they decided they were not interested in Leonard Cohen—because he wasn't a designer of belt buckles or whatever." The interview, which was conducted at the Chelsea Hotel in 1974, would ultimately be published online at PleaseKillMe.com in 2018.

unappealing. That wasn't the way to do it. You didn't call people *pigs* and you didn't say that the government was a fascist government. It wasn't. You know what a fascist government was; it wasn't quite the same.

PAUL: No, but it all came out of an uninformed ignorance.

LEONARD: Yeah, it was a very irresponsible kind of rhetoric.

PAUL: I'll ask Danny. I talk to him once in a while.

LEONARD: Please send him my best if you bump into him. I was very fond of him. He's a very nice guy. I was just a lone stranger in town at the Chelsea Hotel. He introduced me to people. He was very nice, he was kind to me. He introduced me to Edie Sedgwick, who lived down the hall.

PAUL: What years were you in the Chelsea?

LEONARD: I guess it was off and on through about '64 to '66.

PAUL: Well, we were in the Chelsea at one point at the same time. My marriage was going, and I took a room [928] at the Chelsea in a way just to get out of the house. I remember weekly rates at the Chelsea for a room without bathroom were $23.75 a week. It was right around that time, I was on the tenth floor or something, and [composer and critic] Virgil Thomson was right next door. Arthur Miller I used to see in there. I wasn't there all the time, but I was there like half the time, I would say.

LEONARD: Who was the guy who wrote *Tubby the Tuba*? George, uh, Kleinberg. Is that his name? He was there.[119]

PAUL: My room was about the size of a couch.

LEONARD: Did you drink at the Quijote?[120]

119 Composer George Kleinsinger collaborated with lyricist Paul Tripp to create the children's classic.

120 El Quijote, a Spanish restaurant and bar located in the Chelsea, was a favorite spot of Janis Joplin, Patti Smith, William S. Burroughs, Jimi Hendrix, and Andy Warhol.

PAUL: No. I never drank.

LEONARD: Oh, you didn't drink, right. I used to drink.

PAUL: I did. I got drunk a few times. I still can sort of drink if it's vodka or something that doesn't taste like scotch. It just doesn't do anything for me, I don't know why. If I have a pick between vodka or Coca-Cola, I take Coca-Cola. I guess I'm not fond of the loopy state one gets in. Most people are, I guess. I'm not. I don't like the taste of any of it. If I have a drink, I have to pour enough orange juice so I can't taste the liquor at all.[121]

LEONARD: As my band will tell you, I only drink professionally and I never drink past intermission. I always try to sell that idea to the guys in the band. What really takes a toll is the drinking after the concert, because then you're a wreck that night and then you've got the next morning an early call or whatever.

PAUL: Being on the road, I don't know how anybody does it. I've been on the road for stories for a week, week and a half with a band, and they're on the road for a year. After a week and a half I'm wrecked, I don't know what town I'm in, what day it is. It's just the hardest life in the world, I think.[122]

LEONARD: It's very difficult.

PAUL: There was a period where you didn't tour for ten years. Or tour America at least.

LEONARD: I kept on touring Europe but my audience dried up here. Well, even before my '85 tour of Europe, it was very hard to get a promoter for that tour, even in Europe. Seventy-five or '76 was my last tour of America and I didn't come back until '85.

121 Paul was a big fan of orange juice. Crystal Zevon, Warren Zevon's ex-wife, recalls that he used to pour it over his cornflakes in place of milk.

122 As difficult as living the life on the road was for Paul, it yielded two of his best pieces, both *Rolling Stone* cover stories: 1976's "We Are All on Tour: Are You Prepared for the Pretender—Jackson Browne?" and 1978's "Rod Stewart Under Siege."

PAUL: This was a period where you felt your writing was falling off? A bad period as well? Where you were beginning to have doubts?

LEONARD: Seventy-four to '83, around that period, yeah.

PAUL: Did you feel that the albums of that period were not as well done? Or didn't have as many good songs?

LEONARD: I felt the songs were very good. I still feel the songs are okay. Very good I don't know, but certainly they're okay. Do you know what I mean? Just the kind of energy you can summon for any project is very, very limited. You're hanging on by the skin of your teeth in some way through the whole thing and you can't really seem to bring things to completion with a kind of solidity. That it's all just impressionistic. Just like reproductions of the work.

I didn't feel that there was a kind of authority in the singing that I was *able* to manifest when I was singing songs about myself or when they first arose. Some subtraction from strength. But I wasn't strong. There's something there, say, for the truth. I think there's a kind of truth in the records that makes them acceptable. I think the songs are good, but somehow the records weren't *aimed* accurately in the whole thing. I guess *Recent Songs* was when I started to feel good about it again. I don't know if there's any objective reality to these estimations now or whether they're even solid or whether they'll hold for another, you know—I guess there will be one moment, I can't imagine when, when I'll look at the songs. It would never occur to me to reevaluate the work from any point. Maybe if I ever do, I'll look back and say, "Well, those are real nice. They're okay." But right now I feel they weren't *aimed* correctly. They didn't hit the target.

PAUL: Songs can be elusive. Not only one's own songs, say, other songs that you've never got before suddenly sound like different songs many years later. Some of them improve a great deal, it seems like, and some of them that were really favorites now aren't favorites.

LEONARD: Yeah, I think time changes the things. And they reemerge, things reappear.

PAUL: I think one reason why, when I was writing a lot about your records at *Rolling Stone* and the *Voice*, a lot of the younger critics were saying, "Jeez, we don't understand this really." And then Bill Flanagan from *Musician*—I don't know if you've met him, he's the editor at *Musician*—said, "I remember you used to go on and on about Leonard Cohen, and I'd say, 'I just don't get it.'" He then said, "I got ten years older and suddenly I thought, *God, he was right*." He was like ten years younger than I was, and I'd think, *Probably that had something to do with it.*

LEONARD: I think that had a lot to do with it. I remember saying the same thing to Irving Layton. I remember saying to him, "Irving, I always knew you were good but I never knew you were great. Now I know you're great."

PAUL: Yeah, I think just being older and having seen more than someone makes a difference in one's perspective, too.

LEONARD: And I was aware of that at the time, too. Because there weren't very many people—outside yourself, incidentally—who were giving me very favorable attention. There weren't too many.

PAUL: I don't remember.

LEONARD: I do. I do. I mean, they come to me. I did actually take that into my considerations, too, that you have to have a broken marriage first of all to get this. Or as Irv Layton says in one of his poems, "Sad times takes three marriages to season a man."

PAUL: I guess, by using that phrase, you considered yourself married to Suzanne although you were not legally married to Suzanne.

LEONARD: Yeah.

PAUL: Was there a reason why you didn't get married legally?

LEONARD: Never got around to it somehow. We had the children and one's life was filled with that kind of thing. There were a lot of things. One was just cowardice. I was able to find certain ideological justifications. Like, I always consider myself a certain way. Like an old anarchist, I didn't feel like submitting my private life to any public attention or confirmation. I didn't want permission from anybody.

PAUL: Of course it's just a piece of paper, but you considered yourself basically married.

LEONARD: Well, I considered myself in this union. Certainly whatever my relationship with Suzanne was or was not, there was no question about the fact that we were the mother and father of two children. There's never been any question of that. So we might not have been husband and wife all the time, but we were certainly always mother and father.

When there are children around and something breaks up, those things which are commonplace but nevertheless always involve great amounts of suffering, you can't go berserk when there's four people involved. There are repercussions. Very difficult, as you know.

PAUL: Yeah, there was one child involved in my case. Divorces are probably very difficult in any sense, but having children involved is just really murder.

LEONARD: Yeah, it's murder. What I found out, especially when they moved back to New York, which really cooled a lot of the things out because they went to Little Red School House and, you know, half the class came from divorced parents. So it was like a commonplace to them; it wasn't to me. But it was to them and in a certain sense they cooled it out for me. They were going to visit so-and-so, and his father was coming back and he was going to stay with them, and that father had a family, and it was completely within their world. It was commonplace.

PAUL: I just want to jump back to "Joan of Arc" again and "Last Year's Man." "Joan of Arc" has meant a lot to me. We started to talk about it and then got sidetracked.

LEONARD: I finished the song at the Chelsea, we recorded it in Nashville, and then we went to London for Paul Buckmaster to do the arrangements on top of the guitar. But I never thought much about Joan of Arc since then—of course I've always appreciated her—until I read a book called *Intercourse* [by Andrea Dworkin]. Have you ever read it? It is a feminist manifesto. Very brilliant. One of the most passionate books. There's a study of Joan of Arc in it that began to revive my interest in it. I'm reading about it now again.

PAUL: What was it that appealed to you about the figure of Joan of Arc at the time?

LEONARD: Maybe it was Jean Seberg. [*chuckles*] I don't know, I mean, the story always touched me.

PAUL: Ingrid Bergman played her in an early version [1948's *Joan of Arc*] and there's the great Falconetti silent film where Falconetti played her [*The Passion of Joan of Arc*, from 1929].

LEONARD: And then there was the play of Bernard Shaw's [*Saint Joan*, premiering in 1923], which I'd seen and read. The stories were good but there was something about the figure that always touched me.

PAUL: That was a breakthrough song for me. I just took it as, god, it's the story of Joan of Arc in four verses or however many verses, and then someone—Janet Maslin—wrote something about it in the *Times* probably, saying it was a metaphorical song about men and women. That had never occurred to me. I had always somehow thought, *Well, it's about Joan of Arc literally.* Was it a metaphorical song about men and women, in your mind?

LEONARD: I have trouble with that approach to things, although I respect it, that kind of approach to anything, especially when I don't remember it. Yeah, I think it is about men and women also. I think it's a lot about *women*. It's difficult for me to affirm or dispute interpretations of the song. I know it has something to do with men and women—and I know that I can sing it with a woman—or to the male and female aspects of any individual. More the way I'd go if I were forced to look for the metaphor.

PAUL: I guess I saw some of it. I just thought, *He's personalized the historical story*, the man-woman aspect is in it, but she was saying that it's about men and women today, and it never occurred to me that that was the true subject matter, if indeed it was.

LEONARD: It's hard, you know. It leaves me behind, those speculations. And it's not because I don't respect them, because I do, and I often enjoy reading them about, like, especially my own work and certainly other kinds of work when I do enter that mode of investigation into something. Mailer's analysis of things, I'm always interested in. But I remember the struggle with the material, that's what I recall, however it emerges. Of course it's got to have that element in it, of men and women, but it's also got to have that element of the story that touched me as a child. Because, you know, I grew up in Quebec, and she's a figure of Quebec.

PAUL: I thought, *Gee, I'm usually halfway decent about picking up metaphorical things and I just missed this one completely*. I think her viewpoint was a feministic viewpoint. I *could* read it that way.

LEONARD: Yes, I think you could read it that way. And it might even be an authentic impulse in the song. I'm kind of happy that anybody pays it that much attention, but I don't really have a take. I think that if something is worthy of the attention, that it can certainly justify that kind of analysis. For me it's more like, *How do I give life to this material? What is the struggle I have with the story? How can I allow it to live? What do I have to remove from it, what do I have to bring to it?* How do you make it real? How do you bring it to completion so that line after line does not lie, does not violate your sense of its reality.

PAUL: Are you sometimes surprised in the middle of a song that it's going in a direction you hadn't thought of when you started it?

LEONARD: The thing that surprises me most about anything is finishing it. Good or bad. Just the fact that you've come to the end of the song and you can say, "Hey, well—"

PAUL: "That's it."

LEONARD: "That's it." Or as W. H. Auden said, "A poem is never finished, it's just abandoned."[123] Where you can justifiably abandon the song; you know that it has a beginning, a middle, and an end.

She really was a remarkable woman—besides the fact that we have this legend of the little Maid of Orleans. She lived with her captains, she slept on the same straw pallets as her captains. She bathed bare-breasted with them, but nobody *ever* approached her. She didn't permit cussing. She refused to allow the field prostitutes, field whores, to follow the army. The only things that she changed in the army, she didn't permit anybody to take the name of the Lord in vain. And they really loved her, and she really fought.

And apparently what happened, they got her on this thing of wearing male clothes. It was a very big thing. They made her put a dress on. They locked her in a cage when they caught her. And according to this book *Intercourse*, it seemed to come out now that she was raped repeatedly once she was held in captivity, and it's then that she recanted her confession. She said, "If this is what you have in mind for me, forget it. I did hear the voices."

PAUL: In "Last Year's Man" you mention the soldiers.

LEONARD: Yes, I always thought of myself in a military man kind of way.

PAUL: And your father.

LEONARD: And my father. It's just what I'm drawn to, just the organizational milieu. The order and that kind of effort and comradeship, mutual responsibility. You know, they call Zen the Marines of the spiritual world. That kind of training always attracted me. It's just a matter of taste. I always thought of Joan as like the soldier's woman; that relationship her captains had with her and the men had with her.

PAUL: What significance does the book *The Romance of the King's Army* have for you?

123 This quote (or one like it) originated with Paul Valéry in 1933 and was used by Auden, in a forward to a collection of his poetry, in 1967.

LEONARD: I think I mentioned that to somebody somewhere along the line that that was the first book my father gave me. I don't know that I ever got to read it, but I believe it was a study of the military history. The thing I always remember about it, it has this—what is it called?—like a quotation at the very beginning, on the front page. It was: "You would be surprised, my son, with how little wisdom the world is governed."

PAUL: You were a pretty young kid at this time.

LEONARD: Yeah, I was about eight.

PAUL: Are you a Zen master at this point?

LEONARD: No, I'm not even a monk. I mean, I'm not even a lay monk. I'm just a student. No, I don't believe that's in the cards for me. My old teacher, I remember a couple years ago in one of the personal interviews, you have your *sesshin*. A *sesshin* is one of the fundamental teaching practices. It's a seven-day sitting where you sit for about nineteen hours a day, just breaking for meals and three or four hours of sleep, and you sit in the *zendo* most of the day. A very rigorous form. And you see the teacher three or four times a day. I remember sitting in front of my old teacher, and he said, "Oh, Leonard, seventeen years I know you, I never try to give you my religion. Just pour your saki." [*chuckles*] I think he gave up long ago.

PAUL: Is sitting in a particular position required to do this?

> *Leonard retrieves his yoga mat, prefaces with "I don't know if I can do it with my pants on," and gets down and demonstrates the full lotus, half lotus, and quarter lotus positions. He encourages Paul to try it.*

PAUL: And you should let your mind wander?

LEONARD: Well, you let thoughts arise and just acknowledge them as they arise without identifying them, without believing them. Just understanding they're thoughts that arise. Off and on you can place a lot of space between yourself and your thoughts so that, as they arise, you can embrace them as you wish. But that they are just thoughts. You hate this person? It's just a thought. You want to fuck this p— It's just a thought. Then it goes, *Where was that?*

Did you see that beautiful interview with Marlon Brando and Connie Chung [*Saturday Night with Connie Chung*]? It was a *wonderful* interview and there's a certain point where she says, "Mr. Brando, you're still considered perhaps the world's greatest actor." "World's greatest actor," he says. "You know, this goes by and that goes by and you get old and you get sick and one day you say, 'What was that all about?' [*laughs*] This view of myself, this identification of myself with my personality, what a stupid idea that was."

PAUL: Brando apparently has studied also, I gather, a similar thing.

LEONARD: A friend of mine—in fact, the man who introduced me to old Roshi—there was a certain time when a friend of his, a young student, was in a hospital, maybe a mental hospital, and he was visiting him, and he happened to be related to Marlon Brando, and Marlon Brando came to [visit]. They happened to bump into each other outside the hospital. Of course my friend recognized him and they talked for a while. He told Marlon Brando about his teacher and Brando said, "Look, you ask your teacher one thing. What do you do when you wake up at three in the morning with a hard-on?" [*laughs*] "Have you got an answer for that?"

PAUL: You've been studying for twenty years. Was it all gradual understanding or were there breakthrough periods?

LEONARD: I don't know. I think there's something that rubs off on you over the years. You forget it a lot of the time.

PAUL: But there are not sudden periods of leaps of consciousness?

LEONARD: There are, curiously enough. There are sudden moments, very sudden, of tiny illuminations.

PAUL: I was wondering if there were such times around the *Various Positions* period and that being sort of a summation period, as you were saying. And *I'm Your Man*, which sort of started anew. A lot had been happening there.

LEONARD: I certainly couldn't disassociate even my haphazard training with, first of all, my personal survival, and my work. I couldn't—I wouldn't—begin to disassociate the study of Zen.

PAUL: I was just wondering if that contributed greatly to the, I don't know if you'd call it a new beginning or a different slant on things, to *I'm Your Man*. There's definitely a break between those two records, and a new start. There's a particularly active period of growth in the studies.

LEONARD: I think it was. I don't know how to put it exactly. But yeah, it is critical. It was critical to me. It *is* important.

PAUL: I guess you did the Mark Rowland interview for *Musician* like a couple of years ago or three years ago ["Leonard Cohen's Nervous Breakthrough" in 1988], but things you said in that probably don't hold true today.

LEONARD: I don't recall what I said.

PAUL: It seemed you felt like—I know you still feel a great sense of loss—but the great emphasis was on living alone in hotel rooms after Marianne and after Suzanne. Leaving two families, more or less, although there weren't any children with Marianne.

LEONARD: Well, there was a child, not my own [Axel Joachim Jensen Jr., born in 1960].

PAUL: The impression that I got from that interview is possibly second thoughts on this. You were sort of second-guessing the wisdom of this and that you'd had fifteen to twenty years alone in hotel rooms. There seems to be a different sense to that interview in many ways, almost in some ways a different person.

LEONARD: I would say so. Yeah, because my life has changed radically.

PAUL: My guess is that a lot of the studying with Roshi—

LEONARD: Oh, yes. Irving Layton, Roshi, the two older men in my life. Irving Layton as an embodiment of the true artist, of the true writer. The kind of production, the kind of generosity in his life, and the kind of stamina—bravery—of his own life. And Roshi, the embodiment of that space of freedom and love that he surrounds everything with. I've been very fortunate to have those figures in my life. To study with Roshi has been a singular privilege.

PAUL: How old of a person is he?

LEONARD: He's going to be eighty-four next month.

PAUL: Somehow I feel that those are answers you wouldn't give now.

LEONARD: No. This is the first time I've ever had a sofa, in my life. My friends have called me up to congratulate me about having a sofa and two easy chairs. I never had them because I never saw myself as leading a civilian life. I thought, *I need a table. I need a lot of tables for my synthesizers and my typewriter, and* that's *what I need. And a bed.* I don't entertain. I don't lounge around my house because that's not what it is. And I haven't lived in one place—I think for those fifteen, twenty years, whatever it was—ten, fifteen years anyways—I don't think I stayed in any place longer than three or four months. And usually a lot less. I was just moving. All my friends are very pleased for me. Like, the couch is the symbol. To think I actually went out and bought a *sofa* and, like, actually consented to say that I live here. You know, that this is my house and I've got my sofa.

PAUL: It's a symbol of something.

LEONARD: Yeah, the civilian life. I just got it like a month ago. And then carpets, you know, with colors in them.

PAUL: You've been in this house for how long?

LEONARD: I got it with two friends of mine. The three of us were students of Roshi at the time. At 4:30 in the morning it's about eight minutes from the *zendo*, so we got it for its proximity to the center. And there's a training center on Mount Baldy, called Mount Baldy Zen Center, which is a rather rigorous training center. And then they went off on different paths. The downstairs was rented for many years. I'd keep this place for myself because I was working in L.A. a lot, but now I've taken over both floors. But I think we got it in '79.

PAUL: Do you have the feeling now that it will be Montreal and Los Angeles that you'll be living in for quite a while?

LEONARD: Yeah. I love Montreal, and I don't think I'd ever want to cut off my connections to the city. My childhood friends live on the same street as I did in Montreal. And my kids like Montreal. They're completely bilingual, so it's a very nice place for them, too.

PAUL: Los Angeles you have very warm feelings about?

LEONARD: I love the city. I find myself always defending it. But I live more or less the same kind of life in any city: I have a place and some tables and some chairs really. Fortunately, I have a life that doesn't involve having to fight the traffic or the rush hours. I like the light. I found that *it* is somehow connected with not getting enough sunlight. Also, I think they have a word for it now, Seasonally Adjusted Depression or something like that, they call SAD [Seasonal Affective Disorder]. Where part of the therapy is, if you're not in a sunny climate, they expose you to more light every day. I find it's important, so the light means a lot to me. But I'm very fond of the city. And of course I'm able to keep in touch with Roshi and his community, which is very important to me.

PAUL: You described this neighborhood as rather Norman Rockwell-ish. *Saturday Evening Post*?

LEONARD: Yeah, *Saturday Evening Post* cover. It's so very beautiful. Most of the people own their own houses. It's very mixed. There's a Japanese neighbor, a Black neighbor, an Italian neighbor, a Jewish neighbor. I always think it's like an advertisement for America. It's not rich and it's not grand, but it's not shabby either. People take care of their houses.

PAUL: You were talking the other day about *Various Positions*, how after that you cut yourself some slack as a person, I guess. It's really all right to say those things and that your life has had some dignity. It seemed to indicate that you were rather hard on yourself before this, in your work. A sense of alienation.

LEONARD: Yeah, all very strong. Not only that, the swing is very swift and wide, from feeling in love with everything and everyone, and then the second wager: don't even want to answer the telephone for some, you know, dread.

PAUL: Even in the Michael O. book, he's talking about the sense of alienation and yourself as the observer. I think that's probably in both novels also, that sense. This was very early on, I gather.

LEONARD: I've always been in trouble. I had a song: "Well, I've always been in trouble / with a woman or with the law." Yeah, I've always been in some kind of trouble. Not so much now.

PAUL: What would you do if *it* started coming back and winning? Do you think that's possible at this point in your life?

LEONARD: I think it's always possible. I think it's a point that Styron makes, too. He says the only thing that would mitigate the episode would be that you know that it has an end, that it tends to exhaust itself. Do you remember when you came out of it?

PAUL: It was very gradual. I remember being aware, month to month, that I could make sentences better when I talked to people, and I could make decisions better. I could go buy the paper without deliberating all afternoon whether I would or wouldn't go downstairs and buy it. There was never a breakthrough that I could point to—bang—something happened that day. And I was seeing the psychologist and I seemed to have less and less to say, and thinking, *I don't even have any major problems this week. What am I going to talk about for fifty minutes?* But gradual, very gradual.

LEONARD: Well, a lot of it was gradual, too. I'd go to the Zen center and stay there for a month, two months, and my strength would come back, and then I'd go back and it would ebb again. But I remember there were two curious moments toward the end of the affair, and one was I had a conversation with somebody on a personal matter, it really wasn't that specific to the situation, and I put the phone down and I remember collapsing on my bed and I was saying out loud, "I can't take it anymore, I can't take it anymore." And then I heard this little voice come from myself, saying, "You don't have to take this anymore." And I inquired, automatically saying, "What do you mean?" somehow, and the voice said, "You can change your mind about all of this." That was the first time I sort of felt some kind of movement in the logjam. And then about two weeks later I couldn't get out of bed, I was in bed most of the time at that point, and a friend of mine—in fact, the widow of Hershorn, whom I spoke about—she called me up and said, "Leonard, I've got to talk to you." I said, "Francine, I can't see anybody." So she said, "Well, I'm coming over anyways. I want to tell you about a dream." I said, "Look, the last thing I want to hear about is one of your dreams." She said, "Well, I'm coming over anyways." I said, "Well, you can't come over because I can't go downstairs to open the door." And she said, "Well, I'll get Hazel," my neighbor, this old friend of mine, "I'll get Hazel to open the door from the back." We share a common backyard. I said, "Well, do what you want. I don't feel like seeing you or anybody else. And I can't talk." And she came over and she said, "I want to tell you about a dream I had," and I said, "Okay, I'll hear your stupid fucking dream." She said, "I want to tell you about two dreams: the first dream is I dreamt that I was you and it was so horrible I woke up." I said, "Great, thanks a lot." And then she said, "But that isn't the dream I really want to tell you about. I want to tell you about a dream that my father had." I'd met her father three or four times in my life, and he is a wonderful man, a very perky, energetic guy. He played the trumpet and was a postman, I think. She said, "He's been feeling very poorly for the past couple of years. He'd never been sick in his life and found himself sick and went into a depression, and I've been spending a lot of time with him. One morning he woke up completely refreshed, and I said, 'Dad, you must've had a wonderful sleep' and he said, 'Yes, I had a wonderful sleep, but I had a wonderful dream about your friend Leonard Cohen. I dreamed that we don't have to worry because Leonard Cohen is picking up the stones.'" She said, "Do you know what that means? Is there something in Judaism about that, or do you know of anything?" I said, "No, I don't know of anything." *But* as soon as she said that, I allowed myself to think of something that I *knew* was wrong, which was there was some aspect of my own discomfort that had some wider significance. I said to myself, *I can't buy that! I don't like that idea.* So that was one reaction. The other reaction was that there was some use to this condition. I didn't know what it was. I still can't explain why it went some way to dissolving this condition I was in. And then I began to recover. It was curious; I've never been able to figure those two things out.

PAUL: [*sighs heavily*] I think when I said yes to the first story [about Suzanne Vega], it was with some fear that I accepted it, but it seemed like—

LEONARD: You felt capable.

PAUL: —some sort of fate was leading me to that, since I'd just seen Suzanne backstage at your concert and then got the offer to do the story within a week or two. I was afraid if I said no, I'd never do anything again. You know, you just fling yourself out into space.

LEONARD: But at any other point you might not even have considered even those possibilities because the shades are just down, so to say. Yeah, you wouldn't have taken the call probably.

PAUL: I don't think I would've. It seems like there's got to be some relationship to just seeing this woman and then having someone ask about her. I thought all this was put-up or shut-up time.

Leonard notices that his hummingbird feeder is again empty and replenishes it by mixing some instant nectar. While he does, Paul reviews his notes.

PAUL: I just find if one talks, a lot of this stuff just naturally comes up. But some of it doesn't.

We were talking at the Chariot, I think, and you said you had the feeling that there were "great reservoirs of goodwill in the country that haven't been tapped" yet.

LEONARD: Yeah. I'm not American so I have a little bit of a perspective on it. I still think it's man's best hope. There's a kind of resilience here and a kind of genius, a kind of energy and, as I put it, reservoirs of goodwill. I'm not a leader, I don't know how you go about tapping them, but I can certainly affirm them.

PAUL: Yeah, I hope you're right.

LEONARD: I may be wrong.

PAUL: I just see the cities in such trouble.

LEONARD: They are. They are in tremendous trouble. Norman Mailer, in the beginning of that article on *American Psycho*, he says, "The Russians were gracious enough to bow out after seventy years of Communism and say it doesn't work." He says, "It'll probably be 700 years before Capitalism bows out, and there will be nothing left." Maybe I'm just so happy not to be in *it* that I'm looking at the world through rose-colored spectacles.

PAUL: Both of us live in cities. Having come from a small town, I just know that New York and my hometown aren't really in the same country. Everybody forgets Middle America. I don't know what's going on there but there may be great reservoirs of hope *there* for people.

LEONARD: I kind of regret saying that because it sounds Pollyanna and unnecessarily optimistic. But I just bump into people and I see there's some fundamental decency in people that hasn't evaporated. There must be some way of manifesting that on a collective plane.

PAUL: I just feel that something's got to change for the better, because I don't know how much further it can go.

LEONARD: Well, I tried to put those feelings into that song "Democracy." I say, "It's coming from the sorrow in the street / The holy places where the races meet."

PAUL: Seems like there are swings from decade to decade, or number of decades, when one reaches one point, the opposite takes over. It seems like we're almost at that point where the opposite *has* to take over.

LEONARD: Well, I certainly wouldn't write it off.

PAUL: I guess maybe everybody that's lived thinks he's living in the worst time probably and never will things get worse than this.

LEONARD: If you read the Roman Cicero's writings, they're all saying that: "It's never been this bad."

PAUL: In New York it's in a sense isolated from the rest of the country. New York's its own country; it has no relationship to the rest of America in a certain sense.

LEONARD: It's a tricky place.

PAUL: "Don't Pass Me By [(A Disgrace)]" [from 1973's *Live Songs*] sort of anticipated mass homelessness, it seemed to me, as I was listening to it again a couple weeks ago. In a nice way you shift it around: *you're* asking not to be passed by. It's a strange record in a way.

LEONARD: Oh, it's very strange.

PAUL: Planned that way?

LEONARD: I had no plan. Just what I had. As I said, I have little recollection of those days.[124]

124 The photo of Leonard used for the album *Live Songs* is credited to Suzanne B. Elrod.

PAUL: "Passing Thru" is on there. It doesn't sound Pete Seegerish, but it sounds like a real attempt to reach the audience in a Pete Seeger way, in an earlier folk song way than you do now.

LEONARD: I only ever did that song two or three times. It was completely improvised at the time. I just had that chorus: "Please don't pass me by."[125]

PAUL: Yeah, it goes on for a long time, but it drags you into it. I found it a very moving record for some reason. It's got some strange moments that don't appear anywhere else in your career; at least I don't think they do.

LEONARD: No, I don't think so.

PAUL: Do you ever think about another novel?

LEONARD: I do.

PAUL: Since *Beautiful Losers* have you started any?

LEONARD: Yeah, I started one. Kind of like it, too. I won't finish it because I don't really know the thrust, what it was about. Started a few. But it seems that I have something to do in this music racket, you know? Something to do. Maybe it was to sing "Be for Real," I don't know. I feel that, for me, that's [a] real moment for me.

PAUL: "Be for Real"?

LEONARD: That song, yeah. I haven't finished "Always." I think I'm going to feel about that, those two songs, like that's closer to the childhood dream of music than writing all those songs in-between. When I was playing clarinet in the high school band and listening to Guy Lombardo and Duke Ellington and Stan Kenton and the singers with those bands, well, that's what I really meant by being a singer.

125 Though Paul initially asked about "Passing Thru," which was written by Dick Blakeslee and, in 1948, indeed covered by Pete Seeger, Leonard apparently misheard or is conflating that song with the thirteen-minute-long "Don't Pass Me By (A Disgrace)."

PAUL: Interesting it would be in other [songwriters'] songs. You were talking about "Be for Real" like it was a very important song—in the car, we didn't get it on tape—but that *simplify, simplify*, and *be more direct*, you know, like the song's title basically, *be real, be less mystical*.

LEONARD: You know, Jenny gave me the cassette that it was on. Because she knows I love that kind of music. I started playing it over and over and over. I must have played it a thousand times before it occurred to me that I might be able to sing it. But Freddie Knight's version of it is so astoundingly beautiful that I didn't have the courage to do it. And then somehow I met with Steve Lindsey, and I didn't want to give him one of my own songs because I didn't know him. And I said, "Yeah, there's a song I really like." This is the first moment we met, but I knew a little bit about his work from Leanne. Although I'd never heard any, he brought a cassette with him to the studio and dropped in to say hello. He said, "Do you want to hear some of the stuff I've done?" He played a couple of things that were really fine. But still I thought, *I'm not going to lay my own songs on this guy. I don't know him.* So I said, "Do you know 'Be for Real'?" He said no. I had the cassette with me. He played it. He said, "Yeah, I think that's a really good song for you," and then he put together that track. Even then when I heard it, I said, "God, this is a beautiful track. Jenny should sing this, or Frederick Knight." And I gave it a shot.

PAUL: And it came out great.

LEONARD: And it came out. It almost surprised me. Then I was able to say, "Well, that's not quite right there," and I'd correct a phrase and it would work! The correction would work.

PAUL: You said at some point there were also a number of songs that you had wanted to sing. What are some of the others?

LEONARD: There are a lot of folk songs I'd love to use this treatment with. A lot of Stephen Foster songs. Songs like the folk song "Venezuela." Some Spanish Civil War songs: "Viva la Quinta Brigada," songs like that. There are so many wonderful songs, that I was saying to a friend of mine last night, "There's a wonderful song, that song 'Oh How We Danced on the Night We Were Wed.'"[126] [*sings the first line, which is the title*] And then I was thinking of "Golden Earrings."[127] These are old chestnuts that you know. You're from the same era.

PAUL: I'm beginning to love these songs with such passion.

LEONARD: Me, too. That's why I love Irving and Roshi. I like to hear some guys who've actually been around a while. And never mind if they're Zen masters or great poets, I just want to hear the voice of experience. Roshi gave me a lovely moment last year. He walked into one of those personal interviews, bowed, sat down, looked at me and said, "Your generation's over." I said, "What a relief!"

PAUL: [*laughing with Leonard*] Thank god for that. Now I can breathe easy and get on with it. It's been kind of thrilling for me to find a new path to explore.

LEONARD: My son keeps me pretty much—his grasp of his own scene is very, very extensive. "What do you think of this, Dad?" and he'll play Mariah Carey like a year or two before anybody's ever heard of her. He's played me all the rap stuff because he was in it; he was break-dancing from eleven. He's always kept me informed and, you know, it's okay. I know what the Talmud says: "There's good wine in every generation." It's okay, but also I don't have to love it. I say it to him: "I don't have to like it. It's yours." He loves Randy Newman, he loves Joe Cocker.

PAUL: I met a jazz guy recently—I don't know much about it, he's going to teach me about jazz—and he had never heard your music. I said, "Let me just play you two songs, then." I played him "Joan of Arc" and "Famous Blue Raincoat." His mouth just fell open and he immediately went scouting all the used LP bins.

126 The correct title is "Anniversary Song." With lyrics by Al Jolson and Saul Chaplin, and based on the 1880 waltz "Waves of the Danube" by Iosif Ivanovici, the 1946 song was featured in the film *The Jolson Story*.

127 Made famous by Peggy Lee in 1947, it served as the title song to the Ray Milland-Marlene Dietrich film of the same name.

LEONARD: I have some good rock-poet chat with jazzers. I had to have it with Sonny Rollins, like I was telling you. There was no problem. No problem with the voice, with anything. They hear it a completely different way, jazzers.

PAUL: "Famous Blue Raincoat" is another song we haven't really talked about. I'd like to talk about that one a little bit, what the whole idea of that was.

LEONARD: The melody I thought was very, very good. Some of the lyrics, I felt there was a certain lack of clarity about the story. It is forgivable from a certain impressionistic point of view, and okay. But somewhere in my heart I always felt I should've made it clearer, the lyrics should have been clearer. I'm not sure, I'm not sure.

PAUL: That was the one that made the biggest impression on me. You don't expect the end where "my brother, my killer" and then "thanks for"—

LEONARD: —"the trouble you took from her eyes." That's a good line.

PAUL: "I thought it was there for good." And that's unexpected sort of. It reads like a—oh, *rambling* is the wrong word—but a nighttime letter.

LEONARD: Yeah, it *was* that rambling quality that I resisted. But I also recognized—because I subjected it to quite a lot of examination—it *had* something and if I dismantle this completely and start from scratch, it's going to be completely different. There's enough of the time and the place and the story in there to carry it, but I did have some reservations about it. But there are some good individual lines. That's why I didn't want to start tearing it apart. "I see you there with the rose in your teeth"— that's nice.

PAUL: Yeah. I think it's clear enough what happened. It has such a mood to it; tinkering with it might dismantle that as well. It also reads like a very late-night letter that may be somewhat ambiguous or confused, but that's part of the mood, too.

LEONARD: Well, that's how I forgave myself, with those—

PAUL: Well, I didn't have to forgive myself. I think you're being hard on yourself in that case. I think it does work.

LEONARD: I think a lot of it is because a friend of mine—a close friend, a man I respect very much—he said, "It's a beautiful song; however, I can see the carpentry in the lyric." And I respected that because I felt it hadn't really been well-sanded. I thought it's good, the construction's good, the joints are good, but—it's okay, yeah.

PAUL: I guess there are certain points where songs reach when fixing them makes them a different song, and you lose more than you gain, in some senses. So you probably have to leave them at some point if they work ninety-nine percent or whatever.

LEONARD: I'm fond of saying, "The great is the enemy of the good, and the perfect is the enemy of the great."[128]

PAUL: I don't like perfect songs; I like flawed masterpieces. The two words don't seem to go together. Flawed masterpieces are more human than perfect masterpieces. That little crack is where the light comes in in a flawed masterpiece somehow.[129]

Talk turns to folk singer-songwriter David Blue.

LEONARD: David Blue.[130] Our lives came very close together finally, David Blue and mine. I knew him in the old days. And then there was a group called the Centaur Theatre, I believe it was called. Well, maybe that's wrong. But a Montreal theatre group did a play based on my work, kind of an anthology piece.[131] They had an actor in rehearsal, and they

128 Commonly attributed to Voltaire, who was quoting an Italian proverb by Montesquieu: "*Le mieux est le mortel ennemi du bien*" ("The better is the mortal enemy of the good)."

129 Referencing the famous lyric from "Anthem," Paul, in a similar vein thirteen years earlier when reviewing the *Death of a Ladies' Man* album for *Rolling Stone*, wrote: "It's either greatly flawed or great *and* flawed—and I'm betting on the latter."

130 A member of Bob Dylan's Rolling Thunder Revue who also appeared on the front cover of [Dylan and the Band's] *The Basement Tapes* album, Blue was also an actor.

131 In 1980 the Centaur Theatre Group produced a play called *The Leonard Cohen Show*, wherein

brought me down and asked me what I thought, and I said, "I don't really think he's got it." They said, "Well, can you suggest anybody?" I said, "I think David Blue could do this. He knows all my songs very well." And he came up to Montreal and he played the part, and then he fell in love with a friend of Hazel's, a friend of mine, and he married her.

PAUL: Hazel your neighbor.

LEONARD: My neighbor, yeah. And he moved next door, across the street, so I began to see a great deal of him. This is long after he'd abandoned his—not abandoned writing, but he hadn't made a record for years and years. And he started to write again and he made a demo in Montreal. Very beautiful songs. One song was "Wild Canadian Girl," which was written to his wife.

And then they decided to move back to New York. He had no money and he decided the time had come when he had to have a job. So he went to that club, that bar that the man—Mickey [Ruskin]. He'd had Max's Kansas City. And he told me this story: David, he walked into this club and he said, "Can I speak to you, Mickey?" And this is David Blue deciding that he's going to become a bartender now or a waiter, because he's going to make a living. And Mick, says, "Yeah, just give me ten minutes and we'll talk." David's sitting at the bar, and a guy comes up to him and asks him for his autograph. He recognized him. And he said he just couldn't go through with it. He signed the autograph and left the bar. And a couple of weeks later while he was jogging around Washington Square, he had a heart attack and died. I delivered the eulogy at his funeral. His wife asked me to do it. He was a kind of synthesis of a whole lot of stories like that that I'd been in and heard.

Paul puts in a fresh cassette.

PAUL: I never considered your albums gloom and doom and all.

LEONARD: No, I never thought so myself.

---

a Cohen stand-in perched himself in a treehouse and serenaded the audience with Leonard's songs and excerpts from his poems and novels.

PAUL: I thought some of the songs were frightening, but some of real life is frightening, too. And I never considered them to be nihilistic statements or anything like that. I thought the humanity really shone through.

Starting from the beginning, were there particular albums or particular songs—I realize this is too all-encompassing—where you felt like, *This is some sort of a breakthrough*? *It's better than what I've done before*?

LEONARD: Well, I certainly felt that about my last two albums. I think I was so happy to get *Recent Songs* out, on a personal level it represented an achievement because I'd had that Phil Spector album before that. It kind of made me want to never walk into a studio again. I had a great sense of luck during *Recent Songs* because I met [violinist] Raffi Hakopian and John Bilezikjian [on the lute-like oud] during that period, and they really brought a lot of the songs to life; and then Jennifer's magnificent chorus on "The Guests." I really felt I'd lucked into help. In terms of the actual writing, I felt that songs like "If It Be Your Will" and "Hallelujah," "Dance Me to the End of Love" represented some kind of tension I brought to them. Somehow I had the space and the time, somehow my life was sufficiently empty, and then there was some kind of nourishment coming into that emptiness, it was able to work. I felt *Various Positions* and *I'm Your Man* beginning something. I felt that maybe *Recent Songs* was the end of a certain type of concerns. Not the end of them, but the end of the material.

PAUL: Yeah, I can see that. Because *Various Positions* seems to look back and be reassessing, and in a sense be a first step as well. *Recent Songs* I guess has more of a relationship to the themes of the first albums.

LEONARD: And the language. It's very formal. The language is connected to my poetry and to some religious writers like Rumi, the Persian poet. He's a Persian poet of I think the Thirteenth Century.

PAUL: "The Traitor" is very good. The first verse is wonderful. She "yearned me through the summer." That's a big favorite song. Also

"The Guests." I once made a tape loop—forty-five minutes straight—of "The Guests" because I just thought it was a circular song.

LEONARD: You have used the exact words—a friend of mine is a Sufi dancer. She's entitled to teach the Sufi dance in America. I met her and she had the tape with her, and she put on her circular skirt, bells. And she put the record on and she spun—you know that whirling dance?—through the whole thing. She studied in Turkey with the Mevlevi Order of the whirling dervishes, and she came back entitled to teach. The son of the sheik came to check out his outpost and he said to her, "We're dancing to a tune that a Westerner wrote." And she said, "What is it?" and he said, "It's this song, 'The Guests.'" He said, "It has the spirit of Rumi in it." That was one of the best things I ever heard.

PAUL: What would constitute the spirit of Rumi, to someone who's never read him?

LEONARD: Well, Rumi, for my money, is the greatest religious poet since David. Since the Psalms. His poems are astoundingly beautiful, ecstatic poems of love for God and of the path of love. The intoxication of divinity. I think there are a hundred thousand, but I don't know how many he wrote. But there are thousands, and he spoke them spontaneously, or chanted them, and his disciples whirled as he sang.

PAUL: Have you ever considered doing something by Rumi like you did by [Federico García] Lorca?[132]

LEONARD: *Yeah*. I would love to do that.

PAUL: You once said that Lorca was the man who ruined your life because of this song.

LEONARD: [*laughs*] Yeah. Definitely one of them.

132 In 1986 Cohen recorded "Take This Waltz," a translation of Lorca's poem "*Pequeño vals vienés*" for a Spanish tribute album, *Poetas en Nueva York* [*Poets in New York*]. Two years later a slightly rearranged version of the song was included on *I'm Your Man*.

PAUL: Which I gather was an enterprise that you never expected would be as difficult as it was.

LEONARD: Well, I got suckered into it, because I really had decided I wasn't going to do it. But Manolo Díaz, the head of the CBS company, a very sensitive man, a good writer himself—I mean, a musician—he chose the poem for me.

PAUL: The head of the CBS company where?

LEONARD: In Spain. They were doing the project. It was the fiftieth anniversary of his [Lorca's] death, and they were doing this project. He chose the poem for me. It was a very interesting choice. He said, "Do you know Lorca?" I said, "Yeah, I love Lorcas. My daughter's named Lorca." That really went down very well in Spain with him. So I got the poem and I got the various translations that were done of it, and I said, "There's no way I can start this. I mean, it's a huge job." And I wasn't in a very good condition. So he said, "Look, Leonard, what if you come to Spain and we'll just put you in a hotel room for two weeks—it's on us—and we'll send the food up, and you just do it?" I said, "Well, that's really nice of you."

PAUL: Do you speak Spanish?

LEONARD: No, I don't speak Spanish. Then I started it myself. I said, "Forget that, let me give it a shot." I started it. The notebook on that one is really thick. And a friend of mine, a young woman, a Costa Rican woman, came up to Montreal from New York and she read it to me over and over again in Spanish. I asked her about really the details of the language, and I started collecting phrases and things here and there. I totally stopped communicating with the world at that time. Hazel would drag me out for dinner and I'd go along with my Spanish dictionary and my rhyming dictionary and my notes.

PAUL: You didn't go to Spain, then?

LEONARD: No. I went to France to record it because I'd met a man by the name of Jean-Philippe Rykiel, who was a very great synthesizer player and blind. He did the arrangement, but I added the violins and the voices.

PAUL: The fact that it had to rhyme was particularly difficult.

LEONARD: Yeah, because all the translations were unrhymed. And really quite far from it, I thought, because it was a waltz. It's called "Little Viennese Waltz," and it rhymes very rigorously in Spanish and apparently extremely beautifully. Spanish-speaking people love the poem.

PAUL: You had this *huge* responsibility. A beloved poem.

LEONARD: A beloved poem and a poet that had meant a great deal to me. And, well, all the other things that go with writing.

PAUL: It sounds like it would be a good idea to do a poem by Rumi, if it isn't impossible to do.

LEONARD: It's a very good idea. You will love Rumi.

PAUL: I assume Lorca was indeed named after the poet.

LEONARD: Yeah. She does not dishonor the name. There's something very magical about her spirit. You shouldn't praise your children, you know. It's not good. You're not supposed to praise your children.

PAUL: Was every single song on *I'm Your Man* rewritten?

LEONARD: "I'm Your Man" originally started off as the song that became "Waiting for the Miracle."

PAUL: The line about World War II is in that.

LEONARD: Yeah. That was originally in that song—

PAUL: An earlier version—

LEONARD: —an earlier version of "Waiting for the Miracle," to that melody. To that melody. Finally I took that "Waiting for the Miracle" and started working on that with Sharon Robinson for a melody; because it had gotten so confused with my own melodies that I thought I'd better get this out of the whole realm of my own melodies. So Sharon wrote this melody that I'm using on the new record. I have one or two chord changes, but Sharon Robinson came up with the melody. Sharon Robinson, with whom I wrote "Everybody Knows." She and Jennifer were the backup singers of my '79 tour. She's a wonderful writer. We wrote a song called "Summertime" that Diana Ross recorded and now Roberta Flack is recording. We've written a number of songs together. I very much like to work with her.[133]

PAUL: Was "Waiting for the Miracle" changed lyrically a great deal? It still has the line "I haven't been this happy / Since the end of World War II."

LEONARD: Oh, very, very much. That's one of those songs that I have notebooks about. The melody for "I'm Your Man" originally was the melody for "Waiting for the Miracle." Then I felt it didn't work with the melody, so I discarded that lyric and kept the melody. And then I wrote a song called "I've Cried Enough for You." [*hurries through a few lines of the unrecorded song*] So that didn't work, but that whole song was written. It didn't work. And then I discarded that and began another song that resembles "I'm Your Man" and wrote that one, and I discarded that one and then I began writing "I'm Your Man." And as I began writing that, the melody changed again. So eventually I recorded that "I'm Your Man" lyric with a modified melody of the original "Waiting for the Miracle" melody. That was many, many, many changes.

PAUL: And none of these songs went on as originally planned, not a one?

133 In addition to cowriting "Waiting for the Miracle" and "Everybody Knows," Robinson, in 2001, would coproduce, co-arrange, and cowrite all of the compositions on Leonard's *Ten New Songs*. She also appeared on the front cover of the album with him.

LEONARD: Not one. Well, "Take This Waltz" was just a long process. That was the song; there was no other song intervening. "Ain't No Cure for Love" had many, many metamorphoses, and Jenny has one of them [on her 1986 album *Famous Blue Raincoat: The Songs of Leonard Cohen*]. Jenny's version is different than mine, different lyrically and different melodically.

PAUL: I must hear this. It's also got that one song that's never been on any record.

LEONARD: "Song of Bernadette," which I wrote with Jennifer [with Bill Elliott contributing to the music]. Jennifer has an earlier version of the song I did. "[First We Take] Manhattan" was fairly close. There were a *lot* of lyrical changes. I have many, many lyrics that I can't use because they all have the I-N rhyme to rhyme with *Berlin.* I knew just where the I-N rhyme was in the dictionary. But there's nothing I can do about those ones. I can't recycle any of those lyrics. Then there was "Everybody Knows"; a lot of verses for that but no other melody because Sharon did the melody. And "I'm Your Man" has five different elements in it before I arrived at the first one. "Take This Waltz" is pretty much "Take This Waltz." The next one was "Jazz Police." "Jazz Police" went through a lot of metamorphoses. First of all it's part of a very long poem, which I've done in here [his then-unpublished selected-poems], and quite a funny poem. I started working on it with Jeff. Jeff was doing the track—Jeff Fisher, who did the arrangement for "First We Take Manhattan" and "Ain't No Cure for Love." He had done a very, very complicated time tempo that had to be simplified. And then I put in the pads because I couldn't sing to what he'd done. So I put in the vocal pads with Anjani and we changed the melody somewhat.[134] So that was modified, the original treatment was modified. And then the next one was "I Can't Forget," which was a whole other song, *completed* and finished. It had taken me a long time to write and I realized I couldn't get behind this kind of song. It went: "I was born in chains but I was taken out of Egypt / I was bound to a burden, but the burden it was raised." It's quite a nice lyric. If I read it by someone else I would think, *A lot of meat in here.* I

134 Anjani Thomas, Leonard's long-standing backup singer and one-time romantic interest, worked with him on several albums, including *Various Positions*, *I'm Your Man*, and *The Future*. In 2006 he would produce her *Blue Alert*, cowriting with her the album's ten songs.

just couldn't get behind it. But it had some nice lines in it: "I was led to the edge of the mighty sea of sorrow / Pursued by the riders of a cruel and dark regime / But the waters parted and my soul crossed over / Out of Egypt, out of Pharaoh's dream."[135]

PAUL: I guess it could be taken as Israel and Egypt, as well as a personal metaphor.

LEONARD: Yeah. I just didn't feel like having any religious references in that record. I felt I'd done it; it was over. Then the last song, "Tower of Song," of course I showed you the worksheets. I have many, many.

PAUL: That's an incredible song. That's a masterpiece song, I think.

LEONARD: It's a wonderful piece. I like that. Yeah, that one has it.

PAUL: I think you said somewhere that it was like a tribute to the craft of songwriting, or an acceptance of yourself as a songwriter, a Los Angeles songwriter.

LEONARD: Yeah, there was nowhere to go. It just had that *I'm here. It's what I'm doing.*

PAUL: There was never a record where *all* the songs changed on you before this, was there? Not where everything you had planned was all wrong.

LEONARD: Not like that one. That was *so* tricky to do and so tricky to confront finally.

PAUL: That's the last thing you want to find out when you go into the studio, that *I can't sing any of these songs*. That *I have to rewrite the entire thing*. It must have been horrifying to realize that.

135 Having used the music from "I Can't Forget" to craft an entirely new song for *I'm Your Man*, twenty-six years later, in 2014, Leonard would use the original lyrics for the song "Born in Chains" on his album *Popular Problems*. The album would be dedicated "to our Teacher and Companion Kyozan Joshu Sasaki Roshi, 1907–2014."

LEONARD: [*chuckling*] It was terrible. Because you're already exhausted by the time you get through and you think you're finished. *Thank god, it's finished! What? It isn't finished? It isn't started.*

PAUL: There's nothing you hate worse than something you've already finished once and realized you've got to do it all over again. Your soul cries out, *I'm not going near this!*

LEONARD: I cried out!

PAUL: "Chelsea Hotel No. 2" [from 1974's *New Skin for the Old Ceremony*], there's a distancing effect in that song for me that's interesting. I don't know of another song that you've done it on. The end of it when you take a very dismissive—

LEONARD: "I don't even think of you that often."

PAUL: Yeah. Or "I can't keep track of every fallen robin." Why did you do that?

LEONARD: [*thinks hard before answering*] I think one of the reasons, and maybe the only reason, was that was true. That was really how I felt about it. I thought there was this part of my life and I *was* in it, and I was in it deeply when I was writing it. But I think that the kind of mythological tone of a lot of the rock writing at that time was an element in it. You know, that I didn't want to be part of, like, that this was the whole world. One had the feeling at a certain moment, especially if you were in that world, there was nothing else going on. I think mostly it was true, is that this was something that happened to me and it touched me very much—even if it isn't central.

PAUL: It's not something you brooded about.

LEONARD: It's not something I brooded about beyond the song. I remember thinking about it—I was in a Polynesian restaurant in Miami by myself. I remember sitting at the bar and I started thinking about that year in the Chelsea Hotel, and I remember just writing that line down: "I remember you well in the Chelsea Hotel."

PAUL: This was years and years later.

LEONARD: Years and years later, yeah. Just one of those moments when the memory of somebody comes back to you very, very strong and you live in it for a while. It happened to me about Georges Brassens, the French singer. I was sitting at a bar at a bistro in Montreal, and he'd just died. We had some small connection: his publishers wanted me to translate his opus, or some part of it, into English and they'd sent a representative to me with all his records. I never met him, but I respect him very much. A very great French singer. I looked at his songs very carefully and did attempt a few translations, but that was the end of it. That was *all* I ever thought about Georges Brassens until—you know, I'd hear a song now and then, but I didn't hear it too often in the places I was. And then the news of his death came and for an hour, or a half hour, I was with him and his music was going through my mind, and I wrote this poem for him. And then, completely over.

It was like that with ["Chelsea Hotel No. 2"]. Although I worked on the song, the reality of the song was that, once that original deep memory, deep flashback, you know—and I thought it would be somehow dishonest if I left the song with the sense that I lived in this, as you say, brooding, that I lived in this memory that—

PAUL: In fact it wasn't true.

LEONARD: No, it wasn't true. I don't "keep track of each fallen robin." But it was, I suppose, a little bit harsh.

PAUL: I don't know if it's harsh. What you say makes a lot of sense. I guess *distancing* is the way I found it, distancing from the emotion. Strangely it almost makes the song more moving because it's more honest, I think.

LEONARD: There didn't seem to be any question to me when the lines came up. You know that feeling: when a line comes up it may not be the greatest line you've ever written. but you don't have any quarrel with it. Those lines came up—I didn't have any quarrel with it.

PAUL: I don't know how to say this right, but that jolt of distancing at the end almost makes the song more moving because you know the guy is telling you the whole truth.

LEONARD: And that line that preceded the line, "I don't mean to suggest that I loved you the best," it was for Janis Joplin.

PAUL: You almost introduce it with the idea that it wasn't written at the time, I believe; in the introductions I've heard for it anyway. It is a memory piece.

LEONARD: Oh, no, it was written many years later. Many, many years later. And I didn't know Janis Joplin very well.

PAUL: No, I like it, I think it works. It's the one song I can think of that has that distancing effect for the audience.

LEONARD: It turns itself off. It's like a thermostat, it's hot or not.

PAUL: It just strikes me as a very honest song. I don't think most writers would have written the last part. It is harsh, as you say, but it adds to the emotion.

LEONARD: I think it's true. I never thought of it much—in fact I never thought of it again—until you mentioned it this moment.

PAUL: It's the one instance that I can think of where you where you did that. There may be others.

LEONARD: No, I don't think so.

PAUL: I guess proof that it worked—I don't think it works just because it's about Janis Joplin—is doing that. It's a very honest way to write a love song [about someone] that wasn't one's great love but you feel very tender towards at a certain point.

LEONARD: Yeah, I felt very tender towards her. I never knew her very well, you know? I never knew her very well and she was never interested in knowing me any better. Nor I in knowing her any better.

PAUL: Does the Kris Kristofferson anecdote come out of any kernel of truth? Was she looking for Kris Kristofferson?

LEONARD: Yeah.

PAUL: She was? Did you deliver the line that you were in fact Kris Kristofferson?[136] No? [*laughs*] I didn't think so.

LEONARD: When I finally finished the song—I began it in a Polynesian bar in Miami—and I finished it in the Imperial Hotel in Asmara, Ethiopia, which I went to … after the Israeli war. I just was kind of shattered by that whole experience of seeing warfare—

PAUL: And being shelled.

LEONARD: —and everything. And there hadn't been any strong sunlight in Israel all through that time for some odd reason. I wanted to sit in the sun. When I got back to Egypt, I jumped on a plane to Addis Ababa and then from there I went to Asmara, which is a seacoast town. And it was just about three or four months or five months before the revolution hit, the Eritrean rebellion, and there was a massacre in Asmara. Well, the atmosphere in Asmara was very—I don't know what the word is—*tense* hardly begins to describe it. *Ominous*. And I was not feeling very well. I was in this hotel room, and there was nobody in the hotel because the critical events were already destroying the tourist trade. I was there and that's when I finished most of the songs, or brought them to a reasonable completion, the songs in *New Skin*.

PAUL: "Lover Lover Lover."

136 Often, during live introductions to "Chelsea Hotel No. 2," Leonard would recount the playful patter, some of it factual, some of it not, between Joplin and himself in their now mythic elevator ride.

LEONARD: "Lover Lover Lover" was because of the war,[137] and then "Field Commander Cohen" I finished there, and "Chelsea Hotel."

PAUL: Why did you go to Cuba the time during the [1961 Bay of Pigs] invasion?

LEONARD: I can't really sum it up now. I had this sense of myself as an adventurer.[138]

PAUL: Like Graham Greene going to the war zone.

LEONARD: Yeah, or Ernest Hemingway. I don't know what the mythology was, but there was some dismal essence of mythology operating. But one of the things that I thought, I thought there *was* going to be an invasion. Fidel Castro would make these very, very long speeches. There was an atomic object in some way. I don't know why I went down there. I had some interesting adventures down there.

PAUL: Was it truly threatening at any point?

LEONARD: Well, I went to Havana and then I went to the beach called Varadero, and there was no one, there were no tourists in Cuba. The only foreigners there were people from the Iron Curtain countries. And I had a beard, I had a small beard like this, but I was wearing Canadian Army surplus khaki pants and a khaki shirt. And I had a knife, an Army knife, on my belt.

PAUL: Is it something you wore in Cuba all the time?

LEONARD: Well, it was just the clothes I was wearing at the time. It was the evening and I was walking along the beach and feeling very peaceful. There wasn't a soul around. And suddenly I was

137 Performing the song after the war, Leonard sometimes introduced it by saying it had been "written in the Sinai desert for soldiers of both sides."

138 A few years after the invasion, in *Ladies and Gentlemen, Mr. Leonard Cohen*, he confessed that "The real reason" he went to Cuba "was a deep interest in violence. I was very interested in what it really meant for men to carry arms and to kill other men, and how attracted I was exactly to that process. Now, that's getting closer to the truth. The real truth is that I wanted to kill or be killed."

surrounded by about I don't know how many guys—a number of men. I keep thinking there were about sixteen, but maybe not that many; maybe only four or five. I remember suddenly over a sand dune or whatever it was, a whole bunch of guys came up, and I think they had Czechoslovakian machine guns, at the time. They thought I was the first guy off the landing craft. I've told this story many times, but they really were very nice to me considering, like, what the situation was and how mean they could have been. But even when they took me to the station, they were firm and they were stern.

PAUL: They thought you were innocent pretty fast.

LEONARD: Not fast enough for me, but considering the situation. I didn't speak *any* Spanish. I remembered a few of the slogans and I said a slogan to them. So I said, "Do you know '*Amistad del pueblos*'?" "Friendship of the peoples." That was a slogan that was around Havana that I'd remembered, and I said that to them: "*Amistad del pueblos*." And that started to change things around and, before you knew it, they broke out the rum and they put a necklace of shells that the real *Fidelistas* wore—you know, shells?

PAUL: Did you carry a knife in Cuba all the time?

LEONARD: I always had this knife because I wasn't eating in restaurants. I'd buy some bread and cheese, and so I had a knife with me. I stopped wearing it.

PAUL: It could have been quite serious, though. I would imagine the percentage of soldiers keyed up for an invasion to shoot first would have been fairly high.

LEONARD: I was very lucky. And I was very lucky again. I'll tell you the story; it's quite interesting. I went into Havana I *think* with a couple of these guys—I don't remember quite now—with a couple of these guys that I kind of got friendly with. We went into Havana together, and there was a street photographer there. We took pictures. I was with these *milicianos* and I think one of them put his beret on my head. There were three of us and our arms were around each other, and it looked like I was in uniform. And I had this picture with me, okay? So it's in my knapsack and I completely forget about it.

Various things go down in Havana and one of them is that I meet up with a bunch of American Communists, and I get into a vicious argument with them about things. One of them says, "I'm going to denounce you. You are like a bourgeois individualist poet and you don't know anything about the struggle of the people." It was one of those things. Very tough guys.

To make a long story short, I shaved off my beard and I had a seersucker suit with me. I started wearing that suit. The invasion came a couple of days later and it was a fiasco. The guys were on television and everything else. More or less I very much admired the way that the people held themselves. They really *were* invaded. It might have been 200,000 men and not this mad force that arrived. And I was American. People were very nice to me on the street. It was really quite nice.

Anyways, after the invasion, the most humorous thing that happened to me was I was living in this little hotel room—now I'm back in Havana—and I'm getting up in the middle of the afternoon and I'm staying up all night. The only people up are like these out-of-work pimps and gamblers and guys who used to do exhibitions. There are only a few of them left. I'm hanging out with these people and sort of feeling good to be with these people, and a knock comes on my hotel room door. It's a messenger from the Canadian consulate or embassy. I don't know what we had down there—consulate, I think—and they said, "We'd like you to report there tomorrow afternoon." I thought, *I've gotten into some kind of trouble now.* So I went down there and I'm ushered into the second secretary, somebody like that, and he looks at me—I haven't shaved yet, I'm still the same—and he says, "Your mother's very worried about you." [*chuckles*] So my mother had been following the news, and she'd known that I was down there, and she went to a cousin of mine who was a senator. They'd put it in a diplomatic pouch to come down. It was humiliating. And here I was, I was Ernest Hemingway.

In any case, after that I tried to leave the country, but the airports were jammed. There were big signs up in Spanish saying, "Whoever leaves the country now is a traitor and a worm," things like that. There's only one airplane going out every couple of days, whatever it was. So I got to know everybody in the waiting room, waiting for the tickets. Finally got a ticket. I come the next morning with my knapsack, and I'm all shaved by this time. I'm in my seersucker suit. They go through my bags, and I don't hear anything. They start calling out the names of the people who are on the plane. And I knew the person who was in front of me and the person next to me, but they don't call my name. I walk over to the guy—he's reading from a clipboard—and I see there's a line through my name. I go over to him, I say, "Look, I'm supposed to be next." He says, "No, you're going to go over to that table over there." They call it *G2*.

PAUL: Intelligence.

LEONARD: Intelligence, yeah. And they say to me, "There's a picture of you and some *miliciano*." He said, "We can't let you go, we have to question you." My heart really sank. They packed all my bag up and they put it beside me, and they assign me a guard—young, young kid, maybe thirteen or fourteen—with a machine gun. I'm sitting out there and I see all the people are going onto the plane, and I think, *I've had it. I'm never going to be able to explain this*. So it's a very volatile situation, there's no sense of order. The airport has been bombed and the runways are messed up. And somehow somebody's gotten onto the plane that wasn't supposed to be there. A couple. So they pull this couple off the plane and there's this tremendous amount of activity going on about this thing. They're not clubbing them or anything, they're being nice. They're very argumentative and very vocal, the Cubans. In fact their Spanish is known as being extremely elegant and that they delight in their language. There's a tremendous amount of verbal play all the time.

But they're talking back and they're making their case known. And my guard goes to join this little knot of people that are having this wonderful time out in that maybe hundred feet between the place where I was waiting and the airplane. As soon as he leaves me, I make this decision that I'm going to get on the airplane. It's the only brave thing I've ever done in my life. I don't know why I did it, I just said, *I'll never get out of this place.* So I got my bag together, put it on my shoulder, and I just walked across the field. I said, *Don't look back.* I got onto the plane. About ten minutes later it took off. It was my biggest kick. [*chuckles*]

PAUL: But you felt, *Is there going to be a bullet into my back any minute?*

LEONARD: Well, I thought of that. I mean, they were shooting their toes off in a certain way by mistake. They're very gentle. They're not killing people; the Cubans are not that kind of people. Everything I saw in Cuba was very dignified in the way they conducted their revolution. I don't know what goes on behind closed doors. I wasn't so much worried about a bullet in my back as like, "And he's trying to get away, too."

I remember a poignant moment, I had met a young woman who was a Czechoslovakian. She was translating Cuban short stories into Czechoslovakian. There was a cultural exchange going on. We were sitting on the seafront, and at that moment the counterrevolutionaries blew up a big department store. You could hear it and you saw the flames and the firetrucks were going, and she thought it was the beginning of the invasion. She'd heard all these stories about Americans, about how terrible the Americans were, because she'd been brought up in a Communist country. She was saying, "What will they do to me? What will they do to me when they get here?" and I said, "They'll give you chocolate bars and cigarettes. They're really very nice." [*laughs*]

PAUL: That's something, having that message from your mother there.

LEONARD: That was so funny. It was just like my mother, too. She was terrific. Like, "What are you doing there?"

He and Paul enjoy a final laugh on tape together.

LEONARD: I think we better fold.

PAUL: All right, let's fold.

The telephone rings and, as Leonard answers it, Paul turns off the tape recorder. The next time he presses record, it's later the same day but he is alone in his motel room. He snaps his fingers in front of the mic for the last time on this trip.

PAUL: That was a fabulous interview today. A lot of stuff—four hours' worth probably. An awful lot of material. Some really great stuff. I couldn't even begin to remember it all, I'm sure.

He picks me up at the gas station, probably from seeing this woman near here. We go to Burger King and get a double cheeseburger and fries and Coke. He ordered a cheeseburger deluxe, onion rings, and a strawberry shake. He reiterates his generous offer, which could amount to anything—rent, whatever. He tells me this goofy story. Went over to his friend's last night, was playing the songs, from the album, that he's finished. For some reason he left the tape playing, left the car running, and got out of the car and locked it with all of this running inside. He had to call the—I don't know, whatever one calls to get the car opened up again.

Then we go to his house and I guess he changes into black jeans, black t-shirt with *LC*; a European t-shirt, I think, tour t-shirt. Tells me this great story about the first sofa, which is on the tapes. Should be on the tapes. Pray that it's on the tapes. It just went spectacularly well, and I kept telling myself, *Is this is the breakthrough interview I really wanted?* I mean, this one and the last two was a wealth of material. Multi-hours, nine to ten hours probably.

He drives me back again and leaves me off at Outpost Road. Buys some flowers for the lady. Again stopping at Burger King, getting burgers and things, taking with him. I notice the Fatburger and say, "Oh, you have Fatburger! That's good, too." He was a vegetarian in Greece, largely because he'd seen the lambs every day and realizing they were going to be slaughtered, I guess. Leanne, I think, told a story about becoming a vegetarian and being on his boat in Greece filled with sheep, half of them dead. Turned her into a vegetarian. When he goes to the *zendo*, vegetarianism is required there, I guess.

He likes vegetables because they're cooked by people who know how to cook them.[139]

Talked some about Graham Greene, whom he admires a great deal. *Godfather [Part] III*, he felt about the same I did. [*sighs*] What else, what else? Becoming so comfortable that one's eyes start noticing he's gesturing a lot, excitedly gesturing. An animated person. Laughs easily. Again, really zeroed in on going through the breakup, the divorce. My divorce. And Bobbi, really zeroed in on that. He wanted to know about that. Gave me some more stuff: the Mailer article, a book about his Zen teacher. Played him the Baker song; I think he liked it: "Deep in a Dream of You." "Send me your five favorites." It takes him a long time to get into anything. He played "Be for Real" most of the way and then the Baker tape most of the way to his house. We continued talking on the way back, first about his neighborhood. Jackson Browne, he likes Jackson Browne. Something about movies. Graham Greene. Chet Baker book possibilities.[140] That ending with *Godfather III*, as we pulled into Outpost and Franklin. Gee, I don't know, I can't think of anything else. I smoked the Shermans from the silver bowls. I just don't recall any other details now. Later.

Paul presses stop.

139 "Well, it's true that since I stopped eating meat, I feel a lot better among animals," Leonard said in *Ladies and Gentlemen, Mr. Leonard Cohen*. "I feel I can be much more honest when I pat a dog." Paul, on the other hand, was famous among his friends for never eating anything green.

140 Paul received an offer from a publisher for his book proposal, but it wasn't enough to support the enormous research and travel that would be required.

EPILOGUE

Kit Rachlis waited a month or two before reaching out to Paul to see how the profiles were coming. He left several messages but received no response. Then late one California night, the phone rang. It was screenwriter Jay Cocks, a dear friend of Paul's, calling from New York on Paul's behalf. "He is mortified, but he's not going to be able to write those pieces, and he wanted me to let you know."

"Jay, it's okay," Rachlis said. "Tell Paul he can call me. It's not going to affect our friendship."

He never heard from Paul again.

Other than putting them into a box and setting them aside, Paul apparently did nothing with the recordings. That same year he took a job as a clerk at Evergreen Video in the West Village, surrounded by the classic films he loved so much. He'd be there for fourteen years.

During that time his writing sales were nearly nonexistent. In 1992 he wrote four more pieces for *Musician* (profiles of Freedy Johnston, Jude Cole, Chris Harford, and Nicky Holland). Three years after that, and much to his own surprise, saw the publication of *701 Toughest Movie Trivia Questions of All Time*, a book cowritten with Paul's old friend William MacAdams. They had sold it eleven years earlier and the publisher promptly went out of business. After that, in 1997, he wrote four short reviews for *People*, only two of which the magazine published: Guy Clark's *Keepers* and *The Highway Kind* by Townes Van Zandt. Throughout this time he worked on his passion project, a mammoth, forever unfinished screenplay whose characters' company he preferred to those who populated his real life.

Asked to comment, over thirty years after Paul's trip to Los Angeles, Jay Cocks wants to know whether Leonard Cohen and Lucinda Williams or their people were aware that Paul was "struggling in some way. Because basically you're asking these people to invest three or four days of their time—creative time, right? Or professional time—promoting their work so that they can keep working. You're asking them to just get into a car and get into a crash at the end of the dead-end street. You're wasting their time."

According to Fred Schruers, whose time writing for *Circus* magazine in the Seventies coincided with Paul's time there, "I think the [record] companies knew his patterns timing-wise, but the writer's block less so. The latter was something he barely acknowledged even to fellow writers, or at least to me."

"We all love Paul dearly," Cocks says, "but as the years have gone by, I keep thinking back and back to the experience with Clint [Eastwood] ..." From 1979 to 1983, thanks to a personal endorsement from Cocks, Paul and Eastwood met on numerous occasions for a *Rolling Stone* cover story that never came to be. "He spends days or weeks or whatever it was, and he really likes Paul and, you know, nothing happens. So in effect Paul is draining their batteries.

"Let me put it this way: after the experience with Clint, I don't know that I would ever have asked anybody else—let's say Marty [Scorsese] or Brian [De Palma] ... to do this with Paul without first apprising them of the shape that he was in.

"Maybe trying to get Paul to write by doing interviews, in retrospect, wasn't the best way of helping him. Maybe he couldn't be helped. It's a sad and desperate thing, but I'm afraid that's the truth."

"I think that's probably true," says another of Paul's friends, writer and pop culture critic Tom Carson, "but it's useful to remember that Paul never wanted to do straight Q&A's. He wanted to sculpt a sort of cathedral to artists he loved, and it got harder for him once he couldn't do that anymore."

"Look, Paul was a brilliant guy," Cocks continues. "When he was writing, he was a tremendous writer. He was fantastically sympathetic to creative people, but he also sucked the life out of them on a limited basis. It was vampiristic. I think he used their creative juice to keep himself going.

"I feel really sad about this situation, but I'm past feeling guilty about it for myself. I don't know about Kit or Fred or any of these other people; but when you get somebody who desperately needs professional help and won't get it, even if you point them in the right direction or kick them in the direction, then you can't feel guilty. So that's my feeling.

"The other thing is that Paul put his friends at financial disadvantage. Kit as the editor is of course responsible to the paper, the other writers, the readership; he [Paul] put him at a disadvantage. So, you know, I'm sorry I called Kit now. I shouldn't have done it. But I wasn't as tough as I should have been about these things, and it was out of a misguided and desperate affection for wanting to get him back writing. But we should have known that it was a lost cause."

Schruers: "I think Kit and I both felt this was our best shot at reawakening Paul's writing and interviewing gifts and, more significantly, his interest in the trade. As Jann Wenner says of the attempts he and [*Rolling Stone* managing editor] Terry McDonell made to get the late-period Hunter S. Thompson going, 'We both wanted him back at his typewriter.' When it didn't work, there was sorrow but not deep regret over making the attempt. And that's when I came to believe what Dave Marsh said of the entire situation around that time: 'Only Paul can help Paul.'"

Rachlis, the architect of Paul's journey west, says, "I think I both share what Jay feels and probably have slightly different feelings. Which is, I did not know or did not want to believe that this was a lost cause, and which is why I was willing to put my own money for Paul's flight, Fred Schruers was willing to help cover his expenses, why Ariel and I were willing to put Paul up in our house for a week. I didn't face up to the fact that it was a lost cause until Jay called me. It was odd that Jay called me.

"I felt badly that Jay was the one who called me, and read it as Paul did not want to face me directly and Paul feared that he was putting our friendship on the line. The terrible and awful irony is that I recall very distinctly saying to Jay, 'Please tell Paul to call me. This will not affect our friendship.'

"Should we have been tougher? Maybe. Would it have made any difference? Maybe. I don't know any of that, but yes, Paul put Jay in an untenable position and he shouldn't have done it. Paul should have been like the tough-guy heroes that he so admired. He should have called me. But the fact that he didn't I think was a sign of his great fear that he was both letting himself down but letting me down. And I wanted to have him know that there was no way he was going to let me down."

Perhaps it sounds a little cruel, but perhaps Jay Cocks is correct when he uses the word *vampiristic*. And maybe I was on the right track when I wrote in the Clint Eastwood book:

> As different as all these projects were, they were also similar in that they all dealt with artists whom Paul admired as much personally as he did aesthetically. Their opinions undoubtedly meant as much to him as did their work and, fearing that he might fall short in his understanding of them and what they did (for Paul, writing was discovery in the truest sense), the argument could be made that perhaps he was afraid to disappoint them (to say nothing of himself). In terms of the sheer volume of material he gathered on them, just where to begin was daunting. He admitted that sometimes he just had "*too much* to say." If this were the case and it was beyond him to find the right words to describe these artists and their work, well, then he'd rather just say nothing at all.
>
> As much a fan as he was an objective journalist, the frissons that came from spending so much time hanging out with his heroes, talking with them, *trying* to understand them, must have been considerable. (After all, this was a man who, as a result of seeing *Dirty Harry* in 1971, purchased—by way of not entirely legal means—a .44 Magnum.) Maybe, to put it bluntly, writing-wise he'd come too soon. Perhaps his reasons were the same as why, when he worked at Mercury Records in the early Seventies, scouting and developing talent, he'd laid his job on the line with the company brass until they finally relented and allowed him to sign the unruly New York Dolls to the label:

> "I just wanted to be around the damn band—it was as simple as that."

"So I paid for his travel," remembers Kit Rachlis. "Fred paid for most of his expenses, and Paul was never paid a kill fee for the pieces."

Paul Nelson's body was found in his bed on the Fourth of July 2006. His *New York Times* obituary initially cited starvation as the cause of death, but that was corrected based on the medical examiner's findings: heart disease.

Following a fall in the middle of the night, Leonard Cohen died in his sleep on November 7, 2016. He had previously been diagnosed with leukemia.

Like her father, Lucinda Williams was born with spina bifida. On November 17, 2020, she suffered a stroke at her home in Nashville. It initially affected the left side of her body and her ability to play the guitar, but as of this writing she just released her sixteenth album and is touring internationally. She still undergoes physical and occupational therapy.

Neither artist responded to my requests for interviews (Leonard for my first book nor Lucinda for that one and this one). I like to believe that whatever they felt they had to say, they had already said to Paul.

ACKNOWLEDGMENTS

As always, extreme gratitude to Paul Nelson's son Mark C. Nelson for his ongoing support of my mission to ensure that his father, and his father's work, is not forgotten. Towards that end, thanks to Fantagraphics publisher extraordinaire Gary Groth for helping realize this goal and to artist Jeff Wong for his genius eye.

Special thanks to Jay Cocks, Fred Schruers, Tom Carson, and especially Kit Rachlis for their time and encouragement, and to Suzanne Vega for her lovely and generous foreword.

Thanks to Ellis Flink for his lifelong friendship, Thomas Anderson for the occasional, always brilliant music, and Jessica Kaskel for the many insights. Nicole Stansbury was a constant source of inspiration.

Finally, heartfelt appreciation to Don and Elizabeth Avery for their ongoing love and support. And thanks to the rest of my family, past and present.

SOURCES AND CITED WORKS

All American Girls Part 2: In Heat. Directed and written by Bill Milling. 1983. Praexis Productions.

Avery, Kevin. *Conversations with Clint: Paul Nelson's Lost Interviews with Clint Eastwood, 1979–1983*, 2011, Continuum Books; and *Everything Is an Afterthought: The Life and Writings of Paul Nelson*, 2011, Fantagraphics Books.

Avery, Kevin. Interviews and emails with Tom Carson, 2022; Jay Cocks, 2021 and 2022; Tom Pacheco, 2007; Kit Rachlis, 2021 and 2022; and Fred Schruers, 2022.

Berlin, Irving. "Always," 1925, Berlin Irving Music Corp. (ASCAP).

Beviglia, Jim. "Behind The Song: 'Democracy' by Leonard Cohen," *American Songwriter*, September 27, 2021, https://americansongwriter.com/behind-the-song-democracy-by-leonard-cohen/.

Browne, David. "Man Out of Time: The Music and Mystery of David Blue," *Rolling Stone*, June 23, 2020.

Buchwald, Martin J. "Comin' Back to Me," 1967, Icebag Corp. c/o Wixen Music Publishing, Inc. (BMI).

Buford, Bill. "Delta Nights," *The New Yorker*, July 21, 2014.

Cale, J. J. "Magnolia," 1971, Johnny Bienstock Music.

Clark, Stuart. "Leonard Cohen Tribute: Suzanne Vega Gained a Unique Insight Into the Man Behind the Myth," *Hot Press*, December 20, 2016, https://www.hotpress.com/music/leonard-cohen-tribute-suzanne-vega-gained-a-unique-insight-into-the-man-behind-the-myth-19335794.

Cohen, Leonard. "Anthem," 1992, Sony/ATV Songs, LLC (BMI); "Bird on the Wire," 1969, Sony/ATV Songs, LLC (BMI); "Born in Chains," 2014, Old Ideas, LLC (SOCAN), and Sony/ATV Music Publishing, LLC (BMI); "Chelsea Hotel No. 2," 1974, Sony/ATV Songs, LLC (BMI); "Closing Time," 1992, Sony/ATV Songs, LLC (BMI); "Coming Back to You," 1984, Sony/ATV Songs, LLC (BMI); "Dance Me to the End of Love," 1984, Sony/ATV Songs, LLC (BMI); "Democracy," 1992, Sony/ATV Songs, LLC (BMI); "Famous Blue Raincoat," 1971, Stranger Music, Inc.; "Future, The," 1992, Sony/ATV Songs, LLC (BMI); "The Gypsy's Wife," 1979, Sony/ATV Songs, LLC (BMI); "Hallelujah," 1994, Sony/ATV Songs, LLC (BMI); "I Can't Forget," 1988, Sony/ATV Songs, LLC (BMI); "If You Could See What's Coming Next," 1992, Sony/ATV Songs, LLC (BMI); "Light as the Breeze" 1992, Sony/ATV Songs, LLC (BMI); "Night Comes On," 1984, Sony/ATV Songs, LLC (BMI); "Please Don't Pass Me By (A Disgrace)," 1973, Sony/ATV Songs, LLC (BMI); and "The Traitor," 1979, Sony/ATV Songs, LLC (BMI).

Cohen, Leonard. *The Favourite Game*, 1963, Secker & Warburg; "Deep Happiness, A," 1993, McClelland & Stewart; "Embrace, The," 1993, McClelland & Stewart; "My Honour," 1993, McClelland & Stewart; "Paris Models," 1993, McClelland & Stewart; "Robert Appears Again," 2006, McClelland & Stewart; "Stanzas for H. M.," 2006, McClelland & Stewart; and "When Even The," 1993, McClelland & Stewart.

Cohen, Leonard and Sharon Robinson. "Waiting for the Miracle," 1992, Sony/ATV Songs, LLC (BMI) and Sharon Robinson Songs (ASCAP).

Cohen, Leonard and Phillip Spector. "Death of a Ladies' Man," 1977, Sony/ATV Songs, LLC (BMI), ABKCO Music, Inc., and Mother Bertha Music, Inc. (BMI), and Sony/ATV Songs, LLC (BMI).

Cowie, Del. "Watch Leonard Cohen's Heartfelt, Poetic Speech at the 1991 Junos," CBC/Radio-Canada, March 31, 2017, https://www.cbc.ca/radio/q/watch-leonard-cohen-s-heartfelt-poetic-speech-at-the-1991-junos-1.4048637.

Don't Look Back. Written and directed by D. A. Pennebaker. 1967. Leacock-Pennebaker, Inc.

Fields, Danny. "Leonard Cohen Interviewed by Danny Fields at the Chelsea Hotel, 1974," PleaseKillMe.com, January 18, 2018, https://pleasekillme.com/leonard-cohen/.

Furay, Richie. "Kind Woman," 1968, Cotillion Music, Inc. (BMI), Richie Furay Music (BMI), and Springalo Toones (BMI).

Gabriel, Peter. "Leonard Cohen," petergabriel.com, November 11, 2016, https://petergabriel.com/news/remembering-leonard-cohen/.

Hallelujah: Leonard Cohen, a Journey, a Song. Written and directed by Daniel Geller and Dana Goldfine (based on the book *The Holy or the Broken: Leonard Cohen, Jeff Buckley & the Unlikely Ascent of "Hallelujah"* by Alan Light). 2021. Geller/Goldfine Productions.

Hendrix, Jimi. "Angel," 1970, Experience Hendrix, LLC (ASCAP).

Horovitz, David. "Why Leonard Cohen Joined a War to Sing for His Brothers, and Never Spoke of It Again," *The Times of Israel*, March 29, 2022, https://www.timesofisrael.com/why-leonard-cohen-joined-a-war-to-sing-for-his-brothers-and-never-spoke-of-it-again/.

Jolson, Al and Saul Chaplin (lyrics), and Iosif Ivanovici (music). "Anniversary Song," 1946, Shapiro, Bernstein & Co., Inc.

Kraemer, Peter and Terry MacNeil. "Hello, Hello," 1966, Great Honesty Music, Inc. (BMI).

Ladies and Gentlemen, Mr. Leonard Cohen. Directed by Donald Brittain and Don Owen. Written by Donald Brittain. 1965. National Film Board of Canada.

Ling, Ni. "Leonard Cohen Interviews Suzanne Vega in 1993," Dynamic Logic, Probability and Statistics, September 9, 2019, https://logicprobstat.wordpress.com/2019/09/09/leonard-cohen-interviews-suzanne-vega-in-1993/.

Mailer, Norman. "Children of the Pied Piper: Mailer on 'American Psycho,'"*Vanity Fair*, March 1991.

Nadel, Ira B. *Various Positions: A Life of Leonard Cohen*, 1996, Random House of Canada.

Nelson, Paul. "Leonard Cohen's Doo-Wop Nightmare," *Rolling Stone*, February 9, 1978; "The Virginian: Bruce Hornsby Finds His Way Home," *Musician*, January 1991; "Billy Joel's Songs for Swingin' Lovers," *Rolling Stone*, May 1, 1980; "Willie Nile's Good Luck/Bad Luck," *Musician*, May 1991; and "Suzanne Vega: On the Couch," *Musician*, June 1990.

Nelson, Paul. Interviews with Leonard Cohen and Lucinda Williams, 1991.

Night Music (episode #119), "Leonard Cohen/Sonny Rollins – Who By Fire – Night Music," YouTube, February 13, 1989, https://www.youtube.com/watch?v=LCaD6GAQmjA.

No Direction Home. Directed by Martin Scorsese. 2005. Paramount Pictures.

O'Hara, Geoffrey. "K-K-K-Katy," 1918, Leo Feist, Inc. (BMI).

Okun, Milton T., Noel Paul Stookie, Mary Allin Travers, and Peter Yarrow. "Come and Go with Me," 1965, Pepamar Music Corp. (ASCAP).

Ondaatje, Michael. *Leonard Cohen*. 1970. McClelland & Stewart Limited.

Paine, Thomas. *The American Crisis* a.k.a. *The Crisis*. 1776.

Piercy, Maureen. "People," *Maclean's*, June 16, 1980.

Rocca, Jane. "Lucinda Williams: 'My Father Is the Reason I Didn't Go Over the Deep End," *The Sydney Morning Herald*, June 6, 2020.

Rolling Stone (uncredited). "Leonard Cohen's Ex-Manager Sentenced to 18 Months in Prison. *Rolling Stone*, April 19, 2012, https://www.rollingstone.com/music/music-news/leonard-cohens-ex-manager-sentenced-to-18-months-in-prison-248761/

Ronde, La. Directed by Max Ophüls. Written by Jacques Natanson and Max Ophüls (based on the play *Reigen* by Arthur Schnitzler. 1950. Films Sacha Gordine.

Rowland, Mark. "Leonard Cohen's Nervous Breakthrough," *Musician*, July 1988.

Saturday Night with Connie Chung (season 1, episode 3). "Marlon Brando Interview with Connie Chung, 1989, Saturday Night with Connie Chung," YouTube, October 7, 1989, https://www.youtube.com/watch?v=SQRRIgrJBn4.

Scott, Judy. *Leonard, Marianne, and Me: Magical Summers on Hydra*. 2021. Backbeat Books.

Styron, William. *Darkness Visible: A Memoir of Madness*. 1990. Random House.

Tatangelo, Wade. "Acclaimed Artist's Career Started with Kiss from Bob Dylan," *McClatchy-Tribune*, October 20, 2011.

Ward, Steven. "What Ever Happened to Rock Critic Paul Nelson?," RockCritics.com, March 2000.

Webb, Jimmy L. "Up, Up and Away," 1967, EMI Sosaha Music, Inc. (BMI), R2M Music (BMI), and Songs of Lastrada (BMI); and "Wichita Lineman," 1968, Universal Polygram International Publishing, Inc. (ASCAP).

Williams, Lucinda. "Crescent City," 1992, Warner-Tamerlane Publishing Corporation (BMI); "Little Angel, Little Brother," 1992, Warner-Tamerlane Publishing Corporation (BMI); "One Night Stand," 1990, Alpha Music (BMI); "Sharp Cutting Wings (Song to a Poet)," 1980, Alpha Music (BMI); and "The Wind Blows," 1966, Lucinda Williams.

Young, Neil. "Helpless," 1970, Broken Arrow Music (BMI).

ABOUT THE AUTHORS

KEVIN AVERY is the author-editor of *Everything Is an Afterthought: The Life and Writings of Paul Nelson*, *Conversations with Clint: Paul Nelson's Lost Interviews with Clint Eastwood, 1979–1983*, and *It's All One Case: The Illustrated Ross Macdonald Archives* (cowritten with Paul Nelson, with Jeff Wong). Though born and raised in Salt Lake City, Utah, where he now lives, he considers himself a New York expatriate.

Widely regarded as one of the foremost songwriters of her generation, **SUZANNE VEGA** emerged as a leading figure of the folk revival of the early 1980s. Notably succinct and understated, her work is immediately recognizable—as utterly distinct and thoughtful as it was when her voice was first heard on the radio over thirty years ago with iconic songs like "Luka" and "Tom's Diner."

INDEX

INDEX

INDEX

L

M

INDEX

T